CONFES

"I have killed," I say.

Kohler gasps; in horror, surprise, perhaps both. He must think it unlikely, but perhaps the tone of my voice lets him know that I'm not joking.

"How many times?" he asks, more in a croak than a whisper.

"More than once."

"When did you last kill?"

"Now."

I'm up off the prie-dieu and out of the door in a flash, pulling the gasoline can from my bag. I throw open the confessional's other door and see Kohler there. I splash the gasoline on him. For an old man, he still looks strong, but gentle too. Years of turning the other cheek have left him useless in a situation like this.

In another two seconds, maybe three, he might have reacted to the danger; but those are seconds he doesn't have, seconds I won't give him.

"An exciting yarn filled with surprising twists, great characters, [and] vivid descriptions."

—The Mystery Reader

"A nasty little thriller that jets around Pittsburgh at breakneck speed."

—Pittsburgh Magazine

"Incredibly intricate . . . an engrossing drama."

—I Love a Mystery Newsletter

Thou Shalt Kill is also available as an eBook

DANIEL BLAKE

THOU SHALT KILL

POCKET BOOKS

New York London Toronto Sydney New Delhi

Pocket Books
A Division of Simon & Schuster, Inc.
1230 Avenue of the Americas
New York, NY 10020

First Pocket Books paperback edition March 2012

Manufactured in the United States of America

10 9 8 7 6 5 4 3 2 1

ISBN 978-1-4391-9759-2
ISBN 978-1-4391-9764-6 (ebook)

For Michael and Sheila Royce,
whose friendship to my family means more
than they can possibly imagine.

THOU SHALT KILL

1

FRIDAY, OCTOBER 1

Franco Patrese hadn't been inside a church for ten years.

Ironic, then, that his first time back was straight into the mother ship itself: Saint Paul Cathedral, center of spiritual life for close to a million Pittsburgh Catholics.

The bishop himself had insisted. Gregory Kohler had first gotten to know Franco's parents when he, as a young priest, had helped officiate at their wedding. He'd taught Franco and his sister, Bianca, in the days when priests and nuns could still be found inside the classroom, and over the years had become family friend as well as pastor.

Now he'd offered Franco and Bianca the cathedral. You didn't turn the bishop down, not if you were a good Catholic; and Bianca had certainly kept the faith, even if Franco hadn't. How could he have, when he'd seen the depths to which people who professed to be Christians could sink? Bullshit rituals and pious sermonizing in public, and the seven deadly sins plus a few more behind closed doors. Patrese thought the only biblical tenet worth a damn was "do as you would be done by." If every religion followed that, he reckoned, the world would be in all ways a better place.

But the cathedral it was, for Bianca if not for him. Besides, they needed all the seats they could get. Half of Bloomfield—an area of the city so Italian that parking meters were often painted red, green, and white—had come to pay their respects to Franco's parents.

Alberto and Ilaria Patrese had been killed five days before. Alberto had gone to pass a truck on the freeway at exactly the moment the truck driver had himself pulled out to overtake an SUV. The collision had flipped the Patreses' car across the central median and into the path of three lanes of traffic coming the other way.

They hadn't had a prayer.

The police had come to Franco first, since he was one of them: a homicide detective, working out of the department's North Shore headquarters. When two uniformed officers had approached Franco's desk, he'd known instantly that someone in his family was dead. He'd recognized the expression on those officers' faces as clearly as if he'd looked in a mirror. He'd had to break similar news many times. It was the worst part of the job, and by some distance. Nothing ripped at people's lives like the death of a loved one.

Franco had found the immediate aftermath unexpectedly bittersweet. There'd been tears, of course, and shock giving way to spikes of anger and confusion; but there'd also been rolling gales of laughter at the hundreds of family stories polished and embellished down the years. He'd kept himself occupied with death's legion of petty bureaucracies: police reports, autopsies, certificates, funeral arrangements, contacting relatives long-lost and far-flung. Busy meant less time to think, and less time to think meant more time to be strong, to make sure everyone else was bearing up all right, to deflect even the slightest gaze away from himself.

He was doing it even now, during the funeral service, there in the front pew with his nephews and niece tucked solemnly between him and Bianca. Determined to be the rock on which the waves of grief could crash, Franco ruffled the children's hair, and reached across to squeeze Bianca's hand when her jaw shuddered and bounced against the tears.

The last notes of "Amazing Grace" faded, and the congregation sat as Kohler climbed the steps to the pulpit. He was in his sixties, with a mane of hair that would have been the envy of a man half his age. The hands he raised as though in benediction of his flock were large and strong, and they did not shake.

Franco tuned out. He heard the grateful laughter when the bishop said something dry and affectionate, but he was miles away, thinking about the things he wished he'd told his parents while he'd still had the chance, and about the things he was glad he hadn't told them. They hadn't known everything about his life, and he had no illusions that they should have done so. He knew they'd loved him, and nothing was more important. But he knew too that loving people meant protecting them.

Somewhere in the distance, Kohler was talking about God, though it was not a God in whom Franco had believed for many years. As far as he was concerned, his parents' deaths had been blind chance, nothing more. Wrong place, wrong time. Why them? Turn it around: why *not* them? You were born, you lived, you died. Mercy and justice and compassion weren't divine traits; they were human ones, and by no means universal. If you didn't believe it, Franco thought, you were welcome to work homicide alongside him for a while. *Religion* was just a polite word for superstition, and *superstition* was just a polite word for fear.

Franco hooked a finger inside his collar and pulled at it. He felt suddenly short of breath, and his skin was clammy.

When Bianca looked at him, her face seemed to swim slightly in his vision before settling. Her eyebrows made a Chinese hat of concern and query.

"Is it hot in here?" he whispered.

She shook her head. "Not for me."

Franco's ribs quivered with the thumping of his heart. He stood on unsteady legs, stepped over Bianca's feet, and walked quickly down the aisle, looking neither left nor right till he was out the huge main door and into the shouty, safe bustle of students from the nearby university ragging each other and putting the world to rights.

It was the last haven he'd know for a while.

2

MONDAY, OCTOBER 4

The police department had offered Patrese two weeks' compassionate leave after the deaths of his parents. He still had half of it left, but the weekend after the funeral had been terrible. Without the logistics of organizing something to keep him occupied, he'd prowled around his apartment, too lethargic to do anything but too wired to do nothing. The shock and disbelief that always came as sudden death's outriders had hardened into insomnia-twisted anger.

So now, first thing Monday morning, he was back at his desk, to the unsurprised but good-natured exasperation of his homicide partner, Mark Beradino.

"Sheesh, Franco. You don't want your leave, I'll take it."

Patrese laughed, grateful that Beradino knew better than to kill him with kindness. "Thanks, Pop." It was a running joke in the department that they could have been father and son. If you took a photo of Patrese and aged it twenty-five years—voilà! Beradino. The Italian gene, dark and stocky, was strong in them both. Patrese was an inch shorter at five nine, with a lower center of gravity, and he walked on the balls of his feet like the athlete he'd once been. If he wasn't careful, he'd end up running to the kind of mild jowls and spare tire that now adorned Beradino.

Beradino's hair was graying but still all there. Like Patrese's, his features were regular without being actively handsome. He was no Brad Pitt, but neither was he a Michael Moore. You could walk past him in the street without noticing; even if you did notice, you'd have forgotten him five steps later. He'd have been a great spy.

But he was a detective—a hell of a detective, in fact.

As far as Pittsburgh Homicide was concerned, he was practically an institution.

He'd been there since the early eighties—most of his clothes looked as though he'd bought them not long afterward—and he was known on both sides of the law as a good cop. A tough one, sure, one who thought cops should be cops rather than politicians or social workers, but an honest one too. He'd never taken a bribe, never faked evidence, never beaten up a suspect.

Not many cops could say the same.

He and Patrese had been partners for three years—itself a vote of confidence in Patrese's ability—and in that time they'd become friends, comrades. Patrese was a regular guest at the condo in Punxsutawney that Beradino shared with his partner, Jesslyn Gedge, a corrections officer at the State Correctional Institution in Muncy. Beradino and Jesslyn had been among the mourners in Saint Paul three days before.

"But since you're here," Beradino continued, "make yourself useful. We just got a case. Domestic dispute, shots fired, man dead. Zone Five."

There were six police districts in Pittsburgh, numbered with the complete absence of discernible logic that was the hallmark of the true bureaucrat. Zone Five covered the northeastern corner of the city: East Liberty, East End, and Homewood.

Nine times out of ten, an incident in Zone Five meant an incident in Homewood.

Homewood was Pittsburgh's pits, no question. Homicides, aggravated assaults, weapons and narcotics offenses, prostitution arrests; you name it, there were twice as many in Homewood as in any other neighborhood. It was one of the most dangerous places to live in all of Pennsylvania, the worst parts of Philadelphia included, which was saying something.

It was half an hour from police headquarters on the North Shore to Homewood. Patrese and Beradino drove there in an unmarked car; no need for lights or sirens, not when the victim was dead and the uniforms had the scene secured.

You could always tell when you were getting close. First came one splash of gang graffiti, then another, and within a couple of blocks these bright squiggles were everywhere: walls, houses, sidewalks, stop signs.

Our turf. Back off.

Then the pockets of young men on street corners, watching sullenly as the cop cruisers came past; then the rows of abandoned buildings, swallowing and regurgitating an endless stream of vagrants, junkies, and whores; then the handful of businesses brave or desperate enough to stay: bars, barbershops, corner stores, fast-food joints.

Wags from out of town liked to call Patrese's city "Shitsburgh." He usually jumped down their throats when they did—he loved this city—but when it came to Homewood, even Patrese was forced to admit that they had a point.

Tragedy was, it hadn't always been like this.

A century and a half ago, Homewood had been *the* place to live. Tycoons like Westinghouse and Frick had kept estates here. Businesses boomed, a trolley system was built, and people couldn't move in fast enough.

And so it stayed till after the Second World War, when the city planners decided to build the Civic Arena downtown. In doing so, they had to displace thousands of people, mainly poor black families, who'd been living in the lower Hill District nearby. Most of them moved to Homewood; and, sure as sunrise, most of Homewood's whites pulled up stakes and fled to suburbs farther out. The few middle-class blacks who could afford to follow them did.

Then came the riots, here as everywhere else during the civil rights era. With the riots came drugs and gangs, calling themselves names that sounded almost comic: Tre-Eights-Perry and Charles, Sugar Top Mob, Down Low Goonies, Reed Rude Boyz, Climax Street.

Nothing comic about what they did, though. Not then, not now. Drugs and guns, guns and drugs. It was a rare gangbanger who died of old age.

"You okay?" Beradino asked.

"Sure."

"If you're not, if you don't feel up to it—"

"I said, I'm fine."

Up ahead, Patrese saw a crowd of people spilling from the sidewalk onto the street. A handful of cops held them back. Across the way, two more police cruisers were pulling up. The officers held themselves tense and watchful, as well they might. Cops here were the enemy, seen as agents of an alien and oppressive ruling class rather than as impartial upholders of law and order.

Patrese and Beradino got out of the car. A few feet away, a young man in a bandanna and baggy pants was talking urgently into his cell.

"Yo, tell cuz it's *scorchin'* out here today. And this heat ain't from the sun, you know wha' I'm sayin'?"

He stared at Patrese as he ended the call, daring Patrese to challenge him. The police called it eye fucking, when an officer and a criminal stared each other down. As a cop, you couldn't afford to back away first. You owned the streets, not them.

Bandanna Man turned away quickly, spooked perhaps by whatever hyperkinetic pugnacity he'd seen in Patrese's eyes.

Patrese and Beradino pushed their way through the crowd, flashed their badges at one of the uniforms, and ducked beneath the yellow-and-black stretched taut between two lampposts.

It was a three-story row house, the kind you saw all over Homewood, set slightly up from the road level with a porch out front. Every homicide cop with more than a few months' experience had been inside enough of them to know the layout: kitchen and living room on the ground floor, couple of bedrooms and a bathroom on the second floor, and an attic room with dormer windows on the third.

A uniform showed Patrese and Beradino upstairs, briefing them as they climbed.

The deceased was J'Juan Weaver, and he'd been no stranger to the police, the courts, or the prison system. He'd lived in this house with Shaniqua Davenport, his girlfriend, and her (but not his) teenage son, Trent.

Shaniqua and Weaver had been an item for years, though with more ons and offs than the Gateway Clipper Fleet on game day. Before Weaver there had been a string of undesirables, who among them had fathered Shaniqua's three sons. Trent was fifteen, the youngest of them. His two older half brothers were both already in jail.

You'd have been a brave man to bet against him following suit, Patrese thought.

The uniform showed them into one of the bedrooms.

It was twelve feet square, with a double bed in the far corner. Weaver was lying next to the bed, his body oriented the same way as if he'd been sleeping there, with his head up by the end where the pillows were.

The shot that had killed him had entered at the back of his head. Patrese could see chips of white bone and gray brain matter amidst the red mess.

Weaver had been a big man—about six two and maybe two hundred pounds, all of it muscle. There were a lot of sculpted bodies in Homewood, almost all of them from pumping iron while inside. Free gym, three hots, and a cot; some of them preferred to be inside than out.

"Where are the others?" Beradino asked.

The uniform showed them into the other bedroom.

Shaniqua and Trent, both cuffed, were sitting next to each other on the bed.

Shaniqua was in her late thirties, a good-looking woman with a touch of Angela Bassett about her, and eyes that glittered with defiant intelligence.

Trent had a trainer fuzz mustache and a face rounded by puppy fat; too young to have had body and mind irrevocably hardened by life here, though for how long remained to be seen.

They both looked up at Patrese and Beradino.

Beradino introduced himself and Patrese, and asked, "What happened?"

"He was goin' for Trent," Shaniqua said. "He was gonna kill him."

That was a confession, right there.

"Why was he going to kill him?"

Silence.

An ambulance pulled up outside, come to remove Weaver's body. Beradino gestured for one of the uniforms to go tell the paramedics to wait till they were finished up here.

Trent looked as though he was about to say something, then thought better of it.

"We got reports of an argument, then shots were fired," Patrese said. "That right?"

"That right."

"What was the argument about?"

"Oh, you know."

"No, I don't. What was the argument about?"

"Same kinda shit couples always argue 'bout."

"Like what?"

"Usual shit. Boring shit."

"That's not an answer."

Above their heads, the ceiling creaked.

The detectives might have thought nothing of it, had Trent's eyes not darted heavenward, involuntary and nervous. Patrese felt a sudden churning in his gut.

"Who's up there?"

"No one," Shaniqua said quickly. Too quickly. "Just us."

One of the uniforms moved as if to investigate. Patrese raised a hand to stay him, and slipped out of the room himself.

Buzzing in his ears, indecent excitement bubbled in anticipation. *Bring it on.*

Up the stairs, quiet as he drew his gun: a single-action Ruger Blackhawk revolver, .357 Magnum caliber, four-and-five-eighths-inch barrel, black checkered grip.

Surprise was on his side. *Use it.*

He found her, alone, in the attic bedroom.

She was flat on her back, half on the floor, half on a mattress that looked as if it could break new ground in biological warfare. She was wearing a bra and cutoff denim shorts, her right arm flung wide amid the jumble of the rest of her clothes, her right hand hidden from view. Track marks marched like centipedes down the insides of her arms. No wonder Shaniqua and Trent hadn't wanted the cops to find her.

And she was white.

Homewood wasn't a place for white folks.

A few of the more enterprising suburban kids might cruise the avenues in late afternoon and buy a few ounces on a street corner before skedaddling back home and selling it to their friends at a tidy profit—half the amount for twice the price was the usual—but they stayed in their cars the whole time they were in Homewood, if they had any sense. They didn't walk the streets, and they damn sure didn't go into the crack dens.

So this one must have been desperate. And Patrese had been in enough tight spots to know what all cops knew: desperate people were often the most dangerous.

He drew a bead on her, right between the eyes. If he had to shoot, he'd have to do it fast and decisive, which meant either the head or straight down the middle of the trunk, where the vital organs are.

"Hands where I can see 'em," he said.

Her body jerked slightly, and he jumped, his finger tightening on the trigger to within a fraction of the pressure needed for discharge.

Close, he thought, *close. Too close.*

Hand shaking pressure rising expanding from inside need a safety valve pull yourself together you're not a rookie.

Patrese's heart hammered against the inside of his chest.

He was scared. Fear was good; scared cops tended to be live cops.

She opened her eyes and regarded him fuzzily.

Perhaps *too* fuzzily, he thought.

Was she shamming?

Cops had been killed in these situations before. Places like this, you were on your guard, *always.* It wasn't just the guys with tattoos and biceps who knew how to shoot.

"Lemme see your hands," he said again.

She stayed perfectly still, looking at him with an incurious blankness.

This wasn't the way people tended to react, not when faced with an armed and armored cop. Sure, there were those who were too scared to move, but they tended to be wide-eyed and gabbling.

Not this one.

Patrese felt a drop of sweat slide lazily down his spine. He had a sudden desire to crawl out of his own skin; slough it off like a snake's, go find somewhere hot and shady, and sleep. His cheeks burned with the effort of fighting deep fatigue.

Why won't she cooperate?

His thoughts came molasses slow.

Two possibilities.

One, she was so bombed that she didn't know who she was, who he was, where they were, or what he was saying.

Two, she wanted him to *think* all the above, but she was in fact perfectly lucid, and trying to lull him into a false sense of security.

She slurred something low and indistinct, twice. He caught it the second time—"Fucking cops."

The pile of clothes next to her moved slightly.

She was rummaging around in it.

"Hands. *Now*!" he shouted, taking a quick step toward her.

A flash of glinting light as she pulled something metallic from the pile, bringing her arm up and across her chest.

Patrese fired, twice, very fast.

She was already prostrate, so she didn't fall. The only part of her that moved was her arm, flopping back down by her side as her hand spilled what she'd been holding. Something metal indeed, burned on the underside where she'd heated the heroin. A spoon.

3

Patrese could hear everyone shouting downstairs: uniforms barking into their radios, the ambulance paramedics scrambling, Shaniqua bawling out Trent,

Trent yelling back at her. It was all static to him, white noise.

He knew she was dead the moment he fired; cops of his experience didn't miss from that range. But he went over to her body anyway, just to be sure. It was a physical effort for him to stay upright, the room whirling, the floor feeling as though it were being ripped from under his feet like a restaurant tablecloth in a magic trick.

He'd killed a woman who'd been threatening him with a spoon. He'd come back early from compassionate leave, he hadn't slept properly, he shouldn't have been anywhere near a situation like this. Beradino should have stopped him. Patrese should have stopped himself.

And now this woman was dead.

Whether he'd followed procedure or whether he could have done something different, he didn't know. It was his fault whichever way he cut it, no matter what any inquiry said; and there *would* be an inquiry, of course. There always was when a police officer shot someone in the line of duty.

But that was for later. Getting back to the station was their immediate priority, both for questioning Shaniqua and for tipping Patrese the hell out of Homewood.

Patrese squatted on his haunches and put his fingers to the woman's neck.

Nothing.

Wait.

A fluttering beneath his fingertips, so faint he thought he must have imagined it. He pressed harder. *There.* Definitely there.

A pulse.

"She's alive!" Patrese yelled, and at that exact moment Beradino and the paramedics came bursting through the door.

Beradino took charge, quick and efficient as usual. He told the uniforms to stay in the row house with Trent while the paramedics dealt with the girl in the attic. Then he and Patrese took Shaniqua down the stairs and out through the front door.

"Don't tell 'em *shit,* Mama," Trent shouted as they left the bedroom.

She looked back at him with an infinite mix of love and pain.

The crowd outside was even bigger than before, and more volatile. They'd heard Patrese's shots, though they didn't yet know who'd fired or what he'd hit. When they saw Shaniqua being led away, they began to jeer.

"I ain't talkin' to no white man, you hear?" Shaniqua yelled. "I was born in Trinidad, you know? Black folks don't kowtow to honkies in Trinidad, that's for damn sure." She turned to one of the uniforms on crowd control. "And I ain't talkin' to no Uncle Tom neither."

"Then you ain't talkin' to no one, girl," someone shouted from the crowd, to a smattering of laughter.

Trent was standing at the window, one of the uniforms next to him. For a moment, he looked not like a gangbanger-in-waiting but like what he was: a frightened and confused young man.

"I'll be back, my darlin'," Shaniqua shouted. "I love you for both. Just do good."

4

Homewood flashed more depressing vistas past the cruiser's windows as Beradino drove them back to headquarters: telephone-pole memorials to homicide victims, abandoned buildings plastered with official destruction notices. The Bureau of Building Inspection spent a third of its annual citywide demolition budget in Homewood alone. It could have spent it all here, several times over.

Patrese, forcing his thoughts back to the present, tried to imagine a child growing up here and wanting to play.

He couldn't.

He turned to face Shaniqua through the grille.

"Is there somewhere Trent can go?"

"JK'll look after him."

Patrese nodded. JK was John Knight, a pastor who ran an institution in Homewood for young gang members and anyone else who needed him. The place was called the 50/50, gang slang for someone who was neutral, not a gang member. Knight had also taken a master of divinity degree, served as a missionary in South America, and been chaplain of a prison in Arizona. He was a good man but no pushover; even in his fifties, he carried himself like the linebacker he'd once been and shaved his black head to a gleaming shine every morning.

That was it for conversation with Shaniqua till they reached headquarters. Patrese didn't ask what he wanted to: why someone like Shaniqua, with looks, personality, and what he guessed was no small amount of brains behind the front she presented to the world, should have wasted her time on the bunch of losers she'd welcomed into her bed, and her life, over the years.

He didn't ask for one reason: because he knew the answer.

There were always fewer men than women in places like Homewood; too many men were in jail or six feet under. So the women had to fight for the remaining men, and fight they did. There was no surer way for a girl to get status than to be on the arm of a big player.

But on the arm sooner or later meant knocked up, and when that happened, the men were out of there. Some of them even left skid marks. They didn't want to stay around and be what they saw as pussy-whipped; that was bad for their rep. Far as they were concerned, monogamy was what high-class furniture was made of.

So out and on they went, and in time their sons, growing up without a daddy—or, perhaps even worse, with a stepdaddy who cared little and smacked lots—did the same thing. Beneath the puppy fat, Trent was a good-looking boy. Give him a year or two and he'd be breaking hearts wide open, just as his father had done to Shaniqua.

"You'll be okay, Franco," Beradino said. "So will she. The girl."

Patrese nodded, in appreciation of the support rather than agreement with it.

Mind on the job, he told himself. *Mind on the job. Nothing else matters for now.*

At headquarters, Beradino logged Shaniqua's arrest with the clerk, found an empty interview room, and turned on the tape recorder.

"Detectives Mark Beradino and Franco Patrese, interviewing Shaniqua Davenport on suspicion of the murder of J'Juan Weaver. Interview commences at"—Beradino checked his watch—"ten eighteen a.m., Monday, October fourth."

He turned to Shaniqua and gave her the Miranda rights off the top of his head.

"You have the right to remain silent," Beradino said. "Anything you say can and will be used against you in a court of law. You have the right to have an attorney present during questioning. If you cannot afford an attorney, one will be appointed for you. Do you understand the rights I have just read to you? With these rights in mind, do you wish to speak to me?"

Shaniqua nodded.

"Suspect has indicated assent by nodding," Beradino said to the tape recorder.

"You damn right I assent," she said.

5

There's usually a time in a homicide interrogation when the suspect cracks, the floodgates open, and he tells the police anything and everything. That time is often several hours into questioning, sometimes even days; it's rarely right at the start.

But Shaniqua could hardly wait to get started.

"J'Juan dealt horse, that ain't no secret," she said. "And sometimes he'd bring his, er, his *clients*"—she arched her eyebrows—"back to our house, when they were too wasted to get the fuck back to their own homes."

"You were happy with this?"

"You lemme tell you what happened, we'll get done here a whole lot quicker."

Beradino was far too much of a pro to take offense. He smiled and gestured with his head: *Go on.*

"No, I weren't happy. I done seen too much of what drugs do, and I don't want no part of it. Not in my house. Every time he brings someone back—black, white, boy, girl, it don't matter—I hit the roof. Every time, he swears it's the last time.

"And every time, like a fool, I believe him.

"But today, when it happens, I've just had enough, I dunno why. We in the bedroom, Trent and me, sittin' on the bed, chattin' 'bout tings—school, grandma, those kinda tings. We talk a lot, my boy and me; we're tight. He tells me tings, I tells him tings. Only man in my life I can trust. Anyhow, J'Juan comes in, says he off out now, and I says, 'You take that skanky-ass bitch with you, like five minutes ago, or I'll call the police.'

"He looks surprised, then he narrows his eyes. Man can look mean as a snake when he wants to, you know?

"'You do that and I'll kill you, bitch,' he says.

"Trent says to him, 'Don't you talk to my mama like that.'

"J'Juan tells Trent to butt the fuck out, it ain't nothin' to do with him.

"'Come on, Trent,' says I, gettin' up from off of the bed, 'let's go.'

"'Go where?' says J'Juan. 'Go the fuck where? You leavin' me, bitch?'

"'No,' I says, 'we just goin' for a walk while you cool the fuck off.'

"'You leavin' me?' he keeps sayin'. 'You goin' to da cops?'

"'You keep on like this,' I says, 'then yeah, we're leavin' you. Gonna go live with my auntie in Des Moines. Gotta be better than bein' stuck here.'

"I'm nearest the door, J'Juan's standin' by the end of the bed. He's between me and Trent, between Trent and the door.

"He grabs Trent, and says we ain't goin' nowhere.

"And right then, I see he's left his gun on the sill.

"So I pick up the gun, and I aim it at him.

"He's got his back to me, so he don't see straight away; but Trent sees, and his eyes go like this wide"—she pulled her own eyes open as wide as they'd go—"and I say to J'Juan, 'You leave that boy the fuck alone.'

"And he turns to me all slowlike, and he says, 'Put dat fuckin' ting down, you don't know what you're doin' with it.'

"And I say, 'Trent, come on.'

"And J'Juan looks at me, and then at Trent, and then at me again, and he says, 'I'll never forget this,' he says, 'You walk out that door, I'll kill this little motherfucker with my bare hands.'

"And Trent tries to break free, and J'Juan dives for

Trent, and I just shoot him, I said I would and I did, 'cause he was gonna hurt my boy, right before my eyes, and he does that over my dead body.

"Not my boy. Take me, but not my boy.

"Trent's real daddy's about as useless a piece a shit as God ever gave breath to, so no one loves that boy like me. That's why I said I love him for both, you know; I love him as his mama and his pops too. Boy needs a daddy, know what I'm sayin'? Boy needs a father like he needs Our Father in heaven. But he ain't got one. So J'Juan can kiss my ass.

"I shot him, and I ain't ashamed of it.

"Shit, he walked through that door right now, I'd shoot the motherfucker again."

6

Patrese was silent for a moment, and then he laughed; he couldn't help it.

"Now, that's what I call a confession," he said.

Shaniqua looked at him for a moment, and then she laughed too.

"I guess it is. That's the way it happened. But it ain't murder, right? It was self-defense. He was goin' to kill me and my boy."

"How did you feel when you realized you'd killed him?" Beradino said.

"Feel? Ain't nothin' to feel. It was him or me. And if it hadn't been me, it'd have been someone else. He weren't the kinda guy who'd have lived to take out his pension and dangle grandkids on his knee."

Many people freaked at the sight of a dead body, certainly the first time they saw one. Patrese guessed Shaniqua had seen more than her fair share.

Patrese had charged dozens of suspects over the years, and he'd never apologized to a single one of them. But he wanted very badly to say sorry to Shaniqua; not just for what the law obliged him to do, but also for everything shitty in her life that had brought her to this place.

Oh, Shaniqua, he thought. *What if you'd been brought up somewhere else, by another family—by any family worth the name? If you'd never set foot in Homewood? Never opened yourself up to men whose idea of fatherhood starts and stops at conception? Never had your soul leached from you atom by atom?*

"It ain't murder, right?" she repeated.

He was about to tell her that things weren't that simple when Beradino's cell phone rang. He took it from his pocket and answered.

"Beradino."

"Mark? Freddie Hellmore here."

Freddie Hellmore was one of the best-known criminal defense lawyers, perhaps *the* best known, in the United States. A Homewood boy born and bred, he split his cases between the nobodies—usually poor, black nobodies on murder charges—and the rich and famous. He was half Don King, half Clarence Darrow.

Love him or hate him—and most people did both, sometimes at the same time—it was hard not to admire him. His acquittal rate was excellent, and he was a damn good lawyer; not the kind of man you wanted across the table on a homicide case.

"I hear you've got a client of mine in custody," he said.

"I've probably got several clients of yours in custody."

"Funny. Let me clarify. Miss Davenport?"

Beradino wasn't surprised. Someone in Homewood must have called him. "Has she appointed you?"

"Has she appointed anyone else?" When Beradino didn't answer, he continued, "I'll take that as a no. Put her on."

"I have to tell you—she's already confessed."

That piece of news rattled Hellmore, no doubt, but he recovered fast. He was a pro, after all.

"I'm going to have you seven ways to Sunday on improper conduct."

"We did it by the book, every second of the way. It's all on tape."

"Put her on, Detective. *Now.*"

Beradino passed Shaniqua the phone. The conversation was brief and one-sided, and even from six feet away it wasn't hard to get the gist: sit tight, shut up, and wait for me to get there.

"He wants to speak to you again," Shaniqua said, handing the phone back.

Indeed he did; Beradino could hear him even before he put the phone back to his ear.

"You don't ask her another damn thing till I get there, you hear?" Hellmore said. "Not even if she wants milk in her coffee or what her favorite color is. Clear?"

"Crystal."

7

THURSDAY, OCTOBER 7

She'd been in the hospital almost three days now, in the chair beside her sister's bed.

She left only to eat, to attend to calls of nature, and when the medical staff asked her for ten minutes while they changed the sheets or performed tests. Those occasions apart, she was a constant presence at Samantha's bedside.

Sometimes she talked softly of happy memories from their childhood, conjuring up apple-pie images of lazy summer evenings by mosquito-buzzed lakes and licking cake mix from the inside of the bowl.

Sometimes she fell silent and simply held Samantha's hand, as if the tendrils of tubes and lines snaking to and from Samantha's emaciated body weren't enough to anchor her in this world. And in the small hours, she rested her head against the wall and allowed herself an hour or two hovering above the surface of sleep.

People recognized her, of course, though few seemed sure how they should react when they did, especially in a hospital—*this* hospital—after everything that had happened here. For every person who smiled uncertainly at her, there was another who glared and muttered something about how she should be ashamed of herself.

She acted as if she didn't care either way. She was one hell of an actor.

And now, late in the evening, one of the doctors asked if he could have a word.

"Of course," she said.

He cleared his throat. "There's no easy way to say this, so I'll just be straight with you. Your sister is brain-dead. Life support is all that's keeping her going."

"I know."

"To be honest, with the injuries she received, it's a miracle she got this far. Multiple gunshot wounds to the head . . ." He spread his hands.

"So what are you asking me?" she said, even though she knew exactly what.

He swallowed. It was never easy, no matter how often you did it.

"You're next of kin. I need your permission to turn Samantha's life support off."

It was still a shock to hear it stated so baldly, she thought.

"And if I refuse?"

"Then we get a court order."

She thought for a moment. "I understand a certain amount of medical jargon," she said. The doctor nodded, knowing—as did everybody—what she'd been through in the past. "Tell me."

"There's total necrosis of the cerebral neurons," he replied. "All Samantha's brain activity—including the involuntary activity necessary to sustain life—has come to an end. We've conducted all the usual physical examinations to find clinical evidence of brain function. The responses have been uniformly negative. No response to pain, no pupillary response, no oculocephalic reflex, no corneal reflex, no caloric reflex."

"You've lost me."

"Sorry. Eye tests measuring reaction to light, movement, contact, and water being poured in the ears. As I said, all negative. And her EEGs have been isoelectric—sorry, flatline—since she was admitted."

"And you don't want to waste your time keeping her alive."

"It's not a question of wanting."

"It is."

"It's a question of prioritizing. The damage is irreversible. She's not going to get better. She's not going to improve even an iota from what she is now. The only way, medically, we could justify maintaining life support would be to remove her organs for transplant donation, but . . ." He spread his hands again.

"But she was a junkie, and no one in their right mind would touch her organs with a ten-foot pole. I get it, Doctor. You don't have to soft-soap me. Very well."

"Thank you. Please understand—we don't have the capacity or resources to keep her here indefinitely. Even if we did, she has no reason, no consciousness. She's not living. She's existing."

She tipped her head slightly and examined him. "You really believe that?"

"It's fact. It's a medical fact. Medicine's what I believe in."

When she sighed, it sounded to her like condemnation.

"You square it with your conscience," she said.

If she'd got up then and followed the doctor as he left the room, and if she'd turned left at the second set of fire doors and darted into the staff room just beyond, she'd have seen another pair of siblings, these two huddled in anguished conversation.

"You can't go in there, Franco," Bianca was saying. "It's not right."

"I know. I just want to . . . say I'm sorry, I guess."

"If that was you sitting in there, with your sister—with *me*—on life support, and the guy who'd shot her came in, what would you feel?"

"I'd want to kill him," Patrese admitted.

"Precisely."

"But that's just me."

"No, Cicillo, that's most people. You think she cares you're sorry? You think she'll say, 'Hell, it must have been hard for you so soon after your folks got killed, and even though you shouldn't have been there in the first place, I forgive you—could have happened to anybody'? You think she'll say that? Of course not. You tell me one thing it could accomplish, you going in there now. *One thing*."

"I shot her. My fault. Make amends. Take it like a man."

"You want to make amends? Then keep doing what you do. Next time, you'll save a life."

"That won't cancel it out."

"No, it won't," Bianca agreed. "But it'll be a good thing to do in itself. You on the streets, me working in here, that's the best we can do. That 'protect and serve' stuff, keep believing in it. You're a good cop, you're a good man. A lot of guys wouldn't give it a second thought—you know, junkie scum, she had it coming, better off dead. Not you. You still care. I hope you always do. I know you will. You're my little brother, and I love you. But caring about something and beating yourself up over it aren't the same thing."

She pulled him to her. She couldn't hear him crying or feel the tears on her shoulder, but she knew all the same.

8

TUESDAY, OCTOBER 12

The police look after their own. Always have, always will.

The inquiry into what had happened in Shaniqua's house was conducted by Allen Chance, one of a triumvirate of assistant police chiefs referred to, not entirely without irony, as the three wise monkeys.

The Pittsburgh police department boasted three divisions: administration (the backroom bureaucracy that kept the whole place going), operations (uniformed officers), and investigation, Chance's crew, which along with homicide included burglary, CSI, missing persons, narcotics, robbery, sex crimes, and financial crimes.

Not far north of five foot six, with rimless eyeglasses and the neatest of side partings, Chance looked—and thought—more like an accountant than a cop. Murder clearance rates, targets, statistics: Chance crunched them all with a zeal the Federal Reserve would have envied.

He also knew that the quickest way to send those numbers the wrong way was to hammer the morale of his officers, and the quickest way to do that was to leave them dangling when the heat was on.

So his investigation into Patrese's conduct was perfunctory almost to the point of insult. Independent? Not a chance. Pragmatic? You bet.

Beradino, called as a character witness, testified that Patrese was an excellent detective, that the situation had been fast-moving, and that Patrese had done what any other well-trained officer would have.

The suspect had ignored two warnings before making a sudden movement for a hidden object, Beradino pointed out. Patrese's only option had been to shoot.

Beradino asked if he could make a personal observation. Chance acquiesced.

Beradino said he hoped this didn't sound arrogant or fanciful, but he liked to think of himself as Patrese's mentor, a father figure even. He'd seen Patrese change and mature over the three years they'd spent as partners, and Beradino liked to think he'd had something to do with that. As a friend as well as a colleague, he'd been fully aware of Patrese's personal circumstances at the time of the incident. In his opinion, they had not contributed in any way to what had happened.

Chance made appropriate noises about the death being a tragedy. Not the only tragedy of the victim's truncated life, if the toxicological reports were any guide.

Summing up, he said Patrese's actions and behavior had been beyond reproach. No charges would be brought, and Patrese would continue with his duties as usual. A press release to that effect would be prepared and released to the media.

"You really believe that?" Patrese asked Beradino afterward.

"Really believe what?"

"That I didn't come back too soon? That it would have played out just the same if, er, if my folks . . . if everything else had been normal?"

"That's what I said."

"I know. But is that what you *meant*?"

Beradino squeezed Patrese's shoulder—with affection, certainly, but was there something else there? Regret? Pragmatism?

"Ask me no questions, Franco, I tell you no lies," he said at last.

9

THURSDAY, OCTOBER 14

PENNSYLVANIA DEPARTMENT OF CORRECTIONS

REPORT OF INVESTIGATION INTO ALLEGED EMPLOYEE MISCONDUCT

INSTITUTION: SCI MUNCY, PO BOX 180, MUNCY, PA 17756
DATE OF INVESTIGATION: THURSDAY, OCTOBER 14
EMPLOYEE IN QUESTION: JESSLYN H. GEDGE
POSITION: DEPUTY SUPERINTENDENT FOR FACILITIES MANAGEMENT

CASE HISTORY:

Complaints against JESSLYN H. GEDGE were brought on June 23 by inmate MARA E. SLINGER, number A/38259728-2.*

**Subsequent to bringing the complaints, inmate Slinger was released from incarceration July 12 by order of the Superior Court.*

SUMMARY OF ALLEGATIONS:

Inmate Slinger alleges that Deputy Superintendent Gedge:

1. entered into a nonconsensual sexual relationship with her;
2. used her position and influence within the institution to maintain this relationship for several months, substantially against inmate Slinger's will;
3. eavesdropped on inmate Slinger's confidential telephone conversations with her attorney;
4. took revenge when inmate Slinger finally terminated their sexual relationship in the following ways:
   - 4.1. carried out repeated personal searches, strip searches, and body-cavity searches on inmate Slinger, sometimes in public owing to the alleged lack of suitable private facilities;
   - 4.2. scheduled repeated dental examinations for inmate Slinger, knowing that inmate Slinger has a phobia of dentists, and that no inmate within the state DOC system has the right to refuse such an examination;
   - 4.3. otherwise harassed inmate Slinger on repeated occasions, applying maximum penalties for minor infractions of prison regulations, including but not limited to: failure to use the shortest route when traveling between two points in the prison complex; stepping out of line in the dining hall; bringing books or papers into the dining hall; giving part of her

meals to other prisoners; not taking a full set of cutlery at mealtimes; not eating all the food accepted at mealtimes; and talking to inmates working on the refectory serving line;

4.4. withheld packages addressed to inmate Slinger, or removed certain items before handing such packages over;

4.5. repeatedly confiscated inmate Slinger's prison ID card, in full knowledge that inmates must carry said card at all times except when showering, and that inmates must pay for replacement cards if they lose, destroy, or damage said card;

4.6. planted contraband (including money, potential escape tools, e.g. nail files, unprescribed pharmaceuticals, illegal narcotics paraphernalia, weapons) in inmate Slinger's cell during searches, and forbade inmate Slinger to be present during such searches on the grounds that her presence would constitute a threat;

4.7. held inmate Slinger down and forcibly shaved her head;

4.8. refused to hand back personal items upon inmate Slinger's release.

SUMMARY OF RESPONSE:

Deputy Superintendent Gedge responded to the allegations as follows:

1. She admitted that she and inmate Slinger had conducted a sexual relationship, but maintained

that it was entirely consensual and that inmate Slinger had in fact initiated sexual contact in the first instance.

2. The answer to this point is implicit in her answer to point 1.
3. On the occasions that she did overhear such conversations, it was while she was monitoring technical faults in the institution's telephone system, and she stopped listening immediately when she realized the conversation was subject to attorney-client privilege.
4. Termination of the sexual relationship was mutual and amicable, and therefore Deputy Superintendent Gedge felt no need for revenge.
   - 4.1. Deputy Superintendent Gedge carried out all searches in strict accordance with institution policy. On occasion, when all private interview and meeting rooms were being used, searches were carried out in public. Deputy Superintendent Gedge strove to keep these occasions to a minimum.
   - 4.2. Deputy Superintendent Gedge scheduled all inmate dental examinations in strict accordance with institution policy.
   - 4.3. Deputy Superintendent Gedge enforced all regulations in strict accordance with institution policy.
   - 4.4. Deputy Superintendent Gedge checked mail sent to inmate Slinger, removed contraband items, and read letters when she had reason to believe they were being used to plan an

escape or other illegal activity. This was all in strict accordance with institution policy.

4.5. Deputy Superintendent Gedge maintains that inmate Slinger mislaid or deliberately destroyed her ID card on several occasions.

4.6. Deputy Superintendent Gedge absolutely denies planting contraband items in inmate Slinger's cell.

4.7. Deputy Superintendent Gedge maintains that inmate Slinger shaved her own head to remove traces of illegal drugs in her hair follicles.

4.8. Deputy Superintendent Gedge denies this absolutely.

SUPPORT FOR INMATE SLINGER:

Inmate MADISON A-S. SETTERSTROM, prisoner number A/73647829-5, is a former cellmate of inmate Slinger.

She testified that inmate Slinger had repeatedly confided in her that she was unhappy with Deputy Superintendent Gedge's advances toward her, and only acquiesced for fear of negative consequences if she did not.

Inmate Setterstrom said Deputy Superintendent Gedge's behavior after the end of the relationship indicated that inmate Slinger's fears of such consequences had been largely justified.

Several other inmates, speaking on condition of anonymity, also voiced their support for inmate Slinger.

SUPPORT FOR DEPUTY SUPERINTENDENT GEDGE:

Lieutenant VALERIE Y. MARGRAVINE testified that Deputy Superintendent Gedge is well respected among her fellow corrections officers for her attention to discipline and detail.

Several corrections officers stated that Deputy Superintendent Gedge is a devout Christian and a lay minister who presides over services of worship in the institution's chapel on Sundays and other days.

OTHER FACTORS:

Inmate Slinger is a high-profile individual whose original conviction attracted substantial media attention, as did the subsequent overturning of that conviction on appeal by the Superior Court. She remains a newsworthy individual.

Any similar media attention in regard to this procedure would be undesirable. The department therefore believes a quick and final resolution to be in the interests of all parties.

Inmate Slinger has signed a confidentiality agreement preventing her from disclosing details of this investigation and hearing to the press, on condition that Deputy Superintendent Gedge receives appropriate punishment.

Deputy Superintendent Gedge has also been the subject of previous harassment complaints, sexual and otherwise, from inmates (see cases T637-02, T432-00, T198-96, T791-89).

VERDICT:

The Pennsylvania Department of Corrections code of conduct expressly and absolutely forbids all corrections officers from conducting sexual or intimate relationships with inmates.

Irrespective of the validity of the other allegations, Deputy Superintendent Gedge's maintenance of a relationship with inmate Slinger qualifies as gross misconduct and is by itself grounds for immediate dismissal.

Consequently, Deputy Superintendent Gedge is dismissed from her post with immediate effect, and is disqualified from holding any other position within the Pennsylvania Department of Corrections for a period of no less than 10 years.

Signed,

Anderson M. Thornhill

Anderson M. Thornhill
Superintendent, SCI Muncy

10

When Jesslyn pulled in at the service stop just outside DuBois on I-80, she realized with a start that she could hardly remember a thing about the last hour or so she'd been driving. She'd been operating the car on instinct and muscle memory alone, while her thoughts chased themselves into rolling, tumbling tendrils of confusion.

Her career was over. That much—that alone—she knew. She believed in punishment and retribution; that's why she'd sought a vocation in corrections. Taking that from her, and in a way that meant she'd never find work in that sector again, was more than she could bear. It was as though Mara Slinger had first led her into evil, then cut her heart out. Here, truly, surely, was the devil.

She wondered, briefly, whether she should buy a razor here, open the arteries in her wrists, and be done with it all; and even as the thought came to her, she stamped on it with frantic fury, as though trying to beat down a grass fire.

Just the fact that she could entertain such a notion was a deep, shaming sin. As 1 Corinthians, chapter 3, verses 16 and 17 said: "Know ye not that ye are the temple of God, and that the Spirit of God dwelleth in you? If any man defile the temple of God, him shall God destroy; for the temple of God is holy, which temple ye are."

She'd preached that passage repeatedly in the Muncy chapel, knowing that barely a week went past without an inmate trying to take her own life.

Jesslyn stopped her car, a silver Toyota Camry she'd had for a few years, and walked across the parking lot to the service building.

She hadn't eaten all day. She'd been too nervous to eat breakfast this morning, knowing her fate would today be decided one way or another, and afterward she'd been given half an hour to pack up all her belongings, hand in her credentials, and get out. No time to say her good-byes, let alone get some food.

Twenty years' hard work, ripped from her in a flash.

The burger bar smelled like all burger bars do: of cooking oil, sweat, and resentment.

Jesslyn walked up to the counter, where a Hispanic-looking woman whose name tag read "Esmerelda," and who was too young to be as overweight as she was, regarded the world without enthusiasm.

"Help you?" Esmerelda asked, her tone so polite as to be insolent.

Jesslyn mumbled her order and dropped a ten-dollar bill on the counter.

Fat fingers handed her change and food oozing grease through its wrappers.

Jesslyn went to the far corner of the room, past an Employees Wanted sign and a couple of truckers with baseball caps trailing raggedy ponytails.

She was halfway through her burger when the tears came, hot with anger and self-pity. She pressed her hands to her face, not to stanch the flood but in the illogical, childish belief that if she couldn't see the other diners, they couldn't see her.

Through the hot rising of mucus in her throat, she repeated silently to herself the words of Lamentations 2:18. "Their heart cried out to the Lord, O wall of the daughter of Zion, let tears run down like a river day and night; give thyself no rest, nor let the apple of thine eye cease."

11

FRIDAY, OCTOBER 15

Jesslyn left early the next morning, as if she were going to work as usual.

She'd told Mark nothing. It helped that she liked to keep her work and home lives separate—whatever Beradino knew of her job was what she chose to tell him—but still. How could she explain it all to him? Where would she even begin?

She had no idea; and, until she did, she figured it was best to keep quiet, and somehow square up that silence between herself and God.

What she *did* know was that the longer she left it, the harder it would be to ever reveal the truth. Every secret she kept from Mark made keeping the next one both easier and necessary.

She hadn't told him about her affair with Mara, so she hadn't been able to tell him about Mara's complaints, so she hadn't been able to tell him about yesterday's tribunal, so she hadn't been able to tell him she'd been dismissed, so she had to go off today to keep up the pretense that everything was normal.

And going off today meant she'd have to go off tomorrow, and the next day.

She couldn't keep doing that indefinitely—at least, not without somewhere to go and something that would pay her. Corrections didn't pay like Wall Street in the first place, and she didn't have much in the way of savings stashed away.

So she needed a job. Not just any job—a job that offered shifts. Prison work wasn't nine to five; like the police, prison officers worked constantly changing eight-hour shifts, sometimes on the night watch, to provide round-the-clock coverage. She couldn't keep up the pretense for long if she took employment as an office clerk.

It didn't have to be a great job. In fact, it almost certainly wouldn't be.

But as long as it paid and got her out of the house, it would do, at least until something better came along. And she could pass the time by savoring the righteous anger that burned within her. She'd given her life to her vocation, and she'd been cast aside like a piece of flotsam.

That wasn't the way you treated people. There would be retribution; that was not only her right, but her duty too.

She recited to herself the words of Exodus 21: 23–25: "And if any mischief follow, then thou shalt give life for life, eye for eye, tooth for tooth, hand for hand, foot for foot, burning for burning, wound for wound, stripe for stripe."

Burning for burning. Stripe for stripe.

Jesslyn realized she was heading toward Muncy;

reflex, perhaps, or providence. Ahead, she saw signs to the DuBois travel plaza, where she'd stopped yesterday.

She pulled off the interstate, parked the Camry, and went back into the burger bar.

Esmerelda wasn't on duty today. At the counter was a guy with acne and eyeglasses who could barely have been out of his teens. His name tag proclaimed him to be not only Kevin, but also the manager.

"Help you?" he said, in exactly the same tone Esmerelda had used the day before. Must be something they taught at burger college.

Jesslyn couldn't remember feeling as demeaned as she did now. Only her faith that God would provide, and that he moved in mysterious ways, forced the index finger of her right hand up and in the direction of the Employees Wanted sign.

"I'd like a job, please," she said.

12

MONDAY, OCTOBER 18

"You don't recognize me?" I ask.

Michael Redwine shakes his head. He can't speak, because I've put duct tape across his mouth; and he can't take the tape off or lash out at me, because I've cuffed his hands behind his back. The cuffs are those thin plastic ones, good for one use only.

One use is all I need.

Besides, the plastic won't last long, not with what I've got in store for him; but by the time he'll be able to break them off, he'll be long past doing anything at all.

His mouth moves furiously around the gag, spilling saliva down his jaw. It takes me a moment to work out what he's saying.

"You're praying?" I ask.

He looks at me with wide eyes and nods.

"That's funny," I say. "I didn't think people like you believed in a higher power."

His brows contract in puzzlement.

I look around his apartment again.

Nothing much wrong with it, truth be told. He lives in the Pennsylvanian, about the most luxurious apartment building in all of downtown. It's built on the site of the old Union rail station, and the arched canopy that covers the main entrance is often cited as the most captivating architectural arrangement in all of Pittsburgh.

The Pennsylvanian has thirteen stories, the apartments getting ever grander the higher you go. Redwine's apartment is on the tenth floor, where the building's loft homes are located: all elegant arched windows, crown moldings, wood paneling, and intricately detailed fifteen-foot ceilings. The windows give onto warehouse roofs and overpasses swooping toward the Strip. Far below me, streetlights glow low sodium.

This, all this luxury, is what you get when you're one of the premier brain surgeons in all Pennsylvania, possibly in the entire United States.

And all this luxury means nothing when you've done

what Michael Redwine did, and you're going to be punished like I'm about to punish him.

I open my bag and bring out a red plastic container. It can take a gallon, and pretty much everyone in the world recognizes its shape and what it's designed to hold.

Redwine is screaming mutely behind the duct tape even before I open the lid and let him smell the gasoline.

"Remember what you did?" I ask, beginning to pour the gasoline over his head.

He jerks his body across the floor and tries to stand; anything to get away from the pulsing glugs that mat his hair to his forehead and run into his eyes.

He kicks at me, but I skip easily out of reach, still pouring.

The gasoline is drenching his shirt now, rivuleting down his trousers.

"Remember what you said to me?" I ask.

He throws himself against the wall: to knock himself out and spare himself the agony of what he knows is coming, perhaps, or as a last desperate call for help.

Neither works. He's still conscious, and no one's coming.

"And remember what I said to you?"

When the plastic can's empty, I cap it and put it back in my bag.

I take out the juggling torch and the lighter. Then I put the bag by the door, the easier to grab it fast on my way out if I have to make a sudden exit.

I light the torch's wick and look at Redwine. I don't think I've ever seen anyone look more terrified in my entire life.

"Isaiah chapter fifty-nine, verse seventeen," I say. "For I put on righteousness as a breastplate, and a helmet of salvation upon my head; and I put on the garments of vengeance for clothing, and am clad with zeal as a cloak."

The torch flares in my hand like the fount of justice. I take a step toward him.

He backs away until he reaches the far corner and can go no farther.

He curls himself into a ball and turns his face away from me.

I lower the torch to his shoulder.

13

From the point of view of a homicide detective, fire scenes are among the most difficult to work. What fire doesn't destroy, it damages; and what it damages, the firefighters tend to destroy in their efforts to extinguish the blaze. Neither factor bodes well for the preservation of evidence. Only bomb sites boast more destruction and disorder.

The fire department had been on the scene within four minutes of being called, when one of Redwine's neighbors had smelled burning, looked out the window, and seen large black clouds billowing from Redwine's apartment. The firemen had evacuated the entire apartment building and set to putting out the fire.

It had taken them two and a half hours, but they'd managed it, and had kept it contained to the apartment of origin, more or less. There were scorch marks in the apartment above and those to either side, but nothing worse than that, and no serious structural damage, except to Redwine's apartment itself.

The senior fire officer on-site having declared the building safe, Patrese and Beradino pulled on crime scene overalls, shoe covers, and latex gloves, in that order, and entered Redwine's apartment.

They'd been called in the moment the firefighters had discovered both the body—presumed to be Redwine's, though obviously not proved as such yet—and the demarcation line on the carpet next to him.

A demarcation line, in fire terms, marks the boundary between where a surface—in this case, the carpet—has burned and where it hasn't. More often than not, it indicates the use of a liquid accelerant, which in turn means the fire was started deliberately.

And since very few people choose to start a fire and then hang around inside a burning apartment—suicide by self-immolation is extremely rare—it seemed likely that someone other than Redwine, someone long since gone, had been responsible for both the fire and Redwine's death.

This left two possibilities. Either the arsonist had killed Redwine and then set the fire to cover his tracks; or it had been the fire itself that had killed Redwine.

The crime scene photographer was already there. Patrese and Beradino watched as he fired off round after round of shots, changing lenses and films with practiced ease. In close for the serious detail, magnifying things a few millimeters across up to the size of a normal print; midrange images that concentrated on specific objects; and wide-angle shots capturing as much of the room as possible.

He was using both black-and-white and color films. Color was usually better, but gruesome photos were best shown to squeamish juries in monochrome.

Beradino glanced across at Patrese, who read in the furrow of the older man's brow exactly what it meant: concern, that all this would scald Patrese's memories.

Freeway fireball parents' lives snuffed out in a fingersnap the sickening noxious brutality of flames concentrate focus nothing matters but what's here and now.

"I'm okay," Patrese said.

They looked around what was left of the room. It was rectangular, though not by much—fourteen feet by seventeen, at a guess. There were two sofas, a coffee table, and a plasma TV.

All of them burned to the edge of recognition, as was Redwine's body.

His skin was cracked in a patchwork of charred black and bright red, splashed with different colors where his clothes had melted onto him. He was hunched like a prizefighter, arms drawn up in front of him and legs bent at the knees.

This in itself proved nothing, they knew. The position was caused by muscles contracting in response to the heat of the fire, and could not indicate by itself whether the victim had been alive or dead when the fire was set.

But the color of the body could do so.

Reddening of the skin and blistering tended to take place on a victim who was still breathing rather than one who wasn't.

Beradino crouched by the body and took a small voice recorder from his pocket. He was gospel strict about making contemporaneous notes. It wasn't just that he couldn't rely on remembering everything when it came to writing things up a couple of hours later back at the station; it was also that making notes forced the investigator to slow down, think, take his time.

After all, the victim wasn't going anywhere.

Beradino looked closely at what had been Redwine's face.

He didn't think about what Redwine might have looked like in life; that was no longer relevant. If he thought of anything, it was of overbarbecued meat. The less emotive and more commonplace he could make it seem, the better.

Twenty-five years on the homicide squad hadn't hardened him to things, not really. It had merely made him better at coping with them.

There.

"Around the nostrils," he said into the recorder. "Beneath the burn marks. Smoke stains, clearly visible."

The pathologist would doubtless find blackened lungs when he came to do the autopsy, which would confirm it; but for now, Beradino had more than enough to go on with.

Smoke stains meant inhalation. It was this that had almost certainly killed Redwine—breathing in smoke finished people off before burning flesh did—but it didn't alter the chronology of what had happened, or the central conclusion.

Michael Redwine had been alive when the fire was set, and he'd been burned to death.

14

The doorman was dressed in a suit that, Patrese thought, almost certainly cost more than any of his own suits, and very possibly more than all of them put together.

He tried to ignore this slight on his sartorial standards, and instead read the name on the doorman's lapel badge. Jared Foxworth.

Foxworth handed Patrese two lists.

The first showed which apartments were occupied and by whom, though some of the names were of companies rather than individuals. The Pennsylvanian was a popular locale for corporate rentals, allowing companies based outside of Pittsburgh to put up employees or clients here instead of paying for hotels. Freddie Hellmore, Shaniqua's lawyer, was on this list.

The second was a record of every visitor who'd gone up to the apartments today. The Pennsylvanian's rule was simple: you asked at the reception desk, the doorman called the apartment in question, and if you went up, you signed in with him first. If you stayed in reception and waited for a resident to come down before leaving the building, you didn't need to sign in; but

Redwine's killer couldn't have done that, since Redwine had been found in his apartment. Anyway, he'd had no visitors at all today, said Foxworth; none, full stop.

There were, he added, no other ways into the building unless you knew enough about the Pennsylvanian's layout to sneak in through the underground parking garage or up the fire escape; but even then you'd have to rely on doors being open that shouldn't have been and risk being spotted by someone who might ask you what you were doing. Hazardous, to say the least, but not out of the question.

Whichever way Redwine's killer had entered the building, he—of course, it could be a she, Beradino said, but since the majority of murderers were male, they would for simplicity's sake refer to the killer as "he," all the while maintaining an open mind—he had not had to force the door of the apartment itself. The firefighters had broken down the door themselves when they'd arrived, and they were adamant the door had been intact.

Which in turn suggested two possibilities.

First, that the killer had a key with which he'd let himself in. This might have been a surprise to Redwine, or he might have been expecting it. Perhaps the killer had thought Redwine would be out, and the surprise at finding him in the apartment had been mutual.

Second, that Redwine had known the killer, and opened the door to him.

The crowd out front encompassed not just the building's residents, who'd been evacuated and were massed under the canopy waiting to be questioned, but the usual rubberneckers who'd heard that there'd been not just a fire but a death too, which was for a dispiriting number of people reason enough to drop everything and stand behind police barriers for hours on end.

One of the uniforms was subtly filming the latter group. Murderers sometimes returned to the scene of their crime; arsonists often did. The detectives would study the footage later, looking for known troublemakers or simply those who looked shifty.

A film crew from KDKA, Pittsburgh's local TV station, was also on-site. The event was newsworthy because of the Pennsylvanian's prestige as a place to live and the fact that the victim had been a surgeon; but the body language of the reporter and cameraman betrayed their instinct that this was no major story. A big hoo-ha for a few hours, sure, but not the kind of thing that got rolling captions around the clock and a procession of talking heads through the studio. Man dies in fire. Tragic, but happens every day. The TV crew would go through the motions and hope for something bigger, more exciting, or quirkier next time.

Beradino and Patrese went over to the residents. Hellmore broke rank and hurried over to them.

"Detectives."

Beradino nodded, cool to the point of curtness. No love lost between cop and defense lawyer.

"Terrible business, this," Hellmore said. "Anything I can do, be glad to help."

"An officer will take your statement in due course."

Beradino was already turning to the remainder of the residents and asked if a Magda Nagorska was among them; according to their records, she lived directly beneath Redwine's apartment.

She was indeed there, and she looked as old as God, possibly older.

If the way Patrese had to shout every question two or three times was anything to go by, Redwine could have been murdered in *her* apartment, perhaps right next to her, without her having heard a damn thing.

"Did you see or hear anyone go into his apartment?" Patrese asked.

"He was a charming man," she shouted.

"No commotion? An argument? Your apartment didn't shake?"

"It's dreadful, that it happens somewhere like here. *Dreadful.*"

One of the uniforms bit on his hand to stop himself from laughing. It was like giggling in church—the more taboo it was, the more tempting it became.

Patrese didn't think it would do much for the reputation of the Pittsburgh homicide department if the officer fell to his knees weeping with laughter in front of a potential witness.

They continued in mutual incomprehension for several minutes, before Beradino asked in exasperation, "Do you have a hearing aid?"

"Lemonade?"

"HEAR-ING AID?"

"Oh yes, but I don't wear it too often. I'm not deaf. Just a little hard of hearing in one ear, you know."

15

"How did the killer get in?" Patrese asked, when he and Beradino were in the car.

"That's the sixty-four-thousand-dollar question, isn't it? Well, one of them, anyway."

That the fire escape and underground garage were risky methods of entry didn't mean they were impossible. The parking garage had closed-circuit TV; the fire escape didn't. They'd trawl through the footage and see what they could find.

Failing either of those, could the killer have been a resident?

It seemed unlikely. They'd spoken to all the residents, albeit briefly, and none of them looked like they could harm a fly, let alone had an obvious motive to do away with Redwine.

But looks meant nothing, so of course the uniforms would follow up, interviewing every resident properly.

What about one of the doormen? Probably not Foxworth, who had been on-duty—he would have needed to be away from the front desk for too long—but one of the others, who was off shift? A doorman would know all the shortcuts and hidden entrances, and his presence wouldn't be suspicious.

But it came back to the same stumbling block: *why?*

Why had Redwine been killed, and why—the second $64,000 question—why in that way? Why burned, rather than, say, shot or stabbed?

To hide something? If not Redwine's identity, then something else?

To destroy something? Forensic evidence, or something less directly connected to the corpse, such as documentation or other items?

As punishment—a cruel and unusual way of murdering someone?

Or were all these speculations delving too deep into something very simple? Had Michael Redwine been burned to death simply because the killer had felt that was the easiest way of doing it?

Redwine had been a surgeon at Mercy, Pittsburgh's largest and most famous hospital. Mercy was located uptown, a few blocks from the Pennsylvanian.

"We're going to Mercy?" Patrese asked.

"You got any better ideas?"

"Matter of fact, I do."

Patrese flipped open his cell phone and hit one of the speed-dials.

A woman answered on the second ring. "Hey, Cicillo."

"Hey, yourself. Are you on shift?"

"No, at home, all alone; Sandro's taken the kids out. Why?"

"Can we come by?"

"Who's we?"

"Me and Mark."

"Why? What's happened?"

"Tell you when we get there. We're leaving town now. See you in fifteen."

He ended the call. Beradino looked across at him.

"Who was that?"

"Bianca. My sister."

"The one who's a doctor at Mercy?"

"The very same."

Beradino smiled.

There were two ways to find out what Redwine had been like and why someone might have wanted to kill him in such a vile manner. There were formal channels, which involved managers, bureaucrats, and warrants; and there were informal channels, which involved the promise of favors owed if you were lucky and good old dead presidents if you weren't.

Either way, there were no prizes for guessing which method tended to be quicker and more effective.

"You're not as dumb as you look," Beradino said.

"That's the nicest thing you've ever said to me."

16

"What was he like?" Bianca considered the question for a moment. "He was Harvard Med School. That's what he was like."

"You mean he thought he was God's gift?" Beradino said.

"In my experience, most Harvard Med Schoolers think God is *their* gift to the world rather than vice versa."

Patrese laughed. That was his sister in a nutshell, he thought; tell it like it is, no matter the circumstances.

Her patients tended to appreciate her straight talking, particularly when it came to diagnosing the severity of whatever they had. In her experience, most people with illnesses liked to know what they were dealing with.

She'd been shocked, of course, when they'd told her what had happened to Redwine. You wouldn't wish that on your worst enemy—unless, of course, it was that he *was* your worst enemy that had made you do it in the first place.

But doctors saw an awful lot of life and certainly too much of death, so they didn't tend to stay shocked for very long. Bianca was no exception.

So now she sat with her brother and Beradino in her living room and tried to think of who might have wanted Redwine dead.

"How well did you know him?" Beradino asked.

"Well enough, but as a professional colleague rather than a friend. You understand the difference? I spent a lot of time in his company, but almost always at work. We rarely socialized. I knew a lot about his life, and he mine, because those details tend to get shared when you're talking; but if one of us had taken a job someplace else, I doubt we'd have stayed in touch."

"Personal life?"

"Divorced. Couple of teenage boys."

"Nasty split?"

"Quite the opposite, far as I know. In fact, I remember him telling me once that both he and his wife—Marsha, she's called—had been sacked by three successive sets of divorce lawyers because they weren't being greedy enough."

Beradino and Patrese laughed. Cops appreciated a dig at lawyers as much as anyone else; more than most, in fact.

"Wife and kids still in Pittsburgh?" Beradino continued.

"No. They went out west, to Tucson. He used to go and see them several times a year. Hung out with the kids, stayed over at their house."

"He and Marsha still sleeping together?"

"You'd have to ask her that. But I don't think so. Maybe that was why they split up to start with. He told me once he thought of her more as a sister than anything else."

"He have anyone else serious?"

"Not that I know of."

"No," said Beradino thoughtfully, "I can't imagine they'd have been too thrilled with him playing happy family with his ex, whatever the real story."

"But I doubt he ever lacked female company. He was handsome, he was smart, he was successful."

"And arrogant."

"Yes, and arrogant. Most surgeons are. It comes with the territory. You ask them, they'd call it self-confidence. Patients like a surgeon who's sure of what he's doing. The last thing you need when someone's about to open you up is to find they're suddenly iffy about the job."

"He was a good surgeon?"

"One of the best. A real pioneer, always looking for new techniques, new ways to make things better. There are people walking around Pittsburgh today who are still here because of Michael Redwine—not just because he saved their lives, but because he did so with methods and equipment that simply didn't exist several years ago, and that he helped bring into being."

"He ever make mistakes?"

For the first time, Bianca paused.

The house was suddenly quiet, which in Patrese's experience was an event about as frequent as Halley's comet. If it wasn't Sandro's endless practicing—he was a violinist with the Pittsburgh Symphony—it was the noise generated by three kids blessed with the kind of energy that ought to be illegal.

Vittorio was in ninth grade, Sabrina seventh, and Gennaro sixth, and Patrese loved them all to bits. Acting the goofball uncle with them, taking them to Steelers games, playing touch football with them in the backyard till sundown—and telling them that Gramps and Gran were now in heaven, and holding them close when they cried.

"All surgeons make mistakes," Bianca said eventually.

"You sound very defensive about that."

"Yes, well . . . Listen, people expect doctors to be perfect, get everything absolutely right every time. But it doesn't always work like that. We're human, our knowledge is imperfect, some symptoms aren't always clear-cut."

"I don't think Mark intended it to be a value judgment," Patrese said softly.

Bianca might be his big sister, but he was still protective of her; that was the Italian male in him.

And he understood her defensiveness. Doctors

were no different from cops—they looked out for one another. You dissed one, you dissed them all; that was how they saw it.

So they covered one another's backs. Like most professions, medicine was in essence a small world; you never knew when you might need someone to help you out, so you didn't go around making unnecessary enemies. And old habits died hard, even when the person you were protecting was no longer around.

"I'm just looking for why someone might have wanted him dead," Beradino said.

Bianca nodded. "I understand. I'm sorry."

"No need."

"Okay. Every time you lose a patient, you consider it a mistake, even when you know deep down you couldn't have done anything more. That's just the way you feel. And Mike had his fair share of those. I mean, brain surgery, the stats aren't that great. You don't open up someone's skull unless things are pretty bad to start with. But those ones, I'm not counting; they're not mistakes, not really.

"Then there are the ones when, perhaps, if you'd done something different, you might possibly have saved them. But in those cases you don't know till it's too late anyway, and you can drive yourself mad if you dwell on it. If everyone's vision was as good as their hindsight, every optician across the land would be out of work."

"People sue you for those cases?"

"Sure. If you *could* have done something different, they'll say you *should* have done. So the lawyers get involved, everyone starts slinging writs around, and if you can, you settle before it gets to court, goes public, and damages your rep. Comes with the turf, doesn't mean you're suddenly a crappy surgeon."

She paused again.

"And?" Patrese said, not unkindly.

"And then there are the *real* fuckups."

"Redwine have any of those?"

She nodded. "One."

17

The technical term was *wrong-site surgery,* which barely hinted at how catastrophic such incidents were, and how insultingly, ridiculously amateur they seemed.

Wrong-site surgery was, in essence, when the surgeon operated on a perfectly healthy part of the patient's anatomy, and left the offending area untouched.

The consequences tended to fall into two categories: drastic and fatal.

Redwine had been scheduled to remove a blood clot from the brain of Abdul Bayoumi, a professor of philosophy at the University of Pittsburgh.

It was a routine-enough operation, especially for a surgeon of Redwine's standing; he'd done hundreds in his career.

The clot had been on the left side of Bayoumi's brain. Redwine had cut into the right-hand side.

Only when he'd got all the way through the skull did he realize his mistake.

He'd immediately closed up the incision, made another one on the correct side, and removed the clot.

In 99 percent of cases, that would have been it: a near miss, a bureaucratic snafu, and a story on which the patient could dine out when he'd made a full recovery.

But Bayoumi had suffered complications—Bianca wasn't sure of the exact details—on the side of the brain where Redwine had made the first, erroneous incision.

The complications had spread, multiplied, and worsened.

Within six hours, he was dead.

"How the hell can that happen?" Beradino asked. "Don't you guys"—he caught himself—"sorry; isn't it standard procedure to have a checklist or something, so this kind of thing gets caught before it occurs?"

"Sure it is," Bianca said. "There's a three-step procedure, the Universal Protocol, which is absolutely standard. First, you check the patient's notes and make sure they tally with the surgery schedule. Then you use indelible markers to spot the site where the surgeon's going to cut. Finally, the entire operating team takes a time-out before the start and agrees that this is what they're supposed to be doing."

"So how can something like this happen?"

"Because a system is only as good as the people using it."

"And?"

"And in an operating theater, the surgeon is God.

He's captain of the ship; his word goes. So if he says we cut on the right, we cut on the right. And if the notes say otherwise, who's going to tell him and get yelled at, or worse? Shoot the messenger, you know. Everyone stands around looking at each other, and no one does a thing."

"Redwine was one of these surgeons?"

"One of them? He was the archetype. He prided himself on not marking sites—he claimed he could always remember. He didn't think he needed to write things down like the rest of us mortals."

"Christ on a bike," Patrese said.

"Don't blaspheme, Franco," Beradino said instantly. "You know I don't like it." He turned to Bianca. "How often does this kind of thing happen?"

"Per month, per week, or per day?"

Patrese and Beradino looked at her in astonishment.

"Are you serious?" Patrese said.

"I never joke about my work, Cicillo, you know that."

Patrese pursed his lips and blew out.

Beradino shook his head. "And this guy's family—Bayoumi—they're suing?"

"I think so."

"Bayoumi." Beradino turned the name over as though inspecting it. "Arab?"

"Egyptian, I think."

"What kind of family?"

"Wife, one son."

"How old?"

"Early twenties, far as I know. Student at Pitt."

Patrese knew instantly why Beradino was asking. Ask a bunch of Americans chosen at random to play word association with the phrase *young Arab man*, and it was a dollar to a dime that *hothead* wouldn't be far away.

Call it racism, call it common sense; people did both, and more, and they wouldn't stop till white kids flew airliners into skyscrapers too.

18

TUESDAY, OCTOBER 19

Dr. Bayoumi's wife—widow—Sameera, lived out in Oakland, the university district. Her apartment was one of three in a large, rambling house with a porch out front, its roof propped up by Greek columns.

Midmorning—but with all the curtains still closed, as if to block out hope as well as light—she offered them Egyptian tea: hot, strong, and, at least to the palates of two Italian American detectives, undrinkable without three heaped spoonfuls of sugar.

She was darker-skinned than they'd anticipated. Like many Egyptians and Sudanese, she was of Nubian descent, Arab by culture rather than race.

They spoke in near-whispers, mindful of the enforced twilight and the evident numbness of Sameera's grief. They'd introduced themselves, shown their credentials, and explained that they were investigating the murder of Dr. Redwine.

Beradino did the talking. He sensed that Sameera came from a culture more accepting of authority than America's—especially if you were a woman—and that she would expect the elder and more senior man to take the lead.

"As far as you knew, Mrs. Bayoumi, was your husband's operation routine?"

"I think so."

"Dr. Redwine didn't seem unduly concerned when you met him beforehand?"

"No."

"And afterward?"

"What do you mean?"

"How did Dr. Redwine seem to you, after your husband died?"

"I not see him since then."

"Not once?"

"No."

"Have you tried to see him?"

"Of course. But always, he busy. I remember something Abdul always like to say: 'With great power comes great responsibility.' But Dr. Redwine not see it like that."

"Would you say the hospital has been uncooperative?"

"Yes. Very. Not just like that, blocking him from me. I ask for documents, records, and they no interested. Treat me like fly to swat. So I call lawyer."

She handed them a glossy brochure from the firm

in question, a medical malpractice specialist. Patrese glanced at it. Swanky downtown address, shots of a happy but industrious multiethnic workforce that wouldn't have looked out of place in a Benetton commercial, and a commitment in bold typeface to "help you down the path to a better tomorrow."

"What are your motivations for bringing proceedings, Mrs. Bayoumi?"

To many Americans accustomed to a culture where legal representation can seem not just a right but a duty, the question might have sounded odd. But Beradino figured Sameera had enough first-generation immigrant still in her to make her view the law as a last rather than a first option.

The consideration she gave the question before answering showed him to be right.

"Abdul and I, we had our own, how you say, parts in the marriage," she said eventually. "He go to work, I make the home, look after Mustafa. When Mustafa grow up, we keep the parts the same. Abdul still work, I make home, Mustafa live here still. We all happy that way. Maybe not modern, American, but it work for us.

"And now Abdul gone, where will I find job? I'm not educated, not college. Companies, they see my résumé, they say no, no interview even. So how do I live? I can't do it on fresh air and good wishes.

"That's why I call lawyer.

"I want—all I want—is money Abdul earn between now and he retiring. Not a dollar more. I know it not millions, but it enough. That why lawyer, nothing more.

"I know we can do nothing to make Abdul come

back. If you talk of revenge, no, I don't believe in that. And if the hospital say sorry . . ." She made a sound to suggest she thought it unlikely.

"And Mustafa. What does he think?" Beradino asked.

"Mustafa his own man now. You must ask him."

"I understand he's a student at Pitt, is that right?"

"Yes."

"What's he studying?"

"Chemistry."

"So that's where we'd find him now? In the chemistry department?"

"Not today. Today, he on outreach. At mosque, in Homewood."

"We'll go talk to him there," Beradino said. "Thank you, Mrs. Bayoumi."

"May I ask favor?"

"Sure."

"How you say in slang? Go easy on him. For Arab boy, father is most important man in world. To lose that is very hard for him. So for me too. Mustafa is my world now. He my only son. Allah blessed us with him, no more. I lose one man, I no lose another. I do anything for that boy, you understand? *Anything.*"

19

Homewood, Patrese thought; always Homewood. It seemed less a geographical area than a vortex, forever dragging him back in.

On the sidewalk, a handful of youths waved at them, their gestures heavy with sarcasm. Patrese waved back, deadpan, his mind miles away.

After a few seconds, he glanced in the rearview mirror and saw exactly what he expected: a couple of them flipping the detectives the bird, another pair dropping their pants and mooning.

Patrese laughed. Beradino, swiveling to follow his gaze, was angry.

"Stop the car, Franco. Let's go bust their asses."

"Ah, they're just screwin' around."

"To a marked cop car? You let that go, you let anything go. Zero tolerance."

"You don't like black people?"

"I got nothin' against black people. I'm a good Christian man, Franco. Jesus says that we should accept all men equally. I just don't like *these* black people. If they were white people actin' this way, I wouldn't like 'em any better. Shoot, I'd probably like 'em *worse.*"

It was just the kind of thing Patrese's dad would have said, which almost made Patrese cringe. He worked so closely with Beradino, and so often, that sometimes he forgot there was a quarter of a century between them, a gap that manifested itself when he least expected it, like now.

Beradino was no out-and-out racist, no wannabe Klan wizard, but he did have that smear of social conservatism common to people of his age. Basically, Patrese thought, Beradino was suspicious of anyone who wasn't like him. He didn't have any more of a problem with blacks than he did, for example, with gays (probably less of a problem, in fact, given his religious convictions).

But Beradino had also been around long enough to know that most violent crimes in Pittsburgh were committed by young black men; that was a simple, unalloyed, incontrovertible fact. He knew equally well that there were plenty of reasons for this, but as he'd told Patrese more than once, he was neither a social worker nor an academic, so it wasn't his job to figure out how to make conditions better. Besides, when it was a certain type of person giving you static day in and day out, you weren't always going to be full of peace and love for them. That wasn't racism; that was human nature.

Beradino pointed forward. "There, that's the mosque."

There was a plaque on the building's front wall. *In 1932,* it read, *Pittsburgh became home to the first chartered Muslim mosque in the United States.*

"What a claim to fame," said Beradino, deadpan. "Personally, I'd still take the four Super Bowls, you know?"

They stepped inside the main door of the mosque.

It didn't seem like Osama's nerve center, that was for sure. No firebrand preachers hollering death to the Great Satan or burning the Stars and Stripes; no rows of prostrate worshippers facing Mecca. Only the rows of shoes lined up inside on gray plastic shelves gave a hint as to the religion of those within.

It seemed more like a social club than a place of worship. People walked in groups or stood around chatting. Patrese and Beradino, watching this, noticed something pretty much simultaneously: most of the mosquegoers were black rather than ostensibly Arab. They could have been in pretty much any inner city.

"Help you?" a man asked.

"We're looking for Mustafa Bayoumi," Beradino said.

"You'll find him in the outreach center." The man extended an arm to his left. "Through the double doors, then first right."

They followed his directions and, after a couple of further inquiries, found Mustafa alone in an office, entering some data on a computer terminal.

Mustafa was skinny, with cheekbones you could cut your wrists on, hair blacker than Reagan's when he'd been hard at the Grecian 2000, and a neatly trimmed beard. Like his mother, he looked substantially more black than Arab.

Still tapping the keyboard, he looked up. "Help you?" he said.

They sure were polite around here, Patrese thought. That was two more offers of help than he'd usually get in a year in Homewood.

"We're with the Pittsburgh police department," said Beradino quietly, "but we're not going to flash our badges, because we don't want to embarrass you or cause a scene. We just want to ask you a few questions." He nodded toward a couple of chairs. "May we?"

He sat down without waiting for Mustafa's assent. Patrese followed suit.

Beradino gestured around the room.

"What is it you guys do here? Outreach—what's that?"

"It's, er, reaching out."

Beradino laughed, pretending to be offended. "Hey, educational standards at the PD ain't that bad just yet. I worked that one out for myself."

Mustafa smiled too. Patrese said nothing, but he admired Beradino's approach: relax them, put them at ease, find common ground.

"Sorry. Outreach is helping people, mainly. We have a day-care facility, programs for entrepreneurs and released inmates, and a health clinic."

"Pretty impressive." Beradino sounded as though he meant it. "Who funds it all?"

"We receive an annual grant from a nonprofit organization called the Abrahamic Interfaith Foundation. In addition, Islam obligates all those who can feed their families to give two and a half percent of their net worth in alms. Many of us give considerably more, both in time and money. Then there are book sales, telephone fund-raisers, auctions, banquets; you name it, people have pitched in and helped out."

"Very good. We could use some of that community spirit around my way. But listen, Mustafa—you don't mind if I call you Mustafa, do you?—we're not here to admire your work, you know that. We'd like to ask you some questions about Dr. Michael Redwine."

Mustafa's face darkened. Patrese supposed that was only natural.

"The man who killed my father, you mean?"

"I'm sure he didn't mean to kill your father," Beradino said.

"If you shoot someone, Detective, and you mean

only to wound them but instead they die, you've still killed them, haven't you?"

Patrese hoped that neither of them saw him wince.

Beradino chose not to answer the question, and parried it with one of his own. "You know Dr. Redwine was killed yesterday evening?"

"I saw it on the news."

"And?"

"And what?"

"How does that make you feel?"

"Does it matter, how it makes me feel?"

"It does if I'm asking you."

Mustafa took a deep breath. "All right. I hope he suffered more than any of us could possibly imagine. That enough for you?"

"Suffered, as in burning in hell?"

"I don't care how. It's not a fraction of what he's caused my mother and me."

"Okay. Let me ask: where were you yesterday evening?"

"At home. I got back about five, and didn't go out again till this morning."

"Is there anyone else who can confirm that?"

"My mother. Of course."

"Anyone else?"

"No. Just her. I had nothing to do with Redwine's death, so I didn't take the precaution of getting five people to give me an alibi, if that's what you mean."

"I didn't ask whether you had anything to do with his death."

"Why else are you here?"

"Listen, Mustafa, I'm sorry for your loss—"

"That's what people always say when they don't know what else to say."

"—but you being aggressive and giving me static isn't going to help anyone here."

"Your father still alive, Detective?"

"He is, as it happens."

"Then don't tell me not to get aggressive. Not till it happens to you."

"It's happened to me," Patrese said.

Mustafa looked at him quizzically.

"Mine were killed three weeks ago. RTA."

"RTA?"

"Road traffic accident. Car crash."

"Then you know."

"About being angry? Oh, yes. I know. I know very well."

Beradino gave Patrese a look that took him a moment to decode.

Keep your thoughts to yourself. You're getting in my way.

When it came to unsettling suspects, Patrese knew Beradino was a master. His trick—rather, one of his tricks—was to use their moods against them, as a martial arts practitioner will exploit his opponent's weight and momentum to his own advantage.

If a suspect or a witness was calm, so too would Beradino be, looking to lull him into a sense of ever greater security until he, forgetting Beradino was a cop rather than his best friend, let slip something he regretted.

If, on the other hand, he was upset, as Mustafa

Bayoumi was increasingly becoming, Beradino would stoke the fires of his agitation as high as he could until the suspect lost control—and again let slip something he regretted. Patrese's attempts to soft-soap Mustafa risked undoing this strategy.

Beradino gestured around the room.

"You only help Muslims?" His tone was suddenly snappy, all reasonableness and bonhomie gone as though in a puff of smoke.

"We help our community."

"You proselytize?"

Patrese knew what Beradino was thinking. Places like Homewood—poor, deadbeat hoods where those who didn't seek their oblivion via the liquor store or the crack house were open to almost anything that promised to improve their lot—were fertile ground for Islamic recruiters.

And everyone knew what *they* were like, because everyone had seen footage of the Nation of Islam: Farrakhan and his bow-tie-wearing, bean-pie-selling disciples who hated whites, Jews, women, and gays.

"We welcome those who choose to come to us. Your religion does the same."

"Our religion was what America was founded on."

"And what an unqualified success Christianity's been, hasn't it?"

"What does that mean?" Beradino was no longer acting annoyed, Patrese knew; this was the real deal. The two of them had long ago agreed not to discuss religion, because it always ended in arguments—Beradino the devout, Patrese the unbeliever.

"Jesus died for your sins, right?" Mustafa said.

"That's right, yes."

"Then explain this to me. Either that was for everyone's sins right up to the moment he died, in which case we've had two thousand years of some serious bad behavior left unchecked. Or he died for everyone's sins then and for all time, in which case it hasn't helped much, has it?"

Patrese almost laughed. It was a question he'd asked himself, and others, more than once, and no one—not teachers, not priests, probably not even the pope himself—had been able to answer it properly.

"Not to mention the impeccable behavior of priests up and down the country when young children are involved," Mustafa continued.

"A few bad apples. Sinners, as we all are. Everyone in your culture's perfect?"

"I look around here, and I see people brought up to believe in the Christian faith. But I know that, too often around here, BC means before crack and AD means after death. That's not good enough. And it's not good enough just to pray and hope everything will turn out all right. We have to go out and do the work.

"And that work starts here. Islam prohibits drugs and alcohol. You stay off those, you can be a productive member of society. You turn to them, and you're just waiting to die. And if the only way out of that is through Islam, then so be it. Because Islam places paramount importance on the education of our children. To be a teacher is a special calling. When I've finished my studies, I'm hoping to teach at the school we're raising funds to build here, preschool to fifth grade."

"Somewhere to train the next generation of bombers?"

"Not at all. A school where everybody has a strange name, so nobody feels alone. Muslim kids feel like outsiders in public schools. No matter how good those schools are, they can't teach Islamic beliefs and morals. So we will. Kids hate being different; so we'll make them not-different. And you know why?"

"I've no doubt you're going to tell me."

"Because we have to do it ourselves now. Since nine-eleven, we haven't been able to receive money from Muslim countries, even from registered Islamic charities."

"That's damn right. There's a war on."

Mustafa didn't take the bait. Perhaps he hadn't heard.

"We relied on that money a lot, perhaps too much. That was one of the reasons why, before nine-eleven, we—the immigrant Muslims—didn't really have that much to do with the black Muslims.

"Then suddenly we couldn't move because of surveillance, police raids, airport searches, special registration, and so on. All the time, we had to prove our loyalty to the flag. Still do, every day. I look black anyway, but African American Muslims sympathize. They know what it's like—not from being Muslim, but from being black."

He looked at Beradino first, then Patrese, two white men who he obviously felt would never understand, not fully.

"We're all niggers now, basically."

20

THURSDAY, OCTOBER 21

You've seen homicide division rooms umpteen times on the tube, and it's one of the few aspects of police work that TV gets right. There really are desks piled high with report forms and coffee cups, and the detectives sitting at those desks really do crick the phones into their necks while pecking two-fingered at their keyboards.

Amidst the barely controlled hubbub of a major homicide investigation, Patrese read the poster above Beradino's head for the umpteenth time that day.

The Fifth Commandment,
Book of Exodus, Chapter 20 of
THE HOLY BIBLE.

THE OATH OF PRACTICAL
HOMICIDE INVESTIGATION.

Beradino, who'd written and had the poster typeset himself, had clearly never met a capital letter he didn't like.

> Homicide investigation is a profound duty, and constitutes a heavy responsibility. Just as there is no crime worse than taking someone else's life, so there is no task more important than bringing to

justice the people who crossed that line. As such, let no person deter you from the truth and your own personal commitment to see that justice is done. Not only for the deceased, but for the surviving family as well.

And remember—you're working for God.

No, Patrese thought angrily, he was working for the city of Pittsburgh. There were times when Beradino's incessant God-squadding really got on his nerves, and this was one of them—not least because he was pissed anyway.

Every cop knows that the first forty-eight hours after a murder are critical. If they haven't got a good lead in that time, the chances of solving the crime are halved as evidence disappears, suspects flee, and stories change.

Forty-eight hours after Michael Redwine had been torched, Patrese and Beradino had nothing.

Sure, they had an autopsy report, but that just confirmed Beradino's findings—that Redwine, alive when the fire started, had died from smoke inhalation.

And sure, Mustafa Bayoumi's alibi was provided by his mother, and she alone. But it was hard to see what they could do other than take it at face value. Yes, Sameera could have been lying—she'd said she'd do anything for him, after all—but to test that, they'd have to give her the full treatment, on a hunch that was flimsy at best.

It didn't take much imagination to see how hectoring a recent widow that way would look.

Because Patrese and Beradino had to accept Mustafa's alibi, they had no probable cause to search the house in Oakland for anything that might connect him to the fire. Even if they *did* get a warrant, and even if he *had* been involved, he was clearly a smart kid. He'd have ditched any clothing and other items that might link him to the blaze long before now.

That was how they consoled themselves, at any rate; because nothing and no one else in Redwine's life seemed to point to any other suspects.

Every resident of the Pennsylvanian (Hellmore included) had been interviewed, as had all doormen, cleaners, and maintenance workers—anyone with access to the building, in other words. No one had seen anything.

"Either they're on the level, or someone should win a damn Oscar," Patrese said.

It still didn't answer what had started as the $64,000 question and was surely now into six figures: how had the killer got into the Pennsylvanian?

They retraced Redwine's movements on the last day of his life. He'd been at Mercy in the morning, given a speech at a conference downtown after lunch, and been due to go to the opera—*La Bohème*—that evening. Nothing untoward.

They'd taken twelve officers from the regular police department and used them to turn Redwine's life upside down. No friend, acquaintance, or incident was deemed too insignificant or commonplace; everyone was followed up, checked out.

TIE, Beradino told the uniforms, TIE—trace, interview, eliminate as a suspect.

They found zilch. Redwine had been a regular attendee at church, done his part at charity fund-raisers, and enjoyed hiking and fishing in his spare time. No embittered ex-girlfriends, no secret gay lovers, no outstanding sexual harassment cases. Even the professional jealousies were no more than the usual found among surgeons, which was to say at once endemic and excruciatingly professional.

All in all, no reason for anybody to have killed Redwine, let alone by such a horrific method as burning alive.

The fire had destroyed any physical evidence worth the name, so Patrese and Beradino could find no joy there either. Instant forensic breakthroughs were strictly the preserve of TV shows titled with snappy acronyms. Pittsburgh PD didn't even have its own DNA lab. It had to use the FBI's, which had a backlog of cases running into the hundreds of thousands.

The department couldn't use private labs because their results were inadmissible in court, due to concerns over accountability and maintenance of the chain of custody. Only government facilities were acceptable, though the technical standards at private labs were much higher—not surprisingly, given that they were staffed by the best testers, many of whom had left the state sector because they wanted to be paid more, exacerbating staff shortages in public labs and increasing the backlog. . . .

Franz Kafka was not dead, clearly. He was alive, well, and living in Pittsburgh.

Nothing of great value seemed to have been taken

from the victim, ruling out burglary as a motive. Redwine was no serious collector of art, his TV set and computers were still in the apartment (though burned to cinders), and everyone who knew him agreed that he never carried more than a hundred bucks or so in cash.

Every known arsonist within Allegheny County was interviewed, bar those already in prison. All of them had alibis for the night in question. Most of them said they'd pick easier targets than a doorman apartment building, and that they certainly wouldn't kill anyone in the process. Arson was a crime against property, not people.

Self-serving bullshit, Patrese thought.

There was always the possibility that one of the uniforms had stumbled across the crucial bit of information without realizing it. Officers were human, not computers. Long days made them tired; repetitive interviews numbed and bored them. They could miss things and make mistakes, especially toward the end of a shift. But this was the same for every homicide investigation in history. Nothing to be done about it.

There are three nightmare scenarios for cops working homicide cases, and it looked very much as though Beradino and Patrese were facing one of them.

First, that they'd overlooked something so screamingly obvious that, if they ever did find it, they'd almost certainly be castigated from here to Cleveland and back again.

Second, that Redwine's murder was a case of mistaken identity, and that in order to find the perpetrator, they'd need to discover first whom he thought he'd killed.

Third, that the murder was the type of case that was the absolute hardest to solve: a stranger homicide, where the connection between killer and victim was obvious only to one or both of them.

Killer spotting victim in the street; victim in the wrong place at the wrong time; victim who'd caught the attention of killer—any or all of these might happen for reasons unknown to the police, because they simply could never imagine or reconstruct them, short of knowing each quotidian incident and occurrence in the lives of every single one of Pittsburgh's citizens, and even the Soviet Union hadn't managed such overwhelming control over its people.

Redwine's ex-wife and sons flew in from Tucson for the funeral, their eyes rimmed red with tears and fatigue. Patrese met them, sat with them, took them to dinner, told them he sympathized and understood, since his parents had been killed just weeks ago, too recently for him to be able to give any advice. All he could do was share the recognition that, Jesus Christ, it hurt, down in the deep trenches where pain was in the marrow rather than a short sharp surface shock, and though everyone told him it would get better, he was damned if he could see how.

They nodded and laughed in sympathy through their sniffing tears, and asked how the case was progressing.

That was the worst part, Patrese felt—having to look these good people in the eye and say, yes, we're doing all we can to find the murderer, we're following all lines of inquiry, we're confident we'll bring him to justice; when he knew, and he knew they knew, that what he was really saying was this: we don't have a damn clue.

Not a goddamn clue.

21

THURSDAY, OCTOBER 28

Flames leaped high and jagged around the burgers on the grill.

Crammed into a sweltering kitchen, wearing a ridiculous polyester uniform with her hair in a net as though she'd just been caught by a trawler, Jesslyn mashed her anger into tight oblongs.

The interview had been bad enough. Kevin the manager had proved as snotty as he was spotty, sneering at her throughout it all with a contempt he didn't even bother to disguise. Why did she want this job? Why had she left her previous employment? Did she have references? Had she ever worked in the fast-food industry before?

And on, and on, and on, when they both knew this was a minimum-wage job that almost literally a monkey could do, and here was Kevin treating it as though he were personally responsible for choosing the next UN secretary-general.

She even had to work some Sundays, her religious convictions be damned. Not because Kevin had forced her to—she could have claimed her constitutional right to freedom of religion and threatened him with a lawsuit if he'd even tried—but because she'd done Sunday shifts at Muncy so she could preach in the chapel there. Her suddenly spending every Sunday at home would arouse suspicion in a moron, and Mark was certainly not that.

But even if she *did* find a way to tell him about Mara, she thought, he wouldn't understand, not really. Prison was one of those things you could never explain. If you knew what it was like, you didn't need to be told. If you didn't know, mere words weren't enough.

Prison was a pressure cooker, a place of white heat where life had a suffocating intensity. Friendships, still less love affairs, weren't casual, to be picked up and put down whenever one felt like it; they were life rafts of survival in a place that tried to crush the soul, expressions of defiance and pride in being human.

Within prison walls, the rules changed. What went on inside stayed inside. That was why Jesslyn was so careful to keep her two worlds apart. Mark had some of his colleagues over to dinner or Sunday lunch at their condo from time to time; she never did. Mark brought documents home, discussed work problems with her, gave her tidbits of department gossip; she never did any of that either. If he thought it weird, he'd long since accepted it as just the way she was.

And with Mara, who'd been such a bright, shining Technicolor light amid the pallor of endless institutional gray . . . well, Jesslyn had been honored, frankly, that Mara, beautiful, radiant, poised, fragrant Mara, who somehow kept her poise in those conditions, had chosen her when she could have had pretty much anyone.

And then she'd gone. Gone in stages, each of them more painful than the last.

First, Mara had called time on their relationship.

One day, just like that, out of the blue, Mara had said she didn't want to go on with it. Jesslyn had been standing six feet away, yet she'd honestly thought Mara had hit her, such was the physical shock. She'd rushed to the restroom and thrown up her breakfast. Food poisoning, she'd said, before going home. They wouldn't see her cry on the prison floor; not then, not ever. Crying was weakness, and weakness was death.

In the weeks that followed, Jesslyn had begged, pleaded, reasoned, shouted, and threatened, all to no avail. Sometimes she sought Mara out; sometimes she tried to avoid her. Each time she saw her, it felt as though someone had opened up a wound and started scraping salt into it.

Second, Mara had been released, back into the outworld.

If seeing her had been a torment, Jesslyn quickly realized that not seeing her was a hundred times worse. Even after their split, Mara had been the center of Jesslyn's universe, the point around which she oriented herself and her days.

Now all Jesslyn had was the whisper of Mara's name in corridor gossip, and the few of Mara's keepsakes she'd managed to hold on to, inhaling their scent as though it were the breath of life.

Third, Mara had officially complained about Jesslyn's conduct.

Briefly, surgingly, Jesslyn had hoped Mara had brought the complaints as some warped way of trying to keep Jesslyn in her life. But she could only fool herself for so long and, as the process had ground forward, Jesslyn had let her feelings curdle toward hatred, if only in hope that it would harden into a carapace around her heart.

She'd always thought of Mara as the innocent victim of an egregious miscarriage of justice. Now she'd forced herself to damn her as the devil incarnate, vile and evil murderess, fit only for an eternity in hell.

And fourth, obviously, was when Muncy had given Jesslyn her marching orders.

Jesslyn stared into the flames.

Stripe for stripe, burning for burning.

Was it fair, what had happened to her? Was it fair that murderers, rapists, and pedophiles were walking the streets while she was here, frying burgers made of meat she wouldn't give to a dog? Was it fair that she'd given twenty years of her life to trying to make the world a better place, and in return had been given half an hour to pack up and go?

It wasn't just Mara she'd grown to hate, of course. It was everyone who worked the system for their own ends, and then blamed that very system whenever they didn't have the courage to take responsibility themselves. It was lawyers who made people terrified of using common sense; it was media executives who broadcast whatever got them ratings, no matter the harm to those involved; it was judges who gave light sentences; it was doctors who kept alive people any decent society would have executed. It was all these parasites, and more.

Jesslyn sought solace where she always did, in the Book; Ecclesiastes 3:3–8:

> A time to kill, and a time to heal; a time to break down, and a time to build up; a time to weep, and a time to laugh; a time to mourn, and a time to dance; a time to cast away stones, and a time to gather stones together; a time to embrace, and a time to refrain from embracing; a time to get, and a time to lose; a time to keep, and a time to cast away; a time to rend, and a time to sew; a time to keep silence, and a time to speak; a time to love, and a time to hate; a time of war, and a time of peace.

22

SATURDAY, OCTOBER 30

Bianca had gone to dinner with Bishop Kohler. Patrese had turned down the invitation. There were probably ways of spending Saturday night that he'd find even less appealing than listening to Kohler mouth platitudes by way of trying to offer spiritual succor, but he couldn't think of any off the top of his head.

There were many antidotes to death, Patrese thought, but sex was the best of all.

He had a date with a nurse named Erin Fitzpatrick. She worked at Mercy, and he'd met her in an elevator when visiting Bianca at the hospital the other night. They'd chatted, he'd taken her number, and now she was coming over for dinner.

That was the thing about being a cop. He met perhaps a hundred new people a month in a hundred different situations, and so he had a hundred good reasons to give them his number. By the law of averages, some of those people were going to be young women; some of those young women were going to be attractive; and some of those attractive ones were going to want to sleep with him.

For a young, single guy, being a cop was therefore pretty much the perfect job.

Patrese had invited her to his place, as opposed to meeting downtown, for two reasons. Not only was he a good cook—his parents had run a restaurant, after all, and he'd picked up plenty of advice and help along the way—but his apartment had a view of Pittsburgh for which postcard sellers would have killed their grandmas.

He lived in a building called the Mountvue on Mount Washington, the hill on the city's south side that rises so giddily that only cable cars can make the ascent. He paid $1,200 a month for the place, at least a third of which was surely for that vista of the city skyline.

Waiting for Erin to show up, he stood on the balcony of his apartment and looked out. Dusk was his favorite time, the moment when the city was held suspended in all its contradictions: halfway between day and night, sanity and madness, picturesque and squalid.

The heart of downtown was called the Golden Triangle, sandwiched between the Allegheny and Monongahela rivers and tapering to the point where the two met and joined the Ohio. On crisp fall evenings like this it did indeed seem golden, the sunlight making the thrusting skyscrapers glow as though in belief that the day to come would hold more than had the day just passed.

There was the medieval castle of PPG Place, all battlements and crenellations; there the four interlocking silver octagons of the Oxford Center; there the tallest of them all, the USX Tower, a behemoth of exposed steel columns and curtain walls; there the Grant Building flashing P-I-T-T-S-B-U-R-G-H in Morse code over and again; and there the blue light on top of the Gulf Building, which signified that the temperature was falling.

Patrese loved this city. Always had, always would.

He loved the way Pittsburgh held high the best of American values: hard work, unpretentiousness, renewal. Time was, in the heyday of the steel industry, it had been virtually uninhabitable: palls of smoke so thick that streetlights had burned all day; desk jockeys who'd returned to their offices from an hour's lunch downtown with their white shirts stained black; rivers so choked with chemicals that they had burned for days on end.

One writer had called Pittsburgh "hell with the lid taken off." He hadn't found much dissent.

But by the early 1980s the steel industry had shut

down, and now hillsides above the mill sites had grown lush and green again. Pittsburgh was a riot of hills, and valleys, slopes, hollows, streams, gulches, too. It spilled out cockeyed across the landscape's folds, taking its cues from the terrain.

It was therefore a city of neighborhoods, little worlds of their own separated by earth or water and rejoined by bridges. Pittsburgh had more bridges than Venice, something of which the tourist board was inordinately proud; that, and the fact that the Burgh had been voted America's Most Livable City.

That kind of shit was always double-edged, Patrese thought. The surest way to stop it being Most Livable was to attract all the people who came here because it was Most Livable.

There was a sudden explosion of light from below as the sun reached just the right angle to fizz off one of the plate-glass corners on PPG Place. Patrese didn't know whether the architect had designed it so, but he caught his breath every time he saw it happen.

He just wished Pittsburgh looked as good in Homewood as it did from up here.

The doorbell cut through his thoughts: Erin, an entirely predictable fifteen minutes late. Being on time would have been too eager; half an hour late would have been rude.

She had a bottle of Chilean red, which showed she had either good taste or ESP. Patrese loved Chilean red and never drank white wine, no matter where it came from. White wine gave him a headache and bad breath, not always in that order.

Erin was small, with dark hair, blue eyes, and a smattering of freckles; no doubt about her Irish heritage, that was for sure. They kissed on the cheek, near enough each other's mouth for Patrese to know which way the evening was heading.

There were only two certainties in life, he remembered: death and nurses.

He supposed they could have been adults and gotten straight down to it, but for Patrese dinner was a vital and enjoyable part of the ritual: the hunt, the tease, the discovery. He got the same sort of feeling in a police interview room with a suspect. There was always a moment when you knew you had them, when you knew they were going to give it up, and whether that moment was exquisite or humdrum depended entirely on whether they'd made you work for it or not. It applied to confessions and bedrooms alike.

Besides, he found people interesting. Not everyone had hidden depths—some didn't even have hidden shallows—but most had some sort of story to tell, if you knew where to look or how to ask. If he'd simply wanted to get laid, he'd have gone out with the vice squad on a night patrol.

So they ate his pumpkin ravioli, drank Erin's Chilean red, and chatted. They talked about Erin's job: the length of the hours she worked compared to the insultingly small size of her paycheck, tales of detached catheters and drunk doctors.

They discussed that hoary old chestnut, the differences between the sexes, and agreed that the trendy modern sociologists had got it all wrong. Men and women were different, and the sooner everyone accepted that, the happier everyone would be. There was no such thing as a perfect relationship. Every woman had the same ideal man: soft, caring, understanding, and communicative, but also strong, handsome, and rugged. But none of them could have him. He already had a boyfriend.

"You've done this before," she said when the Chilean red was all gone.

"A few times."

"How many is a few?"

He didn't dare tell her the real figure. It wasn't just that it was high, though it was; it was also a little unseemly actually to have kept count. Guys liked to brag about those things, quality and quantity being interchangeable as far as most men were concerned. A bedpost notched like an Alaskan totem pole was supposed to make them feel better.

Well, it didn't make Patrese feel better. He knew why it didn't, and why he kept at it anyway, but there was a country mile between knowing it and actually doing something about changing it.

"A few is a few," he said. "Do you mind?"

She shook her head. "No, I don't mind."

23

SUNDAY, OCTOBER 31

"I'm sorry to disturb you, Father," I say, "but I have some sins I'd like to confess."

Bishop Kohler turns to face me.

I see two competing strands of thought in his expression: the temporal, which says it's late and he wants to be leaving; and the spiritual, which demands he give what succor he can to a sinner.

"Of course, my child," he says, biting down on his annoyance.

"I won't keep you long. I know you must want to get home."

Home, in this case, being an eleven-bedroom mansion set in a couple of acres on the border between Shadyside and Squirrel Hill.

Far too large and ostentatious for a man of the cloth, you might think, and you'd be right. I read an interview where he defended his decision to live there. The mansion was given to the Church just after the war and has been used by every bishop since; Giovanni Cardinal Montini stayed there once, and later he became Pope Paul VI; it's useful for meetings and putting up visiting dignitaries; and on and on and on.

And yet he knows, as I know, as everyone knows, that what he should do, if he were as humble and holy as he makes out, is go and live in a seminary among those training to be priests, and sell the mansion, using the profits to help with the church's work. The place would fetch a couple of million on the open market. Imagine what good could be done with that amount of money.

So forgive me if I doubt the sincerity of Bishop Kohler's spiritual commitment.

Still, in the same interview, he said he liked to spend time alone in Saint Paul Cathedral, the diocese's mother church out near the university in Oakland; that he preferred on occasion to do the locking-up rounds himself, solo, the better to be alone with God in his house.

Which is why I knew I'd find him here, now, and without witnesses.

Kohler leads me in silence to the confessional. He asks me nothing about myself, the better to maintain the anonymity of the confession. He may know my face, but not my name, nor anything else about me.

He's not to know that, in a few minutes, all this will have ceased to matter for him.

He motions me through one door of the confessional and steps into the other side.

The confessional is in classic style, two compartments separated by a latticed grille on which is hung a crucifix. I kneel on the prie-dieu.

I don't know how to begin. I've always thought confession should be between the sinner and his or her God, with no other human present, so this is difficult for me.

"Has it been long since your last confession?" Kohler whispers.

It's only the two of us in the entire place, but the near-darkness of the confessional—and of the cathedral itself—seems to make whispering appropriate.

"Yes," I reply.

"Would you like me to remind you of the purpose of confession?"

"Yes."

"You must confess your sins in order to restore your connection to God's grace and to escape hell, particularly if you have committed a mortal sin."

"What's a mortal sin?"

"A mortal sin must be about a serious matter, have been committed with full consent, and be known to be wrong."

"What kinds of sins are mortal sins?"

"Murder, certainly. Blasphemy. Adultery."

He can't see me, but I smile.

"And what happens if these sins aren't confessed?" I ask.

"It's a dogmatic belief of the faith that if a person guilty of mortal sin dies without either receiving the sacrament or experiencing perfect contrition with the intention of confessing to a priest, that person will receive eternal damnation." He pauses. "These things are known to all Catholics," he adds.

"I'm sorry, Father."

"It must have been a very long time since you last confessed, no?" Another pause. "In order for the sacrament to be valid, the penitent must do more than simply confess her known mortal sins to a priest. She must be truly sorry for each of the mortal sins committed, have a firm intention never to commit them again, and perform the penance imposed by the priest. As well as confessing the types of mortal sins committed, the penitent must disclose how many times each sin was committed."

I know that whatever's said in the confessional stays there; this is an absolute, inviolable rule, even if to do otherwise might save lives. Doctors and attorneys can break their pledges of confidentiality in extremis; a priest, never.

So I can tell him, even if everything else goes wrong.

"I have killed," I say.

Kohler gasps—in horror, surprise, perhaps both. He must think it unlikely, but perhaps the tone of my voice lets him know that I'm not joking.

"How many times?" he asks, more in a croak than a whisper.

"More than once."

"When did you last kill?"

"Now."

I'm up off the prie-dieu and through the door in a flash, pulling the gasoline can from my bag. I throw open the confessional's other door and see Kohler there, mouth open in a perfect circle of outrage, at this violation of religious etiquette if nothing else.

I splash the gasoline on him. For an old man, he still looks strong, but gentle too. Years of turning the other cheek have left him useless in a situation like this.

In another two seconds, maybe three, he might have reacted to the danger; but those are seconds he doesn't have, seconds I won't give him.

I light the juggling torch and touch it to his face.

He screams, echoing loud and bouncing around the cathedral, and the flames rush from his skin and clothes to the walls of the confessional, leaping orange through crackling wood as I step back and close the door on him, holding it shut for as long as I can stand before the heat drives me back.

It's not long, but it's enough.

"Isaiah, chapter fifty-nine, verse seventeen," I shout, so he can hear me above his screaming and through his agonies. "For I put on righteousness as a breastplate, and a helmet of salvation upon my head; and I put on the garments of vengeance for clothing, and am clad with zeal as a cloak."

The screaming stops, and in its place comes a rasped muttering, the words of a dying man, indistinct but their meaning clear if I strain to hear:

"God the Father of mercies, through the death and resurrection of his Son, has reconciled the world to himself and sent the Holy Spirit among us for the forgiveness of sins; through the ministry of the Church may God give you pardon and peace, and I absolve you from your sins in the name of the Father, and of the Son, and of the Holy Spirit, amen."

24

The death of a surgeon in an upscale condo building had merited one mildly disgruntled local TV crew. The death of the bishop brought the national networks out in force. They crammed up against the bumblebee-striped crime tape and turned glaring camera lights on anyone who stepped inside the police cordon.

At the edge of that cordon, a uniformed officer met

Patrese and Beradino and checked their credentials. When he saw Beradino's name, he touched the checkered band on his hat in respect.

"Have you adapted?" Beradino asked.

Adapt, in this case, was a police mnemonic rather than a Darwinian evolutionary imperative. ADAPT: *arrest* the perpetrator, if possible; *detain* and identify witnesses and suspects; *assess* the crime scene; *protect* the crime scene; and *take* notes.

"All but the first, sir."

"Who found the body?"

"Passerby spotted the flames. Kelly Grubb. He's over there." He indicated a middle-aged man sitting on the trunk of a police cruiser.

Grubb's expression was typical of people who stumbled across murder scenes: a mixture, in almost exactly equal parts, of revulsion at the sight and excitement at being part of a police investigation.

"We'll talk to him later. Did he alter the scene in any way?"

"Says he called the fire department straight off. Didn't go in, and they sure as hell wouldn't have let him in once they got here."

"Okay." More degradation of evidence—that was a given once the fire department had done their thing—but there was no point moaning about it. That was their job, to put out blazes, and damn the consequences, forensic or otherwise.

Beradino thought for a moment, looking toward the spot where the fire department had set up an improvised command post. It was right next to where the

TV crews had gathered, and a few uniformed police officers were already shooting the breeze there with the firefighters. Beradino turned back to the officer.

"Throw up another cordon, a hundred feet farther out than this one," he said. "Keep every civilian—TV crews, general public—behind the new one, the outer one. They *start* moanin', threaten to arrest them. They *keep* moanin', make good on that threat."

"Yes, sir."

"Good man."

Patrese understood Beradino's logic. At big crime scenes like this, cops meet up. They haven't seen one another for a while and, since they're used to such situations, they get to chatting, laughing, ribbing one another. They forget there's a corpse nearby. They forget people get offended when they think police officers are being insensitive around the dead. Most of all, they forget there are TV mics around that pick up every word they say.

Patrese and Beradino left the uniform shouting at a colleague to bring more yellow-and-black, and headed toward the cathedral, twin-towered and Gothic, with a statue of Saint Paul mounted on the center pediment.

There was a poster by the entrance:

Saint Paul Cathedral, a foundation of faith, building a future of hope.

Patrese shuddered and stopped. Beradino gripped his forearm.

"Franco, listen. You want me to take care of this one alone? I understand."

Patrese shook his head. "No."

"Come on, Franco. He was a friend of your family's; this is the place you just buried your parents. You got a thousand-yard stare on you. Let me handle this."

"I told you, Mark, I'm fine." Patrese managed a weak laugh. "Vacant stare's probably jet lag."

"Huh?"

"Extra hour's sleep this morning. When the clocks went back."

"Yeah." Beradino looked at Patrese a moment more, and then shrugged. "Okay. You win. Come on."

The cathedral's main door was open. Before Patrese and Beradino were inside, they could smell the burning—the piquant aroma of woodsmoke and the half-sweet, half-acrid overlay of charred flesh.

Patrese puffed out his cheeks and rolled his head in a circle, counterclockwise and then clockwise, preparing the body for what the mind was about to suffer.

A few hours ago, he'd been at Heinz Field, watching his beloved Steelers put thirty-four points past the New England Patriots. Now he was at the holding station inside the door, where he and Beradino put on the usual anticontamination suits, the ones that made the wearer look like a hybrid astronaut and sewage-treatment worker.

Just a normal day in a homicide detective's life, in other words.

The cathedral's nave comprised five aisles beneath pointed arches and ribbed vaulting. The detectives walked between silent pews and past crime-scene officers and firefighters, men whose concerns—secular, scientific—usually had little place in here.

Focus, Patrese told himself, with a ferocity that made his teeth clench. *Focus.* Don't think about Kohler and everything he'd been. There'd be time enough for that later. Just work the scene, the way he did every homicide he handled.

Kohler's body was prostrate on the floor, a yard or so in front of the confessional's ruined timbers; too far simply to have fallen when the confessional collapsed.

He'd tried to escape. Died on his feet, as it were; gone toward death rather than simply waited for death to claim him.

You could mix religion up any way you chose, Patrese thought, believe absolutely in the afterlife and kingdoms beyond this realm; but when it came down to it, simple biological imperatives hardwired into humankind made people fight against the dying of the light. It had nothing to do with soul, or faith, or belief; it was the survival instinct, pure and simple, and it was in you for as long as you breathed.

Kohler looked much as Redwine had: arms raised as though to fight, and clothes—in this case, a bishop's surplice—melted in patches to his skin.

"Who could do this?" Beradino said, and Patrese noted the tremble in his voice. "To a man of God, in the house of God . . ." He shook his head, as though unable to fathom the limitless depths of mankind's mendacity, and then turned to Patrese.

"I know he was a special man, to you and your family—"

"You could say that."

"—and so I promise you, we'll find whoever did

this. Just like when a cop's killed, Franco, we'll pull out all the stops. That's my promise to you, right here."

Patrese nodded.

The photographer was snapping away dispassionately, a vulture with a Canon. He glanced up from his viewfinder as Beradino and Patrese came to a halt.

"No chalk fairies, then," Beradino said.

No one could draw chalk outlines around the body or any other object until the photographers had been and gone. Photographs had to be representations of the crime scene as it was when the incident was reported, or they were inadmissible as evidence. A good lawyer could get a case thrown out of court for less.

"None at all," the photographer said. "You train your cops well."

"Sometimes," Beradino replied.

Patrese looked around again.

The fire damage was substantially less extensive here than at Redwine's apartment. Not only had the fire department been on the scene within three minutes of Grubb's call, but the confessional had also been set against a stone wall to one side of the church. Everything else flammable—pews, pulpits, curtains, altar cloths—was far enough away to have prevented the fire from making the jump.

Patrese swallowed hard, and again Beradino noticed; he knew, too, that Patrese hadn't turned a hair at the sight of Redwine's body, which had been no less horrific than this.

Patrese looked away, more to avoid Beradino's quizzical gaze than anything else.

They set to searching the place.

There were several ways of doing this—spiraling out from or into a central point, dividing the area into zones, shoulder-to-shoulder along designated lines—but Beradino's chosen method was crisscrossing. They'd go up and down the room and then side to side, so that every point was covered twice.

If you missed something the first time, you'd find it the second time.

If you missed it the second time, you were in the wrong job.

They used tweezers to pick up objects and bag them, and their elbows to open and close doors. The fewer traces of themselves they left here, the better.

It was lying on the flagstone floor, and Patrese saw it first.

A piece of wood, with what looked like some kind of sculpture attached to it; and broken, that was clear from the ragged edges, smashed rather than cut.

It wasn't hard to recognize what it was. Half the Western world had one.

A crucifix.

More precisely, the bottom half of one.

The top half wasn't far away. The break ran diagonally across Jesus's chest.

"You got these?" Patrese asked the photographer.

"Every which way."

Patrese squatted down, pulled a transparent plastic evidence bag from his pocket, pushed it inside out, and, with the plastic covering his fingers, carefully picked up one half of the crucifix.

It was broken, but not burned.

Patrese turned it over in his hand.

It felt solid, weighty.

Not the kind of thing that would break if you simply dropped it on the floor.

If you *hurled* it, yes; but not if you just dropped it.

He looked around again.

Nearby, also smashed, were pieces of wood painted bright gold and red.

Patrese found three, and could fit them together in his head without needing to check with the photographer again as to whether he could pick them up.

They looked very like the constituent parts of a medieval icon.

"Mark," Patrese said. "Look at this."

"*You* look at *this*, Franco."

Patrese glanced up, first at Beradino, and then in the direction he was staring.

Beradino was looking at the stained-glass windows high above them; in particular, at the three windows that had been smashed.

25

Sunday nights in Pittsburgh were more or less traffic free, so they had a clear run back from Saint Paul to the North Shore.

"I spoke to him just this morning, you know?" Patrese said, gliding the car through lights turning from green to amber.

"Spoke to who?"

"Kohler."

"You didn't tell me this?"

"When could I tell you this? We've just been at a murder scene. *His* murder. I'm telling you now. I spoke to him around nine this morning."

"About what?"

Patrese sighed, and rubbed the bridge of his nose. "You really wanna know?"

"I don't ask unless I do."

"Okay. This is a little personal, which is why I didn't mention it before. I mean, it's no big deal, it's just . . . I was feeling a bit down, all right? My sister had gone to have dinner with him last night. I had a date. A nurse. She left early this morning, had to work. I was missing my mom and pop, wanted to talk to someone. Bianca was on shift at Mercy, everyone else . . . it was Sunday morning, they'd still have been in bed. So I called Kohler."

"And how did he seem to you?"

"Totally normal. I didn't really pay attention. I was doing most of the talking. He listened. He could have been cooking breakfast at the same time, for all I know."

"How long did you talk?"

"Six, seven minutes, I don't know."

"You speak to your sister today?"

"Yeah. Lunchtime, when she came back from work."

"She say how Kohler was last night?"

"Said he was fine. In good humor, in fact."

Beradino made a moue. "Little did he know, huh? First Redwine, now—"

"There's no guarantee this is even related to Redwine."

"True. Could be copycat, could be coincidence. Method's the same, location's completely different. Only a few people had access to where Redwine was killed. Here, anyone could have come in off the street, literally. Few buildings more public than a cathedral."

"And why the smashing of the crucifix? The icon, the windows? None of that with Redwine, was there?" Patrese pointed out.

"Someone who hates religion? Someone who hates Christianity, certainly."

"Someone like Mustafa Bayoumi?"

Beradino glanced across at Patrese. "He seemed pretty hostile to it, for sure."

"So we look at Bayoumi first."

"Which means we believe the murders *are* connected, until proven otherwise."

"Yeah."

"First, we check his alibi. It's just his mom again, no one else, we get suspicious."

"And we look for any connections between him and Kohler. Did they know each other personally? Did Kohler do something to piss him off?"

"Or *not* do something to piss him off? Something Bayoumi thought he *should* have done, but didn't? Was the diocese in dispute with the Homewood mosque project? Anything like that."

"Perhaps it's something less concrete. If it is Bayoumi, maybe he chose Kohler as a symbol—as *the* symbol, the head—of the Catholic church in Pittsburgh."

Beradino was quiet for a moment.

"Let's not get too carried away with Bayoumi, Franco," he said. "Whether it's him or not, we turn Kohler's life upside down, just as we did Redwine's. Who had a reason to kill Kohler? Who knew both Kohler and Redwine? We cross-reference every suspect, every witness, every friend, acquaintance, colleague. Some of Kohler's parishioners must have been Redwine's patients, and vice versa."

"And what else did they share? Were they members of the same country club? Did they play golf together? Were they on the board of the same charity? Were they members of the same professional association?"

"Exactly. And on, and on, and on. Like I said back there, Franco, back in Saint Paul, far as I'm concerned, this is like a cop killing. We give it full beans. You don't go around burning priests. Not on my watch."

Patrese couldn't help it. It started as a pricking behind his eyes and a flutter in the base of his throat, and then the tears were coming warm and too fast to stop. He wiped angrily at his face, not least so he could keep driving. Tears were weakness.

Beradino was silent, knowing better than to kill Patrese with kindness.

Patrese sniffed hard, twice, and swallowed.

"What kind of man could do those things?" he said. "What kind of monster?"

26

MONDAY, NOVEMBER 1

First thing Monday morning, Chance called Beradino and Patrese into a meeting, the three of them in the room with Mayor Negley on speakerphone like the voice of God.

Howard Negley was a billionaire businessman who'd won the mayoralty a few years back. Drawing a token salary of one dollar, he'd proved himself a dynamic presence in City Hall—too dynamic for most of the old-timers there, who'd swiftly found themselves seeking solace in their directorships. Ostentatiously using his business skills and contacts to help regenerate the city, Negley had consciously set himself apart from the endless infighting of career politicos. The public loved him.

"I'm not having surgeons and bishops murdered in Pittsburgh, you understand?" Negley said. "I *will not* stand by and see it happen. It's bad for the city."

Bad for your popularity, you mean, thought Patrese.

What Patrese could take from Beradino, as good and honest a cop as you'd find anywhere in the lower forty-eight, sounded false and shrill from an elected official. Besides, why did Negley always sound as though he were addressing a political rally?

"Whatever you need to find the killer, you have," Negley continued. "You want more officers, you tell me. You want men from other jurisdictions, I can arrange that."

It was all Patrese could do not to rotate his tongue in his cheek. To judge from the expression on Beradino's face, and even Chance's, he wasn't alone in his opinion.

Yes, they could have more officers, from inside Allegheny County and outside too, but that wasn't within the mayor's power to offer, let alone make happen.

Typical Negley, Patrese thought. No wonder he'd married a Hollywood actress. The only thing more titanic than the mutual appreciation society would have been the clash of egos.

He put it quickly from his mind, and turned his attention back to the room.

"You should bring the FBI in on this," squawked Negley from the box.

Patrese was about to say he'd suggest the same thing—he knew Caleb Boone, the head of the FBI's Pittsburgh office, and thought him a good guy—when he saw Chance look at Beradino, and Beradino shake his head.

"We don't think that's appropriate at this juncture, sir," Chance said.

Patrese knew Chance was a political animal; few people rose as high in the force as he had without being one. But he was also first and foremost a cop. Therefore, as he'd demonstrated at Patrese's disciplinary hearing, he was flatly opposed to anything or anyone that threatened the integrity and independence of the police department.

The FBI was top of that list. Always had been, always would be. It was a turf war, and it was as atavistic and ineradicable as all conflict. There would always be turf; therefore there would always be war.

"Why the hell not?" Negley snapped.

"Because all they'll do is muddy the waters, sir. The more agencies you involve, the more confusion, which helps no one but the killer. Besides, we're perfectly capable of handling this investigation ourselves."

"The FBI has unparalleled resources. It also tracks extremists—Islamic extremists, other religious fanatics—who might have wanted to do this."

"Running to the G-men at the drop of a hat doesn't send the right message, sir. These are crimes against Pittsburghers. Pittsburghers want to see their own police force solve them."

"It's obvious you've got a serial killer here, so you must call in the FBI. The Bureau has infinitely more experience than you in dealing with such people."

Chance actually licked his lips before replying. "I'm afraid not, sir, on both counts."

"I'm warning you—"

"We don't yet have a serial killer, sir, not necessarily. We have two murders, not necessarily linked. If they *do* prove to be linked, the FBI's own criteria establish a minimum of three before a murderer can be considered serial. And even then, we don't *have* to call them in at all. Whether or not to seek the Bureau's help is the decision of the local police department. Right now, we choose not to invite them in."

"Allen, you know me well enough to know I'm not a man you want to annoy."

"And sir, *you* know *me* well enough to know I'm not

a man who needs to be told how to do my job. I don't tell you how to run the city; don't tell me how best to catch this man."

Negley was drawing breath to say something else, but Chance beat him to it.

"Now, if you'll excuse us, sir, we have a killer to catch."

27

Press conferences were usually humdrum, routine affairs: a few crime correspondents, a couple of detectives, and a department press officer who was underpaid and undermotivated in equal measures.

They'd discuss a bar shooting, a domestic murder, a gang hit. The police would give their side of the story; the reporters would dutifully check names and details; the press officer would make random interjections to remind everyone he existed.

Small-time crimes, small-time meetings. Ninety-nine times out of a hundred, they could have convened around a table at Starbucks.

The hacks didn't tend to question the official version of events. If they did, they'd gradually find themselves frozen out of information and access; then their jobs would go to someone else, someone more prepared to toe the line.

Besides, the public appetite for other people's disasters was insatiable. It didn't really matter what the news was, as long as it was bad. Every media man knew the truth of the axiom "If it bleeds, it leads."

But every now and then, those leads slipped from the crime beat to general news.

It could be something shockingly grotesque. There was the floater the cops had pulled from the Monongahela whose skin had slipped off the hands like two gloves; the dog who'd chewed off his owner's face because she'd died and there was no one to feed him; and, most celebrated of all, most gasped at and laughed over, the schizo who'd cut open his own stomach and pulled out his guts before cutting them into neat pieces with a pair of tin snips.

Or it could involve someone important. Someone like Bishop Kohler.

The police department found the largest room available, and even so it was bulging at the seams. Reporters brandishing notebooks and voice recorders annexed every chair; TV cameras ringed the back and sides of the room like a monk's tonsure.

Chance led Beradino and Patrese into the room, holding up his hands as he did so, though whether to acknowledge the assembled multitude or shield his eyes from the popping of camera flashes, Patrese couldn't tell.

Three chairs had been arranged behind a table. Chance sat in the middle, gesturing that Patrese and Beradino should park their butts on either side of him, as though he were Jesus and they the thieves.

Chance's presence was largely symbolic. He was there for one reason only: to show how seriously the police was taking this murder, that an assistant police chief would deign to come and mingle with the masses.

This was a double-edged sword, of course. If Patrese and Beradino found the killer, Chance would share the credit. If they failed, they'd fail alone.

Even though he was the junior man, and even though he'd been up half the night consoling Bianca—predictably devastated by Kohler's murder—Patrese did most of the talking.

Beradino despised the media, and made little secret of it. He disliked being second-guessed by reporters he considered uninformed at best and irresponsible at worst, and he hated their tacit demands that the police work to news deadlines rather than at an investigation's natural pace.

Patrese took a more pragmatic approach. He figured that the media were part and parcel of every major homicide investigation, so he might as well accept it. Better to have them inside the tent pissing out than vice versa. The more he could run them, the less he ran the risk of them running him.

Picking questioners with a practiced hand, Patrese performed the traditional detective's balancing act in such situations: give enough to keep the media happy, not enough to jeopardize the investigation.

He pointed to a man with a mane of hair that would have shamed a lion.

"Ed Sharpe, KDKA. You believe these killings are connected?"

"We're keeping an open mind, but obviously we'd be

foolish *not* to be looking for connections. Burning bodies isn't especially common, either as MO or signature."

MO, modus operandi, was the way a killer went about his business, the things he needed to do to effect the murder as efficiently as possible. Signature was what he needed to do to make the murder worthwhile, be it emotionally, physically, or sexually.

The problem for Beradino and Patrese was that they couldn't be sure whether burning was signature or MO without knowing the killer's internal logic—but finding that logic might be impossible unless they worked out the burning's significance. Had the killer burned Redwine and Kohler because it had been the easiest option available to him, or because he'd felt compelled to?

"Andy Rose, *Post-Gazette.* Were the victims alive when they were burned?"

"Not as far as we can establish." Patrese was proud of his poker face. "We believe they'd been asphyxiated first, and then set on fire."

And so, when the crazies started ringing up—as they would, sure as night followed day—claiming to have used a silk scarf or a gimp ball on the victims, Patrese and Beradino could dismiss them out of hand.

"Jess Schuring, *60 Minutes.* Is it significant that Bishop Kohler was killed in the cathedral? Some kind of religious aspect?"

The poker face stayed on. "Again, not that we can establish. Probably just the place where the killer knew the bishop would be at a certain time."

"But some of the stained-glass windows were smashed."

Patrese thought fast. The broken windows were visible from the street outside, so there was no point trying to deny it. He'd have to give a plausible explanation instead.

"Preliminary investigations suggest that the heat of the fire shattered them."

He didn't mention the crucifix and icons, of course. Nor did he pass on the fact that they'd also found a scorched print of Michelangelo's *Hand of God Giving Life to Adam*—an elderly, bearded God wrapped in a swirling robe, with his right arm outstretched to impart the spark of life into the first man.

Keeping these details quiet was another filter for the lunatics.

"Hugo Carr, *Philadelphia Inquirer*. You think the Human Torch has a previous history of arson?"

"I'm sorry?" It was Beradino, tight-lipped with anger. "The Human Torch?"

"You know. The Fantastic Four?"

"Is this some kind of nickname for the killer?"

"If you like."

"No, Mr. Carr, I don't like. I don't like at all. I don't like giving some cutesy moniker to anyone who does what this man does. I won't be calling him the Human Torch or anything else like that. Nor will anyone else working this case. If they do, they'll be reassigned before they can draw another breath. Is that clear?"

Subdued: "Yes."

Beradino gestured toward Patrese: *Go on.*

"We're interviewing known arsonists in the area, of course," Patrese said. "We've found indications of accelerant at both scenes, but nothing too sophisticated. Certainly nothing that would rule out, you know, anyone but an experienced fire-starter."

Nothing that would need advanced chemistry, either; but Sameera Bayoumi had told them that Mustafa had spent the previous evening with her, had left for Philadelphia first thing this morning, and wouldn't be back till Thursday.

Patrese looked straight down the lens of the KDKA camera. He knew Pittsburghers would appreciate him addressing them through their own hometown channel rather than one of the national networks.

"I'm asking you, the public, to help us on this one. We, the police, can't be everywhere. You can; you *are*. Be our eyes and ears. Please, if you've seen anything, heard anything, noticed anything unusual, call and tell us. Don't worry if it seems too small or insignificant or irrelevant. Let us be the judge of that. You never know—your piece of information could be the one that makes the difference."

That kind of logic—*it could be you*—got people buying lottery tickets, so Patrese figured it was worth a try here. He knew that too much information could, and often did, swamp homicide task forces, but better too much than too little. Given enough time, manpower, and luck, you could always find the needle in the haystack.

But if the needle wasn't there to start with, you had no chance.

28

For a man who'd presumably believed that earthly riches were a bar to the kingdom of God, Patrese thought, Bishop Kohler had sure hedged his bets.

He'd been to Kohler's official residence on several occasions, but it was only now, with the time—and indeed the duty—to search every room from top to bottom, that he appreciated quite how lavish it was.

The house itself was double-fronted, finished in red brick and light gray stone with copper detailing long since oxidized to sea-foam green. Out back, a magnolia tree stood proud in magenta and mauve above perfectly maintained lawns and flowerbeds.

Inside, chandeliers sparkled in shards of silver crystal. Banisters were carved in dark oak and walnut. Intricate reliefs glided across foursquare stone fireplaces.

It wasn't just the quality of the house that struck Patrese, but its size too. Nine thousand square feet over three stories. Eleven bedrooms and six bathrooms, plus a library, a morning room, a living room, a dining room, a kitchen, and a butler's pantry. Patrese had stayed in hotels smaller than this place.

All for one man, living alone.

It seemed to Patrese a terrible waste—no, more than a waste; hypocrisy and cant of the highest order—for Kohler to have had all this to himself. Sure, part of his job had involved entertaining and accommodating visitors to the diocese, but still.

Though it was midafternoon, the high ceilings and

large windows meant that Patrese and Beradino didn't need to turn the lights on just yet. Quiet draped across the house like a blanket; the city might be all around them, but it had been reduced to a gentle, distant hum, no more.

They were looking for everything and nothing—something, *anything*, that might help them discover who'd killed Kohler.

They started at the bottom of the house and worked upward.

In the basement was a makeshift gym with a treadmill, an exercise bike, and a rack of free weights. The bike's crank arms were rusty, and a cobweb stretched across the treadmill's display screen.

The adjacent wine cellar had seen more use. Patrese counted more than five hundred bottles, their racks labeled in Kohler's copperplate: Goosecross Cabernet, Rutherford Merlot.

But there was nothing relevant to the investigation in either room, nor in the living room, the morning room, the dining room, the kitchen, or the pantry.

It wasn't just evidence relating to the murder they lacked, Patrese thought, but evidence of Kohler's life, full stop. If Kohler had read, it hadn't been for pleasure; the only books on the shelves were religious ones. The TV set looked like it dated from the Cuban missile crisis. There were no videos, no DVDs. A handful of CDs, classical and choral music. No family photographs, of course; Kohler had had no family.

You couldn't give your life to God and live among humans, Patrese thought, not if you wanted to do both properly. Making a man go so far from his primal urges wasn't natural. It certainly wasn't healthy.

They went into the library.

"We'll find something here," Beradino said. "Read your Agatha Christie."

He was right. In the top drawer of the antique bureau where Kohler had worked on his papers they found a photo of a young man, probably fourteen or fifteen, dressed in the College of the Sacred Heart football uniform. He was squatting on his haunches, his helmet dangling from his right hand, and smiling up at the camera.

It was a photo of Patrese.

29

Not just Patrese, when they searched the bureau further.

Hundreds of children. Patrese reckoned they ranged in age from eleven to sixteen, give or take. Many were in Sacred Heart school uniforms, purple blazers with an elaborate crest on the breast pocket. Some were in football gear; others wore choir surplices. Boys outnumbered girls by about two to one.

All of them were fully dressed. There wasn't even a bare chest in sight, let alone any nudity, and certainly nothing that could be described as in any way sexual.

Beradino was silent, but even so Patrese could sense his relief. He remembered that Beradino, while arguing with Mustafa Bayoumi at the mosque a couple of weeks back, had dismissed abusive priests as bad apples. Beradino *believed.* It would have devastated him to discover that the bishop himself had been a pedophile, that the apples had been rotten not just to the core but to the top too.

"You recognize these kids?" Beradino asked.

"Some of them, yeah. The ones who were there same time as me, sure."

"The ones you recognize—you guys were his favorites?"

"I guess." Patrese riffled through a few prints till he found a couple of other guys in football uniforms. "Kohler coached the football team. You played football, you were a bit"—Patrese sought the right word—"*special.* Yeah, special. We called him the Pigskin Padre."

"Pigskin Padre. I like that." Beradino laughed softly and let a stack of photos fall gently onto the desk, where they fanned out as though dealt by a croupier. "You have favorite teachers as a kid, so why can't teachers have favorite kids, huh?"

He gestured around the room: not at what was there, but at what wasn't.

"He had no one else, did he?"

30

They boxed the photos and sent them back by police courier to the North Shore, with orders that every child pictured should be traced and interviewed.

Sacred Heart's administrative office would have contact details for its alumni; they should start there.

At the edge of the police cordon around the bishop's house, a woman with immaculately coiffed dark hair was talking urgently to one of the uniforms. He looked in the detectives' direction. When they'd finished giving the courier his instructions, the officer hurried over.

"That lady lives next door," he said. "She wants to tell you something."

Patrese sized her up as they approached. Midforties, a figure that suggested good genes or a fastidious diet, blouse and skirt tailored just so, and a forehead whose perfection screamed Botox.

Typical Squirrel Hill lady, in other words.

"Yesterday morning—" she began.

"Excuse me," Beradino said. "You are?"

"I'm what?"

"Your name."

"My name is Katharine Horowitz. I live there." She pointed to the nearest house, thirty yards away. It was half the size of the bishop's, which still left it four times as big as Patrese's apartment. "Yesterday morning, I heard the bishop shouting."

"Shouting?"

"Yes. Like he was arguing with someone."

Beradino looked across to Katharine's house, then back again. "You heard this all the way from there to here?"

"I was in the garden."

"On a Sunday morning in November?"

"I had some trimming and clipping to finish before

winter sets in for good. Anyhow, it wasn't that cold yesterday. And I could see that Father Gregory had a couple of windows open, overlooking his own garden."

Sunday morning, little traffic noise, no one around. It was entirely plausible she could have heard him at that distance.

"What time was this?"

"About ten."

"What was he saying?"

"I couldn't catch all of it, but something about how this was all dead and buried, you—the other guy—had no right to bring it up now, show some respect and, so on. He was really agitated. I'd never heard him like that before."

"You said 'the other guy.' This was a man he was arguing with?" Beradino asked.

"Yes."

"What was *he* saying? What was this man saying?"

"I couldn't hear."

"You couldn't hear what he was saying, or you couldn't hear his voice at all?"

"I couldn't hear his voice at all."

"So how do you know he was a man?"

"Because I heard his car pull up about three-quarters of an hour beforehand. I'd just started in the garden then."

"That might have been the bishop himself, returning from somewhere."

"No. I heard the bishop greet him and the man say something back."

"You catch a look at him?"

"No."

"The car?"

"No."

"Pity."

"Anyone else see this man?" Patrese asked.

"How do you mean, 'anyone else'?"

"Your husband, perhaps?"

The slightest furrow fought its way through the Botox and rippled the perfection of Katharine Horowitz's forehead.

"I live alone, Detective."

Rich divorcée, Patrese thought instantly, and the look of defensive defiance on her face told him he was spot-on.

"When you heard the bishop shouting, this man was still here?"

"I presume so. I hadn't heard the car leave, if that's what you mean."

"Okay. Thank you." Patrese reached into his jacket's breast pocket and extracted a business card. "You think of anything else, you have any questions, you just call the number here."

"I surely will," she said. "Such a tragedy. He was the best of men, Father Gregory."

Beradino and Patrese walked out of her earshot.

"You phoned Kohler around nine o'clock, you said?" Beradino asked.

"Yeah."

"So by the time you get off the phone, it's ten after nine, give or take. About nine fifteen, according to Katharine Horowitz, Kohler has a visitor. Forty-five minutes later, they're having an argument. You're almost certainly the last person to speak with Kohler before this visitor arrived, you know?"

"I guess. But it doesn't help, does it? Even if Katharine's timings are a bit off, or mine are, I hung up before anyone arrived."

"You're sure?"

"I didn't hear a doorbell, or someone else's voice. Kohler didn't break off to answer the door, try to hurry me off the phone, nothing like that."

Beradino clicked his tongue against his teeth. "Too much to hope for, huh?"

31

TUESDAY, NOVEMBER 2

Patrese and Beradino were supposed to see Mayor Negley at ten. They sat in the antechamber to his office on the fifth floor of the City-County Building for close on two hours, with one or another of Negley's PAs appearing every few minutes to extend the mayor's apologies, reiterate that he'd been caught up in meetings that had gone on much longer than anticipated, and promise he'd be with them as soon as he could.

Standard billionaire behavior. Treat anyone below your own level as supplicants to a medieval king, even when they had a major homicide investigation to run.

Had the meeting just been a progress report, Patrese and Beradino would have gone back to the North Shore long before. If Negley wanted to find out what was going on badly enough, he could make time for them, not vice versa.

But they wanted to see him for another reason entirely.

They'd discovered a connection between him and the two murder victims.

It was almost midday when he finally came bustling in, trailing a comet's tail of advisers and assistants.

He gave both detectives a double-clasped handshake, his left hand clutching their wrists. Every politician Patrese had met did it, presumably in the belief that it made them seem open and sincere. Patrese thought it as phony as a seven-dollar bill.

"Gentlemen, gentlemen. My apologies. This city is a demanding mistress."

Interesting choice of phrase, Patrese thought.

Negley ushered them into his office. Patrese was surprised at how small it was, before remembering it was municipal property. In Negley's billionaire incarnation, he probably worked out of something the size of Heinz Field.

Negley took a seat behind his desk and directed the detectives to a nearby sofa. They'd be sitting lower than him. Corporate Intimidation 101.

A secretary appeared with tea, coffee, and cookies. When she'd gone, Negley clapped his hands together.

"Now. What can I do you for?" He chuckled at his wordplay.

Beradino held up a brochure. Glossy, high-end,

four-color, its cover emblazoned with the words *Abrahamic Interfaith Foundation.*

"You're a member of this foundation's board, I believe."

"Yes, I am. We're all listed in there, aren't we?"

"Bishop Kohler was a director too. We found this in his bureau."

"Yes, he was. But if this is something to do with the murders—the surgeon, Michael Redwine, he had nothing to do with this."

"He didn't, no. But Abdul Bayoumi did."

"I'm sorry, I don't follow. Abdul Bayoumi died a few months ago."

"Only after Michael Redwine had messed up routine surgery on him."

Negley's eyes widened. "I didn't know that. I mean, I knew something tragic had happened in the operating room, but not that Redwine had been responsible. I didn't know Abdul well, I'm afraid. I only saw him at foundation meetings." He indicated the brochure.

"This foundation—what exactly is it that you do?"

Negley switched instantly, perhaps even automatically, into pontificating-politico mode. "Well, Detective, I believe that conflict between the faiths is second only to climate change on the list of issues threatening our society, and therefore resolving that conflict and promoting cooperation is of paramount importance."

"What exactly is it that you do?" Beradino repeated, deadpan.

Patrese had to bite back laughter, both at Beradino's

sardonic tone and at Negley's complete failure to recognize it as such.

"We facilitate symposiums, joint cultural events, exhibitions, seminars, talks, school programs, those kinds of things."

A lot of jaw-jaw, in other words, thought Patrese; a heap of hot air and no action.

"Would you describe any of your activities as controversial?" Beradino persisted.

"Not to right-thinking people, no."

"You don't, for instance, fund mosques?"

"No. Nor churches, nor synagogues—not alone. Every program we fund, either wholly or in part, must involve at least two of the three Abrahamic religions."

"Can you think of anything the foundation does that *would* make someone want to kill two of its directors?"

"Nothing at all."

"Anything about the directors themselves?"

"Quite the opposite. They're all people of the highest integrity. That's why they were invited to join. We picked nine, three each from each of the three faiths."

"We'd like to give protection to you all. To the seven, er, remaining."

"I have my own protection, thank you, so you can save a little manpower there."

"With respect, sir, they're not the police," Beradino pointed out.

"No, they're not. They're ex–Delta Force. They're a lot more skilled than the police, no offense, and they're certainly better paid." He smiled. "I'm sure the other six will appreciate it, however. Is that your strongest lead?"

"At the moment, yes."

Not just the strongest lead, Patrese thought, but pretty much the only one.

It would take a couple of days to trace and eliminate all the people in the photos found in Kohler's bureau, even with the extra manpower they'd been allocated—a fivefold increase in officers, from twelve to sixty.

In the meantime, those officers had already received several hundred calls, all of which they'd have to follow up. Most would be irrelevant. Some, inevitably, were from wives trying to get rid of their husbands by accusing them of the murders.

Patrese had already recognized one voice as that of a woman who had in the past tried to pin ten separate murders on her husband. He'd given her a phone number.

"This your cell phone?" she'd asked.

"No. It's a divorce lawyer."

The cops had studied CCTV footage of the road outside the cathedral, traced cars through their license plates, and interviewed their owners. None had seen a thing.

A homeless man who'd been bedding down opposite the cathedral offered to tell the police what he knew in exchange for twenty bucks. One sniff of his breath had convinced them that the testimony of a man too drunk to remember what day it was would hardly stand up in court, even if by some miracle it *did* lead them to the killer.

They'd checked the list of the cathedral's workers, regular attendees, and supporters against that of Redwine's patients, and interviewed all those who appeared on both. No dice.

They'd discovered that Redwine and Kohler had been members of the same country club in Fox Chapel. They were interviewing the club's management, staff, and members, several hundred in all. One former employee, whom the club had dismissed the previous year for embezzlement, had already come briefly under suspicion—he'd written threatening letters to the club after being fired—until the police had discovered that he was already in custody for mail fraud.

Given the desecration of the crucifix and icons, they were also checking every Muslim recently convicted of any crime, no matter how small. Allen Chance had impressed on them the importance of subtlety here. They had to pick their way through minefields of political correctness and racial discrimination, and avoid turning a murder investigation into a civil rights issue.

What that meant in terms of Mustafa Bayoumi was anybody's guess.

32

WEDNESDAY, NOVEMBER 3

The first forty-eight hours after Kohler's murder were already up. Patrese and Beradino both knew that no joy now meant ever-diminishing returns later.

"Forensics has found a strand of hair in Saint Paul," Beradino said. "Near Kohler's body, but unburned. They reckon Asian origin. Probably Pakistani. Heavily treated, so almost certainly female. And cut neatly, not fallen out naturally, not yanked forcefully."

"A Pakistani woman who'd just been for a haircut?"

"Could be. They're checking hairdressers now. There are no Pakistani women on the cathedral's staff roster, we know that. No Asians at all, actually."

"Which means nothing. The cathedral's a public place. People come in and out the whole time. That hair could have come from anyone, anytime. You could clean that floor for days, *weeks*, and miss something like that. Or you could sweep it up and then deposit it back there again some time later without knowing. Perhaps it got tangled in the broom fibers and then dropped free again."

"Exactly," Beradino agreed. "It's the longest of long shots."

"And the kids in the photos?"

"Sacred Heart has identified most of them, and given contact details for everyone they have in their database. Uniforms are working their way through those people as we speak. About two-thirds still live in Pittsburgh, so they're being given priority."

"And?"

"And nothing, so far. All of them have alibis. Most hadn't seen Kohler in many moons. No discernible motives."

"What are they like now?" Patrese asked.

"What are who like?"

"The people. The ones in the photos."

"How do you mean?"

"Are they, you know, fucked up in some way? Junkies, depressives, suicides?"

"Why do you ask?"

"Looking for a motive for whoever killed Kohler, that's why. Happily married guy with kids ain't gonna wake up one morning and decide to off the bishop, is he?"

"I guess not. Far as I know, they're a pretty standard cross-section. Check the files, if you want. They're in the system."

Patrese logged on, and soon found that Beradino was right; they *were* a pretty standard cross-section.

More than half were married, about a fifth were divorced, some of them shockingly young. A few gays, a handful with drug problems, or at least problems bad enough to have shown up on their records. There'd be a lot more beneath the surface, Patrese was sure, a lot of things that those people wouldn't or couldn't tell the cops. And why should they? Cops were cops, not social workers.

Patrese recognized more names than he'd thought he would. It was like some sort of surreal, virtual school reunion, people whom he'd frozen in his mind at some stage in their teens suddenly reincarnated on the screen in front of him as adults with jobs, and lives, and problems, years and heartbreaks and triumphs and catastrophes away from how he'd remembered them.

"How you've grown!" he recalled friends of his parents saying when he'd been a kid; *of course* he'd grown, he'd always thought. It would have been a whole heap weirder if he hadn't. So too with these people. *Of course* they'd changed.

Later that afternoon, Patrese went back in front of the media and tossed them tasty but fundamentally unfilling morsels.

Yes, they were following up multiple leads. Yes, they were aware the first forty-eight hours had elapsed. Yes, they understood the city's shock and outrage.

No, he wouldn't give operational details. No, he wouldn't commit himself to any predictions. No, he didn't want to send a message directly to the killer.

He didn't say what he really thought: that two murders in and if Mustafa Bayoumi's alibi held when they finally managed to interview him, what they'd need more than anything else was a third.

A third would give them more evidence. A third might persuade Beradino and Chance to call in the Bureau. A third was what they feared and wanted in equal measures.

33

THURSDAY, NOVEMBER 4

Of all Pittsburgh's buildings, the Allegheny County Courthouse was Patrese's favorite. It boasted the quintessential architecture of crime and punishment. Massive slabs of Massachusetts granite ran down long sides punctuated with brooding arches and flanked by half-towers, as though the edifice had been lifted wholesale from city gates in ancient Rome.

Richardson, the architect, had regarded this building as his greatest work. He'd plundered from across Europe for it: detailing from Spain's Salamanca Cathedral for the front tower, still majestically authoritative despite the upstart skyscrapers that now dwarfed it on all sides; Notre-Dame's cornice; the hollow rectangle massing from Rome's Palazzo Farnese; and, from Venice, the rear campanile and the Bridge of Sighs, through which prisoners had been transported from jail to court and back again.

The courthouse interior was even more thrilling than the façade. The main staircase wouldn't have disgraced the Paris Opera. Levels, landings, and staircases seemed to materialize out of nowhere beneath enormous vaulted ceilings.

It was as though Piranesi or Escher had gotten hold of the blueprints and turned it into an arena of spatial paradoxes, a place where the laws of physics were suspended. The Inquisition would have been right at home here, mounting spiked wheels and meat hooks to terrorize the damned far beneath.

In his courtroom on the third floor, Judge Philip Yuricich listened to Beradino making the case for a search warrant against Mustafa Bayoumi—their last, best hope.

Five foot four on a good day, Yuricich held himself slightly hunched, peering out at the detectives from behind big glasses like an elderly tortoise.

"This man, Mustafa Bayoumi, is our prime suspect," Beradino said. "To be honest, he's the only solid connection between the two victims that we have. Both times, his mom has given him an alibi. No one else."

"You think she's lying?" Yuricich asked.

Beradino shrugged. "Who can say? We search the place, we might find out more. I know it might be considered a little, er, premature, but—"

"You don't have to convince me, Mark. Sure, I'll sign your warrant. These people always look out for each other, you know. They got no respect for the law."

These people, Patrese thought, being Muslims; though where Yuricich was concerned, it could just as easily have been blacks, or Jews, or women, or gays, or pretty much anyone who wasn't a WASP like Yuricich himself.

"And when you *do* nail him," Yuricich continued, "I'll do my darnedest to make sure I get the trial."

34

FRIDAY, NOVEMBER 5

They went mob-handed to Sameera Bayoumi's house.

Patrese and Beradino were there, of course, along with ten uniforms. Nine of them were actual police officers; the tenth was Marquez Berlin, whose business card proclaimed him head of the Pittsburgh PD's electronic crime department.

A more honest assessment would have concluded that he *was* the electronic crime department, in its entirety. Blame budget cuts; everyone else did.

Berlin had the pale face and wide eyes of a man who spent a little too much time indoors, and a lot too much time in front of a computer screen. Not that he cared. More than once, he'd spent days online, so absorbed in his work that his body had more or less forgotten its own imperatives to take on food and eject waste.

Now he was draped in one of the department's spare uniforms. He looked an unlikely cop, but that couldn't be helped. All that mattered was that the Bayoumis didn't question his presence there. What Berlin was intending to do might or might not have been unethical, but it was certainly illegal.

Mustafa opened the door. Beradino held up the warrant.

"We have authorization to search these premises. The officers here will conduct this search, while Detective Patrese and I question you and your mother."

Sameera appeared at Mustafa's shoulder, eyes wide in fear. "What's going on?"

"You have no right," Mustafa snapped. "Today is our Sabbath. You are a religious man; you understand the importance of the sacred day. Leave us alone."

"We have every right. We'll talk in the kitchen."

Mustafa took the warrant and started reading it, careful over every line.

"Don't bother," Beradino said. "All the details are correct."

Mustafa ignored him and continued reading till the

end. The details were indeed correct; he couldn't eject the officers on a technicality.

He thrust the warrant angrily back at Beradino. Beradino grabbed Mustafa's hand and pulled him close.

"Any more of that, and we'll do this down at the station. Understand?"

Mustafa's eyes flashed defiance, but he was silent.

Beradino let him go and turned to the uniforms crowded into the hallway.

"Two of you per room. Search *everything*. Turn the place upside down. Pay particular attention to Mustafa's bedroom, you hear? Go."

Patrese and Beradino spent half an hour in the kitchen with Sameera and Mustafa, going through their stories. The detectives asked for the smallest details, time and again: what had been on television that night, what they'd eaten, what time Mustafa had gone to bed.

Tiny, inconsequential stuff, but lies were much harder to remember than the truth. If Mustafa or his mother was lying, and the detectives probed long enough, they'd find it. Interrogation was like dripping water—sooner or later, it found the opening.

And all the time they were questioning Sameera and Mustafa, it sounded as though the house were alive, around and above them. The dull, reverberating thuds of overturned furniture; floorboards creaking under the weight of heavy footsteps; voices muffled yet urgent as they barked to each other.

Eventually, the uniforms came down with three plastic crates of material.

"You can't take those!" Mustafa yelled.

"We can, and we are," Beradino said. "We'll make an inventory and send you a receipt. Thank you for your time." He said it without inflection; impossible, Patrese thought, to tell whether he was being sarcastic or simply polite.

"This is not the America I thought existed," Sameera said.

The police went back out to their vehicles. Patrese made sure they were inside their car, with the doors shut and the windows up, before he turned to Berlin.

"You get 'em all in, Marquez?"

"Sure did. A bug in his bedroom, one in the living room, and one on the landline. And remote spyware on his PC."

35

SUNDAY, NOVEMBER 7

It was the kind of thing that possibly only a trained detective would notice.

Beradino and Jesslyn were in church, their local church in Punxsutawney, the one they'd been attending for years now. The offertory hymn—"Guide Me, O Thou Great Redeemer"—was being played, and the collection bags were being passed up and down the pews. Each worshipper took the bag, put a folded banknote or two in, and passed it on.

When the bag reached Beradino, he dropped twenty dollars in. Then he handed it to Jesslyn, who added her own contribution.

Except she didn't.

Beradino gave no sign that he'd noticed, but notice he had.

She'd reached into her handbag all right, and had brought out her hand with fingers pressed together, as though clasping a banknote.

But in the split second when her hand had gone to the collection bag, Beradino had seen what she'd been holding.

Or, more accurately, what she hadn't been holding.

Her hand had been empty.

Jesslyn always gave money on Sundays, usually ten dollars, sometimes twenty. For her not to do so was out of character. For her not to do so, but pretend otherwise, was doubly so.

Beradino thought he should say something—but what? If it came out wrong, she'd either shout at him or give him the silent treatment. He wasn't very good at dealing with either. Best leave it alone. To start a fight or keep the peace; a dilemma pretty much every couple went through pretty much every day.

Perhaps she was worried about him, given the amount of time he spent regaling her with details of the Redwine and Kohler murders, trying to make sense of it all. Home was a safety valve for him, a sanctuary, the one place he could at least try to switch off. If he disturbed that, he'd have no peace anywhere.

The service ended, and they filed out of the church,

chatting easily with the other members of the congregation. At the main door, the priest shook their hands.

"That was a wonderful lesson, Jesslyn," he said. "Beautifully chosen, beautifully read. Thank you."

"My pleasure," she replied.

She was carrying the Bible from which she'd read. A leather bookmark with silk tassels marked her place. While Jesslyn chatted with the priest, Beradino took the Bible gently from her, opened it, and read the lesson again.

He knew it was one of her favorite passages. She'd preached it several times in Muncy, on the occasions when she was pulling Sunday shifts.

The Book of Isaiah, chapter 59, verses 1–17.

1 Behold, the LORD's hand is not shortened, that it cannot save; neither his ear heavy, that it cannot hear.
2 But your iniquities have separated between you and your God, and your sins have hid his face from you, that he will not hear.
3 For your hands are defiled with blood, and your fingers with iniquity; your lips have spoken lies, your tongue hath muttered perverseness.
4 None calleth for justice, nor any pleadeth for truth; they trust in vanity, and speak lies; they conceive mischief, and bring forth iniquity.
5 They hatch cockatrice's eggs, and weave the spider's web: he that eateth of their eggs dieth, and that which is crushed breaketh out into a viper.

6 Their webs shall not become garments, neither shall they cover themselves with their works: their works are works of iniquity, and the act of violence is in their hands.

7 Their feet run to evil, and they make haste to shed innocent blood: their thoughts are thoughts of iniquity; wasting and destruction are in their paths.

8 The way of peace they know not; and there is no judgment in their goings: they have made them crooked paths: whosoever goeth therein shall not know peace.

9 Therefore is judgment far from us, neither doth justice overtake us: we wait for light, but behold obscurity; for brightness, but we walk in darkness.

10 We grope for the wall like the blind, and we grope as if we had no eyes: we stumble at noonday as in the night; we are in desolate places as dead men.

11 We roar all like bears, and mourn sore like doves: we look for judgment, but there is none; for salvation, but it is far off from us.

12 For our transgressions are multiplied before thee, and our sins testify against us: for our transgressions are with us; and as for our iniquities, we know them;

13 In transgressing and lying against the LORD, and departing away from our God, speaking oppression and revolt, conceiving and uttering from the heart words of falsehood.

14 And judgment is turned away backward, and justice standeth afar off: for truth is fallen in the street, and equity cannot enter.

15 Yea, truth faileth; and he that departeth from evil maketh himself a prey: and the LORD saw it, and it displeased him that there was no judgment.

16 And he saw that there was no man, and wondered that there was no intercessor: therefore his arm brought salvation unto him; and his righteousness, it sustained him.

17 For he put on righteousness as a breastplate, and an helmet of salvation upon his head; and he put on the garments of vengeance for clothing, and was clad with zeal as a cloak.

36

MONDAY, NOVEMBER 8

From: anon@ucanalwaysbeprivate.tv
To: m.beradino@city.pittsburgh.pa.us; f.patrese@city.pittsburgh.pa.us

THIS MESSAGE HAS BEEN SENT VIA A REMAILING SERVICE

Dear Detective Beradino and Detective Patrese

(Mark and Franco seem too informal, you know? We don't know one another that well yet, do we?)

I don't like hearing you or anyone else refer to the victims as innocent. They're nothing of the sort. They deserved everything they got. Pretty nasty way to go, huh? I should think so. They merited nothing less.

Nor are you innocent. I heard you have sixty detectives working on this. Sixty? That's one hell of a lot of cops. Bet you don't assign sixty to a homeless man found shot in an underpass by the Allegheny, do you? Or to a hooker sliced and diced out on the Strip?

Those people, the flotsam and jetsam, the detritus, the losers, they're the usual victims, aren't they? Not for me. They're not my targets.

Oh, I don't think they're angels, far from it. It was their choice to take the first hit of smack, put the extra dime in the slot machine, go with a man they hardly knew and end up with children they can't feed.

But then again, the way they understand choice is hardly the same as the way you and I understand it. Easy to talk about choice when you have a good education and a solid job and a nice apartment. Not so easy when you're born poor and get poorer.

But the people I've killed, and the people I will kill, they had a choice, you can count on that. They have all the advantages in life, but still they choose to behave the way they do.

You call me a psychopath, but those I kill are far more deserving of that title than me.

They're guilty, but do you think they feel guilt for

what they've done? They're charming, but how deep does that charm go?

Their egos are outsize; they think only of themselves, adoring of their reflections like Narcissus. They like to portray themselves as honest, as men of integrity, but they lie and cheat and deceive. They pretend to feel emotion, sympathy, and empathy, but look closer and there's nothing there. And you'll find that whenever anything goes wrong, it's never their fault.

I'm sending this to you two and you two alone, for you to do with it what you will. There are no blind-copy addresses you can't see. I could give it to the media. Even though the papers probably wouldn't print it and the networks wouldn't show it, since they're the worst kind of corporate lickspittles, it'd be on the Internet within minutes.

But I won't give it to the media, because they're almost as loathsome as the people they obsess with. They give this case so much coverage for the same reason you put so much effort into trying to solve it—that you think some people are more important than others.

You don't realize that the more important they seem, the more they deserve to die. I don't believe in the hypocritical, moralistic dogma of this so-called civilized society. Look at all the liars, the haters, the killers, the crooks, the paranoid cowards, trematodes of the earth. You maggots make me sick. I don't need to hear all of society's rationalizations. I've heard them all before. What is, is.

You don't understand me. You are not expected to. You are not capable of it. My experience is beyond you.

Since you clearly have no idea who I am or why I'm doing this, I've made a few suggestions as to how you should go about catching me. I know this is cheeky, but I'll keep taking liberties like this until you find me and take my liberty, if you ever do. Heed this recitation I give you now.

DON'T get too bogged down in details. There's a bigger picture here. Only when you see that picture will you appreciate what you're dealing with.

DON'T believe anything anyone tells you. The only truth is that no one tells the truth.

DON'T trust the officers doing your drudgework. Their aptitude and skills are limited. You're much better than them, though that's not saying much.

DO look inside yourselves. You may find help there.

DO say your prayers at night. You'll need them.

DON'T let your emotions get in the way. They'll only cloud your judgment.

DON'T go with your first judgment, clouded or not. It'll be wrong.

DON'T listen to the drunks, the troublemakers, and the village idiots.

DON'T get frustrated. This is going to take a long time for you to solve.

DON'T think too much about it. Just do it.

Sincerely yours, The Human Torch.

(It's a dreadful nickname, isn't it? I wouldn't have

chosen it myself. I wouldn't have chosen any nickname, in fact. Nicknames are childish and frivolous. But it seems we're stuck with it.)

37

"He's not joking about that."

Marquez Berlin jerked his head in the direction of the first line of the e-mail: THIS MESSAGE HAS BEEN SENT VIA A REMAILING SERVICE.

"Not just one remailing service. Two or three, I'd guess."

The glee in his voice was unmistakable. Like all true computer nerds, Berlin felt inordinately lucky to be paid for doing something that was effectively his hobby. He loved the clarity and logic of computers. By comparison, the real world was messy and absurd.

If there was something to be found in the measureless tracts of cyberspace, you could bet your last dollar that Berlin would find it.

"Which makes the message impossible to trace," he concluded.

"Impossible?" Beradino's tone betrayed the remorselessness of his own logic: computers were created by man, therefore they should have no secrets from man.

"You know how remailers work? If I send you a normal e-mail, I just ping it straight from my account to yours. Even if I don't include my name, finding out where it came from is the easiest thing in the world. E-mails have a heap of information attached—details of the ISP, serial number of the computer that sent it, interface hardware address, and so on. ISPs know everything about you. They justify all their checks by saying they're in the name of security. I always think SP should stand for surveillance project rather than service provider, you know?"

Beradino made a wheel motion with his hand; he wasn't interested in Berlin's opinion of Big Brother. Berlin, for once sensitive to basic human emotions, went on.

"So if I want to keep my identity anonymous, I use a remailer. Rather than send the e-mail to you directly, I send it to a third party, which strips away all those identifying details, replaces them with its own, and sends it on to you.

"But this has its weaknesses, obviously. You know the remailer's details, and he knows the details of the original sender. So if you can lean on him, legally or otherwise, or hack into his system, you can find out where the mail originated.

"So you use multiple remailers.

"The e-mail's sent to the first server. This reorders it and transmits it on to another server, which does the same thing, and so on. Only the first server knows the sender's details, and only the last server—here, ucanalwaysbeprivate—knows the recipient's."

"Why can't you trace each server back from the one it forwarded to?"

"Theoretically, you can, but these servers encrypt

their details. So you're looking at a huge amount of effort to decrypt these. Even if you do manage that, then you have to get every single server to hand over their databases. These servers will almost certainly be based in different countries, which means different jurisdictions, which means different laws . . . you know what I'm saying?"

He did indeed. It wasn't going to happen, at least not this side of the Apocalypse.

"And this remailing," Beradino asked, "it's easy to do?"

"Pretty much."

"By normal standards, Marquez, not yours."

Berlin laughed. "Yeah, I try to remember everyone's not as talented as me."

"That's not the adjective I'd use."

"Hey." Berlin pretended to be offended. "You want my help or not? Yeah, it's easy to do. You have to have a certain amount of basic knowledge, but the thing about the Internet is you can teach yourself. Half a brain and a day on Google, assuming you're moderately computer-literate to start with, and you could work this out for yourself, no problem. Much safer than using an Internet café, for sure. No worries about eyewitnesses, surveillance cameras, trace evidence, any of that."

"And you're sure it didn't originate from Mustafa's computer?"

"A hundred percent. The remote spyware would show us that independently. Hell, the guy doesn't even look at online porn. That's what the web was *invented* for, no?"

"Okay." Beradino tapped him on the shoulder. "Thanks."

He and Patrese went out into the corridor.

"You think it's genuine?" Patrese said.

"Hard to say. On one hand, there's nothing in this to indicate special knowledge, something only the killer would know, that kinda thing. And whoever wrote it is clearly smart, so he'd know that's what the cops look for, to prove bona fides."

"And on the other?"

"Is just that. That he's smart. It's well-written, not the usual rambling illiterate crockashit you get on cases like this. Smart people tend to have better things to do with their time than send crank letters to cops."

"You wanna ask the FBI their opinion?"

"If I want an opinion, Franco, I'll give you one. The FBI will give us some wishy-washy booyah that'll be about as much help as a chocolate teapot. We'll find this guy the same way cops always find bad guys—by being patient and methodical and looking at the facts. No other way. Never has been, never will be."

Patrese batted his fingers against the printout. "What about the people he mentions? The ones he says he'll target?"

"What about them? Do you know how many people he could be talking about? Hundreds, maybe thousands. We can't warn them all, even if we want to; we don't know who they are. Releasing this, even *telling* the great and good . . . all that's gonna do is get a lot of innocent folk worried, which'll cause more harm than anything the killer can do."

"And if he kills again, like he threatens to?"

Beradino sighed. "You know the answer to that one as well as I do, Franco. He kills again, then we got more evidence to work with."

38

TUESDAY, NOVEMBER 9

All surveillance officers sooner or later discover the same thing: that listening to other people's lives is a lot less interesting than it first seems, certainly once the initial voyeuristic thrill has worn off.

Berlin had installed the listening devices and remote computer spyware in the Bayoumi household four days before. Ever since then, the keystroke logs and phone recordings had fed the monitoring technicians—and the translators, for when Sameera and Mustafa spoke to each other in Arabic—unrelenting domestic minutiae.

Sameera asking Mustafa if he wanted anything from the grocery store; Mustafa on the phone to the electricity company; a couple of terse conversations with cold-callers; Jon Stewart and David Letterman on TV before bedtime. Mustafa forwarding a couple of jokey e-mails to some friends, and checking the news headlines.

Nothing remotely concerning the murders. Nothing even about the way the police had come barging in with their search warrant, which was surprising. Most civilians, confronted with the full might of the law, talked about little else for days afterward.

It was almost as though Sameera and Mustafa knew the bugs were there.

The listeners were so desperate not to be thought of as slacking on the job that they called Patrese and Beradino the moment they got something out of the ordinary, a phone conversation between Mustafa and an unknown man.

Unknown man: *You coming to the sanctuary this weekend?*

Mustafa: *Not this weekend, sorry. Need to get my stuff together.*

Unknown man: *You sure? Gonna be a lot of disappointment.*

Mustafa: *Can't do nothing about that. Sorry. Next weekend. Ten days from now.*

Unknown man: *Usual time?*

Mustafa: *Yeah.*

Unknown man: *You wanna meet outside?*

Mustafa: *No. Too cold. See you in there.*

Unknown man: *Okay. See you when I see you.*

Patrese and Beradino played the tape three times, trying to hear beyond the words, listening for inflections, emphasis, anything that might give them a clue as to who Mustafa's interlocutor was, or what exactly they were discussing.

He sounded young, south side of thirty; but then Mustafa was still in college, so it wasn't surprising he'd be talking to people more or less his own age.

"The sanctuary," Beradino said, rolling the word

around his mouth. "The *sanctuary*. He says that in the first line. Does he mean something religious? Kohler was killed in a church. But not in the sanctuary."

"What's the difference?" Patrese asked.

"The area around the altar, inside the railings, that's the sanctuary. It's where God dwells. Kohler was killed in the confessional, outside the sanctuary."

"And how many people know that, Mark? That's a pretty precise definition. What if 'sanctuary' is what Mustafa calls all churches, mosques, synagogues?"

"Could be." Beradino thought for a moment. "He said 'next weekend,' didn't he? So we have ten days till he goes wherever it is he's talking about."

"We haven't got the manpower to put him under visual surveillance till then."

"No. But we *can* start watching him a couple of days before then—say, next Thursday. In the meantime, we keep listening. We listen to every word." He turned to the surveillance officers and repeated, "*Every word.* Anything else like this, you let us know. Don't worry if it sounds insignificant. Better a false alarm than we miss something."

39

WEDNESDAY, NOVEMBER 10

Yuricich comes to the door, unsuspecting.

He has no reason to be otherwise. I don't look in any way threatening, quite the opposite. And this is

Squirrel Hill, one of the city's classier neighborhoods, the kind of place where eminent judges live, side by side with other pillars of the community, secure in the knowledge that the sun has been placed in the sky expressly to shine on them and them alone.

It's not the kind of place where people get torched to death.

Not until now.

Yuricich opens the door and stands on the porch. If I didn't know better, I'd say he's short because he's bowed down by the weight of the evils he's been tasked with judging; but I know there's no evil as great as that which lives within his heart.

He looks at me, and at the reason he thinks I'm here, and he smiles, a smile you'd mistake for that of an avuncular grandfather, if you didn't know better.

"I'm sorry," he says. "I live alone."

Alone. In a big house, with trees out front that shield the front door from the road.

Perfect.

"Not to worry," I say. "You have a good day, now. Sorry to have bothered you."

I half-turn away from him and then, as though an afterthought, say, "I'm sorry, but could I have a glass of water?"

"Surely. Come on in."

I follow him inside, taking care to close the door behind me, and into the kitchen, where he takes an upturned glass from the draining board and runs the tap a couple of seconds to be sure that it's cold.

"You're out early today," he says.

"Yes, sir. Not enough hours in the day otherwise."

His back is to me, and it's the work of a moment to reach into my bag and take out the weapon.

A big old battery in a sock.

Crude but effective, and so easy.

I swing it in a practiced arc, fast through the air till it bounces hard against the back of his head.

Two cracks: the back of his skull where the makeshift cosh hits him, and his forehead as he slumps forward onto the edge of the sink.

40

I worry for a few moments that I've hit him too hard, but he's soon moaning and groaning, and then trying to struggle through what I guess must be a pounding headache as he realizes several things pretty much at once.

First, I've tied his hands behind his back.

Second, I've taped his mouth so he can't scream.

Third, I'm wearing his robe, the one he wears in court.

I didn't expect to find it here—I thought he'd keep it in his chambers in the courthouse—but maybe he took it to be cleaned, or maybe he likes to bring it home with him, I don't know, and it doesn't matter.

The robe is black, with the Ten Commandments picked out in gold lettering on the back. Leaving aside the irony of walking around sporting slogans such as Thou Shalt Not Steal, Thou Shalt Not Commit Adultery, and Thou Shalt Not Lie in a building full of lawyers, judges, and politicians, I know Yuricich wears these on his robe—I know this since he tells pretty much anyone who'll listen—because he believes them to be the basis of America's Constitution and legal system, and because he sees himself as God's representative in the courts.

"Your God will be judging you soon," I say. "Very soon. But before he can judge, there must be a trial, no?"

Terror and puzzlement bounce off each other in his eyes.

"And before there can be a trial, you must take the oath."

I find a Bible in pretty much the first place I look, which is Yuricich's study. I'm guessing there are probably several more about the place. No matter. This one will do just fine.

I maneuver this Bible into his hands. It's not easy, as they're secured tight behind him and I don't want to undo them, even for a second; but after a couple of false starts we manage it, he gripping the leather cover with trembling fingers.

"Now," I say, "repeat after me: 'I do solemnly swear that I will support, obey, and defend the Constitution of the United States and the Constitution of this Commonwealth and that I will discharge the duties of my office with fidelity.'"

He mumbles something incoherent from behind the duct tape.

"Say it," I snap. "That thing's not coming off, so say it as best you can."

More gibberish, but it sounds close enough.

"'So help me God,'" I add.

"Swwwheppmeo."

"I charge you, Philip Yuricich, with failing to do exactly what you vowed to do in that oath. You haven't accomplished any of that, have you? You haven't supported the Constitution, nor obeyed it, nor defended it. And as for discharging the duties of your office with fidelity—it would make me laugh, if it didn't make me sick."

Perhaps there's recognition in his eyes now. I've let my voice slip back to normal again, and maybe he remembers it.

Maybe not. It doesn't matter either way.

"You, Philip Yuricich, have been responsible for more miscarriages of justice than any other judge in Pennsylvania, possibly the entire United States. You've sentenced twice as many people to death as any other judge in the state, even though you've heard fewer homicide cases than most of your colleagues. You don't like blacks, or women, or Arabs, or gays, or pretty much anyone who's not like you. You apply what you call justice according to nothing more than your own prejudices. You're a disgrace to the office you hold. Do you deny any of this?"

He squeaks dissent from behind his gag, but I don't care.

"You're a defendant's nightmare, a prosecutor in robes. Even actual prosecutors have asked you to tone down your favoritism toward them, haven't they? Thing is, no matter how biased and bigoted you are, in your court, there's still a limit to your power. But not to my power, not in my court, not here. I'm not just judge. I'm jury too, and I find you guilty."

He's squirming hard now, desperate and fearful.

"So as judge, I sentence you to death. As executioner, I'm duty-bound to carry out that sentence. And I do so with the words of Isaiah, chapter fifty-nine, verse seventeen: 'For I put on righteousness as a breastplate, and a helmet of salvation upon my head; and I put on the garments of vengeance for clothing, and am clad with zeal as a cloak.'"

I pull the juggling torch from the bag and touch the lighter to it.

It flares, dangerous and inviting.

And he knows. He knows.

He knows what happened to Redwine and Kohler.

He knows it's happening to him now.

He knows it's a dreadful way to die.

He knows who I am.

He knows.

But he doesn't know what's going to happen to him just before the fire comes.

41

Patrese and Beradino bumped into Freddie Hellmore in the line for the metal detector at the courthouse entrance. They were due at a pretrial conference on Shaniqua Davenport's murder charge—first item of business, 9 a.m.

Pretrial conferences—designed to ascertain exactly what charges the defendant would be facing in the trial itself—were usually as dull as dishwater.

Not that either Patrese or Beradino cared too much. Court appearances were almost guaranteed sources of overtime for homicide detectives. If you'd just finished a midnight-to-eight shift, or were scheduled for a four-to-midnight one, an appearance during normal court hours meant you had to do double time.

Some of the more enterprising members of the department had been known to pull down six-figure salaries this way. Collars for dollars, they called it.

Hellmore was wearing a tie loud enough to be heard in New Jersey, and the inner lining of his jacket was patterned in army camouflage. Patrese raised his eyebrows.

"I'm going to war on this one," Hellmore said.

He smiled, but he was serious. Patrese half-expected him to start singing "Soul Man."

They passed through the metal arch—no guns in the courthouse, no matter who you were—and started up toward the courtrooms on the third floor.

Patrese had walked through here hundreds of times before, but this was the first time he'd ever ridden shotgun for Hellmore.

It was extraordinary. They'd hardly gone ten paces before they were surrounded by people. Autograph seekers proffered pens. Young men took hurried snapshots on their cell-phone cameras. Patrese heard business offers, requests for jobs. A couple spoke breathlessly of an egregious injustice that Hellmore alone could rectify. One guy simply wanted Hellmore to read his poetry.

He, Freddie Hellmore, was the Pied Piper, and he dealt with it all without breaking stride: handing out business cards like a croupier dealing poker in Vegas, rattling off phone numbers for people to jot down, promising a meal here, a cup of coffee there.

He might have given each person only a few seconds of his attention, but when he did, that attention was total. He wasn't searching for someone more important to talk to, nor was he signing autographs without even making eye contact, as many celebrities did.

An outsize character, Patrese thought, but in his own way, an authentic one.

Ten minutes later, they made it through the throng to the courtroom, where Shaniqua Davenport was sitting on one of the hard benches, Trent beside her.

Amberin Zerhouni, assistant DA in charge of homicide cases, was already there. She was in her early thirties, perhaps a couple of years older than Patrese. Her eyes were the color and shape of almonds, her upper lip formed a perfect Cupid's bow, and a wisp of jet-black hair curled lazily out from under a crimson hijab.

By DA standards—hell, by most standards—she was a knockout.

She and Hellmore greeted each other coolly. Lawyers who knew each other well were usually cordial, even friendly, no matter how often they clashed in court. Both sides understood that business was business, and cases were nothing personal.

But this one was different. Hellmore seemed to think he'd got a bum deal here.

Patrese knew the story, at least in outline.

Amberin had wanted to press for murder. Hellmore had called it self-defense.

Hellmore's presence on a case—sometimes even just the *threat* of his presence—had scared many a DA into a plea bargain, downgrading the original charge in exchange for a guilty plea. That way, the prosecution got a guaranteed conviction, the court system had one less trial to deal with, and the defendant got a shorter sentence than was likely otherwise. Everyone was a winner.

But in Shaniqua's case, Amberin had refused to bargain. Shaniqua had confessed, and no DA in her right mind was going to turn away a confession. Besides, there'd been only one weapon in the room. Weaver hadn't been holding that weapon. He hadn't even been *going* for it. That didn't sound like self-defense to Amberin.

Hellmore had angled for a compromise: involuntary manslaughter.

Again, Amberin had refused.

They both knew why. It was an election year, when various public officials were obliged to run for office. Being seen as soft on crime was the quickest way to lose the vote. Most DAs would sooner the world knew that they wore their wife's underwear than thought they were bleeding-heart liberals.

If Amberin wouldn't agree to involuntary manslaughter, Hellmore had pledged to run BWS—battered woman syndrome, one of the most emotive of all defenses.

Done well, and with a defendant who pushed the right buttons, it gave the jury a hook on which to hang their collective hat. This son of a bitch deserved to die, he was a batterer, he'd had it coming for a long time, we're not going to put anybody in jail for killing this douchebag. That kind of thing.

Most BWS defense arguments ran that abuse had psychologically traumatized the victim to the point that she was incapable of forming rational thoughts. Therefore, she could not have been responsible for her violent actions.

That Weaver had beaten Shaniqua wasn't in doubt; he'd been indicted before on domestic violence charges. Like many subsections of the American male population, few gangbangers were above using their fists to control their women.

No, the question was whether Hellmore could prove that the abuse had been both severe and prolonged. That was never as easy as it sounded. Most victims didn't report more than a fraction of the incidents that occurred. Even when they did, they were as likely as not to withdraw their accusations a day or so later.

So you could never be sure which way a jury would jump with BWS. Twelve citizens good and true were just as likely to see it as a get-out-of-jail-free card, or even a license to kill. Getting out of abusive relationships was hard, sure, but there were plenty of ways of doing so without putting a bullet in someone's brain.

That was the logic of the case, on both sides.

Now Hellmore sat with Shaniqua, detailing the myriad of motions he intended to bring: one to dismiss the charges altogether, one to suppress evidence, one to change the trial's venue, one to request a jury rather than a judge sitting alone, and so on.

Shaniqua nodded gravely as she listened, all the

while clutching Trent's hand as if her life depended on it.

Perhaps it did, Patrese thought. He gave Shaniqua a little smile.

She regarded him levelly for a moment or two, seemingly more surprised than angry, then looked away.

Patrese felt like an idiot.

Shaniqua didn't care that he had misgivings about her case, he realized. He'd arrested her and charged her with Weaver's murder. He was five-o, the enemy.

That was the thing about courtrooms: they were battlefields. You were on one side or the other. Pretty much the only players in the middle were judge and jury.

There was no jury today. Just the judge. That's who they were all waiting for.

They were waiting for Yuricich.

42

They checked Bayoumi's wiretap and bugs first of all, of course.

The fire brigade had been called to Yuricich's house at exactly eight thirty, when a passerby had reported smoke billowing from the windows. Though the house was set behind a high hedge, it was on a busy road, well-traveled at that time of morning by commuters and school-run moms.

The fire couldn't have been visible for more than a few minutes before the report came in; someone surely would have spotted it. Even allowing time for the fire to spread, Yuricich couldn't have been killed much before seven thirty, if that.

The bugs had Mustafa and his mother holding several brief conversations, in Arabic, at 7:12, 7:37, 8:01, and 8:24 a.m. It was at least ten minutes' drive from the Bayoumis' house to Yuricich's, probably more at that time in the morning.

Whichever way you cut it, Mustafa Bayoumi simply couldn't have killed Philip Yuricich, couldn't have got there and back in the time available. And Yuricich wasn't one of the seven remaining board members of the Abrahamic Interfaith Foundation.

Patrese and Beradino would still go and interview Mustafa, of course. It wasn't just that they might have missed something; it would look suspicious if they didn't. Mustafa had been the prime suspect for the first two murders, and he knew it.

If they didn't follow up on a third, he'd wonder how they knew he hadn't done it. From there, it wouldn't be long before he found the bugs and kicked up a stink.

In the meantime, they called in the FBI.

Pretty much had to, in fact. Three murders meant the Human Torch was now officially a serial killer. Even Allen Chance couldn't defend the department's corner, not with a dead judge on his watch to add to a bishop and a surgeon.

Chance mollified Beradino a little by pointing out

that the Bureau would be involved purely in an advisory capacity. No Bureau personnel would gather evidence, pursue suspects, or attend interrogations without invitation. Those were the rules.

But they both knew things were rarely that simple and clear-cut. The more the Bureau became involved, the more control they'd want. They always did.

Beradino knew arguing the toss would be a waste of breath. Chance's support for this as solely a police operation had gone, and it wasn't coming back. And Beradino hadn't survived on the force as long as he had without knowing which battles to fight and which to cede. Besides, all law enforcement agencies were supposed to be on the same side, weren't they? And Beradino wasn't yet so jaded that turf wars meant more to him than solving crimes.

The procedure for requesting Bureau assistance is the same across the United States. The police department in question fills in a standard thirteen-page Violent Criminal Apprehension Program (VICAP) analysis and submits it to the Bureau.

The Bureau feeds the data from the VICAP form into its central database to see whether any of it matches known incidents, trends, or suspicions. Bureau analysts then pore over everything that comes out and produce a profile of the killer.

VICAP, the Bureau likes to say, doesn't retire, and it doesn't forget.

Since time was tight, however, Patrese sent Caleb Boone, head of the Bureau's Pittsburgh office, a copy of the anonymous e-mail the detectives had received, together with a summary of the murders so far.

"Boone's a good guy," Patrese told Beradino. "We were at college together. All the time I spent playing football, he was in the library."

"Probably explains why you're a homicide 'tec and he's a field office head."

The FBI's Pittsburgh office had federal investigative responsibilities for twenty-seven counties in western Pennsylvania, and all of West Virginia—a sizable beat by any standards. For Boone to be heading it up in his late twenties was some achievement.

Beltway insiders had their eye on Boone. If he didn't screw things up, he could rise very high indeed. Some of them were even muttering about the directorship one day.

Boone e-mailed back pretty much instantly.

Patrese liked that about Boone. He didn't sit on things for hours or days just to make himself look busy, nor did he get underlings to reply on his behalf. If it was urgent, he'd deal with it urgently.

Patrese clicked open the message.

> Give you all the help I can on this, buddy. Have cleared my decks and will go over this with a fine-tooth comb. Get back to you within the hour.

Boone was as good as his word. He rang after fifty-six minutes.

"I'm in the lobby," he said.

43

Boone had come to them, rather than asking them to come to him. It wasn't so much a question of distance—from the Bureau office to police headquarters it was only twenty minutes—as one of priority.

The incident room was here on the North Shore, as were the scores of uniforms working the case. Boone had done the right thing, which wasn't to say he'd done the usual thing. The Bureau's reputation for arrogance wasn't entirely unjustified.

Patrese pointed this out as they went downstairs to meet Boone.

"Darn, Franco," Beradino said. "He jumped in a car, not trekked across the Arctic. We don't have to keel over in gratitude."

Boone shook Beradino's hand and gave Patrese a light fist pound.

In the incident room, they gathered every available uniform—a handful stayed at their desks to man the phones—and introduced Boone, to a smattering of applause, politeness trumping territoriality.

"Thank you," Boone said. He looked genuinely appreciative. "Before we start, I'd like to say one thing. I've completed four behavioral science modules at Quantico, so when it comes to serial killers, I know what I'm talking about. I may not be Sigmund Freud, but I know enough. Any of you have a problem with that?"

When no one demurred, he went on.

"Right. I'm going to tell you what I think about

these murders, and about the kind of person the murderer might be. It's going to be pretty general stuff. That's inevitable at this stage. If you're expecting me to tell you he's six one with a squint, a Pirates season ticket, a Polish grandmother, and a sideline in stamp collecting, then I suggest you go watch *Psych*. All I hope is this: that one of you here today remembers one thing I say, and it's that person, and that thing, that lead us to this asshole."

Boone held up a printout of the e-mail.

"Let's take this e-mail first. First off, I think it's genuine. There's no specific knowledge in there that you could use to eliminate fakes, I know, but everything about it tallies with what I'd expect the killer's personality to be.

"A number of things in this message catch my eye.

"First, look how many questions he asks. Ten in all. Seven of them in the first five paragraphs. Some of these questions are cocky, some sardonic, some disbelieving, some angry, but they're all *questions*. He's inquiring, he's *challenging*. He's got an active mind, he doesn't accept the status quo. He wants to change things.

"He's clearly well educated. Remailing system to remain anonymous. Grammar and spelling, both good. Yeah, you can do spelling with spell-check, but grammar's harder for a computer to correct, especially without sounding like a computer.

"And his vocab is definitely an educated man's. He makes quite a clever pun on taking liberties. He refers to Narcissus, who's from Greek mythology. And he uses the word 'trematodes.' I had to look that one up. It's a type of parasite, apparently. Any of you say you knew that without diving for the dictionary, you're full of BS."

There was a murmur of appreciative laughter. A bunch of cops was hard to impress, but Boone was playing them just right.

"All these are signs of someone who's not just smart, but wants us to know he's smart. And not just moderately intelligent. Not in his mind. He thinks he's smarter than us, for sure. Look how he says we won't *understand* him.

"So he wants to control us, not vice versa. Look at his list of dos and don'ts. You notice anything? Check the ratio. Don'ts outnumber dos four to one. He prohibits, he forbids, much more than he enables." A beat. "Reminds me of my high school principal."

More laughter.

"That's the e-mail. Now the murders. Do they tally? Psychologically? I think so. He's organized in what he does. You know, of course, there are two basic types of serial killer, organized and disorganized. Some killers meld the two, but overall most are pretty much in one camp or the other.

"This one is organized, most definitely. He's planned these crimes in advance. He's visualized each one many times before finally going through with it. He's targeting specific people. That means researching their lives, their habits, their routines. He's not just dragging bums into alleyways whenever he gets the heat.

"What's unusual to me is his choice of *site*. Most organized killers operate in three distinct locations. They confront a victim in one place, murder them in a second, dispose of them in a third.

"But here, he only uses one site each time. Twice it's been the victim's home, once the cathedral. That may be significant, it may not. But the fact that he confronts and murders each victim in the same place *is* interesting. As for disposing—he doesn't. He's not bothered about us finding his victims. Quite the opposite. He *wants* us to find them.

"Two of the three were closed locations, and he got in both times without apparently using force. No broken locks, no shattered doorjambs. How does he do it?"

Boone ticked off the possibilities on his fingers as he spoke.

"One, he knows them personally. Two, he feigns distress, pretends he's been in an accident or something. Three, he poses as—perhaps he even *is*—someone with a valid reason to call: mail carrier, gas man, charity collector, traveling salesman. Four, same idea, but as an authority figure: cop, soldier, teacher, doctor, even a firefighter.

"Which brings me to fire. Is it MO? Is it signature? Bit of both? He doesn't seem to be using it to obscure the victims' identities, since it's obvious who they are. To destroy evidence, perhaps—but if that's the case, why not torch the whole place? But he doesn't. He just sets the victim on fire. Long as the guy's dead, he doesn't seem to worry too much if the fire spreads or not.

"Or we could look at the symbolism of fire. Hell springs to mind—hellfire, burn in hell. Perhaps it's something slightly more obscure. Remember all the crowds outside the prison when Ted Bundy went to the chair? 'Burn, Bundy, burn,' they chanted.

"If the killer sees himself as executing these people, the victims, perhaps he also sees himself as taking over the role of the state, doing something the state should have done but didn't, couldn't, wouldn't.

"Remember too the importance of the homicidal triad: fire-starting, bed-wetting, cruelty to animals. Most serial killers exhibit at least one of these characteristics in childhood, and often two or even all three. Perhaps in this case, he had a childhood obsession with pyromania that has lasted into adulthood.

"There'll be a reason for the fire-starting, that's for sure. What that reason is, we might not know till we find him. Or we might work it out beforehand and find him that way, I don't know. What I *do* know is that the reasoning behind it, whatever it turns out to be, is central to decoding his motivation. Why does he do it?

"In this case—in any case, actually—there are two *whys*.

"The first *why* is what I just mentioned: what drives him?

"In terms of motivation, we divide serial killers into four categories: visionary, mission-oriented, hedonistic, and power/control.

"We can pretty much rule out the last two. They tend to be associated with sexual arousal, sexual dysfunction, and extreme torture, usually with mutilation. There's no sign of any of those here.

"We can also strike visionary. Often as not, visionary killers have schizophrenia or some other mental illness. They get hallucinations, voices in their heads, God talking to them. This makes them unreliable and irrational. But the intelligence and planning our guy's shown—no way he could have done that if he were mentally ill. No way. Not with the kind of psychotic break from reality that real sufferers experience. He might claim insanity when we catch him, but it'll be BS.

"Which leaves us mission.

"Mission killers are organized, stable, and intelligent. They don't usually pose or mutilate their victims; the kill itself is the mission.

"He's already stated why they deserve to die: because they're hypocrites, people in power who should know better.

"This gives us another clue. The victims have all been white males. Most people in positions of power are. That means he's almost certainly white himself. Serial killers don't tend to murder across race lines.

"Then there's the second *why*—why he's chosen to do it *now*. People don't just wake up one day and decide to go on a spree. It festers in them for years, and only comes out when something triggers it.

"The trigger's something stressful or traumatic, usually one or more of the four *d*'s: death, divorce, dismissal, debt. A loved one or close friend dies; a relationship ends, often nastily; you lose your job; financial pressures become crippling. The last two are often related, of course.

"Finally, I want you all to remember something. This is an addiction, simple as that. Nothing alleviates what he's feeling other than the act of killing. The more he kills, the more he wants to kill.

"We can second-guess him up to a point—he's

given us some parameters, but they're too wide for us to protect all potential targets, and doesn't he just know it?

"Gentlemen, this son of a bitch is gonna be a hard takedown, make no mistake."

44

"Can I have a word?" Beradino asked, when the uniforms had returned to their desks.

"Sure," Boone said.

"I didn't want to embarrass you in front of anyone there, but this profile . . . no offense, but it seems like the usual baloney cut-and-paste job to me."

"I'm sorry you feel that way."

Boone wasn't fazed in the slightest, Patrese saw. He probably got this kind of static from a lot of police departments.

"Thing is—about all profiles, I guess, not just this one—thing is, they only exist in statistical probability, right?"

"It's a little less haphazard than that."

"Not much. The moment there's an anomaly, one single anomaly, one deviation from your norm, it all falls down. You say he's a white man, so we're looking for white guys. But what if he's not? What if he's black, or Asian, or a woman?"

"The profile is a guide. It's not ironclad. It's simply designed to show that some people should be examined with greater care than others. Working the percentages is proven to be the best way of proceeding in cases like this."

"Not on my cases. Unless that percentage is one hundred, unless it's an absolute dead cert, there's always a chance you're wrong. Then you might as well get chimpanzees to stick pins in pages of the *New York Times* and spell out the killer's name that way."

"That's not a helpful analogy."

"Way I see it is this. You want us to take your framework—white, male, educated, organized, all that—and fit the evidence into it. To me, that's putting the cart before the horse. I let the evidence speak for itself and guide me to the end. You decide what the end will be, and choose what you need to get there."

"And I bet you we'll end up at the same place."

"If we do, one of us will have got there by luck, and it won't have been me. So, no offense, but since I'm too old to care what the FBI thinks of me, I'm going to tell every man in there"—Beradino jerked his head toward the incident room—"to take your profile and shove it where, er, where the sun don't shine."

45

The main morgue for Allegheny County (including the county seat, Pittsburgh) is located in the basement of one of the government buildings downtown. It's painted a bilious shade of green that is very nearly, if not very actually, the most unsuitable hue possible for such an institution.

There's the land of the living, up and out in the crisp fall streets; and there's this, the body farm, inside and down, down, like an ancient mythological underworld where the walls sweat death and the odors of chemicals and rotting humans cover and tangle with each other like lovers.

Cliff Lockwood, county medical examiner, moved swiftly, economically, and authoritatively around Yuricich's charred corpse.

He placed a rubber body block under Yuricich's back, so that the arms and neck hung down and the chest was pushed up and forward. That made it easier to cut the chest open.

Though medical examiners are always the ones who study bodies and organs for clues as to cause of death, they often leave the actual dissections to their assistants.

Not Lockwood. He cut better than anyone he'd ever met. Some MEs use ordinary kitchen knives to excise organs, or pruning shears to cut through ribs. These are several times cheaper than specialized medical implements, and do the job almost as well. This isn't fancy microsurgery, where one misplaced nick can be fatal. Fatal's already been taken care of.

Again, not Lockwood. He always used top-of-the-line implements, expense be damned. If it was worth doing, he felt, it was worth doing properly. It might have been nothing more than a matter of pride to him, but pride was everything.

He cut Yuricich open in practiced lines, shoulder to breastbone, each side, and down to the waist.

With a scalpel, he peeled back burned skin, muscle, and soft tissue, and pulled the chest flap up over the face, exposing the rib cage and neck muscles.

He made two cuts on each side of the rib cage, dissected the tissue behind it, and pulled the rib cage from the skeleton.

Quick, decisive cuts above the hyoid bone to loose all the neck organs.

Lockwood reached inside the cadaver and brought them out, murmuring their names dispassionately as he did so: "Esophagus . . . larynx . . ." He stopped.

"There's no tongue here," he said.

46

THURSDAY, NOVEMBER 11

It might have been Veterans Day, but it was no holiday for Patrese, Beradino, and Boone, not when reading Lockwood's autopsy report over cups of congealing coffee.

The tongue had been removed antemortem, the report stated.

"I don't need an ME to tell me *that*," Beradino snorted. "The killer could hardly have reached in and taken the tongue once he'd set the body on fire, could he?"

Patrese grunted agreement, and kept reading.

The most likely method of extraction, Lockwood had written, was with a sharp knife, perhaps a scalpel. The killer would have cut down each side in turn and across the back, as though opening a double-zippered suitcase. The frenum, the flap that anchors the tongue to the floor of the mouth, had been severed, and this was visible even through the fire damage.

"Why?" Patrese said.

As in: why had Yuricich been mutilated, when Redwine and Kohler hadn't?

"Gangs? Gangs cut the tongues from snitches who've blabbed, don't they?" Beradino said.

"He was hardly a gangbanger, though, let alone a stoolie."

"No, but he presided over several gang-related homicide cases in his time."

Patrese nodded. He and Beradino had caught some of those killers themselves. "I know. But were those big news? Little local groups, most of them. Hardly crossed the county line. We're not talking Cali or Medellín. Besides, our gangs, Pittsburgh gangs, are almost totally black. A black dude drives around somewhere like Squirrel Hill, half the locals are dialing nine-one-one before he's reached the first stop sign."

Beradino laughed. "Okay. You win. Scratch the gang angle."

Boone got up, walked over to a whiteboard on the wall, and pulled the cap off a marker pen.

What are tongues used for? he wrote.

He penned the answers as they came up.

1. Eating, or at least tasting.
2. Making sounds: talking, shouting, whistling.
3. Kissing, licking, foreplay, oral sex.
4. Insulting others (sticking out one's tongue).
5. Tongue as item of food, e.g., in a meat store.

"Okay," Boone said. "How likely is each one?"

"Number five's really out there," Patrese said. "Tongue as food. There's nothing in any of the murders to suggest cannibalism, right? Quite the opposite, I'd say. Those bodies were burned to a crisp."

"I second that," Beradino said. "Scratch five. Scratch one, too—eating, tasting. Yuricich wasn't a chef, restaurant reviewer, food writer, anything like that. He didn't make his living off of food."

"Could he have been some kind of serious gourmet?" asked Boone.

"Not if he lived in Pittsburgh," Patrese deadpanned.

They all laughed. Pittsburgh cuisine majored in two things: size and simplicity. You wanted nouvelle cuisine, drizzled this and sun-dried that? You could take the next flight to LA, and leave the sandwiches piled with slaw and fries to the hard-core Steel Towners.

"I reckon we can scratch number four, too," Boone said. "Sticking your tongue out at someone, making a raspberry, is hardly the kind of thing you get murdered for."

"Hardly an insult at all, once you're past puberty," Patrese said.

"True. So we have two choices. Sex, and speech."

"Sex first," Beradino said. "Yuricich lived alone. Never married, far as we can tell." He left the implication hanging for a moment, then shot it down. "I only ever met him professionally, but he always struck me as pretty much asexual. If he'd been gay, actively gay, it'd have got out by now."

"And if it *had* got out, it would have been an issue," Patrese said. "This place ain't the Bible Belt, but it's not some kind of freewheeling, anything-goes Frisco either. Folks here are pretty conservative, especially those in Yuricich's circles."

"Maybe he was a secret pussy-hound," Boone said.

"He didn't look the curb-crawling type."

"Three-quarters of a working girl's clientele don't look the type," Beradino said.

Patrese conceded the point with a moue. "So we go through the details of his life, like we've done with Redwine and Kohler. Maybe we'll find Yuricich spent all his spare time down at the whorehouse. Till then, it's a maybe. That leaves speech."

"This is where I'm leaning, I have to say," Boone said. "What else does a judge do, if not give judgment? When he speaks to pass sentence, his word is law."

"Even if you don't agree with what he says."

"And Yuricich could have sparked argument in a phone booth," added Beradino.

"So we look at his cases," Boone said. He tapped a manila folder. "I've got a list of them here."

Beradino's eyes widened in surprise. "Courthouse

records department told me they couldn't pull that together till after the holiday."

Boone's smile failed to suppress the satisfaction of his answer. "The courthouse records department employs two illegal immigrants. I reminded them of that fact."

Patrese managed not to laugh too loudly.

Boone continued, smooth as silk. "These go back a couple of decades or more. Nothing I can see for Redwine. Yuricich *did* sit on a couple of Mercy medmal cases, but both of them before Redwine arrived there. So rule that out.

"With Kohler, it's a little more interesting. *Brennan-Clark v. Roman Catholic Diocese of Pittsburgh.* You remember that?"

Patrese swallowed the last of his coffee and nodded. "Kid who'd been abused by a priest, wasn't it?"

"Kid who *said* he'd been abused by a priest," Beradino corrected.

"Kids don't make that kind of shit up, Mark. Not when it goes as far as a judge."

"Stuart Brennan-Clark claimed he'd suffered abuse at the hands of a Catholic priest, Moss O'Neill, thirty years beforehand," Boone said. "Yuricich ruled there was insufficient evidence to go to trial."

"How was Kohler involved?" Beradino asked.

"Only by virtue of being bishop at the time the case was brought. He wasn't named in the allegations. I don't think he even knew the plaintiff."

"Pretty tenuous, then, to think this might be related."

"Kohler's killer smashed Church artifacts," Patrese

said. "You get abused by a priest, you might want to take it out like that."

"Perhaps," Boone said. "But not in this case. Not Stuart Brennan-Clark."

"Why not?"

"He offed himself a few years ago."

"Because Yuricich threw the case out?"

"Sometime after that. He was an alcoholic, had lots of problems. Moved out to Lake Havasu, threw himself under a train. Phoenix field office sent me the details. So nothing there either."

"Can I have a look?" Patrese asked.

Boone handed him the case list.

It ran for pages and pages. A record of Yuricich's life, nine to five, Mondays to Fridays, year in, year out.

Patrese split the pile roughly in two and handed one of the halves to Beradino. They began to read.

After a few minutes, Beradino said, "Hellmore."

"Hellmore?" Patrese asked.

"Quite a few of these cases, he's defense counsel."

"And?"

"And he lives in the Pennsylvanian, where Redwine was killed."

"But he didn't have anything to do with the Redwine case."

"No, but he must have known about it. All I'm saying, he has a connection to Redwine, and to Yuricich. Probably Kohler too, we look hard enough. Worth bearing in mind."

They went back to reading. After another few minutes, Beradino held up a sheet and pointed. "*Com-*

monwealth of Pennsylvania v. al-Rassar, Malik, and Ben-Kahla. I remember those guys. I helped out on the case."

"They were members of the Homewood mosque, weren't they?" said Patrese.

"Exactly. They were charged under the Patriot Act with endangering national security or something. It wasn't long after nine-eleven. Yuricich found all three guilty."

"Yuricich? What about the jury?"

"He was sitting alone. Terrorist case. Fifteen years each, they got."

Beradino, Patrese, and Boone looked at one another.

They were all thinking more or less the same thing.

Redwine had botched surgery on Abdul Bayoumi, whose son, Mustafa, was a member of the same mosque as the three men whom Yuricich had convicted.

If those three had been Islamic extremists—even if they hadn't—what was to stop there being more where they'd come from? Someone who might want to smash a crucifix, shatter stained-glass windows, deface a print of God and Adam. Someone possibly of Pakistani origin, matching the hair found in the cathedral. To watch the news, to read the papers, was to be told over and again that Christianity and Islam were at war with each other, and that those at either end of the conflict believed there was no middle ground. You were either for or against.

"Caleb, can you give us the list of all the Muslims you guys are keeping tabs on?" Patrese asked.

Boone paused.

"That's pretty sensitive stuff, Franco," he said at length.

"Come on, man. We need to check them all out."

"It's not as easy as that."

"Hey," Beradino said. "You told us you'd help in any way you can."

"And I will. But there's a lot of sensitive stuff here. Surveillance, complex operations, deep cover. I can't have you guys just blundering in somewhere and undoing months, *years*, of painstaking work with a few dumb questions."

"Come on, Caleb," Patrese said. "All we want is what's in your files. Names, addresses, radical connections. We find someone we like the look of, something that makes us think, this guy, he could be our man—then we come to you and check we're not pissing on anyone's shoes. Okay?"

"I don't know, Franco. Terrorism's our number one priority, you know. Everything has to be cleared through, like, nine levels of managers, and—"

"You're head of the field office," Beradino said. "Your word goes."

"Not on something like this. I have to go higher. I have to go to DC."

"This is a perfectly legitimate request," Patrese added.

"The guys we're looking at are suspected of terrorism. This is a serial killer."

"Maybe there's no difference."

"Huh?"

"Terrorists attack innocent people. They create panic.

They attract media attention. They give law enforcement the runaround," Patrese said. "Tell me how that's in any way different to what our killer's doing."

"I have to go higher. I'll ask, and I'll make a good case. That's all I can promise."

"But—"

"But nothing. It is what it is. Take it or leave it."

Beradino clicked his tongue in annoyance. "Every time I deal with the Bureau, you guys are always the same. You swan in and expect everyone else to bend; but the moment *we* ask *you* for something, whoa! You act like we just burned Old Glory."

"Mark—" Patrese began.

"It's okay," Boone said. "I understand your frustration. So please understand mine. I'll do what I can. In the meantime, I suggest very strongly we keep this idea under wraps. This could be a PR disaster if we screw it up. Hell, it could be a PR disaster even if we don't screw it up. We all remember how anti-Muslim sentiment spiked after nine-eleven. I don't want a repeat of that, even on a smaller scale."

"All right," said Beradino. It was as near an apology as he'd give.

There was a pause; not very slight, and not very comfortable.

They all knew that Yuricich had presided over one case more controversial than all the others put together. It had been so controversial, in fact, that the defendant was bringing what would be—what *would have been*, if Yuricich had lived—a landmark case for bias and misleading the jury.

Landmark because, until now, the Supreme Court had always ruled that judges and prosecutors enjoyed absolute immunity, so they could do their jobs without fear of legal retaliation. However, the Third Circuit Court of Appeals had just decided that management failures leading to a wrongful conviction *could* now be prosecuted.

And both Beradino and Patrese had connections to the defendant in question.

47

Her name was Mara Slinger.

She'd been a Hollywood star, one Oscar already under her belt and, if the pundits were to be believed, more likely to come. She hadn't been hardcore, über-A-list—not a Julia or a Nicole—but she'd definitely been on the next rung down, along with the Naomi Wattses and Kate Winslets of this world.

She'd chosen her scripts wisely, mixing popcorn films with serious ones, and she hadn't been scared of taking challenging roles, which was Hollywood-speak for making herself look ugly. Her Oscar had come for a film called *First Lady*, in which she'd played Eleanor Roosevelt, no one's idea of a beauty.

The necessary prosthetics had made Mara unrecognizable, and the way she'd changed her voice meant you wouldn't have known it was her even with your eyes shut. Plenty of actresses would have been too vain to take on the role, but not her, and she'd been good enough to carry it off, her own beauty be damned.

Then Mara had fallen in love with and married a hitherto untamable bachelor, who also happened to be a billionaire businessman and, latterly, mayor of her hometown, Pittsburgh.

Howard Negley.

Their wedding had been a lavish affair, and their honeymoon had trailed paparazzi like the debris from a comet's tail. And if Pittsburgh had liked its new mayor, it had gone crazy for his wife.

Even for a city that was newer, cleaner, and more confident than before, she'd still been an exotic bird. That she'd chosen to live in the Burgh rather than Tinseltown was a vote of confidence in the city that the entire chamber of commerce budget couldn't have bought.

When Mara had said she felt Pittsburghers were the most genuine and hospitable people anywhere in America—and implied, without quite saying so, that Hollywood was chock-full of fakes, charlatans, and weirdos—Pittsburghers had half-considered throwing Howard out and installing Mara as some mayor-cum-queen figure herself.

She'd become pregnant. Supermarket tabloids had rejoiced. The best obstetricians the nation could provide had been summoned to her bedside at Mercy—no Cedars-Sinai or Swiss clinics for Mara—and into a world agog had come Noah, seven and a half pounds of impeccable breeding and genetics.

A month later, Noah had died.

A child's death was perhaps the one thing that could

still stop the rapacious press in its tracks. Coverage of the tragedy had been muted and respectful. Even those selfsame supermarket tabloids had recognized it was something for which no amount of money, power, looks, or talent could compensate.

A year or so later, Mara had become pregnant again. This time around, she'd given birth to a little girl, Esther.

After five weeks, she too had died.

Then had come Isaac, who'd lived for just seventeen days.

The police opened an investigation, with Beradino as lead detective.

Beradino had arrested Mara on suspicion of killing her babies, all of them—three separate charges of murder.

Mara had denied it, of course.

She was a religious woman, a regular fixture at her local synagogue in Fox Chapel. Every movie contract she'd ever signed had barred nude scenes, body doubles or not. She was the last person on earth who'd have killed her children, she'd said.

She'd hired Hellmore to defend her, adamant that all three babies had died crib deaths. She'd refused to plead guilty or claim diminished responsibility, even though she could have got a lighter sentence that way. She hadn't done it, period.

Half the country had agreed with her, and reckoned her the victim of a monstrous witch-hunt. The other half had thought her a baby-killer, evil to the core.

The trial had been front-page news throughout the world.

As prosecuting attorney, Amberin Zerhouni had thrown the kitchen sink at Mara, alleging pretty much everything from Mara's resentment of the enforced hiatus in her career to postpartum psychosis via all points in between.

Not all of it had stuck, but then Amberin hadn't needed it all to. Just enough.

The jury had found Mara guilty. Yuricich had given her three consecutive life sentences.

Howard, having stood by Mara throughout the trial, had filed for divorce.

Hellmore had worked like fury to have the case reopened. Showman he might be, but he also knew how to put in the drudgery off-camera. Somewhere deep in eastern Europe, he'd found one of Mara's grandmothers who'd lost several children in infancy, and he'd set about proving two things: first, that genetic defects had caused the loss of these children; and second, that these defects had traveled down the maternal line, first to Mara and then to her children.

The Superior Court had overturned the original verdict on appeal. On a scorching summer morning a few months back, Mara had been freed from Muncy.

Several thousand people, clearly with nothing better to do than trek to a small town in the middle of nowhere and stand around in the blazing sun for hours on end, had been there to witness her release.

Among them had been Beradino, disbelieving and horrified in equal measures. Of all the homicides he'd worked, this one—three little children dead before they were six weeks old—had shaken him harder than any other. Much harder.

Far as he was concerned, Mara was guilty as hell. He knew when he'd been lied to, and Mara had made Dick Nixon look like the Pillsbury Doughboy.

So that was Beradino's connection to Mara Slinger.

Patrese's was slightly more tangential, but no less traumatic.

Because the woman Patrese had shot in Homewood, the one he'd thought had been going for a gun when she'd just been reaching for her spoon, the one whose death he'd had to stamp down somewhere deep in his psyche, and even then it didn't, *wouldn't* stay hidden, it still seeped little bubbles of anguish and guilt and what-ifs; well, that woman hadn't been just another junkie, just another whitey out of place and out of her depth in the ghetto, certainly not as far as Mara Slinger was concerned.

That woman had been Samantha Slinger. Mara's little sister.

48

FRIDAY, NOVEMBER 12

Mara lived in the resolutely middle-class area of Observatory Hill. Her apartment was right on the edge of Riverview Park, which boasted wildlife; trails for hiking, riding, and cross-country; and the titular observatory itself, an imposing Greek Revival temple in tan brick and white terra-cotta topped by domed telescope enclosures.

Except it wasn't her apartment. It belonged to the Pittsburgh police department.

Pittsburgh PD maintained fifty or so safe houses across the city, which they used for people whose lives were deemed in danger, usually witnesses or snitches due to give testimony in upcoming trials.

Mara wasn't one of those, of course, but her safety had been deemed compromised all the same. Since her release in mid-June, she'd received hundreds of death threats: letters, phone calls, e-mails, even parcels full of excrement or dismembered dolls.

So the police had decided to watch over her till the fuss died down and the hordes of crazies moved on to their next target. They'd put her in this apartment on Riverview Avenue, two officers always inside with her, two more in a cruiser parked outside.

After six weeks, protection had been scaled down to just the two men in the cruiser. Six weeks after that, it had been decreed by whoever decreed these things that there was no longer a clear and present danger to her safety.

The crazies and name-callers had moved on. Only the odd curiosity-seeker was left, and even they didn't tend to hang around too long now that there were no crowds in which to pass the time.

The police had left Mara with two things: a panic alarm, which was routed straight through to the nearest cop shop, and a few months to find alternative accommodations.

A couple of weeks after the police had left Mara, Redwine had been killed, though Patrese and Beradino had yet to find any connection between the two.

And now Yuricich was dead. Coincidence? That was what they were there to find out.

They were almost at the apartment when Patrese's cell phone rang.

It was one of the uniforms in the incident room. "We've found something, sir."

"Go on."

"Two small stones in the judge's house."

"Stones?"

"Yes, sir."

"What kind of stones?"

"Predominantly pink, with areas of red and white mottling, and a smattering of black spots across the surface."

"And?"

"There were similar stones at both other murder scenes."

Patrese sat up straight in his seat. "Then why the hell weren't they noted?"

"They *were* noted, sir. There's an inventory of items found at each scene. They're in both inventories, but not as stand-alone items. That's why we missed them till now. At the first scene, the Redwine case, they were marked as part of a bowl full of semiprecious stones and pebbles that had been on a table in the living room. And in the cathedral, they were categorized as general debris, presumably brought in on the soles of one of the hundreds of people who'd visited that day."

Patrese bit back his anger, knowing it was aimed largely at himself.

It didn't matter that the link had been obscure. His job was to find such links.

"There's a geology department at Pitt," he said. "Send the stones there. Ask the department to tell us what they are, where they come from, what they might mean."

"Yes, sir."

"And good work, whoever spotted the connection."

"That was me, sir."

"Then good work to you. Well done. And whatever you do, keep this away from the press. We can use this as a nut-job filter."

"Of course, sir."

Patrese ended the call and briefly apprised Beradino of the situation.

Beradino nodded, but his mind was elsewhere—Patrese's too, truth be told.

They'd left Boone behind. Technically, they'd done so because Boone's role was purely an advisory one, and having him come along to interview suspects would send out the wrong signals as to the balance of power in this investigation.

They all knew perfectly well that it wasn't the real reason. The real reason was that Patrese and Beradino were probably the two people Mara least wanted to see in the entire world.

Which made them the perfect choices to interview her.

49

There was a picture on Mara Slinger's mantelpiece of her onstage at the Kodak Theatre, gym-honed body swathed in Vera Wang and a little gold statuette in her hand. Her smile flashed two rows of preternaturally white teeth, and her eyes crinkled in the warm joy of her peers' adoration.

She sure as hell didn't look like that anymore.

She was still pretty, of course, if you looked hard enough. But her skin was almost gray, and her eyes had been pulled downward by the weight of the bags beneath them. It was prison pallor, recognizable to pretty much everyone who worked in law enforcement, and it took longer than a few months and a dose of civvy street to shift. Both Patrese and Beradino knew plenty of people who'd never looked the same after even a few months inside.

"I wondered when you'd be making an appearance," she said tightly.

She led them into the living room.

It was large enough, high ceilings, tall windows, neutral décor. Bookshelves on the far wall were crammed with paperbacks. On a side table next to the sofa were three black-and-white photographs in silver frames: Noah, Esther, and Isaac, all scrunched-up baby faces and white blankets.

If Beradino noticed the photographs, he gave no sign; but then his face couldn't have gotten any tighter than it already was without surgery.

"Please." Mara gestured toward a couple of armchairs. "Sit."

She perched on the edge of the sofa, uncomfortable and nervous. She didn't offer them coffee, tea, or even a glass of water. She wanted them out. You could hardly blame her for that, Patrese thought.

"You know that Judge Yuricich was murdered two days ago?" Beradino said.

Mara nodded toward that morning's copy of the *Post-Gazette* on the coffee table in front of her. The front page carried nothing else.

"Would you mind telling us where you were on Wednesday morning?"

"I was here."

"Is there anyone who could corroborate that?"

"No, there isn't. I was here alone, Detective." She paused. "I usually am."

"Do you remember what you were doing on the evenings of Monday, October eighteenth, and Sunday, October thirty-first?"

"Yes, I do."

Beradino raised his eyebrows; polite surprise or rancid disbelief, Patrese couldn't tell. He noticed that Beradino was shaking, quivering with tension as he tried to concentrate on the questions he was asking, and on being fair, and on playing this one by the book, down to the smallest detail, when pretty much all he could think about was that this woman had committed the most heinous crime imaginable—not once, not twice, but three times, *three*!—and that, having got her just deserts, she'd then cheated them through a smart lawyer and the bleeding hearts of the appeals court.

"You do? I don't see no diary. You must have a great memory."

"I was doing the same things those evenings that I do every evening." Mara paused, an actress's nose for the beat. "Nothing."

"Nothing at all?"

"Sitting here. Reading. Watching TV. Going to bed early, hoping I sleep as long as possible. I have no social life. I'm damaged goods, as well you know. No one wants to be seen with me. Not now. Perhaps not ever. I don't go out, 'cause I'm always worried about how people will react. There'll always be people who think I did it." She raised her eyebrows meaningfully in Beradino's direction. "All it needs is for someone to say something, even do something, try to attack me, and that's an evening ruined. So I don't put myself out there. Maybe I'm agoraphobic, I don't know. But after all I've been through, I don't even care that much anymore. So no, I don't have an alibi for the eighteenth, or the thirty-first, or last Wednesday, or any other day you care to mention since I left Muncy, because how can I have an alibi when I never see anyone?"

Patrese was about to say something, but Mara was in full spate.

"No, actually, come to think of it, maybe I *do* have an alibi." She glared at Beradino. "I know your idea of great detective work is taking a woman who's suffered the biggest tragedy a mother ever could, not once but three times, and deciding the only way to make that worse is to accuse her of doing it deliberately—you don't have children, do you, Detective? No, I didn't think so. No father could ever have done what you did. I wonder whether you even like women?"

She went on before Beradino could answer. "Anyway, if you do what detectives are *supposed* to do, why don't you go find some of the freaks who used to gather down on the sidewalk outside? The paparazzi, the stalkers, the haters, the bored, the motley crew who came to gawk at me, day after day, night after night. Go find them, 'cause I bet some of them were here when those people were murdered, and they'd tell you I couldn't have done it, because I was in here all the time, I hadn't left this apartment, and they'd have known if I had, since there's no way out other than right past them."

She was breathing hard, and she didn't break eye contact with Beradino once.

"I don't appreciate you speaking to me like that," Beradino said.

Mara shrugged. "So arrest me."

Patrese almost laughed. He was suddenly conscious that he was being unusually quiet, and realized he was hunching on his seat to make himself appear smaller.

He knew why: because he didn't want to be noticed.

He felt ashamed, the kind of shame he'd known before, perhaps the kind of shame you'd expect when sitting six feet from someone whose sister you'd killed.

"What do you think of Yuricich's murder?" Beradino said.

"What do you mean, what do I think?"

"I mean, how does it make you feel?"

"*Feel?* It doesn't make me feel a thing."

"You're not glad he's dead?"

"Not in the slightest."

"Some people might find that surprising."

"Why?"

"You were bringing legal action against him, is that right?"

"That's right. And?"

"You felt you had a case against him?"

"Very much."

"That must have caused you some upset. Given how, er, how *emotional* this case has been."

"It did cause me, er, some upset, as you put it, yes. But I wasn't suing because I was upset. I was suing because I felt Yuricich had broken the law. If you think I'm happy he's dead, then no, quite the opposite. Yes, I loathed him, with every fiber of my being. But it's a long way from loathing someone to killing them. Too long to make sense, at least in this case."

"Why's that?"

"Isn't it obvious?"

"Not to me."

"Why does that not surprise me? Whoever killed Yuricich deprived me of my justice. I'll never see him in the dock now. Never see him on the wrong side of the law, for once, beholden to someone else's judgment. Never have the satisfaction of holding him accountable for what he did to me. No, the *last* thing I wanted was for him to be killed. Justice denied. You think I don't know what *that* feels like?"

"Did you know Michael Redwine or Gregory Kohler?" Patrese asked quickly.

Both Beradino and Mara started slightly, as if they'd forgotten he was there. Mara stared at him for a moment.

"Redwine, no. Kohler, I might have met him with Howard at some point before—before it all happened, but I don't remember. If I did, he clearly didn't make a big impression on me. If you're asking me whether I killed them—"

"That wasn't what I was asking."

"Come on, Detective. You two aren't here to wish me happy Shabbat. You ask me whether I knew them, you ask me whether I killed them, one leads to the other. No, no, no. I didn't kill either of them. I have no reason to want either of them dead. None at all. None at all."

She glanced out the window. It was late afternoon, and the sky was blackening.

"Now, if you'll excuse me, it's nearly dark, and Shabbat starts at sundown."

50

SATURDAY, NOVEMBER 13

Pittsburgh receives more rain than Seattle, a point it likes to ram home on occasion. Today was such an occasion. Outside the windows of Hellmore's office, the rain came down in sheets, blankets, curtain-rods—hell, practically an entire bedroom suite.

Patrese and Beradino looked around the room. Wall space was clearly at a premium, with hundreds of pictures of the man himself in grin-and-grips with the great and good: Shaq and Magic, Denzel and Will, Jesse and Al. Dotted in the few remaining spaces were framed copies of multimillion-dollar checks Hellmore had won for his clients. Patrese recognized a couple of names from police brutality cases.

Hellmore came in at a quick trot. "Sorry I'm late—and I have to go out again now."

His tie was another marvel in Technicolor.

"Who's your supplier?" Patrese asked. "Stevie Wonder?"

Hellmore laughed, which Patrese took to be a good sign. "The day I take fashion lessons from the cops is the day I know it's all gone to shit."

Patrese remembered the statement aimed at potential clients on the home page of Hellmore's website: *The police and prosecutors do* not *have your best interests in mind after a murder charge is made. Their job is to quickly convict you based on the evidence obtained and move on to the next case.*

It was safe to say Hellmore was not a natural fan of the police force, but equally safe to say he took each member of that force as he found him or her. Patrese made the effort to get along with him; Beradino less so, especially since the Mara Slinger case.

"Listen, detectives, can we do this later? Unless you want to come with me?"

"Where are you going?"

"See my dad."

Beradino and Patrese looked at each other.

"Sure," Patrese said.

"You won't be so sure when we get there, especially if he's refused his pills. Still, on your own heads be it. We'll talk in the car."

"The car" was another integral part of the Hellmore legend: a Rolls-Royce in beige ("racing gold," he insisted) with a license plate that read SUE YOU.

"Don't both y'all sit in the back," Hellmore said as he clicked the remote. "People will think it's *Driving Miss Daisy*."

Beradino pulled rank and took the backseat. Patrese rode shotgun.

Hellmore pulled out into downtown traffic, light on a weekend.

"My right of way, asshole," he hissed at a car passing close across his bow. "Where were we? Oh, yeah. Dad lives in a nursing home—sorry, a senior citizens' home. As if giving it some bullshit euphemism is going to make people forget the residents check out only one way—feet first."

"Good home?"

"Mount Lebanon." Mount Lebanon, southwest of the city center, was about the most characterful of Pittsburgh's more affluent suburbs, with its hilly brick streets and hodgepodge of houses: older mock-Tudors, bungalows, foursquares. "Best that money can buy. Not that he appreciates it. He's an ornery bugger, specially since he had a stroke. Anyway, we'll be there soon enough.

What can I do for you in the meantime? You wanna know who had a reason to do Yuricich?"

"If you would," Beradino said from the rear, deadpan.

"Shit. Take your pick. Half of Homewood, for a start. Yuricich was a racist fuck, man. Didn't like black defendants. Sure as hell didn't like black lawyers. But you guys already figured out that a bunch of black dudes in Squirrel Hill gonna stand out like titties on a pork pie, so it ain't any of the brothers."

"You were bringing a suit against him for bias and misleading the jury in the Mara Slinger case, is that right?"

"Damn right. Not just him. Lockwood, too. You know, the asshole ME."

"Clifford Lockwood is a respected professional," Beradino said levelly.

"Not from where I'm looking. You remember his bullshit statement about the odds against it *not* being murder? That was what sank Mara. But it was bullshit. The math was flawed. One of the math professors at Pitt proved it, right after the trial. But it was too late by then. And Lockwood knew it was bullshit all along. Fucking knew it."

Everyone who'd followed Mara's trial—which was to say, pretty much everyone in the country—remembered that moment.

As well as being medical examiner for Allegheny County, Lockwood was director of pediatric forensic pathology at the Children's Hospital of Pittsburgh, responsible for investigating suspicious child deaths throughout western Pennsylvania. He wasn't just any old expert; he was *the* authority, he was the oracle.

This was what he'd said on the witness stand:

"There's no evidence that crib deaths—sudden, unexpected, seemingly inexplicable deaths—run in families. There is, however, plenty of evidence that child abuse does.

"We work on a simple principle that has yet to be proved wrong. One crib death is a tragedy. Two is suspicious. And three is murder.

"Look at the evidence. All three children seemed entirely healthy before suffering sudden, fatal collapses. The autopsies showed no evidence of illness. I should know; I carried them out.

"In a family like this one—a high-income, professional, health-conscious, nonsmoking family—the odds of an infant dying by chance alone is around one in 8,500.

"The odds of two infants dying by chance alone are therefore this figure multiplied by itself, which works out as one in almost 1.75 million.

"And the odds of three infants dying by chance alone"—*and here Lockwood had paused, as though daring the jury to try and work out in their heads how ridiculously large the next, crucial figure would be*—"are less than one in 600 billion.

"In other words, one in 100 times the current population of the world.

"If you played the lottery every week and those were your odds of winning, you know how long you'd have to play before you could be sure of hitting the jackpot? More than a billion years."

"So Lockwood," Hellmore said, "we're looking to do for perjury. I'd do him for being a smarmy fuck too, if I could. You remember what else that motherfucker did? The bouncy chair Mara had put her babies in was admitted as an exhibit. And that—Jesus, I still can't believe it. Lockwood looked around the room, looking for the laugh, and said loudly, 'I didn't realize we were that short of chairs.' And then, *and then*, he came over at lunchtime and said, 'I always try to be sympathetic toward the mothers. This is terrible for me, it must be awful for you.' I told him to fuck off."

He eased the Roller across the Fort Pitt Bridge.

"We can still get Lockwood, of course. But Yuricich—it would have been legal history, man." His eyes glittered; the words *legal history* were music to the ears of a crusader like Hellmore. "Expert witnesses have long been fair game, but not judges and prosecutors. We'd nailed Yuricich, we'd have opened the floodgates. All those fucked by the system would have had a crack at it too."

"Why not Amberin?" Patrese asked.

"Amberin did her job. I got no problem with that. Neither does Mara. Amberin was there to prosecute. That's what she did. Yuricich *wasn't* there to prosecute, but he might as well have been. I've seen some bent judges in my time, and he was right up there. Too in love with himself, too. You know he used to leave the courthouse during lunch breaks in the trial, go around the souvenir stalls outside, and buy up figurines and T-shirts of himself?"

"And if you'd won? If Yuricich had lived, and you'd taken him to court, and won? What would that have meant?"

"For him? A ruined career, I hope."

"You *hope*?"

"Damn straight. Honest mistakes honestly made are one thing. What Yuricich did to Mara—and lots of others, let's face it—was something else entirely. And you know how much compensation Mara gets for that? None. Zilch. Not a dime. People get millions when they scald their dumb asses with hot coffee from Mickey D's, but not when they spend years inside for something they didn't do. Not in this state, at any rate. All Mara got was a shrug of the shoulders and an 'oops.' She deserves more."

Patrese half-turned and glanced at Beradino.

Beradino was as expressionless as the Sphinx.

51

The Golden Twilight Senior Citizens' Home at Mount Lebanon was clean, well appointed, and lacking any semblance of warmth.

Notice boards were spattered with offers for this, that, and the other, almost all of it costed. The only poster without a dollar sign anywhere to be seen was one asking the residents to become donors for the

UPMC Willed Body Program. Benefit science after you've gone, and so on.

That apart, it seemed to Patrese to be the kind of place where they knew the price of everything and the value of nothing.

The home's manager, Walter deVries, met them at the entrance. A ring of graying hair skirted the flanks of his bald scalp. Beneath it, his face was round and bland.

"Good to see you again, Freddie," he said, shaking Hellmore's hand vigorously.

"You too, Walter. How's Dad?"

"Not too bad this week. A bit up and down. No more than usual."

"Still accusing you of everything bad?"

"A little. But don't worry. We get that all the time, and not just from him. Goes with the territory. It don't mean nothing. You get to that age, folks start losing their faculties. It's sad. We just try to look after them best we can, let them hold on to as much dignity as possible. It's all we can do. All anyone can do."

He gestured through into a sunroom. "He's in there. Have to dash, but good to see you again. Anything you want, you be sure to let me know."

DeVries hurried off. They went through into the sunroom.

Old Man Hellmore was sitting in a wheelchair. He was slightly hunched and looked indefinably shrunken, but there was no missing the dancing sparks in his eyes as he glared at Beradino and Patrese.

"The fuck are these guys?" he snapped.

"Morning to you too, Dad," Hellmore junior said equably. "How you been?"

"I said, who the fuck are these guys?"

Patrese was going to point out that he'd actually said, "The fuck are these guys?" rather than "*Who* the fuck are these guys?" but figured there was a time and place for grammatical pedantry, and this was neither.

"Dad, meet Franco Patrese, Mark Beradino."

"You cops? No, don't answer. Course you are. Clear as the noses on your faces. You carry yourselves like cops. Don't ever do undercover, guys, you want my advice. Okay, Mr. De-tec-tives, maybe y'all can clear up a mystery for me. My son here come see me every week, but he never come on his own. He always gotta bring someone else with him. You figure that shit out?"

"Dad," Hellmore said, in a tone half-warning and half-exasperated.

"'Cause if you can't, you guys ain't much by the way of detectives."

"Dad, let's not do this now. Not in front—"

"Not in front of the guys *you* brought?" Old Man Hellmore never took his eyes off Patrese. "How you doing, hotshot? You worked it out yet?"

Patrese looked at Hellmore, who shrugged apology.

"Families are families," Patrese said eventually. "This is not my beef."

"Then you a chickenshit," said the old man. "You know damn well why he never come on his own. There someone else here, he reckon I can't make a scene."

"I'm a busy man," said Hellmore. "It saves time to

conduct meetings in the car on my way here. That's all it is. I'm not ashamed of you, Dad."

"Then why you shove me in this shithole?"

"This shithole costs eighty grand a year! I could put you in the Hilton for less."

"It's a *shithole.* You put gold plate onna turd, it still a turd. 'S all 'bout the money with you, ain't it? You know where your money goes? I sure as hell don't. It don't go nowhere I can see. Not to employin' anyone who looks like they actually enjoy their fuckin' job, for a start."

"Dad, this is rated one of the best nursing homes in Pennsylvania."

Patrese and Beradino exchanged glances. They both had the impression that this argument had been played out many, many times before.

"Then whoever rates it is a fuckin' moron. Come and stay for a day or two and see what the place is really like. They *abusin'* me, Freddie."

"They're not abusing you, Dad. I come every week, and I've never seen them be anything but professional."

"They *know* you come every week, dumb-ass. They put on a big fuckin' song and dance for you, and the moment you out the door, it's back to the same old shit. They shout at me, they cuss, they ridicule me—when they not ignorin' me, that is. I tell 'em I can't think for the pain, they tell me it's arthritis. I know what arthritis is, damn it. I've had arthritis twenty years, and this ain't it. Assisted livin'? Assisted dyin', more like. They even bitch at me when I try and have a cigarette, like it's some damn crime or somethin'. I have to wheel this damn contraption outside just to light up. No smokin' in the building. It's like the fuckin' Nazis. Come on, Freddie. Take me outta here and lemme come stay with you."

"You're too old for that, Dad. You're too old to be left on your own, and I'm never there, I'm always at work."

"Then work less."

"I can't work less. I made the commitment, Dad. I don't want to sit on the couch scratching my ass and watch things fall apart bit by bit. I try to fulfill that commitment, every day."

"Yeah, commitment to the law, not to anyone who loves you. You wanna use the law, start by suin' everyone in this damn place, from that fool deVries downward. You too busy givin' your time to folks you don't know. You don't give your time to me, or to your women, your kids. Shit, Freddie, between your law and the fact you can't keep your pecker in your pants, 's no wonder you never kept a relationship."

"Choices I made, Dad. Anyway, those folks I give my time to deserve justice."

"Not many of them."

"All of them."

"Some of them, at best. Like that Mara broad. Damn disgrace, what happened to her. Best thing you ever did, getting her off of all that. I don't mind you givin' time to her. You brought more broads like her here, I'd be a happier man."

"You brought Mara here?" Beradino asked in surprise.

"Damn right he did," said the old man before his son could reply. "You couldn't move for slippin' over the droolin' tongues of the old buzzards in here. She sure brightened the place up. Talked some sense, too. You know what she said?"

Hellmore rolled his eyes. "Dad, you bring this up every time I come here."

"'Cause it's *true.* She said even though your parents get like children, they still your parents, they always been your parents, they always gonna be your parents, and forgettin' this is dishonorin' them, takin' their dignity away. Yeah, your relationship with 'em is different from when you was a kid, but it's still a relationship God has made for you." He smiled. "She a fine lady. What she up to now?"

52

SUNDAY, NOVEMBER 14

Beradino, home alone, paced the living room in endless loops.

Seeing Mara Slinger again had shaken him. *Physically* shaken him, as though he had the jitters or something. Beradino believed in evil, as a malevolent force in itself rather than simply the absence of good; and he believed evil was in every molecule of Mara, body and soul. It oozed from her in sludgy trails.

How not everyone could see that, he had no idea.

It was the Sabbath, the day God had set aside for rest and reflection. Jesslyn was on shift, out of reach, but Beradino very badly wanted to talk with her.

He hadn't really slept the last couple of nights, his mind churning in livid eddies: Mara, Mara, Mara. He should have mentioned it earlier, but Jesslyn had seemed preoccupied, as she often did these days, so he'd kept quiet.

He couldn't keep quiet any longer.

He needed to let it out, work it through. Talking to himself wouldn't do it. He needed someone who understood, and that was Jesslyn. Only Jesslyn could make sense of Mara. She'd seen her at close quarters, year after year. She knew her better than anyone. Jesslyn had no illusions about what they were dealing with.

It was through Mara that Beradino and Jesslyn had met, in fact—an irony that never failed to make Beradino wince, that the best thing in his life could have come from the worst.

He'd taken a special interest in Mara's incarceration, wanting to be sure she was getting no special privileges; that every day and in every way, she'd be reminded of what abominations she'd perpetrated.

In the course of this, he'd met Jesslyn, who ran the roost at Muncy and took, if possible, an even dimmer view of what Mara had done than Beradino did.

They'd started exchanging first e-mails, then phone calls, always about Mara, their common purpose. But soon the conversations had begun to last longer and roam more widely, taking in their respective lives, politics, hopes, fears, and, most of all, faiths.

Beradino's Christian beliefs were the bedrock of his life, but sometimes he felt them as something more passive than active: deep strata, always there but rarely called upon.

In contrast, Jesslyn held her Old Testament high, like an army's standard. Born and brought up a Southern Baptist, her father a preacher in Yazoo City in Mississippi, she wanted eyes for eyes, teeth for teeth, fire and brimstone, and woe betide those who didn't repent or acknowledge their misdeeds.

There was another reason why Jesslyn felt what Mara had done so deeply: because she, Jesslyn, had never been able to have children.

For someone who believed so deeply in God, and that children were God's blessings, this had been a terrible blow. Jesslyn had accepted her own barrenness as God's will, imposed for she knew not what purpose; but what she had never been able to accept, not while the world turned, was someone so blessed as Mara turning that fortune back on itself by doing what she'd done to those poor innocents.

Jesslyn had wanted nothing more than for Mara to go to the chair, all appeals over, all pretty human maneuvering and legal technicalities exhausted, an evil woman finally alone in front of whatever God she professed to follow.

She'd wanted to be there, too. She'd have hit the switch herself, if they'd have let her.

But they would never put Mara to death; she knew that too well.

Talking about all this, and much else besides, Jesslyn and Beradino had become friends; a friendship that had soon, perhaps inevitably, blossomed into more. They'd kept their separate apartments for a while, but Pittsburgh and Muncy were four hours apart, too far for regular visits when they both worked odd hours; so, when they'd been sure this was going to last, they'd selected Punxsutawney as more or less halfway between the two places, and moved in together there.

They'd both been around the block: one failed marriage each, followed by a succession of go-nowhere relationships gone nowhere.

Was this a big, passionate love?

Perhaps not, but then they'd found each other at a time when they both expected less out of life than they'd done in their younger days.

Working homicide and corrections, you saw a lot of the worst that human nature had to offer. It knocked much of the idealism out of you, but it also made you realize you were on the side of the angels, no matter what your limitations were. And it made you see how much worse things could be, and how much worse off than you people could be, so you settled for the hand you'd been dealt.

Beradino dialed Jesslyn's cell again, more in hope than expectation.

He was put straight through to voicemail, again. That wasn't surprising. She turned her phone off when she was on shift, and she certainly didn't carry it with her on her rounds. Inmates would have killed for it.

But Beradino wanted to talk to her *now.* He couldn't wait till she came home.

Well, he probably could, but he wanted to be doing something. Sitting around the house was going to drive him insane.

Better to get in the car and go to Muncy. He could meet her when she came off shift, surprise her, take her somewhere nice for dinner.

The traffic was light, and he made good time on the interstate. But near the DuBois exit, he felt a slight quivering behind his cheekbones, and knew instantly what it was: the strain caused by stifling yawn after yawn, testament to his broken sleep.

Best not to keep driving like that. Beradino had seen enough RTAs to know the slogan was true: tiredness really did kill.

Cup of coffee, stretch legs, deep breaths, and he'd be good to go again.

He turned off at DuBois and pulled into the service stop.

There was a burger bar here; he'd get some coffee.

It would probably taste like dirt, but so long as it had caffeine, he didn't really care. Besides, it couldn't be any worse than the department coffee. Nothing could be worse than that; nothing this side of a slurry pit, at any rate.

The burger bar was almost empty. He walked straight up to the counter.

There was only one server there. She had her back to him, arranging paper-wrapped burgers in their various racks. Hair up beneath a ridiculous cap. The things they made these people wear, he thought. As if the salary wasn't demeaning enough.

"Excuse me," he said.

She turned around, corporate smile plastered bright on her face.

53

MONDAY, NOVEMBER 15

Frenzy in the incident room: a Chinese parliament of men barking down phones, passing on leads, checking arrangements for press conferences, or shouting purely to relieve the frustration that still, *still*, they had no concrete suspects, let alone an arrest.

Sound and fury, and nothing.

The only person in any way calm was Beradino, and even that was surface only.

He was far, far away, endlessly replaying in his head everything that had happened yesterday when he'd come across Jesslyn in the burger bar off of I-80.

His surprise. Her surprise. Her embarrassment. His bewilderment. The manager's anger when she couldn't bring herself to serve the next guy in line. Beradino's anger at the manager being a jerk, and at Jesslyn dressed up like a fool, flipping burgers, what the heck . . . ?

She'd quit on the spot, of course. He'd have torn the place apart if she hadn't, and the Lord knew Beradino wasn't a violent man.

Back home, she'd told him what had happened.

Mara had made complaints about her. Muncy, fearing bad publicity, had caved in.

Then we sue the prison, Beradino had said.

No, no, Jesslyn had replied. Mara had a case, loath as Jesslyn was to admit it. Jesslyn had been overzealous;

she had harassed Mara. The Lord knew Mara deserved it, but the Lord didn't make prison laws, more was the pity. Any court was going to side with Mara, particularly after what she'd been through.

Why hadn't she told him any of this before?

Pride, she'd said; pride, shame, guilt. Regular human failings. She'd wanted to tell him, but every day that had gone past—that she'd let go past—had made it harder and harder. She should have told him, she knew; and he'd never realize how sorry she was that she hadn't. But she was telling him now, even if only because she had no choice.

Beradino had forgiven her; that was the Christian thing to do. You love someone, you forgive them their sins. Then he'd told her to be strong. They, perhaps alone, knew what Mara had done; they weren't blinded by her beauty, or in love with her like most everyone else seemed to be.

To give Jesslyn strength, he'd made them recite Psalm 23 together:

> The LORD is my Shepherd; I shall not want. He maketh me to lie down in green pastures; he leadeth me beside the still waters. He restoreth my soul: he leadeth me in the paths of righteousness for his name's sake. Yea, though I walk through the valley of the shadow of death, I will fear no evil: for thou art with me; thy rod and thy staff they comfort me. Thou preparest a table before me in the presence of mine enemies: thou anointest my head with oil; my cup runneth over. Surely goodness and mercy shall

> follow me all the days of my life: and I will dwell in the house of the LORD for ever.

Now, here in the incident room, Beradino had told the other cops he was thinking, searching for some bright spark of an idea that would help them find the killer. They left him alone after that, but they wouldn't do so indefinitely.

He and Patrese had once more tossed around the question of Hellmore as a suspect. They'd found a connection between Hellmore and Kohler: both on the board of the 50/50, the Christian institution for gang members in Homewood that had taken in Trent Davenport following Shaniqua's arrest. Hellmore was quite the philanthropist, and having the bishop on board didn't hurt.

Technically, Hellmore could have committed all three murders.

He'd been alone in his apartment in the Pennsylvanian when Redwine had been killed in the same building.

He'd been at a dinner in town the night Kohler had been torched in the cathedral, but he'd left half an hour or so before Kohler's death; time enough to have gone from one place to the other.

Time enough, too, for Yuricich's murder. Yes, Patrese and Beradino had seen Hellmore in the courthouse the morning Yuricich was killed, but the time frame allowed Hellmore plenty of time to have gone to Yuricich's house, burned him, traveled to court, and waited there for a man only he knew to be already dead.

So, opportunities, yes, and means too; but where were the motives?

As far as Patrese and Beradino could see, there weren't any. They knew of no disputes, professional or personal, that Hellmore had had with either Redwine or Kohler; and though Hellmore had been suing Yuricich, trying to make legal history, he surely would have wanted to keep Yuricich alive to see the case through.

They could arrest Hellmore, of course, in order to question him more thoroughly, but only a fool would take Hellmore on without being 200 percent sure of his ground. If they didn't have probable cause, or if they made just one slipup, Hellmore would be all over them; and right now they didn't have probable cause, not anywhere near. Taking legal chances with the average citizen was one thing. Taking them with Pittsburgh's highest-profile lawyer was quite another.

So they had agreed, first between themselves and then with Chance: keep Hellmore in mind for now, but no more than that.

Patrese's phone rang. He pressed his hand close over his free ear just so he could hear himself speak.

"Patrese."

"Detective Patrese, it's Lionel Wheelwright here." *Great name,* Patrese thought. "I'm professor of geology at Pitt."

"Hi. Thanks for calling."

"No problem. The stones you sent are pink granite."

"Okay. What does that mean?"

"It means they're pink granite."

Patrese laughed. "No, I mean, is there anything special about pink granite?"

"Nothing at all. It's very common worldwide."

"Do you know where they might have come from? What part of the world?"

"Not without further analysis. I can't even tell you at the moment whether they're natural."

"Natural?"

"As opposed to already being cut and treated. Pink granite's used for a whole bunch of purposes. Construction, lot of construction. Like most granites, it makes good dimension stones. You'll find it in staircases, floors, walls, kitchen countertops, that kind of thing. Sculptures and monuments, too, more and more. It's more resistant to acid rain than marble."

"Could you find out where the stones came from? With more tests?"

"Sure, but we'd have to bill you. Those tests can be expensive."

"No problem. Mark the invoice for me and send it here. Thanks."

"Thank *you.* Glad to be of help."

Patrese put the phone down, and immediately it rang again.

Thinking the connection with Wheelwright hadn't been closed properly, he picked up and said, "Professor?"

There was a soft chuckle on the other end; a female chuckle, slightly breathy.

"Not exactly. Probably not ever."

"Who's this?" he asked, though he knew exactly who it was.

"Detective Patrese, this is Mara Slinger."

54

"She did *what*?" Beradino spluttered.

"She asked me over to dinner."

"And you're going to go?"

"Why not?"

"*Why not?* Since when did you become a moron?" Beradino wiped the back of his hand across his forehead. "Because she's a *suspect*, Franco."

"Last time I looked, talking to suspects was our job."

"Talking to them, as in interviewing them, sure. Locking them up and telling them of their right to remain silent, ditto. Having an intimate tête-à-tête with them, no."

"It's not an intimate tête-à-tête."

"What is it, then?"

"It's dinner."

"Just the two of you?"

"I guess."

"Then it's a tête-à-tête. Look, Franco, she's famous, pretty, you're flattered—"

"Don't patronize me, Mark."

"—but she's trouble. Trust me on this. She manipulates everyone around her."

"Come on, Mark. You're not exactly unbiased, are you?"

"No, I'm not. But I'm also right. I don't know what her game is, but there *is* a game, you can bet on that, and she's playing you like a Stradivarius. I know what she's really like. She knows I know. Maybe she wants to get you on her side, drive a wedge between us."

"It's just dinner. Nothing else."

"You're determined to go?"

"Yes. I might get some information out of her. Catch her off guard."

"I doubt it." Beradino sighed. "Well, if you're determined, then okay. But you be sure it's just dinner. You get involved with her—"

"I'm not going to get involved with her."

"—you so much as peck her on the cheek, I'll request a new partner. I'm a Christian man, Franco. I have morals, I have faith. She has neither."

"She's a devout Jew. She asked us to leave before Shabbat the other day."

"She believes in one thing: herself. Nothing else. Be careful, Franco. Here's something to think about. Why on earth does she want to see *you*? You killed her sister. Someone killed my sister, I wouldn't be inviting them over, that's for sure."

"Well, that's part of it, I think."

"What?"

"She said she wanted to talk about that. And so do I. I want to talk about it."

55

TUESDAY, NOVEMBER 16

Something was happening out there, Patrese thought as he drove rain-slicked streets.

It had started with a single Internet tribute site, its tone one of smug, knowing semi-irony. Then it had spread exponentially, the number of Google hits jumping by the hour, replete with semiliterate bulletin boards scrawled in moronic sub-English.

Next, the first T-shirts had appeared, luridly sloganed with hearts and leaping flames, and there'd been a couple of jokey mentions on radio shows, little quips about striking a blow for the little guy, and suddenly it was official.

The Human Torch had become a cult figure.

Patrese took a deep breath and tried to tamp down the churning in his stomach. He was often nervous before going on a date, especially a first one, even if that wasn't the kind of thing you admitted when bantering with the guys.

But this was hardly a normal first date. It wasn't a date at all, come to think of it.

For a start, there was the issue of Mara's sister, which he'd spent so long suppressing and that was now rushing to the surface fast enough to give him the bends.

Then there was the very fact of who Mara was. It wasn't every day you got asked to dinner by an Oscar winner who'd been first convicted and then acquitted of triple murder. Maybe Jack Nicholson would have taken it in his stride. Not Franco Patrese.

He parked outside Mara's apartment building and got out of his car. It was a third-generation Pontiac Trans Am GTA, '87 model; deep burgundy paint, gold flat-mesh diamond-spoke wheels, 5.7 V8, north of 150,000 miles on the clock, electronic gauge cluster. It spent as much time in the garage as out of it and cost him a small fortune, but he loved it, and had vowed to drive it literally into the ground.

He rang the bell, and Mara buzzed him up.

She was waiting for him in the doorway to her apartment. A touch of makeup, not too much; just enough to put color in her face. Simple skirt, simple blouse. Hardly the supervixen of Beradino's nightmares.

A formal handshake, awkward on both sides. He'd brought her a bottle of wine, Chilean red, determinedly neutral; nothing vintage, no cheapo paint-stripper either.

"Here," she said. "Let me take your coat."

"Something smells good," he said, as she hung his coat on a hook by the door.

"Seafood gumbo. You like?"

"Very much."

"November in Pittsburgh, it's the nearest we're going to get to New Orleans."

Mara had a bottle of white already open, chilled from the fridge. She poured two glasses, and clinked hers to his.

"Thanks for coming over, Detective Patrese. I really appreciate this."

"You can call me Franco, you know."

"Franco," she said, as though trying it on for size. "Nice name."

She paused. Patrese felt suddenly vertiginous, the way he always did when about to break up with someone he liked, knowing they'd have to talk it out, and that he'd hate every second of it but find a curious sense of relief when it was all over.

No small talk. No pleasantries. Straight in. Let's get on with it.

"I don't blame you," she said.

He studied her carefully.

"Really?"

"Really. Oh, I *did*, of course. I thought you were just a trigger-happy cop full of adrenaline and testosterone, and that you got your kicks shooting anyone you considered scum. And of course, what I'd been through before with, er, with your *partner*"—it seemed as though she couldn't bring herself to say Beradino's name—"made me hate the cops even more."

"I can see that."

"Then I thought about it a bit. I remembered things I'd seen in Muncy, the way fights blow up"—she snapped her fingers—"bang! out of nothing. Well, not quite nothing, obviously; there's an atmosphere, some tension on the block, but there's always that, there's always something bubbling, you just live with it, but once in a while it explodes, no warning. Not like the movies, where there's a bit of pushing and shoving beforehand. One minute, everything's normal; the next instant it's full-on, women kicking and punching and scratching until the guards come and pull them apart.

"And I wondered if it had been like that for you."

Patrese rotated his wineglass in his fingers, not daring to speak.

"I tried to imagine what it must be like, pumped up so hard you think you're going to burst, and it's like those prison fights, there's only two kinds of people, aren't there? Those who want to hurt you, those who want to keep you safe. So you're there and you come across Sam, strung out of her head—*again*—and you think she might be a danger, 'cause everyone in that house is a danger, right?

"*I* know she wasn't. You know she wasn't, *now*. But not then. And I thought, can I really blame you for that? Thing is, I saw in those fights that these are split-second decisions. I had a sheltered life, I guess, till then. But almost all those girls live their lives like that, minute to minute, never thinking ahead. You do something that takes half a moment, but the consequences live with you for a whole lot longer.

"And then I started wondering what it must be like for you, having that in your head, every day. A split second, and then consequences, running on and on. You seem like a decent man, so I'm presuming it must have affected you."

Patrese nodded, clenching his teeth against the lump in his throat. *If only you knew. If only you knew that I came to Mercy to say sorry, that I see her face sometimes at night. That I shouldn't have been there, whatever the inquiry said. That life doesn't run backward. It's not that you live with the consequences; they live with you, squatting on your shoulder, following you to the bathroom, there, there, all the time, behind your eyelids, in-*

side you, and you can never get away from them, because how can you get away from yourself?

"And if that's so, I want you to know two things. First, like I said, I don't blame you. I did, but I don't anymore. I *can't* anymore. And second—and, and this is even harder for me to say—if it hadn't been you, it would've been someone else."

"Huh?"

"Sam was lost to me long before you shot her."

"That don't make it better."

"It's not supposed to. But it's true, it is what it is. I'm not going to go into her life story—you probably know a lot of it already, it all came out after her death—but basically she had it all. We had a great childhood, loving parents, all that. She had talent, looks. Much more than me. No, no, that's not false modesty on my part; she really did. She was amazing. And she couldn't cope with it, with any of it.

"I've never taken drugs in my life, not one, not even aspirin. They tried to give me antidepressants and all sorts of things after my babies died, and I wouldn't take them. But Sam, she'd do anything going. Drugs I hadn't even heard of, all mixed together. She was in the ghetto when you found her. Nice middle-class Jewish girl. She shouldn't have been there in a million years. You know how desperate she must have been, to end up in a place like that.

"And that's what she was—desperate. She didn't care anymore, Franco. She hadn't cared for a long time, to be honest. She was never going to get better. So whether it had been you, or an OD, or a random bullet in cross fire, or a drunk driver in the wrong place at the wrong time . . . she wasn't going to grow old and read Dr. Seuss to her grandkids, put it that way. And that kills me to say, because I'd give anything for it to be different, but it's true, and it's only right you should know that."

"Can I ask you a question?" Patrese said.

"Sure."

"Why are you doing this?"

"How do you mean?"

"If I were you and you me, I wouldn't be trying to help you, er, *alleviate* your guilt. Seems a weird thing to do. Noble, sure, but weird."

"Sad, isn't it, when noble becomes weird?"

"I didn't mean it that way."

"I know you didn't. And it's a good question. One I've asked myself, too. I guess . . . I guess I've just had enough bad luck and trouble in my life, and now I'm trying to look on the bright side of things, be positive. That, or just go nuts, you know? After everything that's happened to me, I thought, either I can live in the past, chewing on all the bitter stuff, all the injustices and unfairness, or I can leave that behind and look forward. Hatred imprisons you, you know. I've spent enough time imprisoned. Forgiveness sets you free. Sounds like a Hallmark card, but it's true."

Patrese was silent for a long time, trying to find the words that would take him through the door she'd opened.

When the words did finally begin to come, he felt like he was having to pick them out of a minefield, one by one. They came to him reluctantly, haltingly.

Patrese told Mara he felt his life was divided into two parts, before and after; and the moment in the middle was Samantha herself.

She was the first person he'd killed. He could never go back from that.

There *was* a line, but once you stepped over it, the line disappeared. You took a life, and instantly you were apart from the huge majority of the human race who'd never done—who could never do—such a thing.

You weren't like normal people anymore. You were different. You were tainted.

Most of all, you were empty.

He'd never felt such a—such an *absence*, as after killing Samantha.

Beradino had rationalized it for him, of course. Patrese had done what he had to do, no more and no less. It was just one of those things. A lot of guys had been through similar experiences. You just had to pick yourself up and get on with it.

So that's what Patrese did. It was that or go under. But it didn't mean he forgot about it.

Cops like to joke about things, even—especially—things that are beyond the pale. They do so with sick humor, gallows humor, the kinds of remarks that shock normal folks. They mean nothing by it; it's just their way of dealing with the unthinkable. Firefighters and ambulance crews do the same thing.

Patrese could joke with the best of them; but never about Samantha.

He knew the Slingers were Jewish, and he often thought of what the Talmud said: that whoever destroys a soul, it is considered as if he destroyed an entire world. He repeated it to Mara.

"Then think of the very next line," Mara said instantly. "'Whoever saves a life, it's considered as if he saved an entire world.' You catch the person doing these things, these burnings, and you'll save lives, you'll make amends. It won't bring Sam back, but it'll mean someone else doesn't lose a loved one."

Just what Bianca had said, Patrese thought.

He excused himself and went to the john, more to compose himself than through any pressing call of nature. When he returned, Mara was ladling out the gumbo. He took a mouthful, making appreciative—and genuine—noises.

"You're surprised?" she asked, a faint smile wafting around her mouth.

"Should I be?"

"Maybe not. I just thought you might think I think myself too grand to cook."

"That's a lot of thinks there."

She laughed. "Sam always told me I think too much. I get a lot of time to do it nowadays. Not to mention Muncy. A whole lot of time to think in there."

"You come to any conclusions?"

"Lots. Sometimes I reckon none. You don't want to hear about that, though."

"Why not?"

"Well, men never do. You go to a man with a problem, he wants to solve it. Go to a woman, and she listens."

"You want me to listen?"

"It's a long story."

"I got all night."

She arched her eyebrows at him, amused. *All night?*

"Okay." She handed him the bottle of white. "You're

going to need a full glass. Maybe more than one. Where do you want me to start?"

"Begin at the beginning."

"Why not? Why not indeed? But where's the beginning?"

She paused a moment, collecting herself, as if she were about to go onstage.

"The beginning's on Broadway," she said suddenly. "That's where it is."

56

On Broadway I played Medea: daughter of King Aeëtes; niece of the sorceress Circe; granddaughter of the sun god Helios; and wife of Jason, leader of the Argonauts, finder of the Golden Fleece.

Medea, whose husband left her for the king of Corinth's daughter.

Medea, who in revenge murdered the children she'd borne Jason.

In vain, my children, have I brought you up,
Borne all the cares and pangs of motherhood,
And the sharp pains of childbirth undergone.

Of all the roles I've ever played, both stage and screen, it was in every way the most: the most harrowing, the most difficult, the most corrosive, the most exhausting, the most exhilarating, the most horrific, the most fantastic.

Screeching and vengeful, convinced she's given up everything for a man who then betrays her, Medea has violence in that part of the human soul that should be buried forever. She stalks the stage, ranting and raving through the heartbreak and horror of a private hell she's destined never to escape. She's compassionate and intelligent, hateful and insane.

You will nevermore your mother see,
Nor live as ye have done beneath her eye.

Euripides wrote *Medea* almost 2,500 years ago. In all that time, filicide has stood as society's most aberrant act. For a woman to kill her child is the ultimate taboo.

I didn't break that taboo. Whatever they say, I didn't break that taboo. I was never Medea, no matter how hard they tried to prove that I was. I played Medea before I became a mother. I could never, ever have played her afterward.

Far worse to have been a mother and lost your babies than never to have been a mother at all. As a mother, I didn't live life for myself, and now my babies are gone, I don't want to again. I feel aimless and empty, a total, terrifying emptiness in which the absence of anything, *everything*, becomes so oppressive that it generates a force all its own, something atavistic and primal, stripping away thousands of years of evolution and progress and civilization in searing recognition of the fact that we're all animals, we're all part of the natural order, and there's something so terribly, terribly wrong when that order gets ripped apart.

Beradino comes around a couple of days after Isaac, our third, has died. He seems a nice man, offering his condolences and saying how dreadful the whole thing is. Then he asks if I understand why the police need to make an investigation. Of course, I say. Not only do I understand, but I welcome it; maybe it'll give me the answers I crave, and tell me why my babies keep dying. Is it something genetic? Or did the doctors miss something? I've got nothing to hide, I tell Beradino. I know the police will be on my side; that's their job, isn't it, to protect and serve?

"I just can't believe this could happen three times," I tell Beradino.

"Neither do I," he replies.

I should have known then; but I was still blind to the way everything looked. He comes back the next day. He says they've found postmortem abnormalities in Isaac's autopsy that tally with similar abnormalities in Noah and Esther. He's discovered the cause of the children's deaths.

"Well?" I ask. "What did they die of?"

He looks momentarily pained; I think it must be some ghastly disease whose details he wants to spare me. I don't yet realize that what pains him is *me*, or rather what he thinks I am.

"Mara Slinger," he says, "I'm arresting you on suspicion of the murders of Noah, Esther, and Isaac Negley."

57

The strange thing is, even down at the station house, I'm still quite calm. I know I didn't kill the children, therefore there's no way I can be convicted of their murder, therefore this is all a huge mistake, or some crossed wires, or the police department covering itself. I'm bewildered rather than frightened; I've got nothing to hide, so if I cooperate, this whole thing will sort itself out. Nothing to hide means nothing to fear.

I've always believed in authority and its fairness. Sure, mistakes are made, but in the greater scheme of things, good always wins out. I have no history of abuse or mental illness, nothing the police can use to make me look suspicious. I've never been in trouble with the law in my life, not even drunken high jinks at college. I was always a goody two-shoes. Sometimes, when I got invited to parties I thought would be too wild, I said I couldn't go 'cause my mom had said no, even if I hadn't actually asked her.

Beradino brings in three cardboard boxes: one marked Noah, one Esther, and one Isaac. Inside is every trace of our babies' existence: clothes, toys, books, changing mats, cards of congratulations and condolences, certificates of birth and death, imprints of their feet, locks of their hair. It's everything that ever signified they were alive. Before, they were memories; now they're evidence.

Hellmore comes to see me.

"The way I see it," he says, "we've got one chance of beating this."

"What's that?"

"I want you to plead insanity."

Truth is, I've wondered many times since all this began whether I'm going mad. I know there've been cases where people do the most terrible things and somehow completely and genuinely forget every last thing about them, like they're in some trance or fugue state. Of course, I don't think I'm one of those, but then if I was I guess I wouldn't know.

"Women make lousy criminals, by and large," Hellmore continues. "In the US, there's only two types of crime women commit as often as men: shoplifting and infanticide. We still view children as the mother's property, and destroying your own property is the act of a crazy person. So if we plead insanity and the jury accepts that, you'll be sent to a mental health institution, not a jail. In such an institution, your progress will be monitored, and at some point in the future a judge can declare you sane and have you released. And in a mental health institution, you'll get help."

"I don't need help."

"You'll need help if you go to prison, that's for sure."

"I'm not going to prison, I'm not going to a mental ward. I didn't do it."

"The jury might not agree."

"They will if we tell them the truth."

"Trials aren't a search for truth." He holds up his hand against my gasp of disbelief. "I know, I know, they should be, but they're not. Trust me. A trial's a game with complex rules, and whoever plays those rules better wins. It's like football; you have an offense, a defense, and the referees. Or think of it as a stage play, an act. It's all about presentation and prejudice. It's a crapshoot. My job's to get you off, end of story. Anything I can do to that end, I will."

"But if I plead insanity," I say, "won't that be an admission of guilt?"

"An admission of guilt is pleading guilty. This is not guilty, by reason of insanity."

"But I'd still be saying I did it."

"Yes, that you did it, but you weren't responsible for your actions."

"But I didn't do it."

"Like I said, whether you did it or not is irrelevant."

"I'm not admitting something I didn't do."

"Then you're greatly reducing your chances of being acquitted."

But I stand firm. I plead not guilty.

Howard starts to distance himself from me. He does it slowly and gradually, so gradually that he may not even realize he's doing it. When I question him, he denies it. But I know. Maybe he's beginning to wonder whether I actually did it after all; maybe he's just preparing himself in case I'm found guilty. He doesn't ask me straight out whether I killed them, but he doesn't have to. Even if I'm acquitted, he's always going to wonder, deep down, I'm sure of it.

The trial approaches. I find comfort in the scriptures. I receive hundreds of letters pointing me to various verses that the writers think will give me strength. I know there are many people out there praying for me. I have faith; all this is being sent to test me. I don't know why. Maybe I'm not supposed to know.

Every night, before I go to bed, I read the same passage:

> *Even though I walk through the valley of the shadow of death, I will fear no evil: for thou art with me; thy rod and thy staff they comfort me.*

Finally, the trial arrives. I know what the cameramen want: tears, vulnerability, blood. They crowd in on us as we walk into the courthouse, shutters whirring and snapping, reporters yelling moronic questions as the cops elbow a path for Hellmore and me. The cameramen want Hollywood, like I've given often before. I'm not giving it to them today, I won't.

I've learned to numb myself over and over against everything happening to me. I weep, but only behind closed doors. I'm an actress. I can cry fake tears on demand, so I can stanch real tears too. I'll cry for you if you've paid ten bucks to sit in a cinema for two hours; I won't when all you have to do is switch on your TV. Court TV is showing every second of open proceedings. Later, they'll boast that ratings were even higher than for O.J.'s trial, like I should be flattered or something.

I take the oath, swearing on the Old Testament, the Hebrew Bible: the truth, the whole truth, and nothing but the truth.

The prosecutor, Amberin Zerhouni, sets off down looping, swooping lines of questions, designed to catch me out, turning truths into half-truths and doubts into lies, throwing up a myriad of little aspersions, none of them especially convincing in themselves, but weave them all together and they begin to look quite persuasive.

She suggests that having children was damaging my Hollywood career; that I resented the drudgery of looking after newborns; that I didn't get a nanny because having someone else around would have made it difficult if not impossible for me to have killed my children; that I didn't try CPR on any of my children even though I knew how; that I suffered from postnatal depression but refused to accept it or seek treatment; that perhaps that depression mutated into postpartum psychosis, something far scarier, a descent into distorted reality made even more dangerous by the fact the sufferer's often unaware that she's unwell.

Did I ever hear God speak to me? Did God ever order me to do things I wouldn't normally do? Did God ever order me to harm my babies? Did I ever think the world's a bad place and I'd done wrong by bringing children into it? Did I think I was saving their souls by killing them? Did I think God took my children up?

A Muslim questioning a Jew in front of a Christian judge. One nation, under God.

Innuendo and slur from nothing, time and again. It's like a nightmare, where little bits come back in their own time, and never when you want them to. I get small details wrong and contradict myself, and I know these are actually signs of innocence; only the guilty get everything absolutely right, because they've practiced their deception again and again. But tell that to the jury.

Then there's Lockwood.

He starts talking about autopsies and dissection in the cold, impersonal language of medical investigation, and I just take myself away to happy times, little baby things, my darlings asleep on my chest, the wonderful trust and warmth they had for me, an unconditional love that I bounced back to them a hundred times over. They weren't court exhibits or physical shells; they were real, living, breathing people.

And I keep thinking: Lockwood, a man, is talking about mothers and babies like he knows the first thing about us. This is an arena for women. Men don't know, can't know, won't know a fraction of it.

"I'm not afraid to put myself in danger for my beliefs," Lockwood says. "Child abuse is an issue I feel strongly about, even if the public finds it uncomfortable, and they tend to shoot the messenger. People like me who write about it, speak about it, point it out—we're unpopular messengers. But it's a price I'm prepared to pay, over and again if need be. As Jesus said: 'There is no prophet without honor except in his own country.'"

The prosecutor asks Lockwood if he'll demonstrate how I killed my children. A doll is brought in, and Lockwood takes the jury step by step through what he thinks I did. I can't watch; not him, or them, or anyone. It's obscene, revolting—*wrong*, most of all; but when he's finished some jurors are in tears, and one is glaring hatefully at me. The jurors want the drama; they want me to be guilty. They've seen book deals, movie deals; they want to be among those who find Mara Slinger guilty, to be there at this car-crash moment in American culture.

I played Medea, once upon a time, in a different lifetime. I also played Elizabeth Proctor, falsely accused of witchcraft in *The Crucible*. Nothing has changed in three centuries. It's a witch-hunt, and I'm the witch.

Hellmore does his best, and his best is considerable. He describes the case as the most unfair one he's ever come across, one that flies against all known standards of decency and conscience. I've already lost what I prized most in life, my children—and now they want to punish me some more for it? Worse, they want to charge me with something for which they've got no evidence?

And why've they got no evidence? Because no crime's been committed, that's why. In most murder cases, no one disputes that murder occurred; the question's whether the accused did it, or someone else. But here, the facts aren't simply that I didn't commit murder, but that no one did. No one knows why Noah, Esther, and Isaac died. There has to be a reason; three children don't die for no reason. But that reason isn't murder.

Crib death is a mystery, he says. It's baffled the

greatest medical minds for two thousand years. And, not to cast aspersions on the prosecution witnesses, but to be a great doctor, you have to have humility as well as humanity. But the doctors called by the prosecution are arrogant enough to think they know everything; ask them any question you like, and the one answer you'll never hear is "I don't know."

Hellmore brings in experts who propose alternative theories: a vasovagal shutdown of the nervous system, where the baby vomits and the vagus nerve, stopping the child's breathing to prevent inhalation of the vomit, slows the heartbeat down to fatal levels; breakdowns of the immune system; or autosomal inheritance, where a condition is passed from generation to generation, sometimes manifesting itself when the genes are dominant, sometimes lying dormant when the genes are recessive. But that's all they are—theories.

And so to the closing statements. The prosecutor goes first, and she starts by asking the jury to be silent for three minutes so they can experience the amount of time each child endured me smothering it before dying.

Even the showman Hellmore has no comeback to this. He's reasonable, he's calm. With so much divided opinion about this case, he says, whatever you believe could be wrong, and that sounds very much like reasonable doubt to him.

I look at Howard. He's been here every day, but I know that's partly because it would look awful if he wasn't. He doesn't believe in me anymore. He doesn't look back at me. He thinks I'm guilty.

Yuricich could make an indication as to how he's thinking. He doesn't. He's mindful of the need to be fair, he says; unspoken is the implication of another celebrity trial, with everyone remembering the travesty of justice that was O.J. He reminds the jury not to be swayed by high emotions, but instead to use clinical assessment of the facts, even though none of them are clinically trained. He urges them not to flinch from returning a guilty verdict if they think that's the right one, even though they may reach that conclusion with heavy hearts. He sends them out, and says they may not return for days.

They're back in six hours; and I know instantly, just from their faces, that they've found me guilty.

Up till now, I've always thought the verdict would, in a funny way, make no difference, since no punishment could be worse than the all-consuming anguish of losing my babies. I've even wondered sometimes whether death would be a release, and that's something no Jew takes lightly; Judaism teaches that suicide is one of the most serious sins of all.

But now I know it *does* make a difference.

"Have you reached a verdict?" Yuricich asks the foreman.

"We have."

"And is that verdict the unanimous decision of you all?"

"It is."

"On the first charge, the murder of Noah Negley, how do you find the defendant: guilty or not guilty?"

"Guilty."

"On the second charge, the murder of Esther Negley, how do you find the defendant: guilty or not guilty?"

"Guilty."

"On the third charge, the murder of Isaac Negley, how do you find the defendant: guilty or not guilty?"

"Guilty."

58

Says Job:

God has given me over to the impious; into the clutches of the wicked he has cast me. I was in peace, but he dislodged me; he seized me by the neck and cast me to pieces. He has set me up for a target; his arrows strike me from all directions. He pierces my sides without mercy; he pours out my gall upon the ground. He pierces me with thrust upon thrust; he attacks me like a warrior. I have fastened sackcloth over my skin, and have laid my brow in the dust. My face is inflamed with weeping and there is darkness over my eyes, although my hands are free from violence, and my prayer is sincere.

The woman who's waiting for me at the prison entrance wears a Kevlar armored vest to protect her from shanks, spikes, and knives. I expected her to be some big, butch dyke, all shaved head and tattoos, but she's nothing of the sort. She's pretty and petite, no bigger than me. She looks nice, friendly, reasonable; the kind of person who'll be firm but fair, someone who manages to remain conscientious in a place like this. I look at the name on her badge. JESSLYN GEDGE, it says.

She searches me, removing anything that she deems contraband and placing those items in a large envelope, which she says will be returned to me on my release. Is there something in her voice that suggests she doesn't expect that day to come for a very long time, or am I imagining it? Into the envelope go my watch, my wedding ring, pictures of my children, letters, and the Star of David I wear around my neck.

"Can I keep that?" I ask as she removes the Star. "It's for my faith."

She fingers the chain. "What's this made of?"

"Gold."

"Solid gold?"

"That's right."

She puts the Star of David in the envelope. "Chain lengths and medals must not exceed the sizes and dollar amount listed in department policy DC-ADM 815."

"It's for my faith," I repeat, knowing that I sound pathetic.

I'm taken to the RHU, the Restricted Housing Unit. The RHU has four wings, named Alpha through Delta. Alpha is for violent inmates, Bravo has those with mental problems and self-harmers, and Delta houses offenders under the age of twenty-one.

I'm in Charlie—the one where they put lifers.

When someone's in Charlie, you know they did it. You'd think that would make them more violent—that, and the fact they've got nothing to lose, no need to behave well and try to impress the parole board—but the opposite's true. If you're in Charlie, this is your home for life, so you might as well accept it. Rocking the boat just makes things harder.

The first few weeks seem to go on forever. Everything's new, scary, tiring; it's all grotesquely alien, everything planned and circumscribed. Hands through the door opening to be cuffed before we leave our cells; no going anywhere without keys turning in locks ahead of and behind us; plastic cutlery, plastic mugs, plastic food.

Other inmates try to make their cells like home: photographs, pictures, personal items. I refuse. I won't let myself settle in, because I know I'll be out one day, and when that day comes, I want to be able to pack up and go in thirty seconds flat. I learn fast that the only way to deal with things is to harden myself against them, grow a carapace and wrap it around myself.

The choice is simple: shut down, or go under. No anger, no tears. I try to pretend this is happening to someone else, as if the real me's in storage somewhere and a fake me is putting in the time here. I feel like a pencil drawing that's been half-erased, my lines all faint and blurry. It's as if there's a spirit of despair in the prison, an actual spirit, a ghost, moving from inmate to inmate. When it lands on you, when it's your turn, you have to endure it till it moves on again. I'm one of the lucky ones; it never stays around me too long. Others have it much worse; it's no wonder there are so many zombies here, stuffed full of the bug juice of antidepressants and mood regulators whose names sound through the pharmacy like roll call: Phenergan, Vistaril, Elavil, Sinequan, Mellaril, Thorazine, Stelazine, Triavil, Desyrel.

Some women just look blankly into space; some are monkey mouths, talking, talking, talking; some, the smackheads, smash up their cells, so out of it they don't care, they don't feel pain, even when they're dragged away with their arms behind their backs and their thumbs bent back double. Smack's a better bet than dope in here; smack clears the system in three days, dope stays in for a month. What's more likely to beat the urine test?

I'm not really sure what I thought my fellow inmates would be like, but I know now what they're not. They're not big-time gangsters, nor serial killers, nor Mafia kingpins, nor kidnappers, nor embezzlers. Most of them are here because they were accessories to crimes committed by men, or for things like prostitution, pickpocketing, shoplifting, robbery, drugs. Small-time stuff, mainly. Are they criminals, or victims? I'm not scared of them, at least most of them. If anything, I feel sorry for them.

Everyone talks about gangs in prisons, but there aren't many here. Maybe it's because we're all women; forming gangs is tough when everyone wants to be in charge. What violence there is in Muncy is just as often women turning on themselves as it is on others; there's a lot of self-harming.

And a lot of suicides, too. I save one woman, someone just brought into Charlie, who's tried to hang herself with shoelaces. She nearly makes it, too; her eyes are bulging, her tongue lolling between blue lips, the laces so tight around her neck that I can't get my fingers underneath to pry them off, and of course we're not allowed anything sharp. I call the guards, and they come just in time, panicking; they're in a whole lot of trouble every time someone offs herself. I see the woman a day or two later, when she's back from the infirmary. I've heard she was about thirty seconds away from the beginnings of irreversible brain damage, and she comes over to me to say thanks.

"You stupid fucking BITCH!" she yells. "What the fuck did you do that for? Now I'm on suicide watch, and I can't take a fucking step without being watched. Thanks for fucking NOTHING. Next time you poke your nose into my business, I'll fucking KILL you, you understand? KILL you!"

She doesn't kill me, of course. In fact, the next time I see her, she apologizes, and says she's just shocked that I tried to help her, because it's been a long time since anyone has done something decent for her. Her name is Madison Setterstrom, and she's a cop-killer, an unrepentant one at that; she must be about the only person in here who admits she's guilty. Pretty much everyone else claims to be innocent, so much so that it's almost a standing joke; people ask, "What are you in for?" but never "What did you do?" because everyone knows the two are different.

Not Madison. She's proud of what she did, and she can't stand the Pepsi Generation, the newer, younger prisoners who lack respect for the old-school ways. We become buddies. She's my only true friend in here, not least because she's the only one who couldn't give a fig about my celebrity or my story. Everyone else in here is either impressed by the fact that I'm a Hollywood actress or can't wait to tell me what an evil cow I am. Madison's neither. She just takes me as I am.

I never crack, never answer back; do that, and they know they got to you. I just take myself to another place, and say to myself over and over that they're not going to break me. Oh, they try. And every day you have to fight the battle again, because if you break once, you break forever.

One day, Hellmore arrives to see me. He's got good news and bad news, he says; which do I want first? I say the bad news; let's get it out of the way. The bad news is that Howard wants a divorce, and here are the papers. I feel sick. I'd stopped wondering whether this was coming, knowing it was simply a question of when—Howard hasn't been to see me once in all the time I've been here—but it doesn't make it any easier when I finally see it in black and white.

I take a few deep breaths, and ask for the good news. The good news, he says, is that he saw a doctor friend of his last night, and they were discussing this rare, newly discovered gene disorder known as long QT syndrome, which damages the pumping chambers of the heart, sometimes fatally. The thing about long QT is that it can miss a generation or two before striking again, and he remembered something I'd said to him when preparing our defense: that my grandmother had lost several of her children very young.

He wants to go see my grandmother and have her tested for this long QT thing, and perhaps other genetic disorders too. I tell him it's a nice idea, but my grandmother lives in Poland and doesn't speak any English. She lived for a while between the wars in Cleveland, which has a big Polish population—which was why she never had to learn much English, and she'll have forgotten even that meager amount so many decades on—but she and her family went back to Poland in 1938 and never managed to get out again, first because of the Nazis, then because of the Soviets.

So he travels to Poland. Only Hellmore would go that far. He goes to Poland, gets an interpreter from the American embassy in Warsaw, and tracks my grandmother down to the village where she's living now. A remote village in the middle of nowhere, and he turns up, probably the first black man many of them have ever seen. She tells him she had twelve children and lost five of them before they were eight weeks old. Three of those five were born while she was living in Cleveland. He asks her whether they ever found a cause of death for the children, and she replies simply: "This is something Jehovah takes care of. We leave it to Jehovah."

So he explains what's happened to me, and how

he believes in my innocence and wants to get me out, and says that if they can test her and find that she has this thing, or indeed anything else, then that might help me. They take her to Warsaw—she might be ninety-five, but she's tough as old boots, well able to handle such a journey—and they test her. And guess what? He was right. She *does* have this long QT thing.

Suddenly, the whole case is blown wide open. Hellmore returns to America, and comes to visit me pretty much every week, each time with another breakthrough. He says he's found that Lockwood suspected this might be the case, or that it was at the very least a possibility, and hadn't disclosed it to the defense as he was obliged to do. Not just that; Lockwood also withheld research he'd been conducting at the time of the trial, which showed plenty of evidence that attempts to resuscitate children could and did cause rib fractures.

The retinal hemorrhages that he said couldn't have been caused postmortem—and that he therefore held up as evidence of my guilt—turned out not only not to be hemorrhages, they weren't even retinal. They were actually on the choroid, a layer of tissue next to the retina. Lockwood also got the measurements of siderophages in the lungs wrong. Though they were high, they weren't nearly as high as he'd said they were, and were within the limits that could be caused by inhaling blood during resuscitation attempts.

All this, Hellmore says, is easily enough grounds

for an appeal. He has to take it to the state appeals court first, but if that fails, we can go federal. But we don't need to. The state court hears it, and the science is on our side this time. The judge says he can find no convincing evidence that my children's deaths were caused by injury, but he can find a lot of evidence that points to a genetic disorder.

He also slams the way the original trial was conducted. He accuses Lockwood of oversimplifying and withholding relevant data, and of covering up his mistakes; at least one of the autopsies, he says, was a textbook example of how *not* to do one. The state judge says Yuricich was biased and unprofessional; he also criticizes the prosecutor for not being on top of her witnesses, though he recognizes that, not being a medical professional herself, she had to take their findings at face value, and is therefore not as culpable as they are.

I'm going to be released. I can hardly believe it. Madison embraces me. She's originally from Norway, and in Norwegian, she says, the word for a miscarriage of justice is *justismord*—"justice murder." *Miscarriage* is an altogether more forgiving word; it suggests an accident, an act of God. The Norwegians have kept the term "murder" because they know that's exactly what a wrongful conviction is: something dreadfully, horribly destructive. Something deadly.

The day I walk free, what strikes me most of all is the sunlight, so bright and searing, so white, as if it comes from the heart of a thousand atom bombs. I stand outside the gates, next to Hellmore, thousands of people corralled behind hastily erected crash barriers. Half of them are for me, chanting: "Who do we love? Mara!" The other half keep up an endless rhythm: "Guilty! Guilty! Guilty!"

Hellmore takes the microphone, and the crowd slowly quiets down.

"The justice system is like Amtrak," he says. "It can be old and creaky, but it gets there in the end. Today is a victory for all those who believe in justice. I'm sorry it took so long, but better late than never."

He hands me the microphone. I speak in a faint, quavery voice. I'm never as good at speaking my own words as I am other people's.

"With all respect to my fantastic lawyer," I say, "today is not a victory. Not for me, not for anyone. There are no winners here. We have all lost. If I feel anything, it's relief, no more than that. Relief that the courts, and hopefully the people of America and elsewhere too, finally believe in my innocence. That's the only comfort I take. In every other respect, my nightmare goes on. It will never end. I will never get my babies back. I will never know the joys, heartaches, and totality of being a mother. I ask you all for nothing except one thing: that I may be allowed some privacy to grieve for my little ones in peace, and to try to make sense of what's happened to me."

59

Patrese was silent for a long time after Mara finished; so long, in fact, that eventually she prodded him and said, with a weak smile, "Say something."

His face showed his shock. He felt flayed, raw, like an anatomical drawing.

The smile he offered in return was no less faint than hers had been. "Like what? You've just pulled your soul inside out. Tell me one thing I could say that won't sound totally inadequate."

She reached across the table, careful not to knock over a wineglass or trail her sleeve in the gumbo, and entwined the fingers of her right hand with his.

"I'm sorry, Franco."

"You're not the one who should be sorry."

"Well, I am. I didn't mean to lay it on you like that, straight out of the blue. It's just . . . I haven't spoken about it all for such a long time, and so it just came gushing out. Thanks for listening. It means a lot. More than you can imagine."

She made no move to take her hand away. Nor did he.

Patrese remembered what Beradino had said to him about getting involved with Mara, and wondered what Beradino would say if he could see them now. You could probably have heard the explosion in Baltimore.

Patrese figured Beradino had got Mara all wrong.

"I should go," he said.

Mara nodded slowly. "I guess you should."

"Early start tomorrow."

"You don't have to justify it, you know."

"I know I don't. But still."

"Why?"

"Because . . . I've really enjoyed myself." He laughed. "Strange, given what we've talked about, but . . . I'd like to do it again sometime. With a few more jokes."

"Me too."

He took his hand from hers and stood up. She followed him into the hallway.

"Thanks again," he said, shrugging on his coat. "And the gumbo was awesome."

"Take care of yourself, Franco."

He kissed her on both cheeks; and the moment after that was too long, too close.

"Is there anyone else?" she said softly.

Patrese had seen Erin a couple of times after their first night together, and then fobbed her off with some excuse about being too busy for a serious relationship. She'd used language that wouldn't have disgraced a stevedore and called him a whole heap of unflattering names, all of which he'd felt he probably deserved. Since then, there'd been a couple more in and out of his bed, none of whom had lasted any longer. Franco Patrese, always running, always proving.

"No," he said.

"Then do you really have to go?"

He nodded. "No."

60

WEDNESDAY, NOVEMBER 17

It wasn't far off dawn when Patrese left, dazed and confused.

It had been years, Mara had said, since she'd been with a man; since before prison, before the trial, before her arrest, even before Isaac had been born. *Years.* Literally.

Which explained, Patrese guessed, why she'd been so tentative to start with, and why she'd then seemed suddenly unleashed: primal, wild, ravenous.

He could flatter himself and think it was his unique skill and charisma that had set her aflame, but he knew women well enough to know otherwise. If it hadn't been him, it would have been someone else.

What Mara had needed hadn't necessarily been him, Franco Patrese, but simply someone who'd pay her attention, give her a chance, make her feel . . . well, like a woman; but perhaps the more prosaic truth was that she'd simply needed to feel *alive* again.

Or was he just protecting himself from whatever consequences there might be?

Out on the sidewalk, he smiled through a yawn. After all, there were few men alive who didn't, at a basic level, relish the feeling of leaving a new lover's apartment at five in the morning. If Mara had been vulnerable, perhaps he'd needed it too, in his own way. And it wasn't like he'd gotten her drunk and taken advantage of her, was it?

He dug in his pocket for the Trans Am keys.

Suddenly, he was pitching forward and down.

It caught him by surprise, and he was tired, so he was almost on the ground before he realized he hadn't tripped.

He'd been *pushed.* Propelled hard from behind; attacked.

Patrese had played enough football to know how to fall properly, and done enough police training to know how to fight, all repeated so often it had become instinct.

He took the impact on hands and forearms, keeping them loose to absorb the shock; you broke bones when you tensed. The moment he touched concrete, he was rolling, fast onto his left side, because moving targets were harder to hit, and then immediately onto his back with his hands up to block a weapon or lash out. You couldn't fight unless you could see your opponent.

His attacker was a man, that was for sure; but that—and the fact he had body odor that wouldn't have been out of place on a goat—was just about the only thing Patrese could tell with certainty. The man had a baseball cap pulled low on his forehead and a heavy coat buttoned up to his neck.

Patrese kicked out, upward and hard. He heard a sharp crack as his foot connected with his attacker's left hand; and with a yelp the man was gone. By the time Patrese got to his feet, the man was halfway down the street, sprinting toward the main road.

Lunatic? Wannabe mugger who'd reckoned too late that Patrese wasn't a soft target? Patrese didn't know, and to be honest didn't much care. It was the city, it was the small hours, when only the freaks were out. Shit happened.

He patted his pockets. Keys, wallet, cell phone, all present and correct. No broken bones. Probably a couple of bruises.

He could report it, of course, but then he'd have to reveal that he was leaving Mara's apartment at a time when he shouldn't have been there, which would cause way more problems than it would solve.

No report. Forget about it.

He unlocked the Trans Am, got in, and turned the key in the ignition.

Nothing.

He sighed. This was happening more and more. The garage had fixed it a couple of times, but still the starter motor kept cutting out. What did he expect? The car wasn't exactly in the first flush of youth.

He got out of the car and pulled the steering wheel as far around to the left as it would go. Slowly, manually, Patrese turned the Trans Am around in the road, his right shoulder pressed against the windshield pillar, until he was facing back down the length of the street.

With a clear run, he got the car moving at something above a walking pace, leaped in, and turned the key again. The engine fired like it had never missed a beat in its life.

61

Patrese arrived at headquarters a few hours later. Beradino was already there.

They regarded each other levelly, Patrese as deadpan as he could manage. He'd practiced a couple of times in the bathroom mirror before leaving home, hoping the slight traces of red in his eyes didn't betray his lack of sleep.

"Enjoy yourself?" Beradino asked at length.

Serious? Wry? Joking? A bit of all three?

Patrese shrugged. "Interesting."

"You find out anything?"

"Nope. Nothing useful to the case, any rate, if that's what you mean."

"You gonna see her again?"

"It was *dinner*, Mark."

Answering the question by not answering it—a technique used, wittingly or not, by any number of crime suspects over the years. Even before the words were out, Patrese was cursing himself, sure that Beradino would follow up; but either Beradino didn't notice or didn't care, because he changed the subject immediately.

"Okay. We got some good news. Well, a little bit anyway. We managed to connect Kohler and Yuricich."

"How?"

"Well, they knew each other socially, for a start."

"That's hardly surprising. A bishop and a judge. High society and all that."

"I was just about to call you," he said.

"Really?"

"Yeah. About the guys we've got under surveillance."

"That's just what I was calling about."

"Er . . . we can't share the list with you, I'm afraid."

"*What?*"

"I tried, Franco, I really did. I took it as high as I could. I fought your case."

"Why did they say no?"

"Usual BS. Operational security, Chinese walls, compromise possibilities."

"*Jesus.*" Patrese jerked his head in frustration. Beradino rolled his eyes.

"I'm really sorry, Franco," Boone was saying. "If it was up to me . . ."

"I know. And I appreciate that. Listen, Caleb, tell me one thing."

"I can't promise, but try me."

"Is Mustafa Bayoumi on your list?"

"Hold on."

Down the line came the sound of a door closing; Boone ensuring he wasn't being overheard. The walls of Bureau offices had larger ears than most, Patrese thought.

"Okay," Boone continued. "No. Mustafa Bayoumi's not on our list."

"A Muslim chemistry student, and he's not on your radar?"

"He *was*, for a coupla years. But he did nothing suspicious all that time, so we took him off. We haven't got infinite resources, Franco. You know how many people we have under surveillance?"

"How many?"

"Across the entire jurisdiction of this office—western Pennsylvania, West Virginia—about seven hundred."

"Seven hundred?" That was covering just a state and a half of the fifty in the union, not to mention DC. Even allowing for geographical and demographic variations, a conservative extrapolation of that number across the country meant the Bureau must have about thirty thousand Muslims under active surveillance. It really was a war, Patrese thought.

"That's right."

"What kind of people?"

"All this is strictly background, yeah?"

"Course."

"What kind of people?" Boone made the question rhetorical. "Take your pick. Radical mosque preachers. Disaffected youths, some with criminal records, possibly ripe for conversion as they try to find some meaning in their shitty lives. People in sensitive positions—you know, nuclear scientists, defense contractors, those sorts of people. And names passed on by the NSA for inappropriate web use: logging onto jihadist websites, Googling bomb-making instructions, that kind of stuff."

"That can't be legal." Patrese knew it sounded naïve, but he hoped he hadn't yet surrendered himself totally to the cynics. Wiretapping prime murder suspects was one thing; handing over web weirdos was a little too Thought Police for Patrese's liking.

"What can't be legal?"

"NSA. Google history."

"You want legal, Franco, or you want to get blown up?"

62

THURSDAY, NOVEMBER 18

The Cathedral of Learning at Pitt is less a skyscraper than a Gothic totem.

An academic ark of classrooms, laboratories, lecture rooms, libraries, conference rooms, and offices, it rises forty floors above the Oakland campus, high, proud, and stepped. Its hub is not at the top, perhaps strangely for such a magnificent edifice, but right on the ground floor: the Commons Room, a miniature cathedral with ceilings of soaring vaults, walls that echo with the hum of languid footsteps and studious chatter, and an outcircling of smaller rooms decorated according to national stereotype: tenth-century Armenian, folk-style Norwegian, Byzantine-era Romanian.

It was in the Commons Room that Patrese met Wheelwright.

Wheelwright was small and dapper, dressed in a green sport jacket, brown slacks, and dusty brogues. His only concession to mild professorial eccentricity was a red-and-black bow tie.

He had two sheets of paper with him. The first was his invoice, which Patrese folded and pocketed without opening. However much Wheelwright had charged, it wasn't Patrese's problem. The second was Wheelwright's findings as to the origin of the pink granite pebbles.

"Before I tell you what we've found," Wheelwright said, "I want to tell you briefly *how* we found it, so you can make up your mind as to whether we've been accurate enough for you."

"Okay."

It was often this way with experts, Patrese knew. They wouldn't give you straight answers to straight questions; they had to take you through the whole process first, and woe betide anyone who tried to hurry them up. Perhaps it was a legacy of too many exam questions demanding not just the right answer but also that you "show your reasoning."

"First, we found they were from the Arabian-Nubian Shield."

"Which is?"

"An exposure of Precambrian crystalline rock."

"How big is it?"

"It covers most of Israel, Jordan, Egypt, Saudi Arabia, Sudan, Eritrea, Ethiopia, Yemen, and Somalia. Thing is, the shield's actually two subshields, separated by the Red Sea. The Arabian's the east side, the Levant and Arabian peninsula. The Nubian's the west, North Africa. So we had to work out which of the two subshields the pebbles come from. This involved checking microscopic variations in their gravity, magnetic, structural, and isotopic characteristics." Wheelwright indicated the paper. "They're from the Arabian Shield, the eastern side. The figures are there."

"You can't be more specific?"

"Sure we can. And we have. Each shield is divided into microplates or terranes; you know, like individual sectors, areas, but several thousand square miles each. By elimination and subatomic analysis, we've narrowed the place of origin down to the Midyan terrane."

"Which is where?"

"It borders the Red Sea on its east and north shores, and covers the northwestern strip of Saudi Arabia and the northeastern corner of Egypt, the Sinai Peninsula."

"You say Saudi Arabia. Does it include Mecca?"

Wheelwright shook his head. "Too far south."

"Medina?" Medina is the second-holiest city in Islam.

Wheelwright shook his head again. "Too far east. The most popular place for visitors in the terrane is Sharm el-Sheikh. You know it?"

"No."

"On the Egyptian side, right on the Red Sea. Big tourist destination. You dive?"

"No."

"Amazing diving. *Amazing.* Some of the best in the world—hundreds of coral reefs, more than a thousand species of fish. My wife and I go every year. They hold Middle East peace conferences there too, you know."

"Fat lot of good *they've* done."

But Patrese was already thinking something completely different.

He was thinking that Mustafa Bayoumi was originally from Egypt.

63

Patrese found Mustafa in the chemistry department, just coming out of a lecture.

Mustafa's face was briefly, almost comically, thunderous when he saw Patrese; but his classmates' curious glances clearly persuaded Mustafa that discretion was advisable.

Rather than risk an embarrassing scene, Mustafa swallowed his anger and walked over to Patrese.

"You looking for me, Detective?"

"Sure am. You got some time to talk?"

Mustafa looked around suspiciously, as though expecting Beradino to materialize like some malevolent swamp thing.

"I'm alone," Patrese said. Beradino had stayed back at North Shore to keep an eye on any progress in the investigation. "Just a chat. Nothing formal. I'd appreciate it."

Mustafa looked at his watch. "I've got an assignment starting in half an hour."

"That's cool. It won't take that long. Buy you coffee?"

"Sure. There's a café down the corridor there."

"I know. I was a student here myself."

"Chemistry?"

"No. But I had the hots for a chick who did."

A brief, crooked smile appeared on Mustafa's face, and vanished just as abruptly when he remembered that Patrese was the police, the enemy.

The café was almost deserted. Even so, Patrese

instinctively chose a corner table. Corner tables gave good sight lines; they were also harder to eavesdrop.

"So," Mustafa said, when Patrese had returned from the counter with the coffees, "what have you come to talk about?"

Patrese didn't really know, to be honest. He hadn't formulated any plan beyond the vague notion that being conciliatory toward Mustafa might reap more dividends than constantly harassing him.

Mustafa clearly responded better to Patrese than he did to Beradino. Perhaps Patrese could make use of that. If not, he'd hardly have lost much.

"I came to tell you I'm sorry," Patrese said, winging it.

"Sorry?"

"If you think we've been too harsh on you. I know we've got a murderer to catch, but . . . Look, like I told you before, my mom and dad were killed in a car crash a couple of months back. Straight out of the blue, like it must have been for you when your father died. And it's awful, I know it is. I know the shock, the disbelief, the numbness, the anger. It's different for everyone, of course, but I do have some idea of what you must be feeling. And maybe we should have taken more account of that."

Mustafa nodded, but said nothing.

Patrese had a sudden idea; a long shot, but no worse for that, perhaps.

"I know you were close to your dad," he continued. "My parents, for me, were always somewhere I could find solace, love, comfort, all without conditions. They were a, er . . ." He feigned stumbling for the right word, all the while watching Mustafa carefully. ". . . a *sanctuary*, I guess."

No reaction to the word *sanctuary*. None at all.

And Patrese couldn't try again without risking suspicion. The only way they knew Mustafa was intending to go to the sanctuary this weekend, wherever and whatever it was, was through an illegal wiretap.

Mustafa was silent for a few moments, and then said: "You know *The Godfather*?"

"I'm Italian American, Mustafa. It's pretty much part of my DNA."

Mustafa smiled. Perhaps Patrese was getting somewhere.

"You remember the first line?"

"Of course. 'I believe in America.'"

"My father believed in America. Told me a thousand times how lucky we were to be living in the land of opportunity. Every week, he used to read me the Declaration of Independence and the Gettysburg Address. You know the way people who give up smoking are suddenly the most zealous antismokers around? That was my father, about America. He believed America's a place where your name, your color, your creed don't pose barriers to your success."

"And you didn't agree with him?"

"The war on terror is the war on Islam. There are no two ways about it."

"That's not what I asked."

"Yes, it is. How can this be a place of tolerance when Muslim brothers are being killed in Iraq and Afghanistan, while here in America we're stopped, searched, harassed, taken from our homes without evidence, and even shot, all for no reason other than our beliefs?"

Mustafa was still looking at Patrese, but now it was almost as though he were looking *through* him, to a place Patrese could never see. He seemed almost to have been tripped by something; his own queen of diamonds.

"You always cite nine-eleven to us," Mustafa said, his voice rising slightly, "as if that alone is justification for persecuting us until the end of time. Well, I ask you this: how many people died in nine-eleven? And how many have died in Iraq and Afghanistan?"

"It's not about numbers, Mustafa."

"Of course it's about numbers. Whichever side kills more, that side wins. And we have suffered many nine-elevens. *Many* nine-elevens. Enough is enough. You will find an immutable truth not of your religion or ours, but of human nature: that you can only push people so far before they explode. There can be no debate or discussion when you kill Muslims. You attack us, we attack you. You bomb us, we bomb you. You strike at our people, we strike at your people."

"'No debate or discussion'? We're debating now, aren't we?"

"No. I'm telling you what the score is."

"You're telling me nothing. You refuse to debate, you lose the argument."

"How can you argue against the will of Allah?"

"I don't believe in any God, whoever claims him as theirs."

"Then you are even worse than I thought."

"I believe in *man*, his reason, his opportunities, his strength."

"You believe in man? Then who made man? Who made the world? Allah."

"You should try reading Darwin."

"Pshaw! The word of Allah, through the Koran, is true and immutable; and the Koran allows us to fight in armed struggle against those who wage war against us. We must fight and kill the infidels wherever we find them. We must capture them. We must lie in wait for them in every place. Fight against them till there is no more oppression and all worship is devoted to Allah alone. Fight for the future of America."

"The future of America? If you had your way, it would be a caliphate."

"*Precisely.* That is as it should be. Allah created the whole universe; it's all worthy of praise. America doesn't belong to anyone but Allah. He's put us on this earth to live wherever we want, and to implement sharia everywhere. The only laws will be sharia laws, the only courts sharia courts."

"Read your Constitution. Church and state are separate. Religion is free."

"The Constitution is unworthy. Only through sharia can the degeneracy of this country be reversed. Every day and in every way, you see a society without moral standards, without faith, without direction. Drastic measures must be taken, and we must all take them. No one is too small to make a difference. Whoever sees something evil should change it with his hand. If he cannot, then with his tongue; and if he cannot do even that, then in his heart. That is the weakest degree of faith."

The more Patrese let Mustafa rant, the more riled Mustafa became, the more likely he was to say something that might be pertinent to their investigation. Patrese stayed quiet.

"These measures must be taken as follows," Mustafa was saying. "Since Islam, submission to the will of Allah, is the only religion ever given to the human race, all those who follow other creeds must be punished. All those whose characters are flawed because they drink alcohol or consume drugs must be punished. All those who indulge in deviant sexual relations and bring up children out of the sight of Allah, out of his holy institution of marriage, must be punished. All those who injure others, and exploit others, and kill others, must be punished.

"The Koran says those who disbelieve will have garments of fire cut out for them. It says they will have from hellfire a bed and over them from it coverings; thus do we reward the unjust. It says there will be some to whose ankles the fire will reach, some to whose knees the fire will reach, some to whose waists the fire will reach, and some to whose collarbones the fire will reach. And it says the unbelievers will not be able to ward off the fire from their faces, nor from their backs, and they will not be helped. The fire will come to them suddenly and confound them. They will not be able to avert it; nor will they be given respite."

64

It was a sad day—night, rather—Patrese thought, when he couldn't sleep for thinking about religion. But that was the truth.

He lay on his back, watching the headlights of passing cars wash across the ceiling. Mara lay in the crook of his arm, head on his shoulder, fast asleep. She'd come around earlier, laughingly lured by the promise of him cooking for her this time, but they'd never made it to the kitchen table; or rather, they had, but not to eat.

He wanted *her*, and for many of the reasons he knew he shouldn't: because anything they had would have to be clandestine, because she was damaged, because it would be some sort of atonement for what he'd done in that fetid Homewood attic.

And these early days were always heady, Patrese thought, plump and lush with the joys of mutual discovery; and the quickest way—sometimes the *only* way—to kill that excitement was to worry about what came next, weeks or months down the line, when the initial surge had worn off and too much was no longer not enough.

So he wasn't worrying about it, even though he knew it was a bad idea—it, this, them. The judge who'd sentenced Mara had been murdered. Patrese's own partner had originally arrested her. Getting involved with her was unprofessional, to say the least, and much else besides.

But since he'd put that to the back of his mind, he was worrying instead about what Mustafa had said this afternoon, and about the way in which he'd said it. He'd seemed almost *possessed*, Patrese thought.

A surveillance team had been due to start watching Mustafa at eight o'clock the following morning—taking into account the Islamic Sabbath on Friday, the start of the weekend during which he was due to visit the mysterious sanctuary. Patrese had been so alarmed by Mustafa's ranting, however, that he'd brought their start time forward twelve hours. So far, they'd called in nothing unusual.

As far as Patrese was concerned, religion did three things: divided people, controlled people, and deluded people. It didn't matter whether it was the kind of bile he'd heard Mustafa spewing in the café earlier, or Yuricich and Kohler hanging on to their courthouse monument of the Ten Commandments. It ended up pretty much at the same place.

If God had made man in his own image, Patrese thought, why had he made man so flawed—so disrespectful, thieving, covetous, murderous, lying, and adulterous, in contravention of the commandments? Even if you believed in original sin and the fall, why had God let that happen?

Most of all, how could you apply something as proscriptive and inflexible as the commandments to the endlessly complex business of life? That was just bumper-sticker ethics, pure and simple. Surely you should do the right thing because you had empathy and understanding of what was at stake, not because dogma and an outdated set of tribal taboos legislated thousands of years ago compelled you?

Patrese didn't like people who took religion lock, stock, and barrel, with no attempt at separating out its various parts; and he especially didn't like them when they had influence over ordinary people's lives, as Kohler and Yuricich had done.

And yet, and yet . . .

If what Yuricich had told the networks was right, the commandments underpinned pretty much the entire legal system—a system that, as a police officer, Patrese was sworn to uphold.

Patrese might have fallen away from religion, certainly in terms of being a believer, but it—the institutions, the rituals, people's need for faith, pretty much everything—still had a hold on him. It intrigued him, scared him, dragged him back when he least wanted it to—such as now, in the small hours.

Logical reasoning beat blind faith, he told himself.

So he worked out three reasons why the commandments were wrong.

First, they were confusing. Should you honor a father who abused his children or battered his wife? Should you not kill even if killing saved lives? Should you have killed Hitler, for example, had you ever had the chance? What was an image of God, exactly? How could you not covet? You couldn't stop yourself *thinking* bad things, after all, only acting on them. And so on, and on, and on. The commandments were fuzzy; and to unfuzz them, you had to use your own brain, your own moral compass.

Second, they were inadequate. Could they tell us the right thing to do about any of humanity's million and one problems? About climate change, racism, national debt, capital punishment, gay rights, overpopulation, abortion, social breakdown, unemployment, war, terrorism, obesity? Not as far as Patrese could see. You might as well consult the menu of the pizza joint around the corner, for all the enlightenment the commandments gave.

Finally, they were absolutist. Ridiculously, absurdly absolutist, to the point of being immoral. They admitted no exceptions, period. If a man's children were starving and the only way to feed them was to steal food, he must not steal, even if his children died. Imagine running on a road and being told to keep to the road, whatever happens. The road goes off the edge of a cliff. Do you go over with it?

That was that, Patrese figured. Yuricich had clearly been talking shit.

But still, as he finally drifted off, tiny fingers of doubt nipped and pulled at him. What if he was wrong? What if he, knowing what had been done to him, had thrown the baby out with the bathwater?

65

FRIDAY, NOVEMBER 19

The surveillance team outside the Bayoumis' house—more precisely, a new two-man shift, taking over at dawn—reported in to headquarters every hour. They knew that Mustafa was still in the house, because they hadn't seen him leave, but they couldn't tell what he was doing inside.

Marquez Berlin, on the other hand, *could* tell what Mustafa was doing, because Berlin could see exactly what Mustafa was looking at on his computer.

It was a video clip, ten minutes long, an amateur recording. A crowd of men, Middle Eastern by the look of them. It had evidently been taken during the winter, since the men were all wearing thick coats. They were chatting, laughing, singing. A few of the younger men were digging a hole in the ground. One of them paused to exchange pleasantries with the cameraman. He didn't seem to have a care in the world.

After a few minutes, there was a sudden surge of excitement among the crowd. A quick, whirling shot of sky and ground as the cameraman turned to find the source, and then a shape wrapped head to toe in a white sheet was carried into view and placed upright in the hole.

The shape was clearly human, with legs and arms trussed.

Berlin choked back the gag reflex in his throat, and dialed Patrese.

"You better come here, Franco. Like, *now.*"

Patrese was there inside a minute, with Beradino following close behind. They crowded around Berlin, peering at the screen in fascinated horror.

It was impossible to tell whether the trussed shape was male or female. The hole came up to its waist, leaving the torso and head visible.

A loud voice shouted out instructions. The shape was very still.

It only moved when the first stone knocked it sideways.

"Jesus *Christ*," Patrese said.

Beradino was too shocked to notice the blasphemy, let alone admonish Patrese.

On-screen, the shape righted itself again; and again it was hit.

There were stones falling wide or short, but plenty were making contact, glancing blows that barely seemed to register, heavier impacts that each time knocked the shape a little farther left or right, back or forth.

Each time the shape was hit, it took a little longer to right itself again.

Patrese wondered why the shape didn't struggle more. He guessed it was already resigned to its fate.

"It's his Sabbath," Patrese said, meaning Mustafa. "Who the fuck watches this shit on their holy day?"

The sun was behind the camera, and the shadows of the stoners writhed across the ground, grotesque in the exaggeration of their gesturing.

Stones gathered around the shape like cairns.

The white sheet was turning red very, very fast.

Patrese, Beradino, Berlin; they all could barely watch.

Even toward the end, when the shape was lying prone, half in and half out of the hole, no one in the crowd seemed shocked or subdued. None of them seemed to worry that something similar might happen to them, or to appreciate the gravity and finality of such a punishment.

In fact, it looked like it hardly seemed a punishment to them at all, let alone an act of community retribution for whatever crime the poor unfortunate had committed. It was just entertainment, a bunch of guys come to enjoy a good stoning and catch up with some old friends in the process. This was the modern version of family picnics at the old Wild West hangings, or the crowds who used to gather to watch the slaughter of gladiators in early Rome.

"Can you imagine this happening in the West?" Patrese said, as much to himself as the others.

"Savages," Beradino spat. "Darn *savages.*"

"Remember, we don't know Mustafa's watching this," Berlin said.

"This is real time, isn't it? He's watching it right now."

"We don't know, *legally.* We can't do a damn thing about it."

"You can't imagine it, can you?" Patrese continued, gesturing at the screen. "Any of this. It just wouldn't happen here. It's not our mind-set."

Beradino turned slowly toward him. "If that's the case," he said, "and if we're right about this being an Islamic thing, then why shouldn't the burnings be following some equally inaccessible logic?"

"Inaccessible only if you know nothing of Islam."

"Exactly. My point *exactly*. So we need to know something of Islam."

Patrese found a spare terminal and started searching the Koran online.

Pretty much the first thing he found was that *Koran*

meant *recitation.* Where had he heard that word recently, *recitation*?

He thought for a moment, remembered, and checked to see whether he was right. Yes, there, in the anonymous e-mail he and Beradino had received.

Heed this recitation I give you now.

Coincidence? Unlikely. It wasn't exactly a common word, after all.

It didn't take Patrese long to see that the Koran, like the Bible, was open to any number of interpretations, depending on how deranged, literal, fanatical, or autistic you were. Believing every word was inflexible doctrine had driven men to fly planes into the Twin Towers. Patrese found it hard to understand people whose world was so Manichaean; but understand them he might have to, if they were to solve this case.

Reading the entire Koran from start to finish would be too time-consuming, and probably too confusing. If it took scholars a lifetime to understand the Koran fully, as Patrese knew it did, he was hardly going to nail it in a couple of hours flat.

The more he read, however, the more he realized how little he knew. He was learning Islam on the hoof, and it was nowhere near enough for what he needed.

What he needed was an expert, and he knew just where to find one.

66

SATURDAY, NOVEMBER 20

East Carson Street, the main artery of the South Side Flats, is a long drag dotted with bars, restaurants, and clubs. Depending on the time of day it is, successively, not yet open, lively, edgy, and downright dangerous.

Patrese took Amberin Zerhouni there sometime between not yet open and lively.

He'd booked a table at Fat Head's, an unashamedly jock-style bar that was an East Carson institution. Patrese had been going for years with his college buddies. He'd even made it into the Wall of Foam for surviving the beer tour, which had involved working his way through the place's impressive array of craft and specialty beers.

There was much about those visits Patrese couldn't remember, for obvious reasons, but he could still match drinking sessions to the beer in question, their names curiously evocative: Long Trail Harvest, Boulder Obovoid Stout, Southern Tier Pumking, Stone Arrogant Bastard Ale, Rogue Dead Guy Ale, and so on. Small wonder that some people called Pittsburgh a drinking town with a football problem.

He'd worried slightly that Amberin was too sophisticated for this place. Had he met her at college, she'd have been the kind of girl whom football jocks like him jeered at for being too cool and self-possessed, all the time finding her cool and poise intimidating—but that was also part of the reason for taking her there. He wanted to put her slightly off guard. If he'd gone to see her during working hours, the meeting would have been too formal, the two of them circumscribed by their roles. Here, however, they could drop the labels of DA and detective, at least partly.

Moreover, he worried she'd react badly when he told her what he was thinking. He'd made plenty of scenes in Fat Head's in his time, but they'd all been of the drunken antics variety, and none had involved an irate assistant DA.

He worried for two reasons.

First, she might get defensive. Patrese didn't know Amberin well, but it was obvious she was proud of being a Muslim, if only from the hijab she always wore. She could easily regard his theory as a taint on all Islam, even—especially—if he was right. After all, it had taken only nineteen hijackers to spark a war seemingly without end.

Second, it would mean involving Amberin directly with the case, which would bring its own difficulties come prosecution. But he needed a practicing, thoughtful, intelligent Muslim, and she was the most obvious choice. *Not* to have used her would surely have been the greater dereliction of duty. He'd have gone to bin Laden himself if need be.

Amberin looked around her as they sat down. "This is great."

"Really?"

"Sure. That's pretty cool, for a start." She indicated

a collage of people wearing Fat Head's T-shirts in all kinds of weird and wonderful places: a US Marine under the crossed-swords monument in Baghdad; a trade delegation outside the Taj Mahal; people in front of the Eiffel Tower, in Tiananmen Square, even at Everest Base Camp.

"Have you ever been here before?"

"No."

"Would you have ever come if I hadn't invited you?"

"Of course not. Which is why it's great. I might even invest in one of those." She indicated a display case of T-shirts saying *Beer Rescue Squad* on the front and *Saving Society from Bad Beer* around the neckline at the back.

"You're joking?"

"Try me."

They ordered. Fat Head's did all the usual things—burgers, chicken, subs, salads, soups, and so on—but for the full experience, you had to go for one of their trademark headwiches; a sandwich, only bigger. Amberin plumped for a Bay of Pigs—*like an invasion of your stomach,* the menu said, *a Cuban sandwich gone nuclear!*—full of roasted pork, ham, Swiss cheese, pickles, and honey-mustard dressing.

"Pork?" Patrese asked.

"Sure."

"But isn't pork . . ."

"Tasty? Yes." She laughed. "I wear the hijab, but I eat pork."

Patrese laughed too, surprised. "You're the pick 'n' mix Muslim."

"Most of us who live in America are, to some degree or other. We have to be."

Unencumbered by any religious picking or mixing, Patrese went for the Artery Clogger: two fried eggs topped with slices of ham, crispy bacon, melted American cheese, lettuce, tomato, onion, and mayo.

Amberin read the Clogger's description from her menu. "*If Elvis was alive, he'd love this!*" She looked at Patrese. "I can't help thinking that Elvis isn't alive precisely because he *did* love things like this."

"Ain't that the truth."

She was, he thought, proving more fun in two minutes outside of work than in all the time he'd ever known her in it.

"So," she said, "you wanted to pick my brain."

"Yes. And I don't have to tell you that all this is confidential."

"No. You don't."

Patrese told her what they'd found at the murder sites, and the possible connections with Islamic extremism. He mentioned his suspicions about Bayoumi, but didn't tell her about the bugs or the remote computer spyware, or that Beradino was back at headquarters waiting for Mustafa to make a move toward his mysterious sanctuary. She listened to it all without speaking, and waited till he'd finished before replying.

"It's possible," she said.

"That's all? *Possible*?"

"Yes, that's all. It's *possible* that whoever's doing this could be a Muslim, sure. But if you're talking about the stones coming from that part of the Middle East, why not a Christian, or a Jew? Christians and Jews live there too."

"In much lower numbers than Muslims."

"There are fewer Muslims in Pittsburgh than Christians, aren't there? You're looking for a minority, it works both ways. If the hair's from Pakistan, why not a Hindu or a Buddhist? Or he could be something else entirely, like, I don't know, like one of those guys who thought the world was going to end in the tail of a comet; you remember them? Mass suicide cult."

"Hale-Bopp."

"That's the one. The joke's on all of us if it turns out they were right, isn't it?"

Patrese laughed. "Just assume for the moment—"

"You know what they say about *assume*."

"That it makes an *ass* out of *u* and *me*. I know. Detective Training 101. But anyway. Just *assume* for the moment that the killer *is* a Muslim. Then what? Why burn them?"

"Burning has pretty much the same kind of symbolism in Islam as in Christianity, particularly, you know, punishment in the afterlife."

"Muslims believe in hell?"

"Sure. And that the more evil you are, the more you'll suffer. Some people just get smoldering embers under their feet, but they end up with their brains boiled anyway. Others are burned till their skin's roasted through; then they get a new skin, and it all starts again. Or they're dragged into hell on their faces."

"Which kind of people suffer the most?"

"The Koran says that hypocrites will be in the lowest

depths of the fire, and that they'll find no helper there for them."

Patrese started. The anonymous e-mail had referred to the victims as hypocrites.

This thing is also personal, he reminded himself. *Islam will only be a part of it; the other, larger part will be what makes the killer tick.* How could two people read the same religious tract, and one of them used it as a guide to living while the other treated it as a guide to murder? Because their life experiences, their psyches, the way their neurons fired were different. Why did Bianca still believe in God while Patrese was an apostate? Because what had happened to him hadn't happened to her.

"But you can't just pluck these things out of context, Franco," Amberin continued. "Listen, you want to know about the Koran?"

"Yes."

"Then you have to begin at the beginning. The Koran's made up of *ayat*, verses. Some of these *ayat* are clear and unambiguous; these passages are called *mukhamat*. Other passages, *mutashabihat*, are ambiguous or metaphorical. The first ones, *mukhamat*, form the Koran's foundation. They deal with fundamental beliefs, pious rituals, explicit laws, that kind of thing. *Mutashabihat*, in contrast, describe aspects of faith whose nature can't be truly known, is up for debate, and has both outer meanings—*dhahir*—and inner meanings, *baatin*. Scholars have argued about these for more than a thousand years. They'll still be arguing a thousand years from now.

"Now, I can tell you what I believe, along with the vast majority of Muslims. I believe the Koran does *not* say that God belongs to one people. In fact, Islam's the only major faith to be named after not a prophet or a group of people, but a concept, submission to the will of God. The Koran doesn't say that God is wrathful and unloving. It doesn't say that *jihad* is a holy war against the nonbelievers. *Jihad* actually means the struggle for good against evil, and is therefore something everyone should practice, regardless of their faith. The Koran doesn't discourage interfaith dialogue and cooperation. The Koran doesn't hate women. I can tell you all that, and I believe it all to be true. But there are also people with their own take on it, and that take is very different from mine."

"Different enough for them to be doing something like this?"

"There were people who flew planes into skyscrapers, Franco."

Patrese nodded, conceding the point. "And have you come across any?"

"Any what?"

"People whose take on it is very different from yours."

"Here?"

"Yes."

She shook her head. "Not that I can think of."

"Sure?"

"Sure."

"Anyone who comes to mind, no matter how ridiculous it seems."

"Franco, I told you, I can't think of anyone."

"Amberin, this is a murder investigation, and—"

"Don't lecture me. I know full well what it is. I do a lot of sensitive work with people, a lot of it in confidence, and I'm not going to betray that. But I've been around more homicide cases than you, and I know what to look for. If there's something or someone I think might be involved, you'll be the first to know."

"But—"

"But nothing. That's the best you're going to get."

The headwiches arrived, each of them the size of Rhode Island. Tacitly agreeing to a truce, they tucked in.

"Look at the couple over there," she said. "*Without* turning—"

Patrese had already turned his head, of course.

"I can't believe you could be so indiscreet," she exclaimed.

"I can't believe you could see them without turning your head."

"Women have got better peripheral vision than men, that's why."

"Anyway, what about them?"

"*Massive* argument. Massive."

"You heard them?"

"Not here. Before they arrived."

Patrese looked at them again, more subtly this time.

"They look entirely normal to me," he said.

"Franco, how the hell are you a detective?" She drew the sting from the words with a light laugh. "Do you just switch your brain off when you clock off? Can't you tell they've had a fight? It's so obvious."

She went around the room after that. That couple

were bored with each other. Those two guys there were bitching about their wives. That big table, a birthday party, she was with him but wanted to be with the other guy, and so on.

"You haven't noticed any of that?" she said.

"It's a woman thing, clearly."

"Clearly."

"Tell you what I have noticed."

"What?"

"I've noticed every entrance and exit, and how to get there as quickly as possible. There are two blown lightbulbs over in that corner that need replacing. That guy over there has read the same page of the *Post-Gazette* three times."

"Bet you noticed the waitress."

Patrese shook his head. "Not especially."

Amberin laughed again. "I hope you're a better detective than you are a liar."

67

It was almost midnight when the surveillance team finally sounded the alert.

Mustafa Bayoumi was on the move.

If Mustafa suspected he was being watched, he gave no sign. He sauntered out of the house as if he didn't have a care in the world, climbed in his Saturn, and set off without a backward glance, even the one in his rearview mirror required by the traffic code.

The watchers kept an open line to a speakerphone on the North Shore as they tailed Mustafa through quiet residential streets and onto Fifth Avenue, heading southwest.

"That's back toward town," Patrese said.

Mustafa stayed on Fifth all the way past the Mellon Arena and into downtown.

"Making a right on Grant," said the speakerphone.

"Perhaps he's coming to see us," Beradino murmured. "He's going the right way."

Patrese shook his head. "I don't think so."

"Why not?"

"I dunno. I just don't."

"Making a right on Liberty."

Liberty Avenue led away from the bridges to the North Shore and up toward the Strip District. The Strip is a rectangle of about twenty blocks by five, hard up against the cityside bank of the Allegheny. In its time, it's been first the industrial and then the economic center of Pittsburgh. Now it's party central: funky loft apartments, farmers' markets and boutique shops by day, edgy bars and nightclubs by night.

Not exactly the natural stomping ground for a good Muslim boy, Patrese thought.

"Making a left on Seventeenth."

Definitely the Strip. Mustafa had ignored the previous turning, which led to a bridge over the river and up to East Allegheny.

"Left again on Penn. Suspect is slowing. Looking for a parking spot."

Beradino leaned over the speakerphone. "Driver,

stay with the car, please. Shotgun, get out and maintain visual on foot, you understand?"

"Yes, sir." A slight chuckle, and then: *"Sir, you ain't gonna believe this."*

"Believe what?"

"There's a line stretching halfway down the block, people waiting to get in a big-ass new trendy nightclub, and it's called—"

Patrese, suddenly realizing, finished the sentence: "The Sanctuary."

68

The Sanctuary was an old Slovak church, now deconsecrated and converted. Thick brick walls meant little sound leaked onto the street outside, but the lights and lasers thrusting upward through the octagonal cupola rose high into the night sky.

Patrese went in alone. Dressed in jeans and a paisley shirt, he could just about pass for one of the hip young professionals who comprised the club's clientele. Beradino, no matter what clothes he wore, could not. At best, he'd look like someone's dad; at worst, like a cop. Either way, he'd stick out like a pork pie in a synagogue.

The dance floor was packed, several hundred people caught frozen-strobed in an infinity of strange contortions. Patrese was momentarily tempted to join them and abandon himself to primal, sweaty pleasure, to try to dance away all the shit he dealt with every day. That's what everyone else there was doing—stressful, busy jobs five days a week, two nights to enjoy themselves.

A day on homicide shift would show them what real stress was, Patrese thought.

He climbed an elaborate half-spiral staircase up to the mezzanine level, past the DJ boothed in the old pulpit. A smiling waitress dressed as a Catholic schoolgirl stood aside to let him pass. Smiling back at her, Patrese was glad Beradino hadn't come in. Waitresses as Catholic girls; he'd have tried to close the whole place down for that.

An area of the mezzanine was roped off; private party. Patrese checked that Mustafa wasn't among the guests, then leaned on a rail and looked down at the revelers below; those on the dance floor, those by the Plexiglas bar.

There.

Mustafa was standing alone in a corner, nodding his head in time with the music. His eyes darted around the room. Patrese presumed he was looking for whoever he'd arranged to meet here, the voice on the wiretap.

After a few moments, a blond man in a turquoise shirt approached Mustafa.

Turquoise Shirt leaned in close and shouted something in Mustafa's ear; pretty much the only way to be heard above the music.

Mustafa nodded and shouted back, a single word, repeated for emphasis. Second time around, even at this distance, Patrese managed to lip-read perfectly.

Thirty.

Turquoise Shirt nodded. Mustafa slipped past him

and headed toward the stairs that led downstairs. Turquoise Shirt followed.

Downstairs were the bathrooms; Patrese had seen the sign on the way in.

Women went to the restroom in pairs as a matter of course, but men almost never—especially two men who, from their body language, looked to have only just met.

In fact, Patrese could think of only two possible reasons.

If it was the first, why not just go to a gay club?

And if it was the second, who better to deal with than a chemistry ace?

69

During the hour or so in which Patrese watched him, Mustafa disappeared to the restroom seven times. He was dealing something, that much was obvious to a moron, and a dollar to a dime said MDMA. Not only was Turquoise Shirt now dancing as if he'd personally experienced the Second Coming, but Patrese remembered reading about a case in New Jersey where a chemistry major had made about half a million bucks from manufacturing and distributing MDMA. It was one way of funding college, Patrese supposed.

So much for Mustafa hating Western decadence; unless, of course, he justified it with some spurious garbage about helping destroy the system from within.

The easiest thing would have been to bust Mustafa's ass there and then; catch him red-handed, send the pills off to be analyzed, and sling him in the cells. But that could invite explanation as to how Patrese had happened to go, by himself, to the one club in all Pittsburgh that Mustafa was visiting, which would in turn risk blowing the surveillance. Better to be subtle, and perhaps keep the knowledge of what was happening here as a joker to be played at a later date.

Sometime around one thirty, the lights dimmed, the fog machines started belching out enough smoke to hide Mount Rushmore, and the opening bars of Madonna's "Like a Prayer" reverberated around the club.

This was clearly some kind of ritual here, if the crowd's manic cheering and rush to the dance floor were anything to go by. Patrese smirked. The song's video—burning crosses, stigmata, Madonna writhing around the black Jesus—had always made him laugh. He figured Madonna's love-hate attitude to religion was pretty much his own.

Through the smoke, he saw Mustafa pull out his cell phone, read a message—he must have had it set to vibrate, Patrese thought, he'd never have heard a beep above the music—and set off from his corner once more.

This time, however, he wasn't going down to the restroom.

He was heading for the door. Patrese followed.

The night air was sudden and cold after the warmth of the club. Mustafa pressed his cell phone to his ear with one hand and pulled his coat tight around him with the other. Patrese, twenty yards behind, couldn't hear what he was saying, but Mustafa's tone and cadence indicated he was asking for directions, asking where his interlocutor was.

Apparently satisfied with the answer, Mustafa ended the call, shoved his cell phone back in his pocket, turned the corner and headed right, down toward the railroad lines and stockyards by the river. The streets here were much less well lit than the main drag of Sixteenth. It was the kind of place you'd go if you didn't want to be seen; the kind of place you could also get mugged, or worse, if you didn't have your wits about you.

Patrese walked on the balls of his feet, hands loose by his sides, ready for anything.

Up ahead, Mustafa stopped.

A figure materialized from the dark; a black man, Patrese saw, dressed in baggy pants and an orange down jacket. The kind of guy who'd never have got past the rope at the Sanctuary, in other words.

He handed Mustafa an envelope. Mustafa took a step backward, into the pool of watery light from the nearest streetlight, and opened the envelope, the better to count the money inside. The black man stepped forward with him, also into the light, and Patrese saw his face, clear as day.

It was Trent Davenport.

70

Transaction done, Mustafa and Trent went their separate ways; Mustafa back toward the Sanctuary, Trent down toward the Sixteenth Street Bridge. Patrese followed Trent.

The moment Patrese was sure Mustafa was out of earshot, he called out: "Trent!"

Trent spun around, surprised, scared.

"Don't run," Patrese said. "I know what you got. I saw you take it. Running's just gonna make it worse. Run, and I *will* bust your ass."

Trent looked wildly around; not for escape, Patrese saw, but for something else.

Patrese worked it out fast, even as he closed the gap between them.

Homewood was twenty minutes' drive away. It was too late for the buses, and no taxi driver in his right mind would go into Homewood after dark.

So Trent must have got here by car. But he was too young to drive. Someone must have brought him here, and that someone must be taking him home again.

And that someone would have stayed the hell away while Trent was buying the drugs, in case he got caught. Get caught, and you're on your own. That's how the gangs work; they get teenagers to collect and deliver the drugs. Teenagers are less likely to be stopped, so the thinking goes; and, if they do it well, it's part of their initiation. From there, they'll gradually graduate to bigger, better things in the gang.

"Let me see 'em," Patrese said.

"I dunno what you talkin' 'bout, man."

"Let me see 'em, Trent, or I'll slam you against that wall, and it *will* hurt."

"Man, they see you, they're gonna kill me."

Patrese held out his hand, impassive. Trent looked around again. Sullenly he pulled a small plastic bag from his pocket and held it out.

"They ain't for me, man. They ain't personal use."

Patrese took the bag and opened it. A hundred pills, at a guess. Ain't personal use, damn straight.

Trent was gabbling. "You confiscate that, man, I really am dead, I ain't shittin' you. That a thousand bucks' worth, right there, and it ain't my dead presidents."

Ten dollars a pill; reasonable wholesale price.

Patrese thought fast. He had three options here.

One, he could confiscate the pills. But if Trent went back to Homewood with no money and no pills, the gangbangers would think he'd made off with their cash himself. They'd kill him, no questions asked. At the very least, they'd hurt him bad.

Two, he could arrest Trent. But if he did that, he'd be condemning Trent to the endless labyrinths of the justice system. Once you were in, you never got out, not really; not as a young black man in the inner city. Your name was known, you were marked. The cops had their eye on you. That, too, was a death sentence. It was slow, it was insidious, but it was a death sentence just the same.

Three, he could give Trent a thousand bucks, keep the pills himself, and let Trent return to whoever had sent him with some bullshit story about how Mustafa had never showed, and here's their money back. But that would leave Patrese a grand out of pocket, and have made close to zero impact on Pittsburgh's drug supply.

"You recognize me?" Patrese asked while he thought.

"Sure, man. You the cop who arrested my mama. What you here for? You get a bonus for doin' the whole family?"

Don't suggest that to City Hall, Patrese thought. It was just the sort of dumb-ass idea they'd dress up as private enterprise and run with. The justice system, reduced to the lowest common denominator—numbers.

Would that be justice? Of course not.

Did justice always have to be what the state said it was? Of course not.

Then why couldn't Patrese apply his own solution?

Why else had he joined the force, he asked himself, if not to do what Bianca had said to him that night at Mercy while Samantha Slinger lay dying a few rooms away—to make things better?

You could call it taking the law into your own hands; you could call it flagrant disregard for proper procedure. The rule book said it was wrong, but in this case what was wrong was the rule book itself. Homicide detectives were encouraged to think outside the box when it came to searching for suspects; why shouldn't Patrese apply that to other aspects of police work too? What he was thinking of wasn't simply the right thing to do, he felt; it was perhaps the *only* thing to do.

He picked out a single pill, and handed the bag back to Trent.

"Hey, man, they *count*."

"They're not going to miss one. And, Trent?"

"Yo?"

"You got a brain in your head. Think about why I'm doing this."

71

SUNDAY, NOVEMBER 21

Jesslyn broached the subject as Beradino was driving them back from church. She couldn't think of a way to ease into it gradually, so she cut straight to the chase.

"I'm going to see Mara Slinger tomorrow," she said.

Beradino glanced sideways at her, eyebrows arched. "You're doing *what*?"

"I'm going to see Mara."

"I heard what you said. I want to know *why*."

"'Cause she rang and asked me."

"What, and you just *agreed*? After everything she's done to you?" Beradino took his hands from the wheel and clapped them to his temples in frustration. "Shoot, Jesslyn. I've listened to *weeks* of you telling me about how Mara Slinger deserves to die, and suddenly off you go like a puppy dog. What's going on?"

"I'm going 'cause it suits me."

"How's that?"

"There's something in it for me. Something I need."

"Like what?"

"Money."

Beradino looked across at her again, suspicious this time. Wary. "What's that?"

"I've got something of hers. Something she'll pay for."

"Go on."

"Her Star of David."

"What?"

"Solid gold. Wears it around her neck."

"How have you got it?"

"By accident. She handed it in when she arrived at Muncy. It must have got mixed up with my stuff somehow. I didn't even notice till she called to ask me." First lie.

Beradino narrowed his eyes. "How does she have your number?"

"It was on the tribunal documents, under my personal info section." Second lie.

"What on earth was it doing there?"

"Someone messed up. Should have taken it out. Didn't. It happens."

Beradino nodded. He'd seen enough incident statements with the witness's contact details accidentally included to know that this kind of mistake did indeed happen.

"And this Star of David," he said. "You're going to make her pay to get it back?"

"She *offered* to pay." Third lie.

"You shouldn't let her. It belongs to Mara, Jesslyn. You want to give it back, give it back. But it's not yours to sell. Especially not a religious icon like that."

"She *offered*. Darn it, Mark, it's not like she can't afford it. She's still got millions stashed away, I bet. And I need the money."

"We got enough money."

"No, we haven't. Not long-term. Look. Mara cost me my job. Now she wants to pay me. Maybe it's guilt money. No matter. She's paying, I'm taking. End of story."

Beradino thought for a moment.

"You want to hurt her?" he asked.

"I want her to suffer for what she did."

"What she did to her babies, or what she did to you?"

"Both. Her babies more, of course." That, at least, was true.

"The law's the law, Jesslyn. You know that well as I do."

"God's law, Mark. God's law. Not man's law."

"Jesslyn, you go see her, you don't touch a hair on her head, you understand me?"

"Nothing I could do would be a fraction of what she deserves."

"Not a hair on her head. She's a free woman now. I don't like it any more than you do, but she was acquitted by a court of law, and we have to respect that."

"She should never have been—"

"But she is. Take her money if you want, but nothing else. Promise me."

"I'm just going to—"

"Promise me."

Finally, grudgingly, like a sulky teenager: "I promise."

72

Patrese wondered how many lies he told each day. He always lied for a good reason, he thought, but lie he did; and if most of them weren't outright lies, then they were certainly sins of omission.

For example, he'd told Beradino that Mustafa had gone to the Sanctuary to deal drugs, and that he, Patrese, had gotten hold of one of Mustafa's pills to send off for testing. What Patrese *hadn't* told Beradino was that he'd got the pill off of Trent.

And Patrese had told Mara he'd spent yesterday seeking advice about Islam and the Koran, because that was an avenue the police investigation into the serial murders was considering. What he *hadn't* told her, for obvious reasons, was that he'd sought the advice from Amberin.

It was late afternoon. Looped in lazy, rolling cycles of making love and dozing across each other, neither Patrese nor Mara had yet got out of her bed for more than ten minutes at a time. Outside, it was dark again—a whole day gone by without him noticing. Other than being ill, Patrese couldn't remember the last time that had happened. He felt cocooned in a bubble, out of time and place; two damaged people clinging to each other like shipwreck survivors.

"How do you usually spend your Sundays?" Mara asked, propped up in bed on one elbow as she nibbled lightly at his ear.

"Depends whether the Steelers are at home or on the road."

"Seriously?" She stopped nibbling and examined his face. He fought the urge to laugh—he, Franco Patrese, a Steel Town jock, in bed with an Oscar winner.

"Dead straight. Never miss a home game."

"They're not at home today, then?"

He shook his head. "At the Bengals."

She started nibbling again. "And next Sunday?"

"Next Sunday they're back here, against the Redskins."

"And if I offered you the choice between me, here, naked, nice warm bed"—she started dotting light kisses in a line down his chest—"and you standing in some freezing bleachers watching men in stupid pads and helmets, what would you choose?"

"You could always come with me," he deadpanned.

She looked up at him, eyes cartoonishly large in mock outrage. "That's not the right answer." She pouted.

"What if we make love all morning and all night, but go watch in the afternoon?"

She shook her head. "I can't, Franco."

"You come to the game with me, I'll go to the theater with you. Deal?"

"It's not the football, Franco, and it's certainly not you. I don't go to the theater anymore either. I don't go anywhere. I *can't.*"

"Hey. Anyone tries to start something, they'll have to come through me first."

"Franco, you're sweet. But how can you be with me in public when you can't even tell anyone about us? Even if you could, it would make no difference. Let me show you something."

She got up and walked, naked, into the next room. Patrese watched her go.

A moment or two later she was back, carrying a cardboard box that brimmed with sheets of paper.

"There." She handed him the box. "There are two more just like this. Three boxes in all, each of them chock-full."

Letters, Patrese saw. Hundreds of letters, perhaps thousands.

"May I?" he asked.

"Sure. I want you to see them. I want you to *understand.* You're pretty much the first person who's listened to me since I got out. That means something to me. These letters are why that means something."

Patrese tipped the letters onto the bed and flicked through them.

This was one of the things about police work, he knew. You did it long enough, you came across so many wackos, kooks, head cases, nut jobs, screwballs, crackpots, and psychos that you began to wonder whether there was anyone sane left in the country.

The letters Mara had received came from at least forty states (few people put their addresses, but the envelopes had postmarks), and the vitriol expressed in them was staggeringly virulent, if rarely articulate.

Some people had quoted passages from Revelation. Some had attached drawings of what they'd do to her if they ever caught her. Some had written long screeds of verse outlining the myriad of ways in which she'd sinned. One letter consisted simply of the word "BITCH" written over and over again, for twenty-six pages. Another denounced her for being a "Zionist whore" and part of the "Jewish media conspiracy."

Patrese jabbed an angry finger at it. "Conspiracy, *bullshit*," he said.

"You don't believe in conspiracy theories?"

"Not one. Not JFK, not nine-eleven, not Area Fifty-One, the Apollo moon landings, Oklahoma City, Paul Is Dead, the New World Order, the Bilderberg Group, the Illuminati, or anything else you can think of. You know why? In all my time on the force—on this planet, come to think of it—I've yet to meet one person in a position of any authority who could find his own asshole with a mirror."

Mara laughed. "Ain't that the truth."

"Why do you keep all these?"

"Why? To remind me."

"Remind you of what?"

"That no matter how bad my life is, there are plenty of people out there with so little going for them that they get their kicks by spewing hate to total strangers."

Patrese nodded, and turned his attention back to the letters.

An entire section came from Mara's personal stalker; no celebrity was complete without one, he guessed. An unprepossessing Hawaiian man called Alika Manuwai (he was considerate enough to attach his name and address to each letter, and often several photos too), he was quite a scribe, delivering long, rambling, repetitive letters detailing the torrid extent of his love for her, the joy he could bring her (especially as opposed to certain no-good, flaky billionaire mayors), and the inevitability of his and Mara's eventual union.

"What's this?" Patrese asked. "He's written in some kind of, like, child language. 'Peepo tink I mento,' 'I wen cry,' 'God goin do plenny good kine stuff fo yo.' What the hell does that mean?"

"It's Hawaiian Creole. Pidgin language. And Honolulu PD checked him out. Say he's weird, but harmless."

"Harmless? Brainless, more like. If he ever does something, he's practically given you his Social Security number. We could find him in three minutes flat."

"He's no threat to you for my affections, put it that way."

"I should hope not."

"Any case, there's a restraining order against him. He's not allowed within five hundred yards of me."

"I thought you said he was harmless."

"*I* think he's harmless. Hellmore doesn't. And it was Hellmore who filed for the restraining order. He says you can never be too careful."

A couple more letters quoted various passages from the Koran, either on their own or alongside the Bible and the Talmud, as though to prove Mara was damned whichever God happened to hold sway in the afterlife. Another letter suggested that Mara move to Saudi Arabia or Afghanistan, where women were treated as she deserved to be. This, Patrese assumed, was not supposed to be a compliment.

Wondering whether there was any link, no matter how tenuous, between this kind of bile and the killings, he held up the letters in question. "Can I keep these?"

"If you like."

"Come to think of it, why haven't you given these to us before?"

"You? You mean the police?"

"Yup."

"My faith in the police isn't exactly at an all-time high. Present company excepted, of course. Here. Look at these." She fished out two letters from the pile. "These are *really* weird."

Patrese read them. They were unsigned, but clearly both written by the same person. The first one ran as follows:

Dear psycho baby-killing bitch,

Fucking bitch you should suck on a shotgun and do everyone a favor. They should of given a broomstick encrusted with broken glass to the other shitbag's in prison with you and let them use it on you. I would love to beat the ever living tar out of you rip your blackened still-beating heart right out of your chest.

However, the LORD JESUS says I shouldn't, because the LORD JESUS says for us to control our sinful impulse's.

May the LORD JESUS rule over GOD's people forever Amen.

The LORD JESUS says that in the end many false teacher's like Darwin and Mohammad will rise. I will not be swayed because I have met GOD. You say you heard GOD talking to you you're a fucking bitch liar. Only the true believer's can hear the LORD our GOD.

You and your lie's aren't fooling anyone. You're fake through and through that's why you're an actress scum faker not a truthful bone in your body. I saw you on TV with your Oscar acting like it was a big surprise and how humble you felt and I wanted to scratch your eyes out vile woman evil woman so smug and insincere.

You say you didn't kill those poor little babe's you're a filthy filthy liar.

If we claim to be without sin we deceive ourselves and the truth is not in us. If we confess our sin's HE is faithful and just and will forgive us our sin's and purify us from all unrighteousness. If we claim we have not sinned we make HIM out to be a liar and HIS word has no place in our live's.

The word of the LORD our GOD 1 John 1: 8–10.

Those an[illegible] [illegible]t ask to be born you [illegible] them tombstone's before they could talk. Your son's will never play ball learn to drive or give their mother grandchildren. Your daughter will never attend a prom or walk down the aisle in white on her wedding day.

Million's of women would give anything to have children and would love and cherish them every minute of the day but they can't. You were given that most precious of gift's and spat it back. The LORD must have a reason for letting you do this. The LORD is great HE is kind and HE is forgiving.

Well this is not all there is. You are going to be held accountable for your action's. I hope they are worth an eternity in what I hear is a pretty uncomfortable place. All the blood money you and your shyster lawyer make won't help you down there. Fucking kike's scratching each other's back's. You get some big book deal too? Your greed is greater than your shame but your evil will never prevail.

For the word of God is living and active. Sharper than any double-edged sword it penetrates even to dividing soul and spirit joint's and marrow it judges the thoughts and attitude's of the heart.

The word of the LORD our GOD Hebrew's 4:12.

Watch your thoughts for they become word's.

Watch your word's for they become action's.

Watch your action's for they become habit's.

Watch your habit's for they become character.

Watch your character for it becomes your destiny.

Your destiny will be decided by the LORD. Vengeance is mine saith the LORD. Even the most righteous are but filthy rags before HIM.

GOD has granted me great faith and understanding and as long as the earth endures I will fear no evil for GOD is with me. The Truth will shine like 1000 sun's. May the LORD JESUS rule over GOD's people forever Amen.

And the second one:

Dearest darling Mara my precious and sweet one

I'm sorry I should never have sent you that other letter, if I could take it back I would.

I didn't mean all the thing's said there, I wrote it coz I was angry at you coz I thought I'd never see you again after you left without even saying good-bye.

Like all of us I am an imperfect sinner but I know the LORD JESUS will have mercy if we truly repent our sin's.

I want to be with you do you think that could ever happen? Just the two of us like the song goes, we could go live on a beach in Mexico or somewhere where no one would bother us or care or any of that.

But I know you probably don't want that because you misunderstand the way I've behaved toward you. I've tried to explain but word's aren't my strong point as you can probably tell from these letter's!

Well it's not too late, we can always clear the slate and start again can't we?

Can't we say we can say it please?

Most of all I know you didn't do what they said you did with your baby's and that. Your a good person and there's no way you could have done that I know that now. All those men in the courtroom, what do they know of the way women think?

The LORD our GOD moves in mysterious way's and only HE knows why he's sent this onto you but you can rest assured the reason will be perfect.

"The LORD shall judge the people; judge me, O LORD, according to my righteousness, and according to mine integrity that is in me."

Remember too the word's of Job: "Naked I came out of my mother's womb and naked I shall return: the LORD has given and the LORD has taken away; blessed be the name of the LORD."

I've seen you at your window a few time's and you always look so beautiful but sad too, if I could somehow wipe away all the tear's and hurt believe me I would do just that no matter what it cost me.

I stood among all those freak's and idiot's outside your apartment and they all think they know you, but they don't, they're fooling themselves, they read the *Enquirer* and think they know you and it's wrong, no one knows you like I do and certainly no one love's you like I do.

No offense but you're better off without Howard if he never kept the faith and ran off with the little whore next door the moment you were in Muncy.

GOD has granted me great faith and understanding and as long as the earth endures I will fear no evil for GOD is with me. The Truth will shine like 1000 sun's. May the LORD JESUS rule over GOD's people forever Amen.

"Weird indeed," Patrese said.

73

MONDAY, NOVEMBER 22

This will shock them, that's for sure.

It'll shock them because they're too hidebound in their thinking. Since they've already found three dead white men, they assume the next victim will also be a white man. They assume it because that's what the profiler's told them, or that's what they've read in those endlessly tedious screeds of psychology literature: that the chosen, like me, never kill across lines of race and gender. They simply can't appreciate that I'm different, different in every way from what's gone before.

The fear is all too real with this one. She—yes, she—*knows beyond doubt what she's done. Redwine may not have been sure, Kohler probably didn't have time to think, and it would have taken Yuricich days to go through all the people he'd wronged. But this time, I've no need to disguise myself. So she* knows. *She knows who I am, and so she knows what she's done. She knows her scriptures, she tells me; she finds solace in her faith. She'll need it now, I tell her.*

I look around the apartment, savoring the moment.

I remember almost nothing about the first time I killed. There was too much going on in my head—the logistics, the endless checklists to make sure I hadn't overlooked anything, but most of all, the battering in my psyche. Life's so ingrained in our culture. Everything's geared to preserving and prolonging it, from all the doctors and pharmaceuticals money can buy down to the language itself: live life to the full, get a life, life imprisonment, life partner. We're conditioned to make lives and save them, not take them.

So to cross that line is an irreversible shock. When you first kill, in fact, you kill two people, not just the victim but yourself too. Your old self is gone, and in its place is a new persona. I'm no longer part of humanity, not really, nor do I care. I have no faith in mankind anymore. I am the one who will be redeemed, not them, because I am performing the work of a higher power. Those who can't understand that have only themselves to blame.

Most of the world worship at the feet of an all-powerful, no matter what name they use for their deity. And if you believe in a god, then you believe in an afterlife, where the good go to one place and the evil to another.

I know where this one, this victim, is going.

"Isaiah chapter fifty-nine, verse seventeen," I say. "For I put on righteousness as a breastplate, and a helmet of salvation upon my head; and I put on the garments of vengeance for clothing, and am clad with zeal as a cloak."

74

Singing along to Tom Petty loud on the car stereo, roads surprisingly empty for a weekday evening, another night ahead with Mara—Patrese couldn't remember the last time he'd felt so . . . not happy, exactly, he often felt happy, but *carefree*, certainly.

And *carefree* wasn't what he associated with major serial homicide investigations. He still wanted to catch the killer, of course; that went without saying. But he was also beginning to realize that worrying about a breakthrough every minute of the day wasn't necessarily going to make that breakthrough happen any quicker—especially when progress was frustrating. Pretty much all he'd achieved today had been handing Mustafa's pill to forensics, who'd promised him an answer within a couple of days. That apart, it had been the usual rigmarole of dead-end leads and tail-chasing.

Patrese turned into Mara's street, and suddenly Tom

Petty was singing alone on the car stereo, the chorus to "Free Fallin'" vaporizing in Patrese's throat.

At the other end of the street, by the entrance to the park—right outside Mara's apartment building, in other words—three fire engines had slewed across the road.

Beneath flashing blues and reds, the firefighters swarmed like ants, unrolling hoses and raising cherry pickers, their movements shot through with the unflustered urgency of men who did this every day.

Patrese gunned the Trans Am hard, as fast and as close to the fire engines as he dared. He was out and running almost before he'd come to a halt.

One of the firefighters moved to block his path.

"Hey! Fire scene, buddy. Stay out."

Patrese ripped his badge from his belt and held it high. "I'm a cop."

"I don't care who you are, man. That place looks like Saddam torched it."

Panic rose in Patrese's gut, gushing to fill the gap between what was in front of his eyes and what was coming up fast from the back of his mind. He looked around wildly, hoping to see Mara sitting on the back of a fire truck with a blanket around her, shocked and scared but at least still alive.

There was no sign of her.

"Is there anyone left in there?" he blurted.

The firefighter puffed his cheeks out. "We found one."

"Is she alive?"

"Not a chance, bud." The firefighter paused. "You

said 'she.' But we haven't called it in to the cops yet. You know her?"

75

Patrese took himself into the park, away from all the commotion.

Around the back of the observatory itself, he slumped onto a whitewashed stone bench, glacier cold through the seat of his trousers, and inhaled the winter air so deeply and violently that he began to feel light-headed.

Focus, he told himself, *focus.*

Easy to say; a damn sight harder to do when the woman he'd been making love to ten hours ago was now burned to a cinder.

Patrese had seen what had happened to the others. They'd ended up as charred lumps of meat scarcely recognizable as the people they'd once been, the people who had, pretty much until the moment they'd been killed, walked and talked and laughed and loved, paraded their strengths and hidden their weaknesses.

They'd been like the rest of us, in other words. And now they were anything but.

Patrese hadn't known Redwine. He'd met Yuricich a couple of times. Kohler had been a family friend. None of them had evoked in him a fraction of what Mara did.

Mara was dead; the thought ran through Patrese's head like a loop. *Mara is dead. Mara is dead, Mara is dead.* She'd lost her babies, she'd lost her freedom, and now she'd lost her life; pain upon pain upon pain. Why would one person deserve all this? They wouldn't, that's why. It was just chance; and therefore there was no God.

Patrese felt detached. It wasn't the lazy cliché of it being as if it were happening to someone else, but rather that he seemed to be seeing and feeling it all through a thin layer of gauze. He knew it was shock, and he knew too that he must use it while it lasted. Mara's murder would hit him for real soon enough, and when that happened, he wanted to be alone. No one knew about him and her, and that was how it had to stay, even—especially—now that she was dead. Anything else would pose more questions than answers, and the balance between the two was lopsided as it was.

To clear his head, Patrese shook it hard, as though he were a dog shaking off water.

After a few moments, when he was satisfied he'd got his story right and hadn't missed anything, he called Beradino.

"Mark, it's me."

"What's up?"

"We got another one."

"Who?"

"Mara Slinger."

Beradino's silence was loud through the static.

"Mark?" Patrese continued. "You hear me? Mara Slinger. Dead. Fire. *Capisce?*"

"Yeah. Sorry. Mara Slinger. Dagnabbit. You sure? How do you know?"

"I heard the fire called in on the scanner." That Patrese would have been listening to the 911 frequency in his own car was perfectly plausible; lots of emergency-service personnel did. "Hauled ass to Obs Hill."

"You there now?"

"Yup."

"You been inside the apartment yet?"

"Nope. Firefighters still trying to get the thing under control. Be a while yet."

"Wait there for me. Get the uniforms to throw up cordons, and wait there for me."

"Will do."

76

After ending the call, Beradino stared at the wall for a long, long moment, hoping to find an answer in the blankness of white paint.

There had to be an innocent explanation, he thought. Jesslyn had promised him she meant no harm. *Promised* him. And where he came from, that still meant something.

But Beradino knew too that Jesslyn was full of hate, and also that she'd kept her dismissal from Muncy secret for several weeks. In fact, he'd only discovered it by chance. Left to her own devices, she'd still be working in the burger bar.

Since she'd hidden that from him, she'd almost certainly hidden many other things. Working homicide for close to three decades had shown Beradino that, deep down, no one really knows anybody else. If he'd had a dollar for every time someone had told him that the killer was the quietest, nicest guy on the block, he'd be living out his retirement on Grand Cayman.

He picked up the phone again and dialed Jesslyn.

She answered on the third ring, crying great, racking sobs.

And he knew.

Beradino felt his head slump forward, as if his neck muscles were no longer up to the job of keeping it upright.

"What have you done?" he wailed. "What on earth have you done?"

She tried to say something, but it came out as gibberish.

Beradino took a deep breath, trying to compose himself.

"I'll be home later," he said. "I've got to go to her apartment now. Anybody there suspects anything, I'll think of something to head 'em off. When I get home, we'll talk. We'll figure this out. We'll figure out a way, I promise."

77

One man, looking at his dead lover, giving not a hint of the turmoil within.

Like Beradino, Patrese was professional enough to do exactly what he'd been trained to: walk the grid, record his impressions, look for anomalies. He noted that the body was in the middle of the living room, in the same hunched position—half fetus, half boxer—as the others had been. That was fire for you, he thought bitterly.

The fire had ravaged the living room, but the men with hoses, ladders, and a frankly insane amount of bravery had got to it before it could spread much farther. That had spared the kitchen, bathroom, and bedroom the worst of it, and kept the apartment more or less intact.

Kept a lot of Patrese's DNA about the place too, no doubt.

Patrese had spent years cursing the slowness of the overworked forensics system, where getting a DNA sample analyzed could take months. Now that very inefficiency was his best hope. By the time they got around to running the tests, perhaps the whole thing would be done and dusted.

His thoughts were interrupted by a commotion outside the apartment door.

"I know exactly who you are, sir," one of the uniforms was saying, "and you still can't come in."

"The fire department has declared it safe. Let me in."

Patrese knew the voice, but he couldn't immediately place it.

"Yes, sir, but this is still a crime scene, and—"

"Let me see her!"

Patrese recognized it now. The voice was that of Howard Negley—billionaire, mayor, and, most pertinently in this instance, ex-husband.

78

Neither Patrese nor Beradino was quick enough to intercept Negley before he came into the room and saw the carnage.

He took one look, groaned deep in his throat, and rushed through to the bathroom.

Whatever Negley had eaten for dinner, it was all coming straight back up again. Patrese and Beradino listened in silence as he vomited, dry-retched, moaned again, and finally flushed the john.

"That's not acceptable," Patrese said.

Beradino nodded; he knew exactly what Patrese meant.

"You gonna tell him," Patrese continued, "or shall I?"

"I'll do it."

Beradino sounded a little reluctant, Patrese thought; but it was hard to lay down the law to someone like Howard Negley, even when you were in the right.

The moment Negley emerged from the bathroom, Beradino went over to him.

"You've contaminated this crime scene from here to kingdom come," Beradino said. "Your footprints there, your performance in the bathroom." The latter rankled especially, Patrese knew; bathrooms could offer rich pickings for trace evidence. "I've a good mind to arrest you for obstruction of justice."

"That's my wife there!" Negley shouted.

Wife, Beradin[illegible] much in-
stantaneously; not *ex-wife.*

Prison divorce rates were astronomical, [illegible]
for any sentence of more than a year; they ran at something like 80 percent when the husband was incarcerated, and close to 100 percent when the wife was.

But divorce proceedings could last longer than a David Lean film. Even assuming that both parties cooperated, that there was a signed agreement covering all financial issues, that the court wasn't backed up, and that the stars were perfectly aligned, you were looking at six to nine months.

Without those conditions in place, the whole thing could take literally years, especially when rich people were involved. Poor folks never took long to divorce; half of fuck-all was fuck-all. Rich people, as F. Scott Fitzgerald had noted, were different.

Beradino and Patrese drove Negley home, and they talked on the way. It wasn't so much that they suspected him—though they each had reason to try to deflect attention from their differing clandestine involvements with Mara—as that any information from a victim's ex was welcome.

"How did you hear about this?" Beradino asked.

"Allen Chance called me. I was at dinner in town. I came straight here."

He was dressed billionaire casual: pink polo shirt beneath a golf sweater the color of cut grass, and mus-

gh to disembowel

tard slacks ... ar lady? Miss Ellenstein?”

the unwa... river took her home after dropping me

“You think she was upset you wanted to come see this scene?”

“She can be upset all she likes.”

“Okay. Now, you mind telling me how close you were to finalizing the divorce?”

Patrese was momentarily surprised at Beradino’s bluntness, then figured that Beradino was trying to get as much information out of Negley as possible while Howard was still shocked, before he composed himself properly and reverted to his usual master-of-the-universe shtick.

Besides, Negley knew he’d messed up by blundering into the crime scene. Since Beradino would be perfectly entitled to follow through on his threat to arrest him, even now, Negley probably reckoned a bit of cooperation wasn’t a bad idea.

“A couple of weeks, a month maybe,” he said.

“So pretty much a done deal?”

“Pretty much.”

“How much was the settlement?”

“It was complex.”

“That’s not what I asked.”

“You been divorced, Detective?”

“Matter of fact, I have.”

“Then you’ll know Pennsylvania’s an equitable division state.”

"I didn't have too much to divide, equitably or not."

"I'm sorry to hear that." Negley didn't sound sorry in the slightest. "But you'll remember, I'm sure, that each spouse owns the income he or she earns during the marriage, plus the right to manage any property in their sole name. But whose name's on what isn't the only deciding factor. Instead, the judge divides marital property *fairly*."

"And fair don't necessarily mean equal. I remember *that* part."

"You got it. So Mara's holding out for what she feels is fair." Neither detective corrected Negley's errant choice of tense; it was all too common in such situations. "But she and I have rather different ideas about what 'fair' is. And it doesn't help that she has no idea—*no idea*—about money. She's got this agent in LA who's been ripping her off for years, but does she do anything about it? No sir."

"You got this agent's name?"

"Guilaroff. Victor Guilaroff."

Patrese raised his eyebrows. Victor Guilaroff had been a contemporary of his at Sacred Heart. In fact, Victor's photo had been among the hundreds they'd found in Kohler's house. Small world.

"So, back to my original question," Beradino said. "How much are we talking?"

"Neighborhood of twenty million."

Patrese whistled. "That's a pretty respectable neighborhood."

"Ain't it just?" said Beradino. Then, to Howard: "And now she's dead, you hold on to everything?"

"That's right."

"You realize twenty million is reason enough for murder, least where I come from."

"And *you* realize, Detective, what proportion of my wealth twenty million represents? No? I don't wish to sound boastful, but I'll tell you: less than half of one percent. Half of one percent of *your* salary is a few hundred bucks. Would *you* kill for that?"

"I know plenty of people who've killed for much less."

But they took Negley's point. Year after year he rode high on the Forbes list, even though his philanthropy was as legendary as his earnings. He gave away more than $100 million a year—including his mayoral salary, in lieu of which he accepted a symbolic dollar—and liked to compare himself to Pittsburgh's greatest son, Andrew Carnegie. Offing his wife over relative peanuts just didn't seem likely.

"And anyway," Negley said, as though it had only just occurred to him, "I couldn't have killed her. I was at dinner in town. People saw me."

"But you're a man of influence. You could easily have arranged for someone to kill Mara, someone professional."

Howard only just avoided treating the question with the disdain they all knew it deserved. "I *could* have, Detective. But I didn't."

"Had you seen Mara since her release from jail?"

"No."

"When *did* you last see her?"

"The day she was convicted."

"You didn't go see her in prison?"

"No."

"Not once?"

"No. She'd killed my kids. Would *you* go see someone who'd killed *your* kids?"

"But you came here tonight?"

"She's dead. I wouldn't have wished that on her, even her. I wanted. . . . Listen, this is hard to express. It's very confusing."

"Care to be more specific?"

"I'm not sure I can."

"Not sure you can, or not sure you will?"

"Not sure I can. Imagine what it's like, won't you? You go through the biggest nightmare a man can have, you think it's all over, you just about get yourself back on track . . . and then everything you know gets turned on its head. So I tried not to think about it too much. It was easier that way."

"But?"

"But she was still the mother of my children. I loved her once, I really did. I . . ." He trailed off.

Smart enough to make billions, Patrese thought, but not smart enough to unravel the mysteries of the human heart. And if that sounded like criticism, it wasn't meant to be. It wasn't as though Patrese had worked too much of it out himself.

They passed the rest of the journey in silence. There was something bugging Patrese, something not quite right, though he was damned if he could work out what it was. He couldn't quite quell the stab of irrational jealousy he felt at hearing Negley talk about Mara, but he knew that wasn't what was gnawing at him.

Negley lived in Fox Chapel, six miles northeast of Pittsburgh. It would have been more surprising if he didn't. Fox Chapel is the Beverly Hills of Pittsburgh, though without the palm trees. Pretty much anyone who's anyone in Pittsburgh society lives here: the Heinzes; the Kaufmann department store dynasty; and, most importantly as far as Patrese was concerned, Rocky Bleier, former Steelers fullback and four-time Super Bowler. Fox Chapel is 95 percent white and 5 percent Asian. The only black people you see here are either domestic staff, lost, or casing joints.

They glided past ornate gates and manicured lawns: Fox Chapel Golf Club, Pittsburgh Field Club, Fox Chapel Racquet Club. Patrese remembered Groucho Marx's view on such places, and couldn't help thinking he had a point.

The only establishments more in evidence than country clubs were churches. Patrese counted a Methodist, an Episcopal, a Presbyterian, and a Lutheran, all within a couple of blocks. One way or another, he was unlikely ever to end up living here.

They pulled into Negley's drive and stopped outside the house. Beradino got out of the car and opened the rear door for Howard.

"Because you can't do it from the inside," Beradino explained. Negley might not have had to open a car door himself for many years now, but Beradino was damned if he was going to be thought of as a chauffeur.

"Thanks very much," Negley said.

He was halfway to his front door when Beradino called out, "Actually, we'd like to talk to Miss Ellenstein too."

80

Even by Fox Chapel standards, the house was something else. The floor was black-and-white checkered marble, and twin mahogany staircases curved up and around to meet each other at a gallery fifty feet above.

Ruby Ellenstein appeared at the top of the stairs. She was five four and a hundred pounds, of which at least ten were plastic; and her hair, skin, and teeth all came in shades rarely, if ever, found in nature. She and her former husband had lived in the house next door to this, and her swapping horses, as it were, had caused quite a stir in the press at the time.

"Down in a sec," she trilled.

Howard ushered them into a living room roughly the size of Heinz Field. A maid came in with coffee—no alcohol for the detectives, not while on duty—and when both master and servant had left, in walked Ruby.

This was just a chat, they emphasized. Neither she nor Howard was under any kind of suspicion. This was routine police procedure, to interview ex-partners.

She said she understood.

Beradino asked her normal, unthreatening questions to start with. Did she work? She was on a few charity boards. What were her hobbies? She liked going to the gym. What had she had for dinner tonight? Alfalfa sprouts and prune juice.

Patrese somehow stopped himself from laughing out loud at this last one.

"It must be hard," Beradino said.

"What do you mean?"

"Your situation. All the publicity, all the controversy."

Ruby opened her mouth to say something, stopped, then suddenly jumped up, ran over to the bookshelf, grabbed a paperback, ran back, and thrust it at Beradino.

"That's what it's like," she snapped. "It's all in there."

Patrese looked across at the cover. *Rebecca* by Daphne du Maurier.

He remembered the story. A young woman married an older, wealthier man, and found that his first wife—the eponymous Rebecca—still cast a pall over his life from beyond the grave.

"I'm sorry," Ruby said. "I know I should be all calm and collected about it, but you wouldn't be if you were me, and you wouldn't expect me to be, not if you know the first thing about women. She hangs over *everything*. Everybody knows the story, everybody has an opinion on what happened—on what *they think* happened—and more often than not *I'm* the interloper, *I'm* the harlot, scarlet woman, trollop, slut, whore. *I* didn't kill *my* children! She did, and suddenly *she's* Sandra bloody Dee. How did that happen? She killed her children—the worst thing any mother can ever do, bar none—and she *did*, no matter what that clever-ass lawyer and those idiot judges say."

Beradino nodded.

Harden yourself, Patrese thought. *Think without passion.*

He reckoned Ruby could only be this desperate to unburden herself if she hadn't told Howard what she really thought, for whatever reason. Anyone who felt herself heard would never have gone off like this. And Ruby never used Mara's name. It was always *she, she, she*. Never *Mara*.

"Are you glad she's dead?" Beradino said.

"Yeah. Yeah, I am. I hope she's burning in hell right now. That may not be the sensible thing to say to you guys, but it's the truth. I'm *thrilled* she's dead. I'd be even more thrilled if it felt like she was dead."

"How do you mean?"

"She's here, in this house, everywhere; every room's got something of her in it. Her being dead won't change that in the slightest."

"This was where she lived with Howard?" Patrese asked.

"Yup. It's insane that he hasn't moved. He says he won't run away from where it all happened. Like he has to face it down or something. Such a *male* thing to do. I keep on at him, can't we move, can't we move? Somewhere we can start anew, just the two of us. I don't want to stay here. It has bad memories for me too, you know."

"How come?"

"I used to live next door. That's how we got together. I wasn't getting along with my husband, and every day I'd see Howard with all the stuffing knocked out of him, that bitch in jail, his babies dead. All that money and power, they didn't matter. That's when I fell for him. It wasn't because of his money, no matter what people say. I fell for him when all his money meant nothing."

Tell it to yourself often enough, Patrese thought, *and you'll start to believe it.*

81

"What did you think?" Beradino said when they were back in the car.

"She's a piece of work, ain't she?"

"You know it."

"Whichever way you look at it, he's her meal ticket. She got him when he was low. Now she lives in fear he'll be off the moment he stops needing her support, or the moment she loses her looks."

"And he hasn't moved out of the house where his kids died. That had been me, I'd have moved like a shot. Wouldn't you?"

"Sure," Patrese said.

"So where's his motive to kill Mara? Nowhere. But for Ruby, different story."

"Mara out the way, she can try to get Howard to marry her—then she's set for life, whatever happens. She's an operator. She's one of those people who feel they owe it to themselves to be beautiful, skinny, successful, healthy; to be more than—I don't know, to be more than what we all are."

"Which is?"

"A collection of random cells. Ruby figures she can beat that. She reckons with enough aerobics, prune juice, alfalfa, and surgery, she'll live to a hundred and twenty, and by that time science might have worked out how to get her to live forever."

"Jeez Louise." Beradino shook his head at people's unending stupidity. "You eat nothing but alfalfa and prunes, you might not live to a hundred and twenty, but it'll sure feel like it."

They laughed.

"But if it is her, how does it fit in with the other murders?" Patrese said.

Beradino puffed his cheeks. "That, I don't know."

They were silent for a moment; then Patrese said: "Can I ask you something?"

"Sure."

"You asked Ruby whether she's happy that Mara's [illegible] you happy Mara's dead?"

[illegible] questioned, and [illegible] his face softened.

He nodded. "That's a fair question. And good on you, for asking it. Yes, I'm happy, because she killed those babies, and I'd have strapped her into the chair myself for that. But that doesn't mean I don't want to find the killer. I do."

"What if it was just her murder we were investigating?"

"Even then. Sure, I care about the other victims—some more than others, but that's life, even when it's death, if you know what I mean—but I care just as much about the challenge. The murder, this murder, any murder is, I don't know, an affront to my intellectual vanity. Here's the crime, here's the criminal, and he's saying, come on, gimme what you got, let's see if you're up to cracking this baby.

"All those bleeding-heart detectives on TV, they don't exist, not in real life. You know that, Franco. You know that too well. You know which TV detective I like the best? Poirot. 'Cause Poirot doesn't give a hoot. Behind his mustache and his hair lotion and his little-gray-cells, he doesn't—give—a *hoot*. It's a game to him, that's all. That's the best you can hope for from a really good cop, that he cares about the game. Nothing else. You hate blacks, Jews, gays, women, Arabs, it don't matter. City don't employ you to hold hands and be Gandhi. It employs you to catch killers.

"One of the best detectives I knew was a racist all the way through. He'd catch twelve, fifteen murderers a [illegible] victims, [illegible] him. [illegible] the father through [illegible] Not nice. [illegible] charges. It's who he was. [illegible] tell it to the marines."

"I consider my question answered."

Beradino laughed. "I'm sorry. Didn't mean to rant. But you asked."

82

TUESDAY, NOVEMBER 23

It was past one in the morning when Beradino finally got home.

He hoped Patrese had noticed nothing abnormal about his behavior earlier. That business with Negley contaminating the scene had almost caught him out—he'd usually have been on something like that in a flash—but he figured he'd covered up his hesitation well enough. Surely he could be excused for acting a little oddly around this particular murder scene, given his history with Mara and her babies?

And now he had to sort things out with Jesslyn.

Half of him was dreading the confrontation; the other half wanted to get it over with. Even without it, he'd probably get little or no sleep tonight. He always found it hard to rest in the immediate aftermath of being called to a homicide. If you saw the carnage that resulted from one human killing another, and you then slept like the dead yourself, there was something not quite right with you.

He stopped the car in the parking lot outside the building where he and Jesslyn shared a condo. Looking up at their windows, he saw that all the lights were off. There wasn't even the faint curtain-diffused glow of a bedside lamp.

That was strange. Sure, it was late, but after everything that had happened tonight, Jesslyn was surely still awake.

Unless . . .

No, Beradino told himself firmly. *No.* She was a fierce Christian and believed suicide was the ultimate sin. There was no way she'd take her own life, no matter how extreme the circumstances. Absolutely no way.

So why were the lights off?

Maybe she wasn't home.

Come to think of it, he hadn't seen Jesslyn's silver Camry in the parking lot; but then again, he hadn't *not* seen it. He hadn't looked specifically for it. It could easily have been there, and he just hadn't noticed.

Still, if she wasn't home, where would she have gone?

He had no idea.

Or what if she *was* home, but wanted him to think that she wasn't?

Possible; but why?

The answer came pretty much simultaneously with the question. Because Beradino was the only one who knew Jesslyn had killed Mara.

Which made him a target.

Darkened house. Target. Ambush.

He pulled his gun from its holster.

Jesslyn had been incoherent on the phone with him earlier. Panicked, confused, angry, scared . . . she was all these, and any of them could make her lash out. He was bigger and stronger. The element of surprise was all she had. He had to be on guard.

On the landing outside the condo's front door, Beradino scooted silently across the carpet, low to the ground in case Jesslyn was watching through the fish-eye spy hole.

Still crouching, he pushed against the door with a splayed hand.

Shut.

Slowly he pulled his house keys from his fingers spaced between the keys to keep them from jangling against each other.

He found the one for this door, inserted it very slowly in the lock, and turned till he felt the resistance from the tumblers stop.

Absurd, he thought, to be behaving like this outside his own front door.

Beradino tensed, took a deep breath, and flung himself against the door as hard as he could, his momentum taking him forward and down into the room, rolling instantly away from the door with his gun held out in front of him, sighting down the barrel, looking for movement in the dark reaches of the room beyond the pale puddle of light from the hall.

Nothing. No one.

He clambered to his feet and switched the light on.

The room was empty.

He went through the condo fast, checking each room as he'd done a thousand times before on police raids. Empty, empty, empty. No Jesslyn hanging from the shower rod, coming at him with a carving knife, or crouched, shivering tears in the corner.

No Jesslyn at all.

He opened her closets. Half her clothes were gone, as were her toiletries and a couple of suitcases. No sign of her handbag, keys, or phone.

He dialed her cell, and was put straight through to voicemail.

"It's me," he said, hardly waiting for the tone. "You're

ve gone. Call me. Come back. Whatever you think you're doing . . . you can't do it this way, Jesslyn. You just can't. I said we'll sort it out, and we will. But you have to trust me."

He ended the call and wiped his hand across his face.

It was going to be a long night.

83

Long before the first pinking of dawn, Beradino gave up on any prospect of slumber and drove back to the North Shore. He was in good company there, since police headquarters never really sleep. Even on the graveyard shift, when the place is almost empty and most of the people who *are* there move with the deliberate slowness of deep-sea divers, there's no escaping the purposeful, remorseless electronic hum of the platoons of machinery that reduce faces to pixels and individual lives to number strings, but without which the world no longer runs.

It was to this endless network that Beradino now turned.

He requested details of Jesslyn's bank balance and notifications whenever her car was spotted or she used any kind of bank card. To ensure that these alerts went to him and him alone, Beradino assigned them to a case number from the previous year: a homicide in Beltzhoover that remained unsolved but was no longer under active investigation. That way, anything that came in about Jesslyn wouldn't form part of the current inquiry.

The bank information came back inside fifteen minutes. Jesslyn had withdrawn her daily limit of $500 twice in the previous twelve hours: first at an ATM in Allegheny Center, 9:32 last night; and then at an ATM in Punxsutawney, 12:02 this morning.

By now, several hours later, she could be anywhere.

Beradino knew he could still come forward and report what had happened. They'd initiate a statewide, even a nationwide, manhunt for Jesslyn, and a dime to a dollar said they'd have her in custody by the weekend.

That was the sensible thing to do; he knew that. But he knew too that once her name was out, once it was known she was 100 miles and running, she'd never get a fair hearing; not from the cops, not from the public, not from the jurors. Manhunt meant guilty, end of.

Keep this hidden now, and there was no going back. This was his last, best chance. If he didn't take that chance and he was found out, he'd never be able to explain his way out of it. So every moment he waited both reinforced and compounded the lie.

It wasn't a contest. Not really. Not when it was someone you loved. Beradino didn't want to be alone again. He knew there was nothing greater than love, because he knew too how vast and cold was the darkness beyond love.

Beradino walked into the incident room and surveyed the handful of uniforms who'd been manning the phones during the night shift.

He needed alternatives. He needed to keep the pressure on Mustafa Bayoumi as an entirely credible prime suspect, front and center. He needed Freddie Hellmore as a solid backup. Hellmore's connection with the other three victims was nothing compared to his connection with Mara, which meant Hellmore was a valid target for investigation now, no question.

Use it. Use it all. Anything to run interference for Jesslyn.

"Right," Beradino said. "What have you got for me?"

84

If Lockwood had found that performing an autopsy on a woman whom his testimony had once helped convict was in any way strange, unsettling, or simply poetic justice, he made no hint of it in his report. Nor did that report tell Patrese and Beradino anything they hadn't seen in the three previous cases. Mara had been burned alive. Like Redwine and Kohler, but unlike Yuricich, her tongue was intact at the time of death.

Nor did the detectives claim much joy elsewhere. Beradino said he'd already asked Jesslyn whether there could be a connection between Mara's murder and anything that had happened during Mara's incarceration in Muncy, and been assured there couldn't; Mara had been a model prisoner. No beefs, no conflicts, no revenge.

Mustafa Bayoumi had been home all the previous

evening, as he was most nights of the week. Increasingly, it seemed his Saturday night excursions were the start and end of his social life.

"But we keep the Islamic angle in mind," Beradino told the morning progress meeting. "Mara was Jewish, remember. Maybe that makes her just as obvious a target as Kohler and Yuricich; you know, men who were defenders of the Christian faith."

"And maybe we should have thought of that earlier," Patrese said.

"How so?"

"Well, it's not exactly news that Jews and Muslims don't get along, is it?"

"Then maybe *you* should have suggested that before, Franco, rather than being a smart-aleck Monday morning quarterback."

Beradino regretted the words, and the tone in which he'd spoken them, the moment they were out of his mouth. The uniforms were staring at him in surprise, as was Patrese. Beradino never lost his cool; never. That was one of his hallmarks.

"Sorry," he said. "I didn't mean it to come out that way. Sorry, Franco." Patrese raised a hand; *fuhgedaboudit.* "This whole case is getting to me, I guess. Yes, you should have thought about it earlier, but that goes for all of us."

"Even if we had jumped to it, what could we have done?" Patrese said, helping Beradino save face. "Protect every Jew in Pittsburgh? Even every prominent Jew? Of course not. We don't have the manpower. Mara Slinger didn't do anything to piss the Muslims off especially, far as we know, apart from being Jewish. And it's hardly as though the killer's gonna go after Seinfeld and Woody Allen next, is it?"

That got a laugh.

"Okay," Beradino said. "What if we're right about the Islamic connection in the other three murders, but not this one? What if this is a copycat?"

"It can't be. Forensics found two pieces of pink granite, same as before. Copycats don't know about the stones," Patrese pointed out.

"They don't know *officially*; it ain't been in the press. But think of all those who actually know about the stones." Beradino ticked the groups off on his fingers. "Everyone in this room, plus half the rest of the building. Guys at the Bureau. Geology guys at Pitt. Say even one of them has a few beers, has a big mouth, tells his buddies about it—and you know it happens, no matter it ain't supposed to. Those buddies tell other buddies. Sooner or later, it comes to some wacko who wants to get rid of Mara. He thinks if he makes it look like part of this series, it won't point the finger at him. He gets some accelerant and a couple of stones—Wheelwright said pink granite's very common. . . ."

A few of the uniforms were looking skeptical. Beradino couldn't blame them. He was fishing. He knew it, and they knew it, though of course they didn't know why.

"The stones come from the Middle East," Patrese said. "Not the nearest shop."

"So we get Wheelwright to test these, just like the others. In the meantime, we keep an open mind, yeah?"

Anything to keep the hounds from Jesslyn.

There was a knock at the door.

"Come."

Summer McBride, one of the forensic analysts, appeared.

Blond and almost always smiling, she was well named, though sometimes the summer in question seemed to be hurricane season. She could be fearsomely feisty, especially to those who dared suggest that computer technology was making human fingerprint analysts increasingly redundant.

"Got quite a lot," she said. "Too much fire damage in the living room, but in the rest of the apartment, no problem. At least four sets of prints, one of them Mara's."

"How do you know?" Beradino said.

"How do I know what?"

"How do you know one of them was Mara's? Her hands were burned to a crisp."

"I cross-reffed to the prints taken when she was arrested for killing her children."

Beradino nodded approval; smart work.

Summer continued, "The other three sets remain unknown. I've put them in IAFIS to see if there are any matches."

IAFIS was the FBI's Integrated Automated Fingerprint Identification System. The largest biometric database in the world, it was the civil libertarians' bête noire.

Beradino didn't know whether Jesslyn's prints would be in IAFIS. She didn't have a criminal record, that was for sure, but he wasn't certain whether she'd been required to give them in her capacity as a state employee. He seemed to recall a big brouhaha over the issue, and a lot of jumping around about constitutional rights and all that; but he couldn't remember which way the decision had fallen.

"And get this," Summer added. "The other sets, the ones that weren't Mara's? All three were in the kitchen and the bathroom—but only one of them was in the bedroom."

She looked around the room, smiling as they all worked out the implication.

"Mara had a lover?" Beradino's tone suggested that a cure for cancer was more likely.

"She had at least three visitors," Patrese said. Forensic analysts rarely offered suppositions. They regarded their task as simply finding the dots. It was up to the detectives to connect them.

"One of whom looks to have been a lover."

"And one of whom looks to have been a killer," Patrese added.

Beradino looked at him. "Unless lover and killer are the same person."

85

The crowd outside Mara's apartment was growing with every hour that passed following the announcement of her murder. By midmorning, there looked to be around a thousand people out front. Some were making shrines to her, candles glowing softly like votive offerings in front of makeshift photographic triptychs. Others held placards marked BABY-KILLER. In death, as in life, Mara divided opinion.

One of the uniforms was up on the roof of the apartment building, filming the crowd down below. The police had done this for the other murders as well. Killers sometimes returned to the scene of their crime; arsonists often did.

The footage was relayed back via video link to monitors in headquarters, where Patrese and Beradino watched in real time.

In every crowd there's the drunk, the clown, the troublemaker, the junkie, and the fool. They were all represented here, and in multiples.

There was a sound link too, though the officer doing the filming didn't say a word. This was the professional—and the unusual—thing to do. Films like this had to be handed over to the defense if proceedings ever made it to trial, and it didn't look good if the cameraman decided to grade the women out of ten, crack unfunny jokes, or break wind. All three had happened in cases Patrese had worked on.

Berlin was running a face recognition program on the footage. He'd hijacked a copy of the newest software a few months ago and had to be dragged away from using it at every opportunity. He'd once spent three-quarters of a Pirates game filming the crowd at PNC Park, and pronounced himself thrilled when the computer managed to identify more than fifty convicted criminals in the crowd.

Surprised? he'd asked. Only that there weren't more, Patrese had replied.

Not that computer face recognition was perfect. It was pretty good at full frontal faces and anything up to twenty degrees off, but beyond that, farther toward profile, it was hit and miss. The good old human brain and eye combination was much better.

Which was how Patrese came to recognize, standing right in the middle of the crowd and wailing loud enough to have been part of Bob Marley's backup band, a man with eyeglasses and a fat face.

Alika Manuwai. Mara's lovelorn Hawaiian stalker. The one who'd attached photos of himself to his letters. The one Honolulu PD had described as harmless.

Patrese thought fast. Manuwai lived in Hawaii. Mara had been killed around twelve hours ago. Factor in a couple of hours before her death was officially announced, the scarcity of late-night flights, the time spent waiting for connections . . .

If Manuwai had managed to get from Hawaii to Pittsburgh in that time, he deserved his own superhero movie franchise.

Which meant he must have been in Pittsburgh already. Before Mara was killed.

86

Three uniforms lifted Manuwai from the crowd without trouble. He seemed almost pleased to see them, though not as pleased as some of the rubberneckers nearby. Manuwai's caterwauling had obviously been getting on their nerves. Italian mamas at funerals cried and carried on less than he'd been doing.

Real or feigned, Manuwai's distress by itself meant nothing. He could easily have killed Mara before being overcome by grief. Cops saw it all the time, people who murdered their loved ones in red rage and only afterward realized the enormity of what they'd done.

Okay, Manuwai and Mara had hardly been loved ones in the conventional sense; but if his letters were anything to go by, there was no doubting the veracity of his feelings for her—or the tenuousness of his grip on reality.

The uniforms frisked Manuwai, of course. If they found drugs, they'd tell Patrese and Beradino, who could use it as a bargaining chip for information later on. Not that the uniforms had any reason to suspect drugs; so, if it came down to it, they'd claim they'd frisked Manuwai for officer safety, in case he'd been carrying a concealed weapon. Anything else would have violated his constitutional rights.

Then they slung him in the back of a cruiser, brought him into North Shore, printed him, put him in a cell, and called up the incident room squawk box.

"We got your man. Cooling his heels in one forty-nine."

"Thanks," Patrese said into the speakerphone.

"Watch out for his BO, man. Dude's got a half-life like plutonium."

Patrese laughed. "I want my suspects docile, sweet-smelling, and noncontagious, but the world's an imperfect place. One of the three will do just fine. Which one don't really matter."

The cells were in the basement, strung out on either side of a corridor. Patrese and Beradino took the elevator down.

"Gotta take a leak," Beradino said as they passed the restrooms. "See you in there."

Patrese opened the door to cell 149. The uniform had been right about Manuwai's BO, that was for sure. Place smelled like a damn farmyard.

Manuwai was sitting on the cot. He looked up at Patrese, and his eyes widened.

"I know you," he blurted, and then tried to choke back the words, as if he'd said something he shouldn't have.

Patrese was about to assure Manuwai he *didn't* know him when he caught sight of Manuwai's left hand; or, more precisely, what was on it.

A plaster cast.

87

Manuwai started gabbling, the same Creole pidgin in which he'd written his letters to Mara, now spattered out in rapid, machine-gun syllables.

"Oh man, I sorry. I sorry for hittin' ya, I wasn't sleepin' in so long, and you know I love her, fo sure, she an angel on dis earth and now she in heaven and I go kill myself to be with her again, she sent from Holy God above to suffer and save us all, ya know? Ya a good man, sir, ya a lucky man fo goin' with her, of course it don' mean nothin', you nothin' fo her, she jus' waitin' fo me, but . . ."

Patrese was hardly listening. He was thinking fast, knowing he had to get it right first up. Beradino would be here inside a minute, and in that time Patrese had to do two things: first, persuade Manuwai—simple, deluded, possibly mildly retarded Alika Manuwai—to keep quiet about Patrese's sleeping with Mara; second, not to let Manuwai know how important this was to Patrese.

"Alika, shut up."

"I jus' tellin' ya—"

"No. Listen to me, 'cause I want to help you."

"Ya do?"

"Yes. *I* do. But my colleague won't. You're in big trouble, you know. I could have you up for assault and for breaking your restraining order like *this.*" Patrese snapped his fingers. "Combine the two, you're looking at fifteen to twenty, easy. But I don't care too much about that. What I *do* care about is finding out who killed Mara. You help us with that, I'll forget the assault, and see what I can do about the restraining order. But you *don't* help us, I'll bring it all down on you. You understand?"

Manuwai nodded meekly.

Patrese continued, "So if my partner, Detective Beradino, asks you what happened to your hand, you tell him you fell over. He's a real stickler for justice, you know? He finds out the truth, he might decide to press charges himself. Then you're screwed."

Manuwai nodded again.

"Good man," Patrese said.

Beradino appeared at the door. "We ready?"

88

They took the smallest and barest interview room available. This is standard practice. Most detectives like the following: a room with as little space and as few distractions as possible; chairs with no arms to prevent the suspect from getting too comfortable; two detectives there, one talking, one listening; and no table, so they can get close to the suspect, invade his personal space, unsettle him.

"I'll start off," Beradino said sotto voce as Manuwai sat down.

Patrese nodded. Beradino had made his name as a closer, a detective who could close cases by getting the suspect to confess. Some detectives excelled at canvassing, some at forensics, some at finding those who didn't want to be found. Beradino's forte had always been interviewing.

So he'd do the talking; Patrese would listen, take notes, and watch for things Beradino missed. Even someone as good as Beradino found it hard to ask questions *and* get every last detail of a suspect's reactions at the same time.

What Beradino wanted above all from Manuwai was, of course, a confession to Mara's murder, if only to buy him enough time to find Jesslyn.

What Beradino asked, to put Manuwai at ease, was: "You like Pittsburgh?"

"Neat," Manuwai said. "Neat, da city."

"Really? You think it's a dive, you can say, I won't be offended. Franco here, he loves the place, loves it so much he should get paid by the tourist board; but me, I can take it or leave it. What you been up to here?"

"I try fo tink."

"You have to *think* to remember what you did a few hours ago? Come on, man. Your memory's not allowed to be that bad till you get to my age."

Manuwai laughed. "I wen walk round town."

"Where did you go?"

"All round."

"Like where?"

"Er—da Strip. I wen go da Strip."

"What did you do there?"

"I wen chill, man."

Beradino gestured at Manuwai's cast. "How did you do that?"

Manuwai looked at Patrese. Patrese did his best to remain expressionless.

"You don't need Detective Patrese to tell you how you got a plaster cast, I'm sure," Beradino said. "How did you do it?"

Manuwai looked back at Beradino. "I wen fell over."

"How did you do that?"

"Tripped. Too much fo drink, you know?"

"Here? In Pittsburgh?"

"No. Honolulu."

"What were you doing at the Strip?"

"I wen chill, man."

"Where did you go? You remember the names? Bars? Clubs?"

Manuwai thought for a moment, then shook his head. "Jus' places."

Beradino leaned forward and touched Manuwai's knee. As any suspicious wife knows, it's much harder to lie to someone who's touching you.

"Dis importen', ay?" Beradino said.

Patrese almost shook his head in admiration. Beradino was mimicking Manuwai's speech pattern without seeming to be disrespectful. It was a tricky balancing act; Patrese knew he couldn't have pulled it off.

"I know, cuz."

"And we know you weren't at the Strip. *You* know you weren't at the Strip. You came to Pittsburgh to see Mara, and you were outside her house. You can help us here, Alika." Beradino lowered his tone, making Manuwai lean closer to hear him; bonding them by proximity, if not by intimacy. "Tell us what happened. Tell us what you did."

Beradino didn't use the word *murder* or anything like it. Those are very final terms, and suggest to even the densest suspect that there's little way out.

Patrese winced. Accusing Manuwai of killing Mara would make him defensive.

"Honest fo God, I neva done one ting."

Beradino kept his head bowed as he listened, as

though he were priest to a penitent. He was too much of a pro to show an iota of what he was thinking, though both Beradino and Patrese knew Manuwai was lying. The moment a suspect says "honest to God" or anything like that—"honestly," "frankly," "sincerely," "believe me," "I'm not kidding," "would I lie to you?"—it's a sure sign he's as shifty as Dick Nixon.

"You know the story of Pinocchio, Alika?"

Manuwai smiled, the child in him surfacing. "Fo sure."

"You know how his nose grows when he's lying? Turns out it ain't fiction. When people lie, the stress makes blood flow to their extremities. Your nose grows. So does your johnson. Want us to pull down your pants and see if you're messing with us?"

Manuwai giggled. "No, man."

"You think this a game?" Beradino barked suddenly.

Manuwai's head jerked up, his eyes wide with shock. Patrese's were too. Even if this was for effect, it was very unlike Beradino. That was twice in a few hours he'd lost it.

"You think this is *funny*? Tell you what—you wanna have fun, I'll go and call the Operator. You ever heard of him? No? He's a big guy around here. You know why he's called the Operator?" Manuwai shook his head, tears springing from wide eyes. "'Cause he likes phones, that's why. It's good to talk, he says. You wanna know what he'll do to you? First he'll slam a phone book on your head, over and over. Hurts like heck, but doesn't bruise the scalp. You know what that means? *Do you?* It means no one'll believe you when you tell 'em what happened. Then the Operator—he's only just getting into his stride now—next thing he does, he gets one of those old-style crank telephones, you know? They generate electricity when they're wound up. He runs some naked wires out the back of the phone. He puts some on your face, some on your balls. Then he tells you he's gonna make a long-distance call. A hundred bucks says you'll be squealing you killed her before he dials the number. And you know what? Sometimes he dials anyway, just for the heck of it. I'll go get him now."

Beradino pushed his chair back and started for the door.

Through his gulping tears, Manuwai shouted: "I neva kill her, but I see who did."

89

Beradino turned around slowly, and retook his seat at half-pace; trying not so much to intimidate Manuwai as to give himself time to think.

"You were in her apartment?" he asked at length.

"No. Neva."

"You ever try to get in, see her?"

"Neva. Neva, neva. Dat her place. She entitled to her privacy."

Beradino nodded. Restraining order or not, he could tell that Manuwai was way too immature to have approached Mara directly. His passion for Mara was almost certainly genuine, but must have been based on such an artificial construct—movie star, tragic mother, brave victim, stoic sufferer, vindicated heroine—that at the deepest level, he wasn't even interested in who Mara had really been.

"Where were you, then?"

"On da avenue. Riverview Avenue."

"Outside her apartment building?"

"Not quite. Up da street a bit, on da other side."

Keep talking around the issue. If he gets too near to implicating Jesslyn, there might be time to steer him away.

"You didn't want to make yourself too obvious?"

"Dat right."

"Because of the restraining order?"

"Dat right."

"You were on foot, or in a car?"

"Both. I rent car and sit in it. Sometime I go to park."

"Park? Park the car?"

"No. Park, at da end of da street. Wit' da absurdity."

"Absurdity?"

"You know. Big white ting. To watch stars."

"Observatory."

"Dat's what I say."

Beradino smiled thinly. "What were you doing in the park?"

"Walkin' round. Stretch da legs. Fresh air, ya know?"

It would also have done Manuwai no harm to move around like that. If he'd sat too long in the car at any one stretch, one of the neighbors would eventually have seen him and called the police.

"How long had you been outside the apartment?"

"I come over last week. Monday."

"Eight days ago?"

"Dat right."

"You come over often?"

"Time and money. When I have both, I come."

Patrese opened his mouth as though to say something. Beradino reckoned Patrese was wondering why he was beating around the bush this way.

He had to ask Manuwai directly. To delay any further would look suspicious.

"So," Beradino said, "last night. You saw the man who killed her?"

It was a leading question, of course, with the implicit assumption that Mara's killer was male. That was the best Beradino could do. And if Manuwai said Mara's killer was a woman, Beradino would be sunk.

It felt to Beradino as if empires could have risen and fallen in the time before Manuwai answered, though he knew it was probably less than a second.

Manuwai shook his head. "Did na see him."

Beradino blinked quickly; relief.

Manuwai, worried this might not constitute sufficient "help," looked imploringly at Patrese. Patrese nodded as encouragingly as he could.

"You told us a few minutes back that you *did* see him," Beradino said.

"I see his car."

Lord have mercy, Beradino thought.

"What kind of car?"

Manuwai smiled, eager to please. "Toyota Camry. Silver."

Beradino kept his face pluperfectly blank. "You're sure?"

"Sure. I like cars. Wanna Corvette one day. Wanna Z06, yellow."

"You didn't catch the license plate?"

"No. I sorry."

"How come you saw the car, but not the driver?"

"I wen go take leak, 'cause I drink too much coffee. Whole thermos, ya know. Keep me warm, keep me wake. Make me go pipi. I come back, silver Camry's there, right outside apartment. I wait a bit. Den I hungry, so I go get eat. I come back, car gone. Den I see da fire, so I dial nine-one-one."

"You were the one who called it in?"

"Sure. She dying in dere. But dey get dere too late. An she dead. It not right."

Beradino gestured with his head to Patrese: *outside.* They stepped into the corridor.

"He seems on the level," Beradino said.

"I think so."

"You know the Camry's the most popular car in America?"

"Is it?"

"Read it the other day. Sell half a million a year. And silver's one of the most common colors for any car. Some booyah about good resale value."

"So looking for a specific silver Camry's gonna be like trying to find a particular yellow cab in New York City?"

"You got it."

"Well, it is what it is. What do we do with him?" Patrese asked.

"We could bust him for breaking the restraining order, but . . ."

"But what's the point?"

"Exactly. She's dead. He's not going to harm her now, is he?"

The quicker Beradino got Manuwai away from Pittsburgh, of course, the less likely he was to pipe up and remember anything that might point to Jesslyn's involvement. And Patrese had to fulfill his half of the bargain he'd struck with Manuwai.

Letting Manuwai off suited them both, even if each knew only the half of it.

Patrese pulled out his cell and called Summer McBride's extension.

"Hey," she said. "You want his print results?" They'd sent Manuwai's prints up to her for comparison against those she'd found in Mara's apartment.

"No, I just called to hear your voice."

"Flattery will get you everywhere."

"That's what people keep telling me. Yes, print results, please."

"No match. Unless he wore gloves the whole time, he wasn't in there."

"Thanks."

"No problem. By the way, the tests came back on that pill."

"Yeah?"

"MDMA."

"You're sure?"

"I popped it myself, and felt love for everyone. Even you."

Patrese laughed. "Very scientific. Thanks, Sums."

Patrese ended the call and went back into the interview room.

"Dere gonna be funeral fo her?" Manuwai said. "I like fo go."

"Go back to Honolulu, Alika," Patrese said, not unkindly. "Find someone real."

90

Hellmore seemed neither especially surprised nor especially pleased to see them.

"Detectives," he said, not looking up from the papers through which he was sorting. "I wondered how long it would be. You're wasting your time, of course."

"Why don't you let us be the judge of that?" Beradino said.

"As you please." Hellmore gave them his best shit-eating grin, bounced the papers into order, and steepled his fingers under his chin. "Fire away."

"You have a connection with all four victims."

"Yes."

"An increasingly close one, it seems."

"Excuse me?"

"Each victim, each successive victim, has a deeper, er, *association* with you than the one before. Michael Redwine, you live in the same condo building, but you don't know each other. Gregory Kohler, you sit on the board of the Fifty-Fifty together. Philip Yuricich, you've had plenty of run-ins with over the years. And now Mara Slinger. Of all your clients, perhaps the most famous—should I say, *infamous*—of them all."

"Nothing I can disagree with so far."

"For all four deaths, you have no solid alibi. You were home alone for Redwine's. You left a dinner in time to have killed Kohler. You could have killed Yuricich before attending court. And yesterday, according to your secretary, you were en route back from Harrisburg."

"Suing the state government."

"But we checked the trip distance against traffic conditions yesterday, and factored in the time of death the pathologist has given us for Mara, and the two match."

"No."

"Excuse me?"

"The two don't *match. Match* implies that *x* plus *y* definitely equals *z*. That's not the case here. The fact that I *could* have killed Mara doesn't mean I *did*. Same with the others."

"Then it's a hell of a coincidence. And I don't believe in coincidences."

"It's not a coincidence. It's just a pattern you haven't found yet."

Patrese sensed rather than saw Beradino stiffen. Criticism of his work was pretty much guaranteed to rile Beradino.

"You don't seem very upset about Mara's death," Beradino said after a pause.

"Of course I'm upset. But I know what *you* thought of Mara, Detective, and I know what you think of me, so I'm damned if I'm going to give you the satisfaction of showing you that I care. Mara and I went through a lot together. I grieve for that, I grieve for her, but I grieve in my own way and in my own time, and you of all people have no right to tell me otherwise."

"Fine words. But you're a lawyer, so you'll forgive me if my first instinct is to treat whatever you're saying as moonshine. Give me one reason why I shouldn't arrest you right now."

Hellmore gave a snort-laugh. "Never ask a lawyer to give you one reason. We're congenitally incapable of it. The more reasons we give, the more hours we can bill."

"You can't bill for this."

"Damn straight. So I *will* give you just one reason, as you asked. You shouldn't arrest me right now 'cause you don't have probable cause."

"You don't call four victims with increasing links to you probable cause?"

"No, I don't. Because I have no *motive*, and you know that damn well. The only one of those four who'd done anything to piss me off was Yuricich, and you already know that I'd have paid to keep the son of a bitch alive so I could nail his ass. I didn't even know Redwine. I had no beef with Mara or Kohler. I have no history of mental illness, no history of violence. I haven't been through any major trauma lately. And I'm black. Serial killers rarely cross race lines, right? So all the things you must be looking for in your killer's background, none of them apply to me."

"There's still your links with the victims. Can you explain that?"

"No, I can't. And get this. *I don't have to.* The burden

of proof is on you. You find some proper evidence—you find something to show I was at any of those crime scenes, you find some reason I'd have to do these things—then you're somewhere. But as things stand, you don't have probable cause, and you'd be violating my rights under the Fourth Amendment. Don't they teach these things in police academy no more? You want me to quote it to you? You have probable cause for arrest when the facts and circumstances within your knowledge and of which you have reasonably trustworthy information would lead a prudent person to believe that the arrested person had committed or was committing a crime. Probable cause to arrest must exist before the arrest is made. Evidence obtained after the arrest may not be applied retroactively in justification. *Beck versus Ohio 1964, 379 US 89.*"

"Don't patronize us."

"Then don't act like fools. You arrest me, I'll sue your asses to the seaboard and back. I'm not your killer, and you know that perfectly well. Go find who it really is."

91

TRANSCRIPT OF COVERT RECORDING,
HOME OF SAMEERA AND MUSTAFA BAYOUMI,
5:12 P.M., TUESDAY, NOVEMBER 23

(TRANSLATED FROM THE ORIGINAL ARABIC)

Sameera Bayoumi (SB): Mustafa, have you seen the news? Another burning! Have the police been in contact with you?
Mustafa Bayoumi (MB): No, I haven't seen the news. Who is it?
SB: That actress. The one who killed her babies.
MB: Mara Slinger?
SB: That's her, yes.
MB: No, nothing from the police. Maybe they've finally realized it's not me.
SB: Well, for killing those lambs, she deserves it. You remember your Koran? No soul shall bear the burden of another.* Murder must be answered by murder. "Retaliation is prescribed for you in the matter of the slain." What kind of country are we living in, Mustafa, that people do these things?
MB: Don't start that again, Mother. I have to go now, or I won't make it in time.
SB: Where are you going?
MB: The hardware store. I've got to get some stuff to put the shelves up.
SB: Oh yes, I remember. Will I see you for dinner?
MB: Of course. As always.

**Translator's footnote: According to the Koran, humans don't carry the sins of Adam and Eve, the original sin that prompted the fall of man, but only their own good and evil deeds. Therefore, the purest state a human can achieve is that of a newborn baby, who's sinless and whose heart lives in a state of complete submission to Allah.*

The prophet Muhammad said that every child is born in a state of natural inclination to worship Allah alone. Before its earthly incarnation, every human soul converses with Allah. "And whenever your Lord brings forth their offspring from the loins of the children of Adam, He calls upon them to bear witness about themselves. 'Am I not your Lord?'—to which they answer, 'Yes, indeed, we bear witness.'" Babies are born with this original pledge to Allah in their subconscious, and parents must nurture that spirituality into remembrance.

92

WEDNESDAY, NOVEMBER 24

"This is WDVE, one-oh-two point five on your FM dial."

WDVE was the city's most popular radio station, heavy on classic rock, comedy sketches, and sports news—aimed squarely and unashamedly at men under the age of thirty-five, in other words.

"You listen to this stuff?" Beradino asked in mock horror.

"Sure do, Grandpa. Some of us think music didn't end in eighteen twelve, you know."

Patrese was driving them through falling snow to the airport, from which they'd go separate directions. Patrese was heading west to LA, where he'd interview Victor Guilaroff, Mara's agent, whom Howard Negley had accused of stealing from her. Beradino was traveling south, to Mississippi. Among Mara's boxes of hate mail (which she'd kept in her bedroom, and which had therefore escaped the fire) were some from the Magnolia State that were so virulent and unrestrained that Beradino wanted to check them out himself.

That Jesslyn was originally from Mississippi, and that in the past she'd fled home more than once when upset, was of course purely a coincidence.

Both men also felt they'd benefit from a change of scene, no matter how short. They'd be away for at least a couple of days, since tomorrow was Thanksgiving. The world and his wife were traveling across America. Patrese and Beradino had both had to pull rank to get themselves on the flights today, but there was no way they'd make it back to Pittsburgh till Friday at the earliest.

Bianca had wanted Patrese to spend Thanksgiving with her and her family. He'd spent an hour on the phone to her the previous evening, pouring his heart out about Mara, trying to make sense of it all. Was it weird to be mourning a woman he'd hardly known? Was it even just the death he was mourning, or the promise of whatever they might have had together? Bianca hadn't come up with any answers, but then again she'd understood that he hadn't wanted her to. He'd simply wanted someone to listen, and women were in general much better at that than men. Men always tried to find solutions to problems; but sometimes, like when your lover'd been suddenly, brutally murdered, there were no immediate solutions, just a jagged hole where the shadows flared in the shape of a man's desire.

The only solution Patrese could think of was to find the killer; so he'd resolved to keep moving, keep driving forward, do anything he could to bring that about. If it meant being alone in a hotel room on the one day of the year when everyone was with their families, so be it. He had a cell phone; the hotel would have cable. He'd survive.

Patrese and Beradino had left a clear chain of command in the incident room, Boone had promised to lend any help he could, and of course they'd be in constant contact with both North Shore and each other.

Patrese left the Trans Am in the long-term parking lot. In the terminal, they checked into their respective flights, had coffee together, went airside, shook hands, and made for their respective gates.

Crammed onto the last spare seat in his departure lounge, between a wall and a man who spilled over into Beradino's space in cascades of drooping flesh, Beradino tried to stop his mind from racing.

He reminded himself of what he knew for sure.

He knew that Mara's murder was the first to have occurred since he'd discovered that Jesslyn had lost her job at Muncy, and that now Jesslyn was nowhere to be found.

He knew that all four murders had taken place since Jesslyn's dismissal.

He knew that Jesslyn hadn't been on shift at the burger bar when any of the first three victims were killed, since he'd obtained a copy of her records from

Kevin, the spotty, insolent manager. He'd told Kevin he needed them for a tribunal, before slipping him a hundred bucks for his trouble and another hundred for his silence.

He knew that seismic events, such as being fired, were often the trigger for people to start acting out violent and traumatic emotions that they'd previously kept hidden.

He knew that Jesslyn's views on crime and punishment were strong, inflexible, and shot through with her religious beliefs.

That was what he knew for sure.

Then there was what he *didn't* know.

He didn't know why Jesslyn had selected any of the victims bar Mara, apart from the point she'd made in her e-mail about them being hypocrites. Far as he knew, she'd never even met Redwine. She *had* met Kohler a couple of times, most recently at the funeral of Patrese's parents, and each time she'd been thrilled just to be in the presence of a real-life bishop. And Yuricich had been as convinced of Mara's guilt as Jesslyn herself was. It wasn't his fault that Mara had been freed on appeal.

He didn't know why Jesslyn had cut Yuricich's tongue out.

He didn't know what Jesslyn meant with the pink granite pebbles, or where she'd got them from.

He didn't know why Jesslyn, the most God-fearing person he'd ever met, had destroyed the crucifix and icon in Saint Paul Cathedral.

The answers, he reckoned, must lie not just in Jesslyn's obsession with Mara, but somewhere deeper, somewhere in her Baptist preacher's-kid upbringing. Find Jesslyn, and he'd find out *why.*

Finding her, however, was the problem.

93

Patrese was drenched in sweat by the time he reached Guilaroff's office at the Beverly Hills end of Wilshire Boulevard. His flight out of Pittsburgh had been delayed by snow on the runway, but Los Angeles was enjoying an unseasonable heat wave. Even late in the afternoon, the temperature was still in the mid-eighties, a thick, smothering heat beating up at Patrese from asphalt and windshields.

Patrese gave his name to the receptionist before slumping onto a sofa shaped like Mae West's lips. The air-conditioning vent was right above his head, and he shifted position slightly to get as much cold air as possible. It felt like a shower.

"Hey! Franco Patrese!"

Guilaroff came striding into the lobby, arms open wide as though he were a game-show host expecting applause. The little Patrese recalled about him from school—Patrese had been a couple of grades ahead—was of Guilaroff as a short, chubby, nondescript kind of boy. Now, fifteen or so years on, Guilaroff had turned into . . . well, a short, chubby, nondescript kind of man.

Patrese got up and put out his hand.

"Good to see you again, Victor."

"Great to see *you,* man." Guilaroff ignored the handshake and went straight for the hug. Patrese patted his shoulder with a certain bemusement. He and Guilaroff hadn't been friends at school, and they'd probably never have seen each other again had it not been for the coincidence of their respective involvements in Mara's life; yet here Guilaroff was, greeting him like the prodigal son.

"Terrible business about Mara," Guilaroff continued, untangling himself. "*Terrible* business. Help you any way I can. But listen, it's nearly five o'clock, it's Thanksgiving tomorrow, and the office ain't a place to be on a day like this. Why don't we do this thing over a brewski? I know a great little bar around the corner. Whatcha say, bubbaloo?"

Patrese thought fast. Some people were more forthcoming with the police when they were uncomfortable and disoriented; others were more prone to let things slip when they were relaxed. He reckoned that Guilaroff, used to endless meetings of bluff and brinkmanship, would fall into the second category. Besides, Patrese needed a beer badly enough to qualify for a remake of *Ice-Cold in Alex.*

"Sure," Patrese said.

94

Hollywood agents take movie stars and bigwig producers to the Polo Lounge or the Four Seasons, but they sure as hell don't take out-of-town cops there. They take them to the Coronet in West Hollywood, where the lights are low and the booth walls high.

Guilaroff clinked his bottle of Coors against Patrese's.

"So. Mara. Like I said, help you any way I can."

"What did you do for her?"

"I was her agent. I represented her."

"Which involved what?"

"Sending her scripts, pitching her to studios, negotiating her contracts, making sure she was happy with her career path, holding her hand—"

"Metaphorically or literally?"

"Strictly metaphorically. Rule one: Never fuck the client."

Like Mara would have given you the time of day, Patrese thought.

"And she paid you—what? A retainer? A salary? A commission?"

"Fifteen percent."

Patrese whistled. "Nice rate."

"I'm worth every dime, I assure you."

Patrese wasn't sure, but he thought he remembered Guilaroff as having been on the end of some nasty bullying at Sacred Heart one time; nasty enough to have gotten the police involved, let alone the school board. That kind of thing could work one of two ways. Either you let it destroy you, or you nursed the hatred, moved away, reinvented yourself, and worked toward success with a furious ambition.

"How did you get to work for her?"

"Excuse me?"

"Hey, I don't mean it as an insult. I'm just curious. How do agent and star meet?"

"Oh. Okay. The agency I work for, she was with us already. The guy handling her retired—got burned out, went to Montana, Idaho, someplace like that. I'd met her a couple of times, and she liked me."

"This was all before her court case, obviously."

"Sure."

"So you must have been young back then."

"Twenty-four years old, when I first started working with her."

"Vote of confidence in your ability."

"I guess she saw I was talented. And she liked that I was from Pittsburgh, you know? Steel Towners stick together, and all that. So there we are."

"Your fifteen percent. How does that work? When she got paid, who got the money first? Her? You? Both of you?"

"Me. The agency. Everything came to me first; that's standard."

"Then you deducted your percentage and transferred the remainder to her?"

"You got it."

"There can't have been that much coming in when she was in jail, right?"

"Not true. A lot of back-end stuff—you know, payments tied to a movie's gross—kept coming in from things she'd done earlier in her career. Complex stuff. Hollywood accounting procedures make rocket science look like the two times table."

"Would you say she was financially savvy?"

Guilaroff cocked his head slightly, trying to work out where this was going. "How do you mean?"

"I mean, you said this stuff is complex. Was she on your ass the whole time, questioning this and that about her finances, or did she just accept what you sent her?"

"She trusted me, so she knew what I sent her was correct."

Interesting, Patrese thought. That wasn't what he'd asked. He swigged his Coors.

"Her husband reckons you were ripping her off."

Guilaroff's eyes flashed wide. "Her husband's talking shit."

"You don't sound surprised to hear this."

"I'm not. He called me personally one time to tell me just that."

"How did you react?"

"I told him we had better lawyers than him, and if he wanted to find that out for sure, all he had to do was repeat it."

"And did he?"

"No."

"What would you say if I wanted to take a look at your accounts?"

Guilaroff laughed. "I'd say you're out of your jurisdiction here, you haven't got a warrant, and you probably don't know your way around a balance sheet anyway."

Asshole, Patrese thought. He kept his expression and tone neutral, though. Just two old school buddies having a beer.

"And I'd say you're right on all three. But say I could find a way around all those, what then? You'd be happy for me to look at your accounts?"

"My accounts in general, no. We deal with big stars, and they don't like people knowing how much they have. But Mara, now she's dead? Sure."

It was the smart answer, Patrese knew. It made Guilaroff look cooperative, but they both knew it would take weeks for a warrant to work its way from Pennsylvania to California, and months while Guilaroff and his lawyers used every stalling trick in their no doubt extensive playbook.

Still. Playbook meant game, and game meant tactics.

"Great. I'll get on it the moment I get home."

"When you heading back?"

"Friday. No available flights tomorrow."

"You're gonna miss Thanksgiving?"

Patrese shrugged. "Demands of the job. My family understands. Yours?"

"Mine what?"

"Your folks. They still live in Pittsburgh? You come back home a lot?"

"My folks still live there, yeah. Same old house as they ever did. But I haven't been back in, like, forever. Eight, nine years, I guess. My folks come see me here from time to time—not this year, this year they're with my sister in Michigan—but I don't go back there. Home is here, my man."

"You don't like Pittsburgh?"

Guilaroff was silent for a second. "Honestly?"

"Honestly."

"I *hate* it. Why do you think I came out here? I got sunshine, money, chicks."

"Why do you hate Pittsburgh?"

"I hate the weather. I hate the people. I hated school."

"Sacred Heart?"

Guilaroff finished his Coors and gestured to the bartender for two more.

"I wasn't like you, Franco. I remember you from school, man. First-string running back for, what, two years in a row? Three?"

"Three."

"I remember you on the grid. Whole school used to come watch, you know? Every time Sacred Heart was on offense, we didn't look for the quarterback. We looked for you."

Patrese remembered it too: the handoffs from the quarterback, the heart-pounding rush into the tunnel of bodies in midfield, ducking, weaving, muscles working faster than thought itself as he jinked toward the glimmering chinks through the darkness, run to daylight, run to daylight, as if the noise from the crowd was physically prying open the gaps in front of him, and then out onto the open prairie and the long run for home, defenders floundering in his slipstream as the crowd rose and stamped and his teammates thrust their arms skyward, *Go, Franco, go, go, go.*

Nothing else in his life had ever come close.

"I was just a nobody," Guilaroff continued. "Bet you don't even remember me from school. Before this whole thing came up?"

"Sure, I remember you."

"Really?"

"I recognized your name when I heard it. I recognized your face in the photo."

"Photo?" Guilaroff looked puzzled. "What photo?"

"The photo we found in Kohler's desk."

"No one told me about this." Guilaroff sat forward, his face flushed. "What the hell? What kind of photo?"

"You got something to hide?"

"No. No, not at all. But . . . it sounds weird. What would *you* say, if you found your photo in the desk of a man you hadn't seen for fifteen years?"

"I did."

"You did what?"

"Find my photo in his desk. And yours, and hundreds of others, kids from Sacred Heart. Normal photos, yearbook photos. Someone should have been in touch with you earlier; I'm sorry. I thought we checked out everyone involved, to see if they knew anything about his murder. You know he was murdered, right?"

"Yeah. I read about it."

"How did it make you feel?"

Guilaroff dug the heels of his hands into his eyes and rubbed hard.

"I hated that school, Franco. I was unhappy, and I got no support from anybody who should have given it to me, Kohler included. For a man of God, he sure didn't behave in an especially Christian way. So I didn't feel anything when I heard. Okay?"

"I get you."

"If you ask me, school's bullshit, deep down. Take

someone like me. Total nobody at school. Look at me now. I do well for myself, I reckon. I do more than well. What you are at school don't determine shit."

Patrese wondered what Guilaroff was implying, if anything. That it worked in reverse too? That it was a fall from grace for someone like Patrese, one of the school demigods, to be now eking out a public-sector salary as a Steel Town cop?

Guilaroff gestured around him. "You should come here too, Franco. To LA. Plenty of opportunities for a guy like you. Hollywood homicide. Beverly Hills cop. I know some guys on the force here, I could help you out. You interested?"

Patrese shook his head. "Your demons don't vanish just 'cause you run from them, Victor," he said.

95

THURSDAY, NOVEMBER 25

Beradino's life was neatly parceled into a triptych: good, nondescript, and bad.

Good was the view from his window: open roads and rows of crops marching out of Yazoo City like ants to the horizon, and the start of the Mississippi Delta.

Nondescript was his room. Typical chain motel: neat, clean, less than no soul.

Bad was pretty much everything else.

He'd trawled Yazoo City, hoping against hope that

he'd see Jesslyn walking down the street, or eating in one of the restaurants she'd taken him to on their trips here, or praying in church, or . . . or anything, really.

He'd called Jesslyn's sister, LeAnn, who lived outside the city with her husband and what seemed like a million kids. The conversation had told Beradino everything he needed to know, and nothing he'd hoped for.

"Hey, LeAnn," he'd said. "It's Mark, your brother-in-law."

"Hey, Mark! Happy Thanksgiving, honey."

"And to you."

"Bet it's cold up there in Punxsutawney, hey?"

"Matter of fact, I'm in Mississippi."

"You are? You nearby? Come on over. We got food for plenty."

Which meant Jesslyn almost certainly wasn't there. If she had been, and if she'd been lying low, LeAnn wouldn't have invited him over.

"I'm too far away, I'm afraid. I'm in McComb. Working some interstate case."

"On Thanksgiving? Hope they're giving you double time. It's not right. Not on Thanksgiving. How's my sister? She home alone? I called her earlier, but no answer. She never calls, she never writes. . . . You tell her not to forget her family, you hear? Spending all that time with those wack-jobs inside must be messin' with her head."

LeAnn was many things, but an actress, never. No way had Jesslyn got in touch with her since Monday, let alone confided in her.

Beradino had been sorely tempted to leap in the car and go over there anyway, with due regard for how long his supposed journey from McComb would have taken. Under normal circumstances, he could think of few things he'd rather do than be surrounded by love and laughter while stuffing his face—and in LeAnn's house, your face stayed stuffed, most of all on Thanksgiving, when you could hardly see over your plate once you'd taken your share of turkey, cranberry sauce, stuffing, gravy, winter squash, sweet potatoes, hominy, green bean casserole, corn bread, pumpkin pie, and pecan pie—but there was no way he could go there and pretend everything was okay.

The motel was doing a special dinner, but that was hardly the same. Besides, he'd be eating on his own, and Thanksgiving was all about family. Other diners would either pity him or invite him over, and he didn't want either.

He remembered reading somewhere that the name Yazoo was a Native American word meaning "river of death." It seemed bitterly appropriate.

96

FRIDAY, NOVEMBER 26

Patrese and Beradino met back at Pittsburgh International Airport, by the statue of Franco Harris, the Steelers' greatest-ever running back and the man after whom Patrese had been named.

Franco Harris Patrese, that was his full name, and damn proud of it he was too.

Harris—the original Harris—had in his prime looked like Othello, with fierce dark eyes and an aquiline nose. He'd had a black father and an Italian mother (they'd met in Europe at the end of the war), and as a result had been wildly popular with Pittsburgh's Italian population, some of whom had dubbed themselves "Franco's Italian Army" and worn army helmets with his number, thirty-two—the one Patrese had worn through high school and college—painted on them.

Patrese's father had been just about the biggest fan in all the Italian Army; such a fan, in fact, that the day Patrese had been born, Alberto had been not at his wife's bedside but a thousand miles away in New Orleans, watching the Steelers win their first Super Bowl and Harris be named MVP.

Waiting by the statue, Patrese thought about Harris, and football, and Pop. He thought about how Pop hadn't been there when he'd been born, and hadn't been there when Patrese had needed him most; and he thought about how the first had never bothered him, and the second always would.

They drove back into town.

"Your sister understand about you going away for Thanksgiving?" Beradino said.

"I guess. First one after our folks died, she wanted the family together, for the kids as much as anything."

"Of course. They love you, no?"

"Especially when I play the goofball for them. Long may it last. A couple of years' time, they'll be old enough to start asking why they haven't got any cousins yet."

"You want my advice?"

"Always."

"Don't get married. Not now, not ever. You know what? I used to play my wedding video backward, so I could see myself walk out of church a free man. Don't get me wrong; marriage has its good side. It teaches you loyalty, tolerance, restraint, patience, selflessness. All the things you don't need if you stay single. You wanna spend the rest of your life being nagged? All women nag. They just do. It's in their genes or something. Men talk shop, women nag. And a nag ain't just a nag."

"It isn't?"

"No way. It's an art form. My wife—this is a long time ago, mind—she had a whole heap of 'em. I can think of"—Beradino counted them off quickly on his fingers—"at least five.

"One, there's the single-subject nag: take out the trash, take out the trash, like a stuck record.

"Two, the multi-nag: you need to put up the shelves, fix the toilet, mow the grass, go to the store, fill the car with gas, and this, that, and the other.

"Three, the beneficial nag: stop drinkin' beer and eatin' cheeseburgers, 'cause they're bad for you; start eating, I dunno, tofu or some garbage, start exercising, start lookin' after yourself, 'cause they're all good for you.

"Four, the third-party nag: look at x and y, look at those guys, they earn more than you, they're in better shape than you, they have bigger houses and nicer cars than you do, why can't you be more like them?

"And five, the advance nag. This is the gold medal of nagging—to get it in even before the event you're nagging about actually happens. You believe that? This one ain't for amateurs; you have to be an experienced nagger to pull it off. Don't do this, or that'll happen. Darn, Franco. It was like *Minority Report* by the end. The day I signed the divorce papers, happiest day of my life."

"Really?"

"Really. Huge sense of failure, sure. But even huger one of relief. It felt like—I dunno. Being reborn, I guess. Starting again." He looked out the window. "But don't let me put you off."

Patrese laughed.

The road snaked through rolling hills and countryside, past outlying towns and hints of creeping urbanization, but with no sign of Pittsburgh itself. You could see Manhattan pretty much all the way in from JFK; but here, a few miles from Pittsburgh, you could be anywhere.

Then they dived down into the Fort Pitt Tunnel, drove through half a mile of claustrophobic darkness, no sense of the outside world, and *wham!* Pittsburgh in all its glory; city, skyscrapers, and bridges suddenly exploding into view as if they'd materialized from nowhere.

There was no city in America, perhaps the world, that had an entrance so thrilling. Each time Patrese came through it, it was like a rebirth.

He thought of what Beradino had just said, about being reborn after his divorce.

That was what they needed right now, Patrese suddenly realized. A rebirth, a reboot—an entirely new approach to the Human Torch. They had to accept that everything they'd assumed might be wrong.

They had to start again.

97

"Of all the victims, which one was most likely to be killed?" Patrese asked.

"What do you mean?"

"I mean, who had the most enemies?"

Beradino thought for a moment. "Mara, I guess."

"Yeah. Mara, by miles. Half the country hated her, it seems sometimes."

"So?"

"You remember when Boone first did his profile? Remember what you accused him of? You said he was making the evidence fit the theory."

"Yes, I remember."

"That's what *we've* been doing. We've been chasing Bayoumi, and Muslims, and this, that, and the other, and we've gotten *nowhere.* We've got to go back, do it the other way around. Evidence first, then theory. And which victim has the most potential evidence? Mara."

"So what do you propose to do?"

"Turn her life upside down."

"We've done that already."

"Not all of it."

"What have we missed, then?"

"Muncy." Beradino opened his mouth, but Patrese cut him off. "I know what you're going to say, but hear me out. I just thought of it, driving through the tunnel, coming up here into the city. I wondered whether that was what Mara felt when she was released. You're used to walls, darkness, no view of the outside world, and then in an instant everything's in your face, there's a million ways you can go. System overload. So I thought of Mara and Muncy, and that made me think in turn: where better to look for clues to a murder than in prison? And I know you already asked Jesslyn. But she's a guard. I bet she doesn't know a fraction of what goes on in there."

"She knows *everything*. She rules the roost there. And she said Mara was a model prisoner—never got into trouble, sat in her cell, read her scriptures, had no beef with anyone. Too much of a chicken to take on anyone who could fight back, you ask me."

"Well, double-checking can't do any harm."

"You're wasting your time, Franco."

"It's my time to waste. Let's find out what the brass *doesn't* want us to know."

"How? You want to infiltrate? You want to go undercover as an inmate? It's an all-female prison, Franco. What the heck you think this is? *Some Like It Hot*?"

"Not infiltrate."

"Then what?"

"Use someone already there."

"A prisoner?"

"Of course."

"Yeah, that'll work. 'Cause prisoners really love cops, don't they?"

"They do if we find an incentive."

98

MONDAY, NOVEMBER 29

The incentive Patrese had in mind needed both Amberin and Hellmore to okay it, so he had to wait till Monday to pitch it to them. He'd spent the weekend hanging with some of his old college buddies, watching sports, drinking beer, and telling well-worn tales that seemed to get a little taller with each airing; in other words, therapy.

Monday morning, cops and lawyers met in Amberin Zerhouni's office in the courthouse. Beradino had told Patrese several times this was a nonstarter, but Patrese was determined, and Beradino knew he couldn't keep pouring cold water on the plan without Patrese eventually getting suspicious of his motives. So Beradino went along, and hoped that either Amberin or Hellmore would nix it.

Coffee poured and cookies offered, Patrese outlined his idea.

Background first. Mara had told Patrese that she'd made one particular friend in Muncy: an inmate named Madison Setterstrom. So if there *was* a connection between these murders and something that had happened to Mara in prison, Setterstrom was the most likely person to know something about it.

Thing was, Setterstrom wouldn't tell the cops directly. Not in a month of Sundays. Beradino had pointed out that cops weren't the flavor of the month in prisons, and in Setterstrom's case they could magnify that tenfold. She was doing life for killing a cop during a convenience store robbery, and had said at the trial that her only regret was that she hadn't taken out more of the fuckers. Her exact words.

The admission had scuppered her not-guilty plea, but that was another matter.

So the cops had to get Setterstrom to talk without letting her know she was talking, as it were. The best way—perhaps the only way—was to get her to share a cell with someone who'd pry the information out of her, over a period of weeks or months if that was what it took, and then report it all back to them.

Of course, that someone would need an incentive.

That was why Patrese was here. He wanted Shaniqua Davenport to be their informant.

Shaniqua was a damn sight more intelligent than people gave her credit for, he said. She'd be good at tweezing out information without making it obvious. She could talk, exchange confidences, do all the things women did so well. The plan would never have worked in a male prison; put two men in a cell together, and two years down the line they'd still be discussing beer, football, and sex.

In return, as the carrot, the incentive, Patrese wanted Amberin to downgrade Shaniqua's charge from murder to voluntary manslaughter.

Voluntary manslaughter was the most Patrese knew he'd get. There wasn't a prosecutor in Pennsylvania—in the entire country, in fact—who'd agree to involuntary manslaughter, the next step down, in any case where a firearm had been used.

If Amberin agreed to voluntary manslaughter and Shaniqua accepted that, they'd be in business. It might all come to nothing, but at least Patrese would have tried, done something rather than just chase his tail around headquarters.

What Patrese didn't say was that downgrading the charge would also help Shaniqua, and that was the least he felt she deserved.

Amberin listened to the plan, all the way through, without saying a word.

"Absolutely not," she said when Patrese had finished.

Hellmore jumped in. "Why not?"

"We went through all the options first time around. What's changed between then and now? Nothing. So the charge stays the same."

"You've got no sympathy for Shaniqua?"

"Personally or professionally?"

"Both."

She blew her cheeks out. "Personally, yes, a little. Sounds like Weaver was a terrible man. But no one forced Shaniqua to be with him. No one held a gun to her head and said, 'You must be with this man.'"

"Well, he did. Weaver did."

"So *she* says. That's a matter for the jury. My job's to uphold the law, not be some spokeswoman for the sisterhood. So professionally, no, no sympathy. Sorry. I can't afford to."

"Can I try to persuade you?" Patrese said.

She laughed. "Sure. I'd like to see you try."

"Me too," Hellmore said. "She's a hard-ass, Franco, in case you ain't noticed."

"Okay," Patrese said. "Let's start at the beginning. Self-defense is a complete defense against any charge of murder, isn't it?"

"Yes."

"Now, I know this case isn't self-defense pure and simple."

"No."

"But isn't it also true that if a person acts in the honest but unreasonable belief that self-defense justifies the killing, then this is a deliberate homicide committed without criminal malice—in other words, manslaughter?"

"Yes."

"And that the word *malice* is used in the definition of murder where the act is both an intentional killing, and without legal excuse or mitigation?"

"Franco, you been raiding Grisham's backlist again?" Hellmore said.

"Yes," Amberin said, in answer to the original question.

"Well, that was Shaniqua's situation. She thought she had to kill Weaver to prevent him from hurting her or Trent. She was wrong, but she still held that belief honestly."

"Or she'd just had enough and thought this was an easy way out."

"It wasn't like that."

"Oh, you were *there* when it happened? It was the kind of argument Shaniqua said they'd had a million times before, if I remember rightly. She hadn't felt the need to blow Weaver's brains out on any of those occasions, had she?"

Probably not the need, Patrese thought, but almost certainly the urge.

"Come on, Amberin," said Hellmore. "You know as well as I do that women are much more likely to kill a male partner than they are to kill anyone else, especially when that partner's abusive. You know too that recidivism rates for such crimes are extraordinarily low."

"I'm not prosecuting Shaniqua on what she might do in the future, Freddie. I'm prosecuting her on what she did in the past, on what she's done already."

"I know that. But look at it from her point of view."

"That's your job, not mine."

"Damn it, Amberin," Patrese snapped.

She rounded on him, eyes wide with fury. "Don't you *dare* talk to me like that."

"Then *listen.* What happened in that bedroom just before Shaniqua shot Weaver, you can't treat that like, I don't know, like an altercation in a bar between two guys who can't handle their beer. It wasn't a fair fight. She's smaller, she's weaker, she's scared for her son. She *can't* walk away."

"She could call the police."

"In Homewood? On a domestic violence charge? Would you? Ghostbusters would come quicker, let's face it."

Amberin was silent. Patrese and Hellmore exchanged glances; first blood to their cause? Patrese hurried on, anxious not to lose momentum.

"So what's Shaniqua supposed to do? Wait till he hits her again? Or *stabs* her? Or *shoots* her? She does any of those, and all she's agreeing to is murder by installment. Her murder, and probably her son's too, if he's a witness. So we come back to the start. Was Shaniqua's fear of Weaver correct? On this occasion, probably not. But was it *reasonable*? Yes. And that's what matters. That's what matters in law, isn't it?"

She was silent. Wavering, Patrese felt—he *hoped.*

He'd done the heartstrings. Hellmore weighed in with the pragmatics.

"Come on, Amberin. We both want to maximize our opportunities here. You can't be sure a murder charge'll be sound, can you? But a manslaughter charge will stick, I bet you that. And I'll take voluntary manslaughter like a shot, you know that. You've got a good conviction rate. You want to jeopardize that?"

Another pause, and then Amberin smiled. "Franco, you should be a lawyer."

"I'm presuming that's a compliment."

She laughed. "I guess it's normally the most heinous of insults—sort of like 'You should be a realtor' or 'You should be a politician'—but in this instance, yes, it *is* meant as a compliment. All right. I'll do it. I hope it works out for you."

Beradino's face wouldn't have shamed a veteran of Texas Hold'em.

99

TUESDAY, NOVEMBER 30

Patrese went to Muncy alone. It was both his choice—he figured his chances of persuading Shaniqua were better on his own, as he reckoned he'd had something of a rapport with her—and Beradino's. Beradino had said he'd had a few run-ins over Jesslyn's pay scale with Anderson Thornhill, the prison superintendent, and would therefore prefer it if Patrese didn't mention his name. Best to keep Beradino and Jesslyn out of his altogether, they'd agreed.

Beradino had asked before he left whether Patrese had the hots for Shaniqua too. What was it with Patrese? Did he have to hit on every woman he met? Was he trying to prove something?

There was no answer to that—or rather, there was an answer, but it was long and complex, and Patrese didn't think Beradino was necessarily the right person to hear it.

The journey to Muncy was almost all interstate, and Patrese had his brain as well as his car on cruise control as the signs rolled past the windows: I-79 North, I-80 East, I-180 West, Route 405 South. All four compass points. He found that oddly pleasing.

The final road into Muncy, lined with maple trees, was unexpectedly, disarmingly tranquil. The limestone administrative building, all faded charm and white cupola, could have been the heart of a small rural college;

not an Ivy League hothouse, perhaps, but somewhere in the second or third rank, where the pace of life was gentler and the students probably much more content.

Patrese parked in the parking lot, where he could see things that shattered the illusion—things like fences, razor wire, security cameras, even searchlights.

His status as a police officer didn't exempt him from the usual searches, which in an odd way reassured him. Visitors were searched not just to stop them from deliberately bringing in contraband, but also to be sure they had nothing on their persons that could be used as weapons if they were taken hostage.

So Patrese surrendered his Ruger Blackhawk, his keys, the change in his pocket, his cell phone and what seemed like half the accoutrements without which he, along with 99 percent of his fellow Americans, couldn't get from dawn to dusk and back again.

Thornhill was a thin man with eyeglasses and a studious air who appeared much more suited to the college campus of Patrese's alternative Muncy than the realities of a state correctional institution. He wasn't especially happy about Patrese's request, though this seemed to be more resentment at police interference than any great concern that Patrese might disrupt the running of the prison.

Patrese understood Thornhill's attitude, and didn't hold it against him. Most police officers would be similarly ambivalent if a prison superintendent marched into *their* office and started trying to shift *their* personnel around.

Thornhill made some noises about the difficulty of

housing a remand prisoner like Shaniqua with a convicted killer such as Setterstrom, but found a solution to this in the very next sentence. Prisoners were always being moved, sometimes for their own safety, sometimes through sheer weight of numbers. The authorities could think up several plausible excuses for unlikely pairings.

Curiously, perhaps, Thornhill didn't want to know *why* Patrese wanted Shaniqua moved. Perhaps he'd guessed. Perhaps he simply preferred not to get involved, and figured that Patrese must have decent reasons if he was asking in the first place. If Shaniqua agreed to it, he said, that was fine with him. Patrese wondered whether Thornhill was this hands-off in all aspects of his superintendence. Maybe all those women cooped up together frightened him.

Patrese met Shaniqua in the visitors' room. It took him a moment to recognize her. It wasn't her features that had changed, but her expression: a wariness to the set of her jaw, a deadness in her eyes. Three and a half decades in the ghetto hadn't knocked the sparkle out of her, but a couple of months in jail had.

"My favorite detective," she said.

"What's my competition?"

She laughed. "Not great. Now, why you here? You ain't come four hours from the Burgh for the good of your health."

"I've come with an offer from the prosecutor."

Shaniqua hissed with her tongue against the back of her teeth. "The fuck that bitch offerin' me? Rat poison?"

"Plea bargain."

"Plea bargain?"

"She's prepared to downgrade your charge. If you plead guilty to voluntary manslaughter, she'll drop the murder charge."

"The fuck does that mean?"

"It means that instead of facing life behind bars, you'd be looking at four and a half to seven. You behave yourself, you'd be out earlier."

"And in return?"

He smiled. "How do you know there's an 'in return'?"

"Don't shit me, Detective. Ain't no such thing as a free lunch. Everybody here knows that. Shit, half of them are in here for tryin' to prove there *is* a free goddamn lunch, one way or the other."

"Okay. In return, we want you to get information from another inmate, and we want to put you in the same cell as her."

Shaniqua regarded Patrese levelly for a few moments.

"I know what you're thinkin'," she said.

"What am I thinking?"

"You're thinkin' I was gonna say to you straight off, fuck that, I ain't doin' that, I ain't no fuckin' snitch."

Patrese shook his head. "No. I wasn't thinking that."

"For real?"

"That's what I'd expect most people to do. But I don't think you're most people. Which is why I want you to do this."

"Well, I figure you ain't a bad guy—shit, by the standards of the police"—she pronounced it almost as two words, *poh-lease*—"you're practically Captain America. So I figure you must have a good reason for aksin' me."

"I do."

Patrese explained about Mara and Madison Setterstrom, and what they were looking for—which was to say, they didn't really *know* what they were looking for, so all they wanted Shaniqua to do was get in there, get to know Madison, don't push too hard, but try to become friends with her and get her to open up slowly, gradually, naturally, unsuspectingly. Put that way, it sounded easy. It might be anything but.

"Deal?" Patrese asked.

Shaniqua shook her head. "Uh-uh."

His shoulders slumped. "Can I ask why not?"

"Sure you can aks. I might even tell you." She laughed. "I ain't takin' no plea bargain from no one, for one simple fuckin' reason. *I didn't do it*. Not murder, not manslaughter, none of that. It was self-defense, end of. That's what happened, that's what I'm pleadin'." She held her hand up. "I don't give a fuck it might be the sensible thing to do, to take that skanky old plea bargain. I'm doin' what's right. It's nothin' but a game to them, and I ain't playin'."

"Please, Shaniqua. Mara didn't do what she was accused of either, I'm sure of it."

"Don't try that emotional blackmail shit on me. You're better than that."

"Okay. But I wouldn't ask you if it wasn't important."

"Oh, I'll share a cell with that Madison ho, no problem."

Patrese felt his forehead knot in confusion. "You will?"

"Sure. But I ain't pleadin' guilty to no manslaughter. And 'cause I ain't takin' the bargain, I want somethin' else."

"I'll have to get that authorized," Patrese said. "Don't worry. There are procedures for this kind of thing, it won't be a prob—"

"You think I mean *cash*?" Her eyebrows arched like an angry cat's. "You think I'd aks you for dead *presidents*? Shit, Franco. Who the *fuck* you take me for?"

Patrese couldn't remember the last time he'd felt so small. People talked about wanting the ground to swallow them up or wishing they could rewind time. It was moments like this when Patrese realized these weren't simply figures of speech. He'd rather have run buck naked around Heinz Field than underestimated Shaniqua like that.

He looked at the floor. He couldn't bear to meet her gaze. "I'm sorry."

Shaniqua exhaled. "Accepted. Forget about it."

"Thank you. So what do you want in return?"

"I want you to keep an eye out for Trent."

100

It was on the tip of Patrese's tongue to say, "Is that all?" but he caught himself just in time. He could get away with being crassly insensitive once but not twice, not with someone as sharp and proud as Shaniqua.

He debated whether to tell her about Trent, Bayoumi, and the MDMA.

On one hand, it would show him, Patrese, in a good light, that he'd already tried to show Trent the right path. On the other, it would anger and alarm Shaniqua, and she'd be able to do nothing about either.

For now, at least, he decided not to mention it.

"Of course I will," he said, "but why me? Hell, Shaniqua, I'm not even from Homewood. I'm not even black."

"Exactly." She wagged her index finger at him. "*Exactly.* Homewood's the damn problem. When you last see a U-Haul movin' someone *into* Homewood? You know the world outside, Franco. You ain't in that Homewood state of mind. You know there's more'n the choice between sellin' drugs and workin' at Taco Bell, and you know that choice is only a damn choice if you're not the one havin' to make it.

"I want Trent to respect the law. I want someone to show him the police don't have to be the enemy all the time. You're a good man, you can show him that. You know why? 'Cause you believe. Maybe you don't even know that yourself, but you *believe.* I know you seen some bad things, I can tell that just by the way you hold yourself, but you wake up each mornin' believin' today'll be better than yesterday and worse than tomorrow. You do, don'tcha? And you can't put a price on that.

"Don't get me wrong. JK's a good man too—you know JK, the pastor who's lookin' after Trent?—he's a helluva good man. But he's got a whole heap of boys to look after. Will Trent be special to him? No. He can't be. Shit, Franco, I don't want you to adopt the little man or shit like that. Just keep an eye on him now and then till I get out. And that ain't gonna be in four to seven on no goddamn plea bargain. That's gonna be when the jury acquit my ass first off.

"Lemme tell you somethin', Franco. The other night in here, I made myself a promise. I promised myself I ain't never gonna love another man again. Every man I ever loved, they're all dead, or they're in jail, so they might as well be dead, 'cause those prisons kill your ass quicker than rat poison. And why are they inside? Because of bullshit, man, over kids' stuff. You call me this, I call you that. It's all bullshit.

"But Trent's different. He's my *son,* man. I don't have no choice about lovin' him. You have kids? No? Then you don't understand. You don't, not really. The moment you become a daddy, you'll understand. You'll understand you can't *not* love your kids. Every day, if I don't get up and say a prayer, I can't make it. And I say that prayer for him, for Trent, no one else.

"And I tell him, he better not be a gangbanger. Not now, not ever. I'm gonna hurt him if he is. They better not give him nothin', he better not do nothin' for them. I told him, 'I know some of your friends are dealers. You can talk with them, but don't let me catch you hangin' on the corner where they sell. I done struggled too hard to try to take care of you. I'm not gonna let you throw your life away.' That's what I told him. But I know how hard it is. Boys don't become gangbangers 'cause they're bored after school and need somethin' to do. Shit, no. Gangs ain't no fuckin' *playgroup*. You seen them toolin' up for a rumble, ain'tcha? They goin' to *war*, man. They goin' to fuckin' *war*, and it's bullshit, like every war ever is. Some of those kids wanna die, Franco; they wanna be remembered as a goddamn fallen soldier, they wanna be put out of their misery, but they sure as hell don't wanna do it themselves, 'cause that's the coward's way out, ain't it? So they go to war hopin' they catch a bullet. They're scared, but they ain't *allowed* to be scared. So what do they do? They dress it up into bullshit about retaliation and honor. But bullshit is bullshit. I always been knowin' that. I refused to be a straight G, you know, a girl who gets to be a big-shot gang member by doing the things the boys do. Always refused. You know what my biggest fantasy was? You wanna know? You'll laugh your ass off. I'll tell you. I wanted my life to be just like *Ozzie and Harriet.*"

Patrese didn't laugh. He knew all too well what she meant. Gangs are like pedophiles. They draw you in subtly, grooming you, a little here, a little there, carry a message, paint a graffiti tag, run some drugs, take a gun, one step further each time, one more brick in the wall of your resistance knocked away, so it's hard to tell even where the point of no turning back is, let alone whether you've passed it.

By the time you get to the initiation ceremony, the formal acceptance of your status, you're pretty much in anyway. And once you're in, you're in forever, both as far as the law's concerned—penalties and jail time are bumped up almost automatically whenever a crime is considered gang-related—and also in the eyes of your fellow members. Gangs are like lobster pots: there are several ways in, but only one way out, and you don't tend to be around to see that route.

Patrese remembered a case where a couple of Homewood gangbangers had found religion and decided to leave the gang. They'd been executed. They'd had no intention of ratting on their former comrades, but that had made no difference. Patrese had arrested the man who'd shot them, and asked him why he'd done it. "There's no getting out of this motherfucker," he'd replied. "Not Jesus, not nothin' gets you out."

Cure is therefore pretty much impossible. Once you're in, you're in. The outlook for prevention—catching them before they make it through the door—is slightly better, and slightly better is pretty much all you ever get in Homewood. If Patrese had thought that busting Trent's ass would make a difference, he'd have done it; but he knew that arrest, caution, even jail had never stopped a single person from joining a gang. All they did was make sure the police were on your case too.

There was a wailing from the other side of the visiting room, a wailing so visceral that every head snapped around toward the source.

Another inmate was with her children—two little girls, hair in bunches, the elder one no more than five—and they were clearly at the end of their visiting time. The debris of their visit—plastic bricks, coloring books, jigsaws, fairy tales—was scattered across the floor, and the little girls were clinging to their mother as if they'd never see her again. She was down on her haunches, the better to clasp them to her, and her entire body was shaking, as though racked not by ordinary sobs but by tremors of the earth itself.

Everyone else in the room stopped their conversations; not just because they could hardly hear themselves think over her wailing, let alone hear someone else talk, but also because it seemed somehow discourteous to the intensity of her agony to do anything other than hold themselves in suspended animation.

Three guards pulled mother from daughters, not without kindness, and ushered the children out of the room. Patrese looked at the guards as they went past. Their faces were blank, absolutely wiped of expression. It was the only way they could deal with it; the only way anyone could deal with it, if you saw it as often as they did.

The woman staggered out of the room in the other direction, back toward her cell, toward another week before the whole thing would happen all over again.

"Happens every day," Shaniqua said. "You can't touch them afterward, not for hours sometimes, else they just break down. Just don't say anythin' when they go quiet. We all have it here, man. Everyone just clampin' down on all that shit inside them. If we all overflowed at once, this place'd need a nine-one-one to Noah and his ark."

Patrese's time with Shaniqua was up soon afterward. He reclaimed his belongings from security at the entrance and walked back to his car—a squad car, not the Trans Am, so there was at least a vague possibility he might make it back to Pittsburgh without breaking down.

He had a vague, uneasy feeling that took several minutes to crystallize, and it slightly surprised him when he managed to articulate it. The responsibility Shaniqua had given him, he felt, was the equal of the task he had in solving these murders.

He started the car, turned the headlights on against the darkness, pulled out of the gate, and headed up Route 405. It was a couple of miles to the interstate, no more.

He wasn't halfway there when a massive bang sent the car slewing across the road.

101

Police driver training had its uses.

Patrese didn't panic. He battered down the lurch of surprise in his stomach, steered into the skid, felt the front wheels regain their grip, and eased the car straight again.

His first thought was that he'd had a blowout, but he scotched that a moment later. The car was still riding smoothly, with none of a flat tire's shuddering and listing.

And the bang hadn't sounded like a blowout. It had been more of a metallic report, as though something had struck the car.

A deer? Animals could be a hazard pretty much anywhere outside built-up areas.

He slowed and pulled toward the side of the road, intending to get out and examine the damage to his car and whatever had hit it. If it was an animal and it was in pain, he had his sidearm; he'd do the humane thing and put it out of its misery.

He was just coasting to a stop when the car was hit again.

102

This time, Patrese saw him.

Well, not *him*, exactly. He saw a nondescript sedan with its headlights off, which was why he hadn't seen it first time around. In the darkness, with all that was happening, he couldn't get any more than a glimpse of the driver, not even enough to tell if it was a man or a woman.

Patrese hit the gas and fishtailed away from him.

He came again, clipping Patrese's offside rear and sending him into a half-spin.

It was bizarre, but Patrese felt as though only half of him was concentrating on driving. The other half was trying to work out who the hell his assailant was.

Was it Patrese in particular he was after? Then he must have been lying in wait for him, either in the Muncy parking lot or in a turning off of Route 405.

If that was the case, it begged the question of who knew Patrese was there. Beradino, Amberin, and Hellmore were the first three who sprang to mind, followed by a good proportion of the police department and the DA's office. Patrese had hardly advertised his trip, but it wasn't a state secret either.

Then, of course, there was the prison staff. They all knew he was here. If one of them was worried about him finding something, how better to nip it in the bud than try to kill him, or at least give him a warning serious enough to make him think twice?

So the answer to Patrese's question—who knew he was there?—was, give or take, around two hundred people.

The other possibility was that the attack wasn't aimed at him personally at all and was just dumb chance; some junkie or dipso bombed out of his head and having his own kind of fun.

Patrese corrected the spin. The sedan came again, and this time Patrese was ready for him. He yanked the steering wheel hard over, and caught the sedan flush on the fender. The sedan veered across the road and onto the verge, sending clouds of gravel and dust billowing into the arc of Patrese's lights.

This was fun, Patrese thought; no, more, it was *exhilarating*. He was enjoying it. He felt *alive*. He shouted something, half challenge, half exhortation.

Once more the sedan aimed for him. Patrese hit the brakes, watched as the sedan sailed across his bows, then stood on the gas and took the assailant broadside. The sedan spun across its own axis, off the road and out of sight.

Patrese pulled to a stop and took his Ruger Blackhawk out of the glove compartment; turning off the engine, he pocketed the key and got out of the car, low to the ground in case the mystery attacker had other means of finishing what he'd started.

He crouched by his open door, checking that every bit of him that should be working was. There'd be a few bruises in the morning, possibly some whiplash, but right now there was far too much adrenaline chasing itself around his body for him to feel any of it.

He counted a minute. No sign. If the attacker was coming for him, he'd surely have been here by now.

Patrese went across the road in a half crouch, so as not to reveal his silhouette against the night sky.

The sedan had come to a halt in a field about thirty yards from the road. Patrese approached it cautiously, trying to keep himself to the driver's blind side.

When he was a couple of yards away, he took a deep breath and launched himself at the car, grabbing the door and yanking it open in one movement.

The sedan was empty.

Patrese looked around, but couldn't see anyone.

For a moment, Patrese thought the attacker might have hit him with the oldest sucker punch in the book—drawing him out so he could make off with Patrese's car—but then remembered he'd been smart enough to take the keys out, which automatically set the immobilizer.

That minute Patrese had spent waiting by his car had allowed the attacker to escape.

Ah well, Patrese thought. He had the man's car, and presumably a whole heap of forensic evidence inside.

He called the Muncy police and got them to send a trailer for the sedan. They said they didn't have the facilities to test forensics, so he told them to take it all the way back to Pittsburgh. They'd run tests there, and sign off on all the jurisdictional hoo-ha later.

Then Patrese got back into his car, which was a substantially more interesting shape than it had been ten minutes previously, checked that everything that should work did work—as indeed he'd done with his own limbs—and set off for Pittsburgh.

He was shaking half the way home, and it wasn't with anger.

103

WEDNESDAY, DECEMBER 1

The sedan that had run Patrese off the road outside of Muncy was in the pound the next morning. Patrese rang Beradino, and they agreed to meet down there.

A quick check once the mud had been scraped off the license plate had given them the owner's name and details. He was a Thomas Monroe of Muncy, and he'd reported the car, an aging Chevy Nova, stolen a couple of hours *before* the attack had taken place.

Muncy PD had checked him out and said he was genuine. He worked nights as a security guard and had been on shift when Patrese had been reenacting the Indy 500.

That the car was from Muncy suggested local involvement. This, if true, would mean that the culprit was either simply some joker who'd picked Patrese at random, or one of the prison staff. If it was the latter, they must have moved very fast, given that the car had been reported stolen two hours before the attack and that Patrese hadn't been at the jail much longer than that.

When Beradino arrived, he cast a weary eye over the damage.

"What does yours look like?" he asked.

"Pretty much the same."

Beradino opened the Nova's door and hauled himself inside. "Right. Let's see if we can find anything that might tell us who this punk was."

Clutching the steering wheel for balance with one hand, he leaned across and opened the glove compartment.

"Er, Detective?" said one of the tech boys.

"What?"

"We haven't dusted it yet."

Beradino sat upright again and glared at him. "Why the hell didn't you say so?" He pulled himself out and gestured toward the car. "All yours."

104

Patrese called Amberin and Hellmore to tell them that Shaniqua had agreed to his plan.

"Didn't think it was gonna happen for you, I have to be honest," Hellmore said.

"Why not?"

"'Cause Amberin ain't in the takin'-shit business. But you didn't let her play you. I'm impressed, man. I know there's some static between cops and defense lawyers, so sometimes you need to cut through the bullshit and give props where they're due. For what it's worth, I'm impressed."

"Thank you," Patrese said, and meant it.

"Hope Shaniqua finds out whatever it is you want her to. Oh—that reminds me. About Mara. She never changed her will."

"Huh?"

"I was clearing up some loose ends yesterday on her estate. Turns out the will she wrote when she and Howard first got married, she never changed it."

"Which means what?"

"Under state law, if you're getting divorced, an existing will's valid right up to the moment the judge signs the final decree. If your will leaves everything to your spouse, as Mara's did, and if you die before the divorce is over, as Mara did, then the spouse gets everything."

"Everything?"

"Everything. It don't matter if proceedings have been going on for years, it don't matter if one or both of you's living with someone else, it don't matter if the whole thing's gonna be signed off in twenty minutes' time. You're in or you're out. No such thing as legal separation, not in Pennsylvania."

"How much is 'everything,' in this case?"

"Close to ten mil."

"*Ten mil?* Jesus. Why didn't she change her will?"

"You tell me. I kept on at her to do it—even got one of my associates to draw one up for her—but she always said yeah, yeah, she'd do it, and then just left it till I bugged her about it again."

"Did she want to get Howard back?"

"Get him back as in 'win him back,' or get him back as in 'punish him'?"

"I meant 'win him back,' but I guess either."

"She never said so, but I reckon. She didn't want the divorce to start with; she stalled it as much as she could. But what did she expect?"

What indeed, Patrese thought; what indeed?

105

Negley hadn't just saved himself $20 million with Mara's untimely death; he'd actually made another $10 million, whether he knew it or not.

Patrese wondered if he and Beradino had been too hasty in taking Negley at his word the other night, when he'd told them that even millions of dollars was a drop in the ocean for him. In Patrese's admittedly limited experience of dealing with very rich people, he'd worked out two things. First, as far as most rich people were concerned, too much was never enough. Second, most fortunes looked a lot less secure on closer inspection than they did at first glance. Extravagant net-worth assessments were always impressive, but as often as not they were at best exaggerated and at worst downright fiction.

Either way, it was easily enough reason to go see Negley again.

Patrese called Negley's office. Howard wasn't there. His secretary explained that he was in a meeting at the Renaissance, downtown's newest and swankiest hotel, a brownstone building of rather severe beauty hard by the south bank of the Allegheny, from where it looked across the river right into the diamond of PNC Park baseball stadium.

Patrese and Beradino headed for the Renaissance.

The hotel doormen gave them the once-over, expressions suggesting the detectives were a couple of rungs down the social ladder from the Renaissance's usual clientele. Patrese resisted the urge to flash his badge. They had every right to be here.

"I need to take a leak," Patrese said once they were inside. "Too much coffee."

"Okay. You find the john, I'll wait for you here."

They approached reception, intending to ask where they could find the restrooms. A young woman was a few paces ahead of them.

"I'm here to see Mr. Negley," they heard her say.

They stopped dead.

"Is he expecting you?" the receptionist asked.

"Oh yes."

"Can I have your name?"

"Ava."

Patrese and Beradino looked at each other. Negley's secretary had told them he was in a meeting. Some kind of meeting.

The receptionist dialed a number. "Mr. Negley?" she

said brightly. "I have an Ava for you. Yes, yes. Thank you." She replaced the receiver and turned back to Ava. "Room nine fifteen. Ninth floor."

"Thank you." Ava headed toward the elevator bank on the far side of the lobby.

The receptionist looked at Patrese and Beradino. "Can I help you?" she said.

"No," Beradino replied. "Thank you. We know where we're going."

Ava pressed the button for the elevator. One set of metal doors slid open, and she stepped inside. The detectives quickened their strides to make it in with her.

She gave a brief smile, the way you do at people who've just sneaked in between closing doors. "Which floor would you like?" she asked.

Patrese glanced at the control panel. The number 9 was illuminated.

"Looks like we're already going there," he said.

"Are you staying here?" Beradino asked, playing the jovial conversationalist.

She hesitated for a moment. "Yes. Yes, I am."

"They got some of those fancy credit-card keys here? I bet they have. I love those things. Mind if I have a quick look at yours?"

She stared at him without speaking.

The floor indicator pinged, the doors opened, and they all stepped out onto the landing. Ava glanced at the signs on the wall and headed in the direction of room 915. Patrese and Beradino followed.

All the way to the door of 915, in fact.

106

Negley's reaction to their appearance followed an entirely predictable sequence. Open-mouthed shock gave way to self-righteous anger, which in turn elided into a cold-eyed assessment of the situation, the second transition given a helping hand by Patrese's suggestion that, if Negley didn't want to cooperate, they could just call Ruby and let her know where they all were and what a fun time they were having.

There was a bottle of champagne open, and Howard had poured two glasses. He offered them to Beradino and Patrese with a smile, as if he'd been expecting them all along. They shook their heads, but Patrese smiled back. The mayor had style.

Negley came clean pretty much immediately. As they all knew, Ava was from an escort agency; and, again as they all knew, escorting is legal. An agency can dispatch individuals to provide social or conversational services. What it *cannot* do is arrange a contract for sexual services, or even hint that such an option might be available. If the escort and the john agree to have sex once they're in each other's company, that's neither the agency's fault nor its problem, at least technically.

The whole thing is shot through with hypocrisy, of course. Everyone knows what's really on offer and how best to skirt the legal line in providing it. No one in their right mind pays thousands of dollars for a little small talk and no action. Hell, if all you want is conversation and intellectual stimulation, you can hire Henry Kissinger.

Terms and conditions vary from agency to agency, but it's not uncommon for the girls and the agency to split the fees fifty-fifty, with the girls keeping anything they earn on top, like tips or extras for rough stuff. So the state makes agencies gain licenses and pay taxes, both of which swell government coffers, and directs the police to crack down on streetwalkers instead.

"Come on," Negley said. "This happens all the time. People like me, with high-powered, high-pressure, high-stress jobs, we need an escape, a release. How do you think we get these jobs, hey? By having sex drives the size of Texas, that's how." It sounded like something from Dr. Ruth, but he didn't seem embarrassed in the slightest. "You elect men with big balls and high testosterone, and then expect us to behave like eunuchs?" He shook his head. "Uh-uh. No, sir. It's high sex drives that get you into positions of power to start with."

"And they can get you out of them, too," Beradino said.

Howard turned on him. "What are you, Detective? The moral majority?"

"I'm not making a judgment. I'm simply pointing out the truth. If this came out, how long do you think you'd last as mayor?"

"And you think that would be a good thing? You don't think I'm a good mayor? You think it's just coincidence that the city budget's gone from a billion-dollar deficit to a billion-dollar surplus on my watch? Or that more police are on the streets and crime's down? Or that all the America's Most Livable City stuff just *happened*?"

He didn't once ask them to consider whether he'd suffered enough already. Many people in Howard's situation would have fallen back on the trauma of the Mara case and tried to lay on the emotional blackmail that way. For all his money, power, ambition, drive, and intellect, what had happened to his wife and children had clearly cut Howard to the core, and he was as much a fuckup as anybody else who'd undergone that kind of ordeal. But he didn't use it as an excuse, and Patrese admired him for it.

They had the fate of one of America's richest men in their hands, at least potentially. It felt almost headily surreal. For the first time, Patrese appreciated a fraction of what it must be like to have the power of life and death over someone; to be a surgeon, a soldier, a serial killer.

"Did you know your wife hadn't changed her will?" Patrese said.

Howard didn't look fazed in the slightest. "Mara's affairs were her own business," he replied. "She never listened to me about money, about lawyers. Nothing."

"Her entire estate goes to you. Ten million dollars."

He shrugged. "I'll give it to charity."

"All of it?"

"Every last cent."

"As part of your annual philanthropic efforts?"

"*On top of* my annual philanthropic efforts."

Patrese was suddenly conscious he still needed to take a leak. "Excuse me," he said to Negley. "Could I use your bathroom?"

"Sure," Howard said, and pointed to a door across the room. "Just in there."

"Thanks."

Patrese walked in, turned on the light, shut the door—and had a sudden, almost muscular flash of realization.

While driving Negley back to Fox Chapel from the scene of Mara's murder, Patrese had thought that something was wrong, that he'd missed something.

He now knew what that was.

107

Patrese shook, zipped, flushed, washed, and stepped back into the hotel room.

The atmosphere was so awkward it was almost comic. The other three were standing around like strangers at a cocktail party who'd exhausted their reserves of small talk. Howard was gazing lustfully at Ava; an encounter with the law was too trivial to derail his libido, clearly. Ava looked slightly concerned; probably wondering if she was still going to get paid. And Beradino had the air of a chaperone from a bygone age, knowing that the other two wanted him to leave and that they'd be getting it on pretty much before the door had closed behind him.

"Well," Patrese said, "that's good, isn't it? Everything sorted out." He went over to the table and picked up one of the champagne glasses. "This calls for a celebration, no? Anyone want to join me?"

They all looked at him as though he was mad.

"No?" Patrese shrugged. "Okay. No problem. Mark, can I have a word? Outside?"

Patrese and Beradino went out into the corridor. Patrese was still holding the champagne flute and hoped Howard hadn't noticed the unnatural way in which he was gripping it: very lightly, and as near the rim as possible.

"I'm going to call Summer and tell her to expect us at headquarters," he said.

"Huh?"

"I want her to check some fingerprints."

108

"Yup," Summer said.

"You're sure?" Patrese asked.

"Positive."

She'd dusted the champagne glass, which had Negley's fingerprints all over it from when he'd offered it to Patrese. That was why Patrese had picked it up by the rim.

Once Summer had found a good print, she'd checked it against those found at Mara's apartment. There had been four separate sets there: one belonging to Mara, the other three as yet unidentified.

Howard's prints were a dead match for one set.

"The set that was found in Mara's bedroom?" Beradino asked.

"No. Not that one," she said. No, Patrese thought; he knew who *that* set belonged to. "His prints were in the kitchen and the bathroom."

"Still," Beradino said. "The night Mara was murdered, Howard told us he hadn't seen her since the day she was convicted, right? When he saw her body, he went to the bathroom to throw up, which explains his prints being there. But he *didn't* go in the kitchen, did he? Which means he must have visited before, to have left prints there. When Mara was alive." He turned to Patrese. "How did you know?"

"From when he threw up. Like you said, he took one look at her body and rushed to the john. But he didn't ask *where* the john was. He knew already, even though he said he'd never been to her apartment before. When I asked him tonight if I could use the bathroom, he showed me which door I needed—even in a room with only two doors, the bathroom door and the main door, and we knew which one the main door was because we'd come in through it."

Beradino clapped Patrese on the shoulder. "Well done, young man."

Patrese felt absurdly proud.

109

The whole fingerprint thing had taken so little time—ten minutes each way between the Renaissance and headquarters, and twenty minutes of Summer working her latent-print magic—that they were back at the hotel within the hour.

"You think he'll still be there?" Beradino asked on their way up in the elevator.

"Heck, yeah," Patrese replied. "If I'd paid the going

rate for Ava, *I'd* be getting my money's worth, even if an entire SWAT team was kicking down the door."

Ava was in a robe that revealed less of her undoubted charms than most men would have liked. Howard was in a shirt and underpants, looking rather less like a master of the universe than usual.

"Get your clothes on and get out," Beradino said to Ava.

She grabbed her dress from the floor and hurried into the bathroom. Beradino and Patrese waited in silence till she came out. She picked up her handbag, glanced around the room to see whether she'd left anything, walked up to them, spat in both their faces, and left the room.

"Classy," Patrese said.

"Very," Beradino replied.

Beradino explained to Howard what they'd found. He said they must be mistaken. His legs and arms were crossed, his hands hidden. Underdressed, or something to hide? Or both?

They probed a little more, and still he parried. But his eye contact, his Clintonesque *you're the most important person in the room* shtick, was gone. He kept looking toward the door as if he couldn't wait to get out.

There are three tells to a liar's voice: pitch, speed, and volume. The pitch gets higher as stress contracts the vocal cords; the speed slows as the liar tries to formulate the lie; and the volume decreases as the liar thinks things through, being careful not to trip himself up.

Howard's voice was high, slow, and quiet. In addition, he touched his nose, rubbed his eyes, pulled his ears, and scratched his neck—none of the gestures sinister in themselves, but a pretty powerful indication en masse that right now he was telling more porkies than Pinocchio.

"This is how it is," Beradino said. "We'll keep on here, or we can go down to the station. We'll grill you for three hours, then we'll bring in some new guys. Just when you think you might have convinced us, you'll have to start over again with another pair who won't want to believe a word you say. And they'll be fresh and alert. They're used to this kind of stuff. There's two types of people in this world, you know? ESSO guys and non-ESSO guys; ESSO, in this case, being every Saturday and Sunday off. Homicide 'tecs are non-ESSO guys. They're in good shape, because they have to be. You, on the other hand, will be tired, trying to remember what lie you told and who you told it to. They'll ask you the same old questions again and again. You know how demoralizing that is? I'll tell you; most suspects, if they haven't spilled already, confess within an hour of the first shift change. That's how demoralizing it is.

"There you go," Beradino concluded, ever reasonable. "Your choice."

"I didn't kill her," Howard said.

"I'm not saying you did. You hear me say you did? Franco, you hear me say he did?" Patrese shook his head. "No, Franco heard nothing neither. I'm just saying your prints were all over Mara's apartment. You disputing that?"

"I didn't kill her."

"But you were there?"

"Yes," Howard said, so softly that they had to strain to hear him.

110

It all came out after that.

Howard had gone to see Mara just once, not long before she'd been killed but after the police protection had been lifted. He hadn't told Ruby, of course. She'd have gone *apeshit*; she wouldn't have understood, not in the slightest.

To tell the truth, he wasn't sure he understood either. Why had he gone? He didn't really know. No reason. Lots of reasons. To see how Mara was doing, after everything she'd gone through. To apologize for having doubted her, and explain why he'd done so. The evidence against her had seemed so incontrovertible; he'd been so distraught; he'd wanted someone to blame, and she'd seemed the obvious person.

How had Mara reacted to his visit?

God, that was the worst part, he said. She'd been so goddamn gracious and understanding, it had made him feel ten times worse. She'd said she didn't blame him, it wasn't his fault. No, he'd said, it *was* his fault. He shouldn't have abandoned her, he should have stuck by her. Maybe they should try again—not for children, of course, but as a couple, try to put it all behind them and start over.

His suggestion, or hers? His, definitely. His.

They'd cried, and hugged, and . . .

The cold knot that suddenly clenched tight in Patrese's stomach told him where this was going.

. . . somewhere, somehow, the hug had turned into a kiss, and the kiss into—well, they could guess, couldn't they? Both of them shaking with tears even before it was over. And afterward? Go away and think about it, she'd said, and she'd do the same. They had a lot to sort out.

Patrese clenched his jaw so hard he thought his teeth would break.

Liar, he wanted to say. *Liar. She never mentioned you, not once. You might have been in the apartment, but you never made love to her.*

111

They'd checked Negley's alibis for all four murders not long after Mara had been killed, but for form's sake they checked them again. Watertight, the lot. At the time of the murders, Howard had been, respectively, at a cocktail party, giving a television interview, at a breakfast award ceremony, and out having dinner. His attendance was corroborated by at least twenty people for each occasion. His "meetings" with the likes of Ava aside, Howard lived a life that was almost unrelentingly public. Good for a mayor; bad for a serial killer.

"You read that thing in the paper the other day?"

Beradino said. "About how politicians and millionaires exhibit typical characteristics of psychopaths?"

"No, but I can imagine. Charm, narcissism, egotism, manipulation, low boredom threshold, promiscuity . . . the list goes on."

"You want it to be him? You want Howard to be our man?"

"It would solve our problems." *We wouldn't be looking for Mara's lover anymore.*

"It sure would." *Sure would take the heat off Jesslyn.*

Patrese wondered whether—hoped that—Howard was lying about having made love with Mara. He remembered what Mara had said about Howard's lack of reaction to their children's deaths. Pathological deceit and absence of empathy are also high on psychopathic checklists. It's not that psychopaths don't know how to show emotions, Patrese knew; it's that they don't even know how to *feel* them.

112

THURSDAY, DECEMBER 2

Patrese had asked to be informed if Trent Davenport was ever brought into Central Booking. He got his first notification a little over twenty-four hours later, when two patrolmen arrested Trent for tagging—spraying graffiti markers.

Patrese went down to the basement and checked for

the number of Trent's cell on the list. He was right at the end, the last cell. Patrese walked all the way down the corridor, unlocked the cell door, and went in.

For a moment, he thought he'd got the wrong room. There was only one place to sit, a concrete bench, and that was empty.

Then he saw the dangling legs away to the right, just above his eye line; kicking hard, spotless and laceless Timberlands beneath baggy jeans.

Oh no. Oh, Jesus, no.

Patrese moved quicker than thought, one arm around Trent's waist to take the weight, the other reaching upward for whatever Trent had used as a noose. Damn it, Patrese thought, the uniforms were supposed to take laces and belts from suspects. It was pretty much the first thing you did after fingerprinting them.

There was no noose. No belt, no cord—nothing. Just a hand that batted angrily at Patrese's, and a voice shouting, "Get off me! Get off me, man!"

Trent wasn't hanging himself. He was trying to escape through the ceiling panel.

113

Patrese wrestled Trent down and onto the concrete bench. Trent lashed out a couple of times, but Patrese was too quick and smart for him. He swayed easily away from the blows and pinned Trent's wrists to the bench. Trent tried to kick Patrese's back.

"You do that one more time," Patrese snapped, "you're gonna be in more trouble than you can possibly imagine."

"Fuck you, man. Let go of me."

"You stop thrashing around like a dying fish, I'll let go."

Trent gradually subsided. Patrese pushed himself away and stood up. Trent sat upright, adjusting his clothes with sullen defiance.

Patrese saw a pair of gloves sticking out of the back of Trent's jeans—cloth gardening gloves. A lot of young men wore them to protect their hands during a fistfight; either that, or Homewood had more budding Theodore Paynes than River Farm ever did.

"This your first offense?" Patrese asked.

"First one I been *caught* for." Sullen bravado.

"Okay, so you probably won't be charged this time. Next time, different story. If I'd busted you outside the Sanctuary the other night, you'd already be on remand, you know? This is not the way you want to go."

"How the *fuck* you know which way I wanna go?"

"I'm telling you. This is not the way."

"And *I'm* tellin' *you*—"

Patrese grabbed Trent's collar and pulled his face close. "You're telling me *nothing*, you understand? You're in a police station. My turf. While you're here, you'll listen to me. Is that clear?"

"Listen, man—"

"Is that fucking clear?"

Trent looked briefly like the frightened, confused young man Patrese had seen the day they'd taken Shaniqua away.

"Yeah," he said. "Yeah. Sorry."

Patrese let Trent go. Trent picked at his shirt again.

"Sorry," Trent said again.

"Why do you do it?" Patrese asked.

"Man, it weren't nothin'. We was just—"

"No. Not why *did* you do it, the tagging. Why *do* you do it?"

"What you mean?"

"Why the gang? Why do you want to be in the gang?"

Trent smiled. "Man, *everyone* wanna be in da gang."

"Why?"

Patrese knew the answers, of course, but he wanted Trent to say them out loud. Maybe that way he'd think about them, question them.

"Respect," Trent said. "Dead presidents, hos. Be the big man. It's excitin', yeah?"

"Hanging out on street corners is exciting?"

"No, man. Goin' for a rumble is excitin'."

"You spend a lot more time hanging out on street corners than going for a rumble, I can tell you."

"Man, what you know about it anyway?"

"I work homicide, Trent. Homicide means gangs, often as not. I know more than you think. I know more than you do."

"Man, I get this shit off of J-Dog all da time." J-Dog, Patrese presumed, being John Knight. "This make-yourself-a-better-citizen shit."

"You keep on like this, Trent, you'll end up in jail, or you'll die, or both. You can't do a thing with your life if you're dead or serving twenty-five. Think of your mom."

"My mom's in jail. *Remember?* She ain't here with me."

And that was it in a nutshell, Patrese thought, whether Trent knew it or not. Trent wanted the gang because he wanted a family. All his real family were either locked up, dead, or otherwise long gone from his life. The gang was a substitute for all that, even though it would eventually eat itself; because how could a gang compensate for all the brothers dead or inside, when so many of its members would end up going the same way?

You joined a gang to belong, and it turned out to be undependable. You joined it for excitement, and it turned out to be boring. You joined it for protection, and it turned out to make you more vulnerable.

Shaniqua was right, of course. Homewood was the problem—the place, the mind-set. It was all very well Patrese telling Trent not to get involved, but Trent would only listen when he had alternatives, and alternatives meant getting him out of there.

After the arresting officer had cautioned Trent and told him he didn't want to see him back here, not *ever*, not unless he'd just graduated from the police academy, Patrese said he'd drive Trent back to Homewood.

"This your car?" Trent said as they approached the Trans Am.

"Yup."

Trent pursed his lips and nodded. They got in. Patrese turned the key. The starter motor turned over wheezily, considered its options for a few moments, then decided that today was a good day to actually do some work and start the V8.

"It always sound that bad?" Trent asked.

"Always. Half the time, it don't even start."

"You should get another car."

"No way. Not till the rust is all that's holding this thing together."

As they passed Heinz Field, Patrese nodded toward it. "You ever been?"

Trent snorted. "No, man."

"You don't like football?"

"I *love* football, man. But when a brother like me gonna get to Heinz Field?"

"You play?"

"Sure."

"What position?"

"Safety. Free safety, mainly."

"You like playing there?"

"Yeah, man. Love it. Stand back, watch the play unfold, see it all before me. I got all the options. Cover the receiver, smack the halfback, blitz now and then. *Love it.*"

By Trent's standards, Patrese figured, that was a veritable soliloquy.

"Yo, man, can I aks you somethin'?" Trent said.

"Sure."

"J-Dog said you won the Heisman at Pitt." The Heisman was the trophy for the best college player. "That true?"

"That *is* true. I did."

"Man. *Man.* The Heisman, that's some serious shit. But you a bit short for bein' a quarterback, ain'tcha?"

"Why do you think I was a quarterback?"

"Why? Only quarterbacks and runnin' backs ever win the Heisman, right?"

"Not always—you might get a wide receiver now and then—but pretty much, yeah. But why can't I have been a running back?"

Trent laughed, as though this was the most ridiculous thing he'd ever heard. "'Cause you *white,* man. White folks don't play runnin' back."

He had a point. Not a single NFL team, and precious few college outfits, had a white running back on its starter roster. No one really discussed it, because it—the Great Disappearing White Running Back—was all bound up with America's great unmentionables, race and culture.

Scientists will tell you it's racial, that blacks have denser bones, less body fat, narrower hips, thicker thighs, longer legs, and lighter calves than whites. Then in the next breath they'll tell you whites are more intelligent, so no one can accuse them of bias—give with one hand, take with the other.

But it was just as much a question of social pigeonholing. The fewer whites who played as running backs, the fewer whites who were encouraged to. It worked the other way too, of course. There hadn't been a black NFL quarterback, not a regular starting one, at any rate, until the late seventies. Not because they hadn't been good enough, but because they hadn't been white enough.

"I did," Patrese said. "I played running back."

Short and stocky, sharp and elusive, low to the ground; a scat back. The big fullbacks tend to run north-south, straight lines up and down the field. The smaller ones, the halfbacks, run east-west, looking for the gaps. I ran every which way. I'd have given a compass motion sickness.

When I ran, I imagined his face beneath my feet. Stamp, stamp, stamp. When I was hit and got hurt, I'd imagine his face at the point of impact; whichever linebacker had taken me out had also smashed his face in. I ran ahead of this tsunami that was on my heels, because I feared it would swamp me the moment I stopped. Keep running. Never stop, never face it, never let it catch me.

At Pitt, I made the Panthers, the varsity football team, in my freshman year. Out there, on the grid, I was free. I didn't have to worry about him or my studies or even the laws of physics, it sometimes seemed, as I dodged half the defense to score searing touchdowns.

I loved everything about it; not just the games, but the razzmatazz, the feeling that I was one of the big men on campus. At home games, students would carry banners and form a tunnel for us to run through onto the field while the Pitt band played "March to Victory."

In my senior year, we won the Sugar Bowl and I won the Heisman. There was some serious pedigree in that little trophy. O.J. had won it; so had Tony Dorsett, Earl Campbell, and Marcus Allen. If I could have been half the player those guys were . . .

"They give you static about it?"

"Did who give me static?"

"Anyone."

"Sure they did. Coaches, mainly. Told me to bulk up and play tight end, or I'd never get a place on the starting roster."

"They told you that 'cause you were white?"

"That's right."

"Just 'cause you were white?"

"Just 'cause I was white."

"Nothin' to do with some other guy being better than you?"

"Just 'cause I was white."

"Shit, man." Trent smiled. "Then you got a small idea what it's like to be a nigga."

114

SATURDAY, DECEMBER 4

Mustafa Bayoumi was working with a fury that was controlled, ice cold, and, above all, righteous.

The chemistry department at Pitt was deserted, which was how he liked it when doing things that weren't strictly legal. He had an entire laboratory to himself, and he laid out his ingredients across the workbench with the precision of a television chef.

First, hydrogen peroxide and acetone. When he mixed them together, they'd make acetone peroxide, a by-product of MDMA. It was his MDMA-making that had first given Mustafa the idea for what he was doing now.

He continued arranging his precious items. Chapati flour. Cardboard tubes. Flashlight bulbs. A nine-volt battery. Electrical wires. Metal pipes cut to various lengths. Ball bearings, washers, nuts, screws, tacks, nails. And a camouflage hunting vest bulging with pockets: six bellows on the chest, a hand-warmer on each side, two on the inside, and a couple on the back.

The camouflage pattern was immaterial to Mustafa's purpose—he'd be wearing the vest under a bulky overcoat, so it wouldn't be on show—but the vest's shape was important. Explosives belts tend to "print"; their sharp edges catch the fabric of the clothing outside them, thus revealing their shape. Vests fit both body and clothes better, and are therefore easier to conceal.

Once Mustafa had all the items where he wanted them, he stepped back from the bench and took several deep breaths to keep his thoughts clear.

He had no doubts that he was doing the right thing. The Human Torch had shown him that; this way, the public way, was the only way.

Look how the serial killer had everyone in his thrall. The cops, the media, people in the street, the whole city seemed to talk about little else. They didn't know exactly who the Human Torch was, but they sure as anything knew *of* him, and took notice of what he did. The apparently random, one-off killings took lives, gained vast amounts of attention, and set a city on edge.

Mustafa wanted to do just the same thing. He wanted people to take notice of him too, give him some of their minds. And not the kind of attention the cops had been paying him, either, thinking he must be involved in all those murders. What gave them the right to keep on and on at him, when they had absolutely no evidence?

It was just as he'd told the detectives right at the start, when they'd first come to see him at the mosque: all Muslims were niggers now. If it wasn't these murders they were on his tail about, sooner or later it'd be something else. If it wasn't him on the receiving end, sooner or later it'd be someone else, hassled, harassed, never given a moment's peace, all because they were Muslims, wore beards, didn't believe in what the Americans did, didn't want their way of life.

The Americans wouldn't want his way of death, that was for sure.

If Mustafa's father had still been alive, he'd have said Mustafa was insane to be doing this. Abdul had believed there was always a route to compromise, if only both sides were prepared to seek it. But Abdul was no longer here to turn the other cheek. Mustafa believed in an eye for an eye. He'd had it with bowing down to the infidel. The infidel would bow to him.

Americans would doubtless wonder how a son could do this to his mother, especially not so long after she'd lost her husband. But Americans were weak. All the wastrel, self-indulgent fools who'd bought Mustafa's pills in order to find brief respite from the soulless, godless vacuums of their lives had shown him that. They were weak, but they believed their lives to be of paramount importance.

Mustafa knew his life, like that of everyone in the world, belonged only to Allah. It was Allah for whom he was fighting, and Allah for whom he'd die. His mother would understand. And she'd be all right financially, for a while at least. Selling MDMA had made him somewhere north of $40,000, which he'd stashed in a bank account for her.

Mustafa cast all this from his mind. It was time to make the bomb, for which he needed every ounce of concentration he could muster. Making the bomb wasn't difficult, but it needed precision, patience, and time.

He'd chosen acetone peroxide as the base for several reasons. He'd worked with it before, it was the easiest of several possible explosives to get hold of and prepare, and it was undetectable to sniffer dogs. But it was also dangerously unstable—so much so that Palestinian bomb-makers, many of whom were missing hands or had skin streaked with burns from where they'd misjudged preparations, called it something else entirely.

They called it Mother of Satan.

115

SUNDAY, DECEMBER 5

Patrese had two season tickets to the Steelers. One he always used himself, but who he took with him varied. He'd gone with Pop quite often before this year, and also with Beradino. Sometimes he'd take Bianca, or perhaps a college buddy.

What with one thing and another, however, he hadn't yet asked anyone to today's game, even though it was the Turnpike Rivalry, the Steelers against the Cleveland

Browns, the most visceral of all Steelers matchups. Hardcore Steelers fans would accept losing to every other team on the roster—even their two other great rivals, the Cincinnati Bengals and the Baltimore Ravens—as long as they beat the Browns. It was always hammer and tongs, a special day whether your team won or lost, whether the game itself had been close or a walkover.

With this in mind, Patrese knew *exactly* who he'd take to Heinz Field.

116

There was a grim constancy about Homewood. Summer or winter, spring or fall, you saw the same faces in the same places doing the same things.

On each corner ran a conveyor belt of drug deals. It wasn't as obvious as it sounded, of course; even in Homewood, people don't sell drugs in plain view. But if you know what you're looking for, the players aren't hard to spot.

There are always five of them, not including the boss, who if he has any sense (and he usually does, or he doesn't stay boss for long) keeps himself well away from the scene.

There's the lookout, who keeps his eyes peeled for the law and whose cell phone has the quickest speed-dial in the west. There's the steerer, the buyer's first point of contact, the maître d' of the street corner, rattling off menus and prices. How much? How much for how much? Next comes the moneyman, who takes the buyer's cash.

Now we're at the sharp end, because here comes the golden, cardinal, number one, forget-your-own-name-before-you-forget-this rule of drug deals: keep the money and drugs separate.

Once the moneyman has your cash, and not till then, the slinger gives you the drugs. The slinger's the only one of the gang who physically handles the drugs in this transaction, and is therefore the most liable to be arrested, which is why gangs often use juveniles as slingers, because the courts treat them more leniently.

And finally comes the gunman—hidden, of course, on a rooftop or behind a hedge—watching, waiting, trigger finger at the ready in case the whole thing goes to shit and he has to shoot his way out of it.

Patrese counted this scene, with minor variations, on six consecutive street corners.

This life, this so-called life, was what Shaniqua feared for Trent.

It wasn't only Trent either, Patrese thought. He saw a young mother, couldn't have been out of her teens, two little boys already, and she was cooing sweet nothings into her cell phone while her kids tugged uncomprehendingly at her leg, seeking the attention she was giving to the guy on the other end of the line.

That was the next generation of steerers and slingers right there, those two cute little boys. You didn't need to be Nostradamus to predict their future.

Patrese arrived at the 50/50 and got out of the car. There was no point locking the Trans Am's doors; if someone wanted to break in, they'd do so anyway. Locking the doors only meant they'd have to cause damage.

Patrese found Knight in his office, changing out of his priest's robes; he'd just finished his Sunday service.

"I've come to ask Trent if he wants to go to Heinz Field with me," Patrese said.

"I'm sure he would. Heck, if he doesn't, I will." Knight laughed. "No, it would be good for him. He was talking about you the other day, you know."

"Who? Trent?"

"When you brought him back from the cop shop. Talking all about the crazy white dude who won the Heisman for being a running back."

Patrese felt ridiculously, stupidly proud.

"But listen," Knight continued, "you can't just go in there and ask him if he wants to come, not in front of his buddies. They'll think he's a snitch, or you're a fag, or both. He'd never live it down."

"So what should I do?"

"Say you want to talk to him some more about that tagging incident." He paused. "Can I be frank here?"

"Sure."

"Franco, I don't know you from a bar of soap, but you seem a good man. What you're doing for Trent—not too many people do those things these days. But be careful. Kids like Trent, they don't trust adults, period. They especially don't trust men. Too many men come and go in their lives. They're there with them, then they're inside, or six feet under. No one hugs these kids. They think everyone's out to get them; they'll hustle you just to stop you hustling them first. So once you start this, you can't stop. You can't start on trying to help Trent and then walk away because you're too busy or he's being a jerk. You got to be in it all the way. If you're not, if you haven't got that commitment, then go now. I won't think any the worse of you, Lord no. The only thing I won't let you do is raise his hopes and then shatter them again. That's worse than having no hope in the first place."

Patrese nodded. He knew Knight was right, and he appreciated him saying it.

Patrese found Trent in one of the communal rooms, sitting on the floor with three other youths about his age. They were poring over a copy of *Guns and Ammo.*

Trent looked up and smiled for half a second before remembering that his buddies were watching.

"Yo," he said, voice dead neutral.

"Yo," Patrese replied, feeling about as uncool as a dad dancing at a wedding. "Can I have a word? About the tagging?"

"You wanna word now?"

Patrese nodded. "Now."

"Okay." Trent got up and walked toward Patrese. The other three watched warily.

Patrese gestured for Trent to follow him from the room. When they were out of the others' earshot, Patrese stopped.

"Hey, man, I got a caution for that," Trent said before Patrese could speak, "and you told me that was it. So what's this about?"

"I'm trying out a new interviewing technique."

"Yeah? The fuck am I, some sorta guinea pig?"

"I thought we could discuss it further at Heinz Field this afternoon."

Trent was about to snap something back when he realized what Patrese had said. "Heinz Field?" he asked.

Patrese nodded.

"The Browns are playin' there, that's right?"

Patrese nodded again.

"Yo, lemme check my calendar." Trent paused half a second. "I checked. I'm free."

117

Everyone has a last morning of their life, thought Mustafa, but only the privileged ones know for sure exactly when that last morning is, and can therefore make all the arrangements they need for entry into paradise.

The last tufts of his beard lay clumped in the sink. He ran his hand around his jaw, wincing slightly at the tenderness of skin clean-shaven for the first time in years. The face that returned his gaze from the mirror looked younger and more innocent than he knew it was.

No one would give him a second glance; not till it was too late, at any rate.

Mustafa washed the remnants of his beard down the drain, sluicing with water and fingers till the sink was clean again. Then he took a vial of flower water and dabbed it on his face and hands. As with the removal of his beard, this was a vital part of correctly preparing his body for what awaited him.

He returned to his bedroom and dressed carefully: underpants, socks, pants, shoes, two T-shirts, and the camouflage vest. Each of the vest's numerous pockets contained one or more of the metal pipes he'd cut to length, and every pipe was filled with an assortment of ball bearings, washers, nuts, screws, tacks, and nails. The vest was heavy on Mustafa's shoulders, and he had to adjust it several times before he found a comfortable position that didn't dig into his skin too much.

He was proud that he'd done all this himself, without a single bit of help. Some attacks needed a whole team of people: one to select the operative, one to select the target, a couple of engineers, one to plan logistics, one to get the operative to the target, and so on. Not this time. Mustafa was a pure solo artist. A legend.

He'd set his video camera on a tripod in one corner of his bedroom. He went over to it, switched it on, pressed the record button, and returned to his chair, already placed so as to be dead center in the picture.

When he spoke, his voice was clear and strong, and he didn't stutter.

"My religion is Islam, obedience to the one true God, Allah, following the footsteps of the final prophet and messenger Muhammad. To Allah belongs the power and the majesty. I beg Allah to accept this action from me, knowing I make it in all sincerity, and to admit me to the highest station in paradise, for verily he grants martyrdom to whomever he wills.

"To my mother, I beg you not to cry for me, but

instead rejoice in happiness and love what I have done, for Allah loves those who fight for his sake. Mother, keep your heart sealed to this religion. Hold tight to the rope of Allah, and don't let go. Pray your five daily prayers so you may be saved from hell. My father would be proud of your steadfastness.

"I am pursued, left unable to go about my daily business by a godless government that perpetrates atrocities against my people all over the world. My creed and color deny me the freedom your Constitution promises. I salute the man known as the Human Torch who's killing the prominent people of this city. Between us, we'll make you listen. I salute the Human Torch especially for killing the surgeon who murdered my father. I hope the fires that consumed Dr. Redwine are only a forestate of what he is experiencing in Jahannam. He was too arrogant to accept he might ever be wrong. Had he lived, he would have hired lawyers as deceitful as they are expensive to help him escape the consequences of his action. My father was a good man. My father believed in America. I thank Allah he did not live to see his belief destroyed.

"We are at war, and I am a soldier. *Allahu Akbar.*"

118

Patrese found it amusing, and touching, to see Trent out of his natural environment.

Trent walked around Heinz Field with his eyes wide

and his mouth hanging open, as though he were witness to an alien invasion rather than to one of thousands making a weekly pilgrimage. He gawked at everything: at the scalpers selling tickets outside the stadium, at the tailgate parties in the parking lots, at the sea of black and gold in the stands. Here, Trent wasn't a gangbanger in waiting, or a teenager trying to cover up confusion with masks of toughness, or even a young man whose mother was going on trial. Here, he was just a kid at a ball game, knocked sideways by the sound and the noise.

Patrese had been to watch the Steelers probably more than a hundred times in his life, but the wonder and excitement in Trent's eyes made him feel somehow that he too was seeing it through fresh eyes. For the first time, Patrese felt he understood why men loved being fathers; he understood the vicarious, deep-rooted thrill at the everyday and familiar being made new and enthralling again.

It was more than that with Trent, he knew; certainly more than just because Shaniqua had asked Patrese to look out for him.

It was protection, and protectiveness, and you only really sought the first if you'd felt denied the second.

It was a recognition that Shaniqua's life would have been much different—much better—if she'd been raised somewhere else.

It was an appreciation of the sacrifice Shaniqua was making for Trent.

It was a kicking against all the deaths in Patrese's world, an affirmation that saving someone's life didn't always have to be as dramatic as pulling them from a fast-flowing river or a burning building.

It was a perfect storm of elements that had brought a confluence of people, place, and time; Patrese and Trent, at Heinz Field, right now.

"Could have been you, man," Trent said.

Could have been me. I was placed in the NFL draft. Every night for a month, I prayed the Steelers would get me. But I guess I was no longer sold on God, and God knew this; because the Steelers missed me, and in the second round I was picked up by the Minnesota Vikings, the team the Steelers had beaten to win the Super Bowl the day I was born, January 12, 1975. You had to laugh.

Summer in Minneapolis, preseason, the press on my ass, as they always were with the Heisman winner. Routine training session, nothing special. A running drill, two linebackers closing in, and I'd already seen the gap between them and was shifting to get through it.

But the grass was wet where the sprinkler system had been left on too long. My cleats caught in a patch of mud. I went one way. My knee went the other. It sounded like a shot. I collapsed like a cheap deck chair.

The surgeon who operated on me said it was the worst knee injury he'd ever seen. In time, I'd be able to walk again, even run—in a straight line. But jink, twist, dodge, and swerve—no way.

I was never going to be a pro football player.

Here came the Dawg Pound, the Browns' most hard-core fans, decked head to foot in orange and brown, singing loudly and posing for TV cameras. Here were stalls selling ranks of Terrible Towels, yellow hand towels that had become staple items for any serious Steelers fan.

Everywhere was laughter and anticipation, a rivalry that came from similarity: two industrial towns, both with waterfront stadiums, both with rabidly partisan fans. The rivalry was about battles played hard, won hard, and celebrated hard. It was about not just the desire, but the atavistic *need* for a rivalry like this. When it had at one stage looked as though the Browns franchise might be relocated away from Cleveland, Steelers fans had joined the protests in huge numbers, standing alongside their oldest and bitterest rivals. Both clubs needed the juice of such an ancient contest, understanding that they were diminished without each other.

Patrese didn't insult Trent by making explicit the unspoken message of all this: that if you need rivalry in your life—and most people, certainly most young men, do—then make it this rather than what you're heading for. People die in gang shootouts. They don't die in stadiums on the banks of the Allegheny or Lake Erie.

Everyone was here to celebrate, honor, and renew that rivalry.

Everyone except one.

119

In purely scientific terms, a bus would probably have been Mustafa's best target, especially at this time of year when all the windows were closed to keep out the cold. A sealed environment would intensify the force of the blast and maximize its killing potential; the shock wave tearing lungs and crushing other internal organs, a hail of shrapnel piercing flesh and breaking bones, an exploding fuel tank causing burns and respiratory damage.

But in terms of the wider psychological effect Mustafa sought, a bus was a nonstarter. He knew he had to hit the people of Pittsburgh where it hurt, which meant targeting something they loved.

People didn't love the bus. They rode it to work and back, a purely functional way of getting from A to B. Catching the bus was no more exciting than breathing.

People liked their public buildings—their theaters, their galleries—and their parks, sure, but attacking these places would sting the city rather than tear its guts out.

No, there was only one thing all Pittsburghers loved.

The Steelers.

120

Marquez Berlin didn't often come into work over the weekend, but he was running a big diagnostic check on the department's crime database, and it needed checking every twenty-four hours. If he left it unsupervised all weekend and something went wrong, it would take him half the following week to fix; but this way, he'd lose a day's work at most.

The system was running slowly, and it took him a

few moments to work out why. Someone had switched the download destination of the Bayoumi bugs to the hard drive on which Berlin was running diagnostics. The department didn't have people listening to the taps around the clock anymore; it was just too much manpower. Now they were simply saving the files and checking them every day.

Sound files took up a lot of memory, and saving them to the wrong drive was a simple mistake, easily corrected. Berlin clicked on the mouse to move the files, but his finger was too fast. The mouse registered a double-click and opened the first file before he could cancel the command.

Mustafa Bayoumi's voice came through the computer speakers.

> *"My religion is Islam, obedience to the one true God, Allah, following the footsteps of the final prophet and messenger Muhammad. To Allah belongs the power and the majesty. I beg Allah to accept this action from me, knowing I make it in all sincerity, and to admit me to the highest station in paradise, for verily he grants martyrdom to whomever he wills."*

Berlin listened all the way through, hardly daring to breathe. It was a joke, surely? Or perhaps some kind of weird rehearsal? A film, a play?

He listened again. It sure didn't sound like a joke.

He called up to the incident room, skeleton-staffed on a Sunday.

No, said the bored uniform manning the phone,

neither Beradino nor Patrese was there. Their cell numbers? Sure. Hold on a sec. A shuffling of paper, the sound of coffee being slurped, then the uniform was back on the line, reading out the numbers. Berlin scribbled them down with a shaking hand.

He dialed Beradino's first.

"Beradino."

"Marquez Berlin here. You gotta listen to this. It's from the Bayoumi surveillance."

Berlin played the sound file for the third time.

"Jeez Louise," Beradino said when it had finished. "This was recorded when?"

Berlin looked at the time code on the file. "Coupla hours ago."

"That's all there is? Nothing else?"

"I'll check."

There was only one file recorded more recently. Berlin clicked on it. Two voices this time: Mustafa and Sameera, speaking in Arabic.

Down the line, Beradino sucked his teeth in frustration. "Doggone it. Translators aren't in today, are they?"

"Doubt it."

"Okay. Marquez, listen to me. I'm home in Punxsutawney. I'm leaving now, but it's a couple of hours from me to you, and we might not have that time. Call Patrese and play that file to him. Then I want you to take a couple of uniforms and haul ass to the Bayoumis' house. You remember where that is?"

"Sure."

"Tell Patrese to meet you there. Find out from Sameera where her son's gone."

121

Patrese wasn't answering his phone—it just rang and rang before going to voicemail—so Berlin went to the Bayoumis' house with only the first uniforms he could find.

Sameera answered the door with a strange cowering defiance.

"What you want?" she said quickly. "Why you not leave Mustafa alone?"

"Where is he?"

"He not here."

"Where? Where's he gone?"

"I don't know. He not tell me."

"We're going to have to search the place."

"You need warrant."

"We have reason to believe your son intends to perform a suicide bombing."

Sameera's eyes opened wide, like a cat's. "*What?*"

"You heard. Now let us in."

She stood aside a split second before they barreled through the door.

If her reaction had been genuine, and there was no reason to suppose otherwise, Sameera clearly hadn't heard Mustafa's suicide message, which meant he'd probably recorded it in his bedroom. Berlin led the uniforms up there.

The video camera was in the corner. One of the uniforms turned it on and began to scroll through the recordings, while Berlin looked around the room. There was a handful of prints on the walls, scenes of deserts and mosques. The books on Mustafa's shelves were either scientific or religious. His jackets, shirts, and pants hung in the closet; underwear was folded in drawers. It was all very neat and tidy—unnervingly, unnaturally so. Hell, Berlin thought, even the trash can was empty.

Almost empty.

There was one thing in there: a label, trailing a plastic tag. Berlin bent down and picked it out.

Congratulations on buying genuine official Steelers merchandise, the label said, next to the three-starred Steelmark logo.

The shop sticker was on the back. *LGE STLRS JCKT, BLK/GLD. $149.95.*

Berlin walked out of the bedroom. Sameera was standing in the corridor outside.

"Mrs. Bayoumi, was your son wearing a Steelers jacket?"

She nodded.

"Was it new?"

"Yes. He buy it the other day. I don't even know he like football."

Berlin went back into Mustafa's bedroom and looked in the closet. There were two overcoats in there, both more than up to the job of keeping the wearer warm even in a Pittsburgh winter.

"Why would you buy a brand-new Steelers coat," Berlin mused, "when you've got two perfectly good overcoats here, and you don't even like football?"

"To blend in," one of the uniforms said.

"Like, at a football game," added the other.

122

It was turning into one hell of a game.

The Browns had gone out of the blocks at a fearful pace: ten points up after the first quarter, fourteen at halftime, back to ten up going into the last quarter. The Steelers had hardly got a look in. Passes had gone to ground, tackles been missed, punt returns fumbled. Patrese hadn't seen them play this badly in a long time.

And the crowd had kept singing and shouting, louder and louder.

That was what had really grabbed Trent in his vitals, Patrese saw—that the Steelers fans hadn't gotten down on their team because they were losing, but instead had ramped up the support, up a gear, and another, and another. Each time the Browns had scored, when you might have expected a deflated hush, the stadium had erupted in defiant noise: Come on, Steelers, *come on,* back at 'em, we shall overcome, we love you whatever, cut us and we bleed black and gold.

It was part of Steelers folklore that the team never thrived more than when they were dissed, knocked, kicked to the curb. The surest way to make them lose was to tell them how good they were and get them complacent. It was that old Steel Town thing; they were always underdogs, and they loved it. The Steelers liked being in a corner, they said, because in a corner no one could come at you from behind.

And now, slowly, with the clock running down, back they came.

Third and goal, a flurry of movement behind the scrimmage, and suddenly there was Ben Roethlisberger, Big Ben, the first Steelers quarterback to be spoken about seriously as a successor to the legendary Terry Bradshaw, scrambling over from a couple of yards out for the touchdown.

Trent was on his feet, his arms rising to punch the air—and the upswing accidentally knocked Patrese's cell phone out of his coat pocket and onto the ground.

"Shit. Sorry, man."

"No worries." Patrese bent down, picked the phone up, and checked it for damage. It looked okay.

Missed calls: 11 the screen said.

Patrese raised his eyebrows in surprise. The noise of the crowd must have masked the ringing, and the thickness of his coat deadened the vibrations. He scrolled through the menu to see who'd called.

Beradino, North Shore, a couple of numbers he didn't recognize.

He phoned Beradino first of all rather than wade through endless messages. Beradino picked up almost before Patrese had heard it ring.

"Franco! Where the heck have you been?"

"I'm at Heinz Field. Sorry, didn't hear—"

"Heinz Field? Holy moly, that's where Bayoumi is."

"What?"

Another breaking wave of crowd noise. Patrese jabbed his finger into his free ear so he could hear Beradino properly.

"Mustafa Bayoumi. He's there, at Heinz Field. He's going to blow himself up."

Patrese was too much of a pro to waste time asking Beradino if he was joking.

He thought fast. Heinz Field held sixty-five thousand people sitting close together, side by side and front to back. An explosive vest could kill perhaps fifty people first off, injure a whole heap more, but that wasn't the half of it. The blast would set off the mother of all stampedes to get out of the stadium as fast as possible, and that would kill the same number of people again, maybe even more.

"I'm on it."

"Get your butt over to the stadium control room. There's a bunch of uniforms on the way. Stadium security's been told to look out for anyone acting suspicious, but not why, or what he's doing."

"How come?"

"Fewer people who know, fewer people who can panic. But they need you to ID him, Franco. You're the only one there who knows what he looks like."

"Where are you?"

"On the interstate, hauling ass. *Go.*"

Patrese ended the call and turned to Trent. "Stay here. I'll be back."

Trent was so engrossed in the game, he barely noticed.

Patrese hurried from the stands and into the bowels of the stadium. A steward in a vest fluorescent enough to be seen from space directed him to the control room.

Four times along the way, unsmiling men in suits blocked doorways and asked with menacing politeness whether they could help. Four times Patrese showed them his police badge, and four times they swung open the portals for him.

In the control room, screens were banked high on every wall, showing the crowd parceled into endlessly shifting sections. Whoever you were, wherever you were sitting, you were being watched.

"We've already checked the ticket sales roster," said one of the stadium staff. "There's no record of a Mustafa Bayoumi. So either he booked in a false name, or he bought a ticket from a scalper outside."

Patrese nodded. The game was in its fourth quarter, so the scalpers would be long gone. No point looking for them, let alone questioning them.

"What do you want him for, anyway?" said someone else.

Patrese didn't answer. He ran his eyes from screen to screen, skimming the sea of faces. Bayoumi's skin tone alone wouldn't be enough to mark him out, especially on a day when people were wrapped up tight beneath hats and scarves. Bayoumi looked more black than Arab, and plenty of Steelers fans were black, as were half the team.

No; what Patrese was looking for was something that *jarred.*

Sporting crowds are homogenous entities. They move more or less as one. Heads swivel in synchronicity to follow the action; bodies tense in communal excitement or frustration. It was the anomaly that Patrese was seeking, the one who looked like everyone else but wasn't behaving like it.

There.

A man with eyes lifted high and unfocused in a thousand-yard stare. A genuine fan would never have worn an expression like that, especially during a game like this.

"Zoom in there," Patrese said.

Buttons tapped and trackballs spun. A face filled the screen. It looked like Mustafa, but the man had no beard.

"Can you go in closer?"

Another zoom.

Through the cluster of pixels, Patrese could see what looked like mild tan lines, a lighter area of skin around the jaw and mouth.

The kind of mark a freshly shaved beard would leave.

"That's him," Patrese said. "Where's he sitting? Where's that camera?"

"Lower Level West. Block 135."

"No one is to approach that man but me, do you understand?"

Patrese left the control room at a jog. By the time he was back in the wide concrete walkways under the stands he was running fast, almost knocking over a pregnant woman with a sign over her bump saying "Baby's First Game."

He wondered why Mustafa hadn't detonated the bomb already. Perhaps he was plucking up the courage to do it. Perhaps he was waiting for the game to reach its climax, for maximum effect.

Patrese didn't know, and he didn't much care. All that mattered was that he got to Mustafa before Mustafa decided to detonate. That was their only option. Anything else—a public address, a SWAT team, an attempt to clear the stadium—would simply alert Mustafa to the fact they were onto him, and that would be it. Mustafa would never let them take him alive.

Patrese saw the entrance to Block 135, and headed toward it.

No. Going that way would put him straight in Mustafa's sight line. Better to enter the stand at the next block along and come at Mustafa from the side and behind.

Patrese went in at 136. A short flight of stairs took him into the main body of the stand, where he turned back on himself and climbed to the highest row of seats in the block, hard against the overhang of the level above.

From here, he could get to Mustafa as quickly and stealthily as possible.

Two minutes to go, three points between the teams. The Steelers on offense, second and ten, thirty-two yards out.

Patrese looked through the crowd, trying to sort through the visual clutter—towels, arms, movement—and get a fix on Mustafa.

Roethlisberger took the snap from the center, backpedaled into the pocket, and surveyed his options.

There. Mustafa, his mouth working furiously. Talking to himself. Praying.

Roethlisberger waited, and waited, and waited, arm cocked, checking events downfield; looking at the patterns his wide receivers were running, looking for the angle, the space, all the time keeping half an eye on the frothing, churning maelstrom of the big guys in the middle of the park, the Browns' linebackers grappling with the Steelers' offensive linemen, thousands of pounds of muscle and aggression colliding like crazed rhinos.

Patrese was on the move now, hurrying along the clear aisle behind the final row of seats. He held his left hand ahead of him to barge past anyone who got in his way. In his right, he gripped the Ruger Blackhawk tight inside his coat.

One of the Browns' linebackers broke clear. A Steeler's hand clutched in desperation at the linebacker's ankle and banged the turf in fury when he missed; and *still* Roethlisberger waited.

Patrese ran down the stairs toward Mustafa's row.

The linebacker was still a stride away from Roethlisberger when the quarterback, with a sniper's deathless cool, finally saw the opening downfield he'd been waiting for. He shimmied half a pace to his right, just enough to clear the linebacker, and in the same moment he launched the ball, the power coming not just from the sling of his arm but all the way through his twisting trunk.

Every pair of eyes in the stadium followed it, apart from two.

Patrese was at the end of Mustafa's row now; ten yards away, maybe less.

Roethlisberger's throw wasn't a perfect spiral, but it didn't matter. It went just where he'd been aiming, the exact spot where wide receiver Hines Ward was arriving in the middle of three defenders.

Patrese pulled his gun out, and even with the drama on the field, the people nearest him saw what was happening and began backing away, shouting, staring, shrieking.

Ward leaped, reached, caught, tumbled to the ground, and bounced straight up again, the ball held above his head and his mouth gaping in triumph. Touchdown. *Bedlam.*

Mustafa turned toward the commotion at the end of his row and saw Patrese, the Ruger held in two hands front and center, bead drawn on Mustafa.

It seemed to both of them, locked deep in their concentration, that all the noise and tumult faded away.

Mustafa moved his hand toward his pocket.

Detonator, thought Patrese. *Detonator.*

"Hands out!" he yelled, loud as he could, louder than he'd ever yelled before, just to be heard above the torrent of noise in the stadium. "Show me your fucking hands!"

Patrese would have to go for the head. A body shot could still allow Mustafa to press the detonator, or the bullet might even set it off if the detonator was sensitive to heat or shock.

No; head shot, or nothing.

"Hands where I can see 'em," he shouted at Mustafa, *again,* that was the third time, and in that moment Patrese realized why he hadn't taken the shot yet: because *hands where I can see 'em* was exactly what he'd said to Samantha Slinger before he'd shot her.

He'd been wrong then.

But he wasn't wrong now, was he?

Take the shot, goddamn it, he told himself; *take the fucking shot.*

The Muslims call it *bassamat al-farah*, the smile of joy; the luminous, transcendental ecstasy brought on by the impending martyrdom of a true believer. When Mustafa gave Patrese this smile, he looked so happy that, just for a moment, Patrese didn't see Mustafa's hand dart into his pocket.

Just for a moment; no more.

Patrese squeezed the trigger, faster than thought, and Mustafa's head exploded.

Not all of him. Just his head, split like a watermelon and gone in puffs of blood.

123

MONDAY, DECEMBER 6

Boone was a one-man Big Brother, on your screen no matter how often you switched channels. Sharing a sofa with Diane Sawyer on *Good Morning America*; behind a desk with Matt Lauer on the *Today* show; video-linked to Harry Smith on *The Early Show*, not to mention *Fox and Friends*, *BBC World News Today*, and probably even MTV and the Cartoon Network, given half a chance.

Boone's line, as agreed with Chance, was that the shooting of Mustafa Bayoumi had been a Bureau operation carried out after receiving specific intelligence about the Heinz Field attack. This was the only way to sidestep any tricky questions about how Mustafa's intentions had been known ahead of time. The Bureau's powers of surveillance under the Patriot Act were vastly greater than the police's.

Boone declined to be drawn out on the exact nature of the intelligence received, the name of the agent who'd shot Mustafa, or any other operational specifics.

The networks tried to link the attempted bombing with the Human Torch murders, of course. They wanted Boone to connect the dots for them: Mustafa had killed Redwine in revenge for Redwine's botched operation on his father before murdering the others and trying to go out in a blaze of glory. That's how they wanted it.

Sorry, Boone said, but that simply wasn't plausible. Yes, there were similarities. The triggers that could turn a serial killer's fantasies into reality applied to terrorists too. Mustafa had always flirted with radicalism, but he'd only made an irrevocable leap to it following his father's death. Increasingly disillusioned with mainstream America, bereft of the man who'd been his rudder and anchor no matter how often they'd argued, and angry at the way Abdul had died, Mustafa had struck out in the most destructive way possible.

Thing was, Mustafa's anger had been diffuse, unfocused. He'd ranted and raved about the evils of American society, but (Redwine apart) hadn't singled out any individuals for opprobrium. On the other hand, whoever was doing the burnings—and no, Boone wouldn't use the nickname he knew the media was fond of—was very focused indeed.

Mustafa had alibis for each of the killings. None of the forensic evidence found at any of the scenes matched him. Far as they could tell, he'd shown no special interest in the case—no newspaper clippings scrapbooked at home, no discussions with friends or colleagues. Many serial killers loved talking about their cases, returned to the scenes of their crimes, even tried to insert themselves into the investigation by hanging out at police bars and discussing the case with off-duty officers.

Whichever way you cut it, Mustafa was not their man, not for the burnings.

The killer could still be a Muslim extremist, of course, but it hadn't been Mustafa. He'd been a failed terrorist, and he'd never been a serial killer. He'd wanted to kill hundreds. As it was, he'd killed no one at all. Not even himself.

124

Pittsburghers reacted to what had happened at Heinz Field with indignation, affront, and fury. Crowds gathered at each of Pittsburgh's seven mosques. Protestors railed against Bayoumi's actions and demanded arrests, deportations, executions, the lot. Muslims gathered in counterprotest, furious that they should all be tarred with one brush, and pointing out that they had American passports and paid American taxes. A rally downtown turned into a riot. Muslims were attacked on the streets for no apparent reason other than their religion. That the victims were of Arab origin rather than black, and therefore more obviously and visibly Muslim, seemed to bear this out.

Inevitably, there were those in the Muslim community who wanted to—and did—strike back. A bunch of hotheads went on a rampage in Homewood, and it needed almost half the city's riot squad to stop the carnage turning into civil war. Central Booking hadn't seen anything like it in years.

Meanwhile, Patrese spent three hours in debrief with Chance and Boone, recounting every last detail he could remember about the shooting. They told him he'd done a hell of a job, but they couldn't recognize it publicly, given the official line that this had been a Bureau operation. Patrese couldn't have cared less. He didn't particularly want to play the hero, especially if putting his name out there would encourage another disaffected Muslim to seek revenge on him personally.

He thought of something Mustafa had said in his video message: *"I am pursued, left unable to go about my daily business by a godless government that perpetrates atrocities against my people all over the world. My creed and color deny me the freedom your Constitution promises. I salute the man known as the Human Torch who's killing the prominent people of this city. Between us, we'll make you listen."*

Had Patrese been too zealous in his pursuit of Mustafa? Was that what had tipped Mustafa over the edge—that Patrese had come around after every murder, probing, questioning, worrying away at him like a terrier?

There was no way of knowing for sure. But even if he *had* been the difference, what else could he have done? He'd been doing his job; yes, with zeal and thoroughness, but those were what usually got cases solved. Except this one.

Patrese was leaving North Shore when his cell phone rang. He looked at the caller display and his eyes widened in surprise: Amberin.

"I'm calling to see if you're okay," she said the moment he answered.

"Yeah, I'm fine. Er . . . thanks." He couldn't keep the curiosity out of his voice. He hadn't expected her to phone, hadn't even wondered whether she would.

"That was a heck of a brave thing you did, Franco. I'm sure lots of people have told you that already, but I—hold on a second."

Patrese heard a shout in the background.

"Amberin?" he said.

"I'm here." Her voice was strained and twisted.

"What's wrong?"

"I'm being followed."

125

"Where are you?"

"Just left the courthouse. Crossing Smithfield at Fourth. Franco, there's three of them, three guys, and they're—they're shouting things, racist things. . . ."

"Stay on Smithfield." Smithfield was a large street,

well-lit and busy. "Find a shop or something, a department store."

"Franco. *Hurry.*"

The naked fear in her voice on that last word had Patrese sprinting to the nearest cruiser. No matter that Amberin was a kick-ass assistant DA who'd faced down psychopaths across a courtroom. On her own, at night, with three men behind her, she was a woman, no more and no less, and as vulnerable as all women were to the stupider and cruder end of the male species.

Patrese turned on his blues and sliced through the North Shore traffic.

He trusted there were enough people around Smithfield for the men following Amberin to think twice. They were probably just punks, too much beer inside them and picking on someone they thought was an easy target. Every cop had met hundreds like them, assholes who looked tough and talked loud but took off like scalded cats at the first sniff of a real fight. That's what he *hoped* they were, at any rate.

It took him six minutes to get to Smithfield. As he pulled up, he called Amberin's cell phone. No answer. No sign of her either.

What he *could* see was a crowd of people gathered on the pavement.

For a moment, Patrese thought it must be the men who'd been following Amberin, but there were too many of them for that, and the crowd was largely static. Someone was making a phone call; another person was crouched down. Their body language reeked concern, and they were massed around something.

Someone.

Patrese leaped from the car and shouldered his way through, shouting: "Police officer, I'm a police officer, let me through."

Amberin was curled on the ground in a fetal position. Her face and hijab were covered in blood. Her eyes were open, and she was both conscious and lucid, telling those around her that she was okay, that all she needed was not to be rushed.

"Franco," she said when she saw him.

The others stepped back a bit to allow Patrese to crouch at her side.

"I came as fast as I could." It sounded desperately inadequate.

"They jumped me. Called me an Arab bitch, told me to go back to my cave."

Patrese looked around at the crowd. "Anyone see what happened?"

Two or three people said they had. Amberin's attackers had hightailed, but they'd still have enough eyewitness statements to get descriptions of them.

An ambulance and a patrol car arrived. The cops started taking witness statements; the paramedics put Amberin on a stretcher and lifted her gently into the back of the ambulance. Patrese followed them to Mercy, where he ignored Amberin's protests that he should go home and waited while the doctors patched her up.

Erin Fitzpatrick—the nurse with whom Patrese had slept a couple of times back in the fall—was on duty, and when she saw him she marched over and bawled him out for being a total shit, never calling her, fucking her and chucking her, and so on.

She then launched into a long explanation of how Patrese was a rooster, because a rooster could screw sixty hens in a given mating, but could never screw the same hen more than five times. No matter how much he wanted to, he could never get it up sixth time around; but if he was presented with a new hen, then suddenly the problem was gone.

By the time she'd finished, Bianca had appeared. She looked at Erin, then toward the triage room where Amberin was being treated, then back at her brother.

"I can't keep up, Franco," she said, rolling her eyes theatrically.

After the doctors had checked Amberin for concussion and broken bones—negative on both counts—they sent her on her way. Patrese said he'd drive her back to her apartment.

"Thanks, but you don't have to. You've already done more than enough."

"You want to wait half an hour for a taxi? Or you want a lift courtesy of the city?"

"You must have better things to do than go out of your way to drop me home."

Patrese thought for a second, then shook his head. "No, I don't, actually."

Amberin laughed. "Okay. Then yes, I'd like a lift, thanks."

She winced as she settled in her seat and fastened the belt.

"Where to?" Patrese said.

"South Side. Above the Flats."

It wasn't too far from Patrese's own stomping ground of Mount Washington, at least as the crow flew, though the roads tended to take rather more circuitous routes through, across, up, down, and around Pittsburgh's extravagant topography.

Patrese pulled out of the hospital parking lot.

"I don't mean to state the obvious," he said, "but . . ."

"What?"

He gestured at her bloodstained hijab. "Don't you think it might be wise not to wear that for a while?"

"I've got plenty more at home."

"Not that particular one. The hijab, period."

She chuckled. "I know what you meant."

"Well?"

"You're probably right, but I don't care. I'm going to keep wearing it."

"Why?"

"Because I *want* to. I wear it to show my attachment to my culture. My pride in my religion. My identity, something a little bit separate from this McDonald's world."

"It's not, er, a bit—"

"Oppressive? No. You want to see oppression? Every American woman is forced to look the same way—not through law or force, but through something just as potent, the relentless bombardment of images saying this is how you must look, this is the ideal, always be skinny, wear short skirts, look hot, let guys know you're up for it."

"It's not the same."

"It *is* the same. You're a man, you don't understand; it doesn't hit you where it hurts. But it does for girls, and *that's* oppression. The hijab is feminist expression, because it forces people to judge me by my character rather than my looks. It protects my dignity. If that's not liberation, then what is?"

"Men don't have to wear them though, do they?"

"No. No, they don't. But Muslim men have to do things that Muslim women don't, and vice versa. And before you tell me women are second-class citizens under Islam, no, they're not, and if you think they are, you don't know what the hell you're talking about. You know when Muslim women were given the rights to keep their surnames when married, receive and bestow inheritances, manage their own financial affairs, get divorced? The seventh century. Parts of the West didn't grant those kind of rights till the sixties. The *nineteen* sixties."

Amberin in full flow, brimming with passion and energy even after having the stuffing knocked out of her by pond scum; Patrese shook his head in admiration, and more.

"But the Koran—" he said.

"You want to see sexism? In the Bible, Eve comes from Adam's rib, and she lures him into eating the apple. In the Koran, she's created equal, and she doesn't tempt Adam. Satan tempts them both."

"What about Afghanistan? What about Saudi Arabia?"

"What about them?"

"Women covered head to foot. Banned from driving. Can't go anywhere unless there's a man with them. You support that?"

"Not at all."

"But that's Islam."

"No. That's *culture*, that's oppressive governments, and I hate it far more than you ever could. But it's nothing to do with religion. Look at it the other way. What are the three countries with the biggest Muslim majority in the world? I'll tell you: Indonesia, Pakistan, and Bangladesh. And they've all had female leaders. How many women presidents has America had?"

Patrese held up his hands. There was no answer.

"That's far more serious than what I choose to wear on my head. See, Franco, you look at the hijab and think of it as gender discrimination. You see cultural restraints on individual behavior and call it oppression, because you're American and that's the way you see the world. No, don't dispute it, I'm not saying that's right or wrong; it is what it is. But for lots of cultures, mine included, communal standards *aren't* seen as inhibiting individual freedoms. Quite the opposite, in fact; they're seen as part of belonging to a group whose cultures and values are important to those individuals."

"But your head?"

"What about my head?"

"Your head's where your face is, your individuality. You subsume those?"

"I cover my head, Franco, not my brain. Does your brain stop working when you put a hat on?" She laughed. "Don't answer that. Listen, I may be a Muslim, but I'm an American too, just as much. This country lets me practice my religion, wear what I choose and be respected for my choices. To me, that's real empowerment. I'm sorry Mustafa Bayoumi felt otherwise, and I'm especially sorry he chose to show it the way he did. But he's not me. He's not the vast majority of Muslims, either." She pointed toward a side street ahead. "Make a left there."

It was an eclectic neighborhood, where new condo buildings touched shoulders with teetering rickety row houses one room wide and four stories high.

"There." Amberin indicated a block on the right. "The Angel's Arms."

The Angel's Arms was a deconsecrated church turned into condos, a stern and handsome redbrick building in the Romanesque revival style with a tall square entrance tower that rose glowering from the Slopes.

"A *church*?" Patrese said. "Interesting choice."

"I like to think so."

They pulled up in the parking lot.

"You hungry?" she asked.

"I guess."

"Then I'll cook you some supper."

"You don't have to do that."

"And you didn't have to give me a lift."

126

There were towering columns in Amberin's kitchen; the vast main windows of the living room were arch-topped beneath a domed ceiling with ornamental plasterwork; and a seven-foot stained-glass rosette looked to be a fully restored original.

It was quite a place.

Amberin cooked chicken and rice. Here, on her own turf and free from the endless demands of being a woman in a man's world, she seemed much softer. She was no longer wearing her hijab. Her white shirt was rolled up to the elbows and slightly creased across the shoulders, and thin strands escaped from the clip that held her hair up. When she smiled, it was with a soft crinkling of skin rather than a sharklike flash of teeth.

Not that it made her easier to read; quite the opposite, if anything. It made her even harder to read than before.

In other circumstances, Patrese might have assumed that any woman who invited him up to her apartment at night was interested in taking things further. But with Amberin, he couldn't help feeling that it might just have been a mixture of professional interest and a caring personality, and that she'd have done the same for anyone.

He couldn't get a lock on her intentions, not at all; and it was almost with a start that he realized he liked her.

Yes, he'd been drawn to Mara too. Funny that he

should have had designs on two women who'd faced each other across a courtroom in the most bitter and charged of circumstances; or perhaps not so funny, whether peculiar or amusing. And yes, dating Amberin would come with its own difficulties. But he liked her.

Not just because he couldn't work her out; not just because she was dusky beautiful and altogether too exotic for a hardscrabble Pennsylvania steel town; not just because she was bright and feisty and principled; and not just because she straddled two cultures, and even she didn't know where the boundaries between the two were.

It was all of these, of course, but more too.

She *felt* right. She *smelled* right.

And when Patrese realized this, he realized something else too: that all humans are animals and, like animals, they sense things at a gut level. So either he felt and smelled right to Amberin or he didn't, and either way there was nothing he could do about it.

By happenstance, *First Lady*—the film about Eleanor Roosevelt for which Mara had won her Oscar—was showing on cable. Patrese and Amberin sat on the sofa with their plates, close but not touching, and watched it together.

"You forget it's her, don't you?" Amberin said during the first commercial break.

You did indeed, Patrese thought.

The most famous scene in the movie was about halfway through. Eleanor and FDR have both just begun affairs—Eleanor with her bodyguard, Earl Miller; Franklin with his private secretary, Missy LeHand. In the marital bedroom that night, both husband and wife not only recognize the arrangements, but also accept and even encourage them, knowing that the extent to which they want each other to be happy is matched only by their mutual inability to provide such happiness.

It was one of those scenes during which you held your breath, and only realized you'd been doing so once the scene was over.

But there was nothing spectacular about it, no flashy shots, fancy camera angles, or extravagant monologues. It was underwritten and underplayed. Neither Eleanor nor Franklin ever alluded to the situation directly. Instead, they did it all with euphemism, pauses, and minuscule adjustments of their bodies and faces. It was magic.

When Amberin turned toward Patrese, her eyes were wet.

"It's such a tragedy," she said. "For someone that talented, to do what she did—"

"*If* she did."

"She did. I know she did."

"She was acquitted."

"She did it, Franco. Some cases you just know they're guilty, and this was one of them. Why are you so determined she was innocent?"

"Perhaps because everyone else around me has her nailed as a baby-killer."

Amberin smiled. "Contrary. That makes sense."

"What's contrary?"

"You're contrary."

"I am?"

"Sure you are. I deal with a lot of cops, and you're not like most of them. You pretend to be sometimes, but you're not, deep down. More sensitive. More *secretive*."

"Secretive?"

"Secretive. I always feel there's something you're hiding."

"Everyone's hiding something, What are *you* hiding?"

"We're still talking about you."

"You show me yours, I'll show you mine."

Her laughter trailed away into charged silence. Patrese was suddenly aware that they were both holding themselves very, very still, each waiting for the other to move first.

It was Amberin who broke the spell, but not in the way Patrese had hoped.

"I've got an early start tomorrow," she said.

127

TUESDAY, DECEMBER 7

"Can I help you?" he says.

"Yes. I think you probably can."

His eyebrows furrow. "Are you a resident here? Are you one of ours? I'm afraid I don't recognize you, and I pride myself on knowing everyone here."

"I'm just visiting."

"Then I'm afraid you'll have to come back another time. Visiting hours are over for today. You can visit the residents between ten a.m. and six p.m."

"It's not the residents I've come to see."

"No?"

"It's you."

He's puzzled, I can see, but not alarmed; not yet.

There's a watercooler in the corner of his office. I gesture toward it.

"Could I have a glass of water, please?" I ask.

"Of course." He goes over to the watercooler, pulls a cup from the dispenser, and holds it below the spigot.

One smack on the back of the skull with the battery in the sock, and down he goes.

I don't worry about witnesses; we're alone in the office, and the rest of the complex is an old people's home. The few people who can see well enough to give the police a description of me probably can't remember what they had for lunch today—hardly the most reliable of witnesses.

I cuff his hands behind his back and slap him back to consciousness. He peers at me with woozy eyes.

"Scream, shout, do anything other than talk, and I'll hurt you," I say.

"I don't understand."

"I think you do."

"Are you confused? Would you like help?"

"I know what you do to the residents here."

"What are you talking about? We provide them with care that's second to none."

"You take their dignity from them."

"This is absurd. Let me get you some help."

"You take their dignity in life, and you take their dignity in death."

"We—"

"SHUT UP! Do you know what your staff do? Let me tell you. They don't give the residents the medicine they need. They deny them food. They restrain them forcibly and leave them like that for hours. They wrap towels around their heads to stop them from breathing. They let them wallow in their own waste. You think that's dignity?"

"That's not true."

"Residents have complained, haven't they?"

"There are always complaints, in any senior citizens' home."

"That's not an answer."

"Okay. A few people have complained, yes—but they're not in good health. They're senile, distressed, prone to fantasy. Every single allegation we get, I check it out. Every one is baseless. I'd know if there was something like that going on."

He's gabbling now, he's nervous.

I pull the torch from my bag.

"Oh no," he says. "Oh no, no, not that. No. Please. Please. I beg you."

"Isaiah chapter fifty-nine, verse seventeen," I say. "For I put on righteousness as a breastplate, and a helmet of salvation upon my head; and I put on the garments of vengeance for clothing, and am clad with zeal as a cloak."

He screams. It's no use. They're all deaf as posts here. No one will hear him.

128

The fire brigade had evacuated the Golden Twilight nursing home while they tried to stop the blaze spreading from deVries's apartment to the rest of the building. By the time Beradino and Patrese arrived, the residents were huddled in small groups on the driveway. Most sat in wheelchairs, all of them wrapped in as many blankets as they could find against the savage, clear coldness of a December night.

"Hey! Hotshot!"

Patrese recognized the voice at once. It was Old Man Hellmore.

Each victim had been linked to Hellmore junior more closely than the one before; and now they had the manager of the home where his father lived. How much more entwined could these choices get?

But Patrese had just called Hellmore's cell phone, and Hellmore was in Philly. Patrese hadn't just taken Hellmore's word for it, of course—on a cell phone, he could have been anywhere—but had taken the name of the hotel, dialed the switchboard, confirmed that Hellmore had checked in several hours before, and then been put through to his room to talk to the man himself.

So Hellmore couldn't have killed Walter deVries. Was someone trying to frame Hellmore? Was someone *working for* Hellmore? Either way, where was the motive?

Patrese went over to the old man.

"Fuck the fire, man." The flames, reflected, danced in Old Man Hellmore's eyes. "A few more minutes, you gonna have folks here dyin' of hypothermia. Y'all gonna keep us outside, least let us move a bit nearer the fire so we can get warm, you know what I'm sayin'?"

"I'll have a word with the fire department."

Patrese was halfway toward the firefighters when he heard Old Man Hellmore shout out again: "Full marks for compassion, hotshot. No marks for doing your job."

Patrese turned around. "Huh?"

"Don't you want to know who killed deVries?"

"Sure."

"I was out here having a cigarette. Had to give the smokin' Nazis the slip, 'cause there's some damn-fool curfew, everyone in their room by nine thirty, like we're damn schoolkids or something. Can't smoke in the room, or it sets off the alarm and all hell breaks loose. I fought at Midway, for Chrissakes. I'd known I was fightin' for a country a man can't even have a smoke in, I'd have gone over to the Japs.

"Anyhows. Out I come, just there, ten feet from where we are now, and I spark up. Hell of a headrush, smokin' when it's this cold, you know? I'm enjoyin' my smoke when, right over there"—he indicated the door to deVries's apartment, about twenty yards away and swarming with firefighters—"I see this little old lady come out."

Patrese and Beradino looked at each other.

"I think she must be one of ours, one of the residents here, but I don't recognize her. Sure, it's dark, and she's a ways away, but we got the streetlights on, and my eyes aren't too bad, least not for distance vision. Can't read a damn thing close up, mind. I wonder who she is, but I'm not, like, suspicious or nothin'. She comes out of the apartment, gets in her car, and drives away."

"Did she look agitated? Did she drive away fast?"

Old Man Hellmore shook his head. "Cool as you like. So I didn't pay it no mind. I thought maybe she come to see deVries about livin' here—I could tell her a few home truths, if she asked me—maybe she was a friend or somethin', I don't know."

"Could she have been a former resident?" Beradino asked.

Old Man Hellmore laughed. "This a one-way street, man. When your residency goes from current to former, it's 'cause you're six feet under. Where was I? Oh, yeah. She drive away. Few minutes later, I see the first flames, just as I'm finishin' my cigarette. I wheel the chair inside like I'm Mario damn Andretti and hit the alarm."

"Did you see what kind of car she was driving?"

"Sure I did. Toyota Camry. Silver."

129

WEDNESDAY, DECEMBER 8

It wasn't just the car that Old Man Hellmore had noticed. He'd also remembered the first two letters of the license plate, DG, and that the plate itself had blue letters on a white background, with a blue band across the top and a yellow one along the bottom. That was the design of the Pennsylvania state plate. Cars registered in Pennsylvania were given license numbers with three letters, a period, and four numbers.

The license number of Jesslyn's silver Camry was, Beradino knew, DGY•7462.

For reasons obvious to him, if to no one else, Beradino took personal charge of the vehicle hunt. He confirmed with the Pennsylvania Department of Motor Vehicles that the plate design in question had come into force near the end of 1999—before that, it had been yellow lettering on a solid blue background—and that numbers were issued sequentially, beginning with DAA•0000 and ending with DXX•9999, before moving on to the F series (no E, for reasons best known to the bureaucrats). A DG beginning, which could cover anything from DGA to DGX, indicated a 2001 issue.

There were more than eight thousand silver Camrys that matched the description.

"Let's start with the cars registered in Pittsburgh and Allegheny County," Beradino told the uniforms. "If you get no joy there, then move wider."

Jesslyn's Camry was registered to their home address in Punxsutawney, a couple of hours' drive from Pittsburgh. It would give Beradino a couple of days' breathing space, which was the best he could reasonably hope for. He'd already tried to delete Jesslyn's details from the DMV database, but the department's remorseless computer had advised him that he didn't have the requisite authorization. Sooner or later, therefore, the uniforms would find Jesslyn on the list.

"Any of those cars that have been reported stolen, of course you check them immediately," said Patrese. "Nothing to stop our killer having stolen the car first."

"What about looking at the owner's age?" asked one of the uniforms. "If it's, like, an old lady we're looking for."

Patrese shook his head. "It's not an old lady. No old lady I've ever met could carry out killings like this. It's someone *disguised* as an old lady. That's how she gains entry into the victims' houses. Who turns an old lady away? No one, that's who. No one feels threatened by them. Hell, no one even *notices* them."

Every cop knows it's better not to be noticed than not to be recognized. No one recognizes a man running down the street with a stocking over his head, but they sure as hell notice him. Old ladies, on the other hand, are about as invisible as you can get.

"Maybe it's not even a woman," Beradino said. "Could be a fellow in drag."

Patrese shook his head again. "No. It has to be a woman."

"Why?"

"Because her disguise is good enough to get her into victims' houses, and then keep those victims off guard for as long as it takes to subdue them. Putting on some dowdy clothes, plunking on a white wig and giving herself a stoop wouldn't fool Stevie Wonder, let alone a five o'clock shadow and hairy arms. In fact, you ask me, this isn't even just basic makeup. This is professional stuff."

"Professional stuff?"

"Heavy-duty makeup. Theater stuff."

130

Patrese went to the O'Reilly Theater downtown, where a quick phone call had secured him a slot with Maxine Park, one of their makeup artists.

Maxine Park was built like a shipping hazard and sported an orange bandanna above purple eye shadow, which made Patrese fear for her cosmetic skills—did she ever look in a mirror?—but he needn't have worried. She knew her stuff, and then some.

"You can get old-age kits online or in stores," she said. "Anything from kits for kids' parties, which are fun but no more, to real theatrical ones, as good as anything we use here. I'll give you the names of the main manufacturers, if you like."

"Please, yes. But this is something the person in question would need to apply regularly, probably by herself. Would that be possible?"

"Sure. Difficult in parts, but easily possible, if you've got time and patience."

"How long would it take?"

"To apply? Coupla hours on, twenty minutes off."

"Would she need to be skilled?"

"Not really. You can get videos showing you the process, either on their own or as part of the kits. A little practice goes a long way in this business."

"And good makeup would fool people?" Patrese knew the answer, but he wanted to be doubly sure; the killer had tricked quite a few people along the way.

"That depends."

"On what?"

"On how suspicious they are. Most people, they see an old lady, and they think, that's an old lady. If they've got no reason to be suspicious, then they won't be, not even when you're quite close to them. People see what they want to see. You could make it good enough to pass any normal encounter, no question."

"You're sure?"

"I can prove it, if you like."

"How?"

"I can age you so people who see you every day won't recognize you."

131

First Maxine cleaned his face with something called Sea Breeze, to remove surface oils that might stop the latex stipple she was going to use from sticking.

Using a makeup sponge for even coverage, she put on Patrese's face, neck, and ears a base layer slightly lighter than his natural skin tone. Elderly complexions tend to be on the pale side, she explained. Next, she used highlighter and shadow on his forehead, nose, and cheeks and around the eyes to make his skin look saggy. White makeup took care of his eyebrows, with transparent powder taking the shine off.

Then came the main part: stretch and stipple. Stretching each section of his face, neck, and hands in turn, she stippled on a modified latex solution, two layers each time. Still holding the skin, she ran a hair dryer over the section in question, powdered it, and finally let go.

The effect was amazing. Suddenly Patrese's entire skin was wrinkled—truly wrinkled, old-person wrinkled.

Then it was just touching up: deepen some lines with greasepaint, add liver spots and freckles to break up the smooth areas, put a pad inside each cheek to sag and pouch them, and fix the wig on top.

"This wig feels really natural," Patrese said. "Is it real hair?"

"Sure is. Asian."

"I'm sorry?"

"Ninety-nine percent of wigs come from Asia."

"Why's that?"

"Economic, mainly. There are many more people there than in America or Europe. Certainly many more who need to sell their hair for money."

He thought for a moment. "Anywhere particular in Asia?"

Maxine tipped her head slightly, as though unbalanced—or impressed—by the specificity of the question. "The best ones come from India and Pakistan. Their hair's less stiff and forms slight waves, which looks good on wigs."

The hair in Saint Paul Cathedral had come from Pakistan, Patrese remembered.

Wig in place, Patrese looked at himself in the mirror. He'd expected to see some likeness, but he literally couldn't recognize the man who stared back at him. He felt so dislocated that he had to say something out loud to reassure himself it was still him, but all that did was freak him out that an old man was speaking in his voice.

Maxine said she'd get a list of old-age kit manufacturers and fax them over.

"Go on," she said. "Go back to the police station, and see how long it takes till someone recognizes you."

She loaned Patrese an old man's jacket from her props store to make the disguise even more convincing. Still in makeup, he left the O'Reilly, got into his car, and drove north across the Allegheny. He used his swipe card to get through the security gate at headquarters and went up to the homicide department, where he walked through the middle of the room, in Maxine's makeup, an old man's jacket, and his best effort at a doddery geriatric gait.

He'd been working day in, day out with these people—all police officers, all trained to be observant—for more than two months.

Not a single one recognized him. Not a single one.

132

Maxine Park faxed over the list of companies that manufactured old-age makeup kits within the hour. Patrese gave it to a couple of uniforms who weren't checking the Camrys, and told them to get these companies' mailing lists and order records. Pay special attention to any kits sent to Pennsylvania addresses in, say, the six months before the first murder, he said, and make sure to cross-reference with the license plate lists. If a name and address appeared on both, that was a red flag right there.

Patrese and Beradino took themselves to an empty room and tossed ideas around.

There were now five victims. All of them had connections to Hellmore, but Patrese and Beradino couldn't for the life of them see what motive Hellmore would have to kill them, or by extension to order the killings. And if someone was trying to frame Hellmore, why kill deVries when Hellmore had a cast-iron alibi?

Think laterally. Hellmore. Case. Mara Slinger.

Two of the victims were directly connected to Mara's case: Mara herself, of course, and Yuricich. A third, Walter deVries, was also linked, albeit very tangentially; he'd run the nursing home where the father of Mara's lawyer was living. For the other two, Kohler and Redwine, nothing.

If these killings had something to do with Mara's case, and they were looking for a woman, there were at least two people in the frame: Ruby Ellenstein, the mayor's girlfriend, and Amberin, who'd originally prosecuted Mara.

If either of them owned a Camry or had sent off for a professional makeup kit, she'd be a prime suspect. But neither seemed likely—again, where was the motive?—which probably meant these murders had nothing to do with Mara's case at all.

Make the theory fit the facts, Patrese remembered, *not the other way around.*

Given that they had precious little by way of theory, that was hardly a problem.

By the end of the day, they didn't have much more by way of facts either. Neither list, the license plates or the makeup kits, had yet thrown up any likely suspects, let alone a name that appeared on both. Though they still had a long way to go checking through these lists, and they both knew this was how many crimes got solved—through repetitive, clerical drudgery—that didn't stop the lack of speed and results from being immensely frustrating.

For Patrese, at least. For Beradino, of course, it was his only hope.

133

THURSDAY, DECEMBER 9

"Mark? It's Summer."

This was the call Beradino had been dreading. He knew it straight away, just from the tone of her voice. She had news for him, and he wasn't going to like it.

"Hey." He tried to keep his voice as neutral as possible.

"Can I come and talk with you?"

"Sure. Now?"

"Please. And if you've got somewhere quiet, that would be best."

"Secret stuff, huh?"

"You got it."

In the couple of minutes before Summer made it up from the basement, Beradino tried to work out how best to play this.

Summer must have found Jesslyn's fingerprints in Mara's apartment. They'd have to interview Jesslyn. She wasn't around. They'd ask Beradino when he'd last seen her, and either he'd lie, and they'd bust that one open soon enough, or he'd tell the truth, and bring seven tons of Shinola down on his head. Either way, his career would be finished. He probably wouldn't even qualify for the police pension.

By the time Summer arrived, Beradino was no nearer finding the answer.

They found an empty interview room. Summer looked terrified, torn.

"I don't know how to say this," she began, "but we've got a match from Mara's apartment, and I don't know who to talk to, I don't want to be the one who tells tales out of school, but I can't hide what we found. I double-checked it, *triple*-checked it, because I couldn't believe it at first . . . and, well, you should know, I guess, you're in charge of this investigation, and it impacts directly on you."

Beradino felt for Summer. It wasn't her fault that things had come to this, nor was it fair on her that she should have to be the one to break it to him.

This was it, he guessed.

A strange sense of calm came over him. He was out of options. All he could do now was tell the truth. Everything else was history.

"You found her fingerprints?"

Summer looked puzzled. "Mara's? Of course. It was her apartment. No, the match I'm talking about is the semen."

Beradino's head felt as though it were plunging down a roller coaster. Semen? Mara's lover? This wasn't about Jesslyn at all.

"You found her lover?"

"Yes."

"Well, who is it?"

Summer looked as if she was going to cry. "It's Franco."

134

Beradino was far too smart and streetwise to confront Patrese immediately. This was information, and information was power—especially when it proved that his deputy had not only jeopardized the integrity of an investigation, but had also lied to Beradino about it when directly questioned.

That Beradino's own record on lying and jeopardizing the investigation wasn't exactly spotless was neither here nor there. He knew about Patrese; Patrese didn't know about him. It was the Eleventh Commandment: Thou shalt not get caught. When this was all over, Beradino would find a way to square it with God and with his own beliefs, but he didn't have time for that right now.

All police officers have to give fingerprints and DNA samples, so their traces can be eliminated from consideration by crime-scene analysts. Patrese's fingerprints had also been found in Mara's apartment, but that was easily explicable. Even Beradino knew Patrese had been there three times: when the two of them had first gone to interview her, when Patrese had gone to dinner there, and when they'd attended the murder scene. He'd been wearing gloves only on the last occasion.

But there was absolutely no reason for traces of Patrese's semen to have been in the apartment—apart from the obvious, of course.

Summer would be expecting him to do something about Patrese. She hadn't given Beradino the information for the good of his health. If she saw Beradino covering this up, who knew what she might do? She might accept it; she might cry blue murder.

So inaction was not an option—but Beradino didn't have to rush thoughtlessly into things. He had a few hours, a couple of days maybe, to work out his next move.

He went back into the incident room. Patrese was on the phone, grinning across his face and hopping from foot to foot.

"Okay. Okay," he was saying. "I'll be there as soon as I can."

He ended the call and turned to Beradino, eyes shining.

"That was Shaniqua," he said.

And there went Beradino's safety margin, vanished in a fingersnap.

"What did she say?"

"Her exact words?" With affection, Patrese imitated Shaniqua's voice. "'I gots somethin' for you, detective man.' That's what she said."

135

Beradino sat down, thinking furiously.

Two escapes in direct succession was too much to hope for. He'd dodged a bullet with what Summer had found; it wouldn't happen again. Why else would Shaniqua have called, except to tell Patrese about Jesslyn? Prisons were rife with gossip, even more so than offices. At least in offices, people had something else to do. Not so in prison. An hour's exercise, ten hours' sleep, thirteen hours' gossip.

Beradino had already tried to put the frighteners on Patrese by running him off the road outside of Muncy, but that hadn't worked. So maybe now was the time to bring up Patrese's involvement with Mara. He could throw Patrese off the case for misleading him. Someone else would have to go interview Shaniqua, sure, but Beradino himself could do that, then make up something back at headquarters about what she'd told him. By the time anyone found out the truth, this case would be long over.

Mulling all this over, Beradino was only half listening to what Patrese was saying.

Patrese was on the phone to Thornhill, the super

at Muncy, trying to fix a visiting time. It was already late afternoon; there was no way Patrese would make it from Pittsburgh to Muncy before the inmates were confined to their cells for the night. Beradino could only hear Patrese's side of the conversation, but it was clear that Patrese's attempts to bend the rules weren't going smoothly.

"No, I understand that, but . . . I'm asking for one exception . . . It's hardly a precedent, is it? I mean, how often do you get this kind of request? . . . No, of *course* I don't want a wasted trip. . . . This is urgent police business. . . . By the time I get a warrant, it'll be tomorrow anyway, so I might as well wait till then, right? . . . No, thank *you*. Fuck you very much."

Patrese slammed the phone down.

"Fucking petty jobsworth *asshole*." He pointed at the clock. "I've been here ten hours today. I'm outta here. I'll go see Shaniqua first thing tomorrow, so I'll be back here in the afternoon. On my cell except when I'm in jail."

A few uniforms laughed, waving sketchy good-byes to Patrese.

Beradino didn't even notice. He'd just realized something.

Something absolutely critical.

136

I see him come home—find a parking space, get out of his ridiculous car, head for his apartment building. His movements are shot through with anger's jagged jerkiness. He must have had a bad day at work.

Behind and below me, Pittsburgh spreads low and wide. Like him, I love this city, I really do—just not some of the people who live here.

It's only been two days since deVries, so they won't be expecting another one so soon. That's the trick, I know: mix it up a bit. I left ten days, give or take, between each of the first four. Let them get used to a regular rhythm, then pull the rug from under their feet. A couple of weeks from the fourth to the fifth; leave it longer, get them worrying. And now this one, hard on its heels. Slow, slow, quick quick, slow. Keep them on their toes and off balance.

Patrese's now twenty yards from the Mountvue's front door. His hands are stuffed in his pockets and he's walking fast, with his head down against the cold. I break cover and begin to shuffle along the sidewalk toward him, slow and pained, making myself as decrepit and unthreatening as possible. It's not enough just to dress as an old lady. I have to act the persona all the way through.

137

Hunched against the cold, Patrese only looked up when he got to the Mountvue. When he did, there was someone right in his face, materialized from nowhere. He jumped back, startled and breathing hard.

"Jesus Christ! You almost gave me a heart attack."

"I told you before, Franco. Don't blaspheme."

Beradino's here. Where did he come from? What's he doing? What does he want? He looks grave. They're talking. I have to abort this run. I've missed my chance, at least for today; can't go through with it this time. I'll have to reschedule.

Turning around or stopping would look suspicious, so I keep shuffling, right past them, without missing a beat. Just another little old lady heading back to her lonely apartment. They don't even notice.

They're on their way inside the apartment building, their faces both furrowed: Patrese's in puzzlement, Beradino's in concern, or at least that's how it looks to me. What's happened? What's going on? If it's something drastic, it'll be in the news.

I take deep breaths. Calm, steady. No drama. There'll be other opportunities.

138

Patrese took off his jacket and holster and hung them in the hall. In the living room, he removed his tie and watch, placing them on the table. He offered Beradino a hook for his coat, a beer, and an armchair. Beradino took none of them.

"I hauled ass here for a reason, Franco. There's no way of soft-soaping this, so I'll just get straight to it. Forensics has matched the semen found in Mara's apartment."

"Yeah, we know that already. To Negley."

"No. To you."

"Don't be ridiculous. That's impossible." Patrese's voice sounded shrill, even to his own ears. "Impossible."

"None of Negley's semen was found there. Either he was lying about making love to her, or he used a rubber. Your semen *was* there. Just dinner, you told me."

"Just dinner. That's all it was."

"And?"

"And what?"

"And what else?"

"There must be a mistake, Mark. Forensics makes mistakes. Look at what Lockwood said during Mara's trial, about the odds of her killing her children being billions to one. That turned out to be bullshit, didn't it?"

"There's no mistake here. It's a DNA test. It matched yours exactly. *Exactly.*"

"I still—"

"Don't insult my intelligence, Franco. You're not

some two-bit punk who reckons people will eventually believe you if you just keep lying. You're better than that. If you're not, I certainly am. So let's do this the easy way, eh?"

Patrese was silent.

"You want to think about it?" Beradino continued. "Okay. No hurry. I got all night. But while you think, there's something else you should be aware of."

"What's that?"

"You remember Katharine Horowitz?"

"Who?"

"Kohler's neighbor."

"Oh, yeah."

"She told us someone came over the morning Kohler was killed. Someone Kohler had a huge fight with."

"I remember."

"I know who that person was."

"You do? Who?"

"You."

139

"It was you arguing on the phone with Thornhill just now that gave me the clue.

"I was thinking how disjointed conversations sound when you can only hear half of them, and I remembered something Katharine said: that when Kohler was arguing that morning, she could only hear his voice, no one else's. We'd presumed the other person was cowed, or trying to be placating, or whatever, keeping his or her voice low.

"But what if that person wasn't there at all? What if he was on the other end of the phone? That would explain why she'd only heard one voice, wouldn't it?

"The records show Kohler wasn't using the phone at the time Katharine said, around ten o'clock that morning. The nearest call, either before or after that time, was the one you yourself had made an hour earlier. *Exactly* an hour earlier.

"Then something else you did just now gave me the second half of it. You pointed at the clock in the incident room and said you'd been in the office too long and were going home. The clocks had gone back an hour the morning Kohler was killed, hadn't they? And whenever they go back or forward, folks often forget to change the time, especially that Sunday morning. What if Katharine was one of them? What if the times she gave us were still daylight savings, not winter time?

"She said she heard a car arrive at around nine fifteen, Kohler greet the visitor, and then the argument at ten. But what if that person—*you*—had arrived at *eight* fifteen, left sometime before nine, and *then* called Kohler and had the argument? That would match the time on the phone records, wouldn't it? And the phone records would always have the right time; they're automated.

"There was still one thing that bothered me. If Katharine heard the visitor's car arrive, why didn't she hear it leave? But if the visitor was you—in fact, *especially* if it was you—that's perfectly plausible. You'd have gone there in the Trans Am, which makes up its own mind about whether or not it's going to start each time. The drive from the bishop's house slopes down to the road below. If the Trans Am didn't start when you left Kohler, you'd have had to roll it down the slope and get enough speed in the wheels to turn the engine over. By the time the ignition caught, you'd have been pretty much at the road, out of Katharine's earshot."

The fight had gone out of Patrese's face. Beradino knew he had him.

"So, Franco, what's this all about?"

Patrese was silent for a long time, but it was the silence of someone standing on the edge of a precipice, trying to find the courage to jump, to work out the right words, rather than that of a determined stonewaller. Beradino let it play out.

"I couldn't do it face-to-face," Patrese said. "I still felt like a little boy. On the phone, he was just a voice. On the phone, I could tell him."

"Tell him what?"

"Tell him I was going to bring him to justice."

140

I wanted to be a priest when I was growing up.

I wanted to be a priest because Kohler was our local priest in Bloomfield, and he was a cool guy. He wasn't some fat, balding weirdo like lots of priests.

He was quite young and athletic, and he didn't patronize us. He told us silly jokes and played ball with us.

Bloomfield's about as Italian as Rome, and Kohler was Irish, but no one ever held that against him. My father used to joke with Kohler that he was like Tom Hagen in *The Godfather*—you know, the Robert Duvall character, the Irishman who becomes Don Corleone's right-hand man.

Kohler did everything. He baptized the young, conducted Mass and first communions, performed wedding ceremonies, taught religious studies at school, took us on outings. Everything. I can't remember a time when he wasn't around. We'd have trusted him with our lives. All our parents did.

I became an altar boy—hard to imagine now, I know. It may even have been at Kohler's suggestion, I can't remember. I *do* know, now if not then, that he was very good at working out who was vulnerable, who'd be amenable to his advances. He was a Jedi master at that shit, seeing who had a vacuum in his life that needed filling. I was one of the ones he homed in on.

Pop was rarely there—not really, not the way you need your pop to be. Oh, he was *there*, of course, he wasn't one of those deadbeats always trying to dodge child support. Quite the opposite, in fact; he worked his nuts off to provide for us. But restauranting ain't an easy job, and if your peak work hours are other people's social time, your own spare time—your own family time—is what suffers.

Pop treated everyone like his best friend. It was great, of course, and it said a lot for him, a lot that was good; but it got so I felt if everyone was special, then no one was special. Pop paid all his customers so much attention, it felt like there was none left over for us. Sure, Pop was jovial, demonstrative, flamboyant, but all my life, I can't recall a single conversation we had that you could call intimate. Not one, on either side, when he poured his heart out to me, or vice versa.

Kohler identified this very fast. He'd been to our house often enough to see it. And he was very, very good at doing what he did.

I don't mean that grudgingly. I mean that, years on and knowing what I know now, I can see how skillful he was. He *groomed* us. All of us. He was a family friend in the truest sense of the word, a friend to the whole family and everyone in it. Different things to each of us, of course; but he left me in no doubt that I was the one he thought was very special.

He groomed me most of all, and he did it with sophistication, professionalism even. He didn't just force himself on me one day. No, that would have been too vulgar.

Not one step until we'd taken the step before. Inviting me to stay behind after choir practice to watch some football on TV. Sharing with me the dregs of his whiskey nips. Asking me to sit on the arm of his chair and rub his sore shoulder. Each one very innocent on its own, little parts of the kaleidoscope of growing up.

Then a porn mag, which he claimed he'd confiscated from one of the other boys. A short lecture about the evils of temptation and the devil. "Are you aroused? Are you aroused? Let me see. Let me feel if you are.

"You *are*."

Of course I was. I was just about starting puberty. I got aroused by a gust of wind.

"No, Cicillo"—he used my family nickname—"this won't do. You're too special a boy to get your kicks from looking at this filth. I'll show you the right way. I'll help you. I'll *protect* you. You're lucky to have this opportunity. You might find it uncomfortable at first, but don't worry. You'll get used to it. It's like your first beer, your first cigarette. They're rites of passage, and if they seem horrible at the time, it's only because you're not used to them."

The first few times were just kisses and cuddles. Then clothes started to come off; first shirts, then pants, finally underwear. He'd fondle me, and ask me to fondle him. Fingers, hands, mouths.

Finally, one day, he said: "This might hurt a bit."

And it did.

You hear that pause, Mark? That's not silence. That's the sound of a child's spirit being broken.

When something like that happens, that act—you see, I still can't say it out loud, what he did—there's no way back.

I was like a broken vase. I put myself back together again, I glued the cracks up, and from the outside I looked the same as I ever did. But I was never the same again. I was never whole again.

Even then, I knew the exact details of what Kohler was doing weren't the important things. What was important wasn't what he was doing, but that he was doing it at all.

Each time, afterward, he'd ask me, "Did you enjoy that?" I always said yes. Sometimes I even meant it. That was the worst part—no, not the worst part, but certainly the most confusing part. I got erections. I came. I was with a man when I did these things, so I figured I must be gay. And gay was the one thing you could never be at school.

When the other guys were bragging about getting with girls—almost total bullshit, of course, though at the time we all took it as gospel, little forays into an unknown world—I was with Kohler. I was submissive, I was dominated, it was my job to give him pleasure rather than the other way around.

But I also enjoyed it sometimes. I'd let him do it to me. So it must have been my fault in some ways. Must have been. Because otherwise I could have stopped it, no? I played football. I could look after myself, I could protect myself from harm.

And yet I chose not to.

I don't know how long the abuse went on for, I honestly don't; must be one of the things I blocked out. More than a year, less than two, if I had to guess. Not every day, of course, not even every week. When and how often wasn't the issue. The issue was that every time, there'd be a next time, until I got big enough to say no, that was enough, there'd be no next time.

And when I *was* big enough, that's what I went to tell him. He must have sensed something—shit, he was that good at seeing who was ripe for it, he sure as hell should have been good at seeing who wasn't going to take it anymore. Before I could say a word, he told me it was over—"it," like it had been some big love affair. I'd lost my looks, he said. I no longer gave him pleasure.

I should have been relieved, and I was; but I was also hurt, as he knew I'd be. He'd had the power from the start, and he made sure he still had it at the finish. Not a single thing in my dealings with him had been on my terms, and he made sure it ended that way.

I fucking *hated* him for that.

I thought stopping it would be the end of my problems. It wasn't. In some ways, it was just the start.

I started to have nightmares, and even bizarrely violent daydreams, when moments I'd had with Kohler came back to me at the most random times. I became numb and number. I'd go through the motions, but I'd sleepwalk through each day. I'd look at everyone around me reacting in all the ways you're supposed to, all the hundreds of emotions human beings can experience, and I couldn't feel a damn thing. I couldn't concentrate, I couldn't sleep, I jumped at the slightest sound.

Football was my salvation, and my torture. My torture because, even more than in normal life, there was no bigger sin in the locker room than being gay. If someone called someone else a fag and meant it, that was an act of aggression not far short of Pearl Harbor. Being gay was being someone the others couldn't trust, the weak link in the team ethos. Watching your buddy's back was good. Checking his butt was bad.

I worried all the time in the showers that I'd get a boner. All those naked guys, and me thinking I was gay. It was bound to happen sooner or later, wasn't it? Unless you did what I did, which was hang around in the locker room, chatting with the other guys so as not to make it too obvious, until everyone else had finished their showers and I could go in alone. Meant I always got a cold shower, 'cause everyone else had used up all the hot, but that was a price worth paying.

And football was my salvation, because I loved it—right up till the moment I shattered my knee and, with it, my ambition to go pro.

I'd invested so much of myself in that ambition, not least in trying to flush Kohler's poison out of my system. Football had been keeping me sane. Without it, I had to find some way of letting out all the poison.

141

I went to see a therapist, after much agonizing; after all, seeking psychotherapy wasn't the manliest thing to do, was it? And I'd had more than my fair share of worrying about not being a man, hadn't I? Ironic, that seeking help for not being a man made the problem worse.

I asked for a woman therapist, of course. I tried to seduce her; but I was clumsy about it, and my ineptitude saved me. She brushed me off with eloquence and grace, and over the course of many sessions, she unpicked the mess that was my head.

She was the very first person I'd told. It wasn't just for me that I kept it secret. It was for my family too. They loved Kohler, they'd had him over to the house a hundred times, he was their friend. They'd entrusted all their children to him at one stage or another. To tell them what had happened would be to tell them that they'd failed as parents. You're supposed to protect your children. They hadn't protected me—but how were they to know? How could they have known what Kohler was really like? If they *had* known, they wouldn't have let me anywhere near him.

Would they?

I'd tried to find out whether Kohler had ever done anything to Bianca, but she always seemed uncomplicatedly pleased to see him whenever he turned up, so I guessed he hadn't. It had only been me who made excuses never to be alone in a room with him—football practice, studying, upset tummy, whatever.

The therapist told me I was feeling guilt, which came from believing I'd done something wrong. I'd done nothing wrong, she said; that was where this started and stopped. I wasn't responsible for the abuse. It had been Kohler's decision, all the way along. And even if I *had* initiated some of it—I hadn't, but even if I had—it would still have been Kohler's responsibility to say no. He was the adult, I was the child; he had the understanding and the experience that I didn't.

I also felt shame, which was like guilt but also quite different. Shame was a painful feeling of inferiority, of unworthiness, of being ridiculed or held in low opinion by somebody. Shame carried the fear of being judged and disapproved of. I was ashamed because I'd enjoyed some of my trysts with Kohler, but that was no reason, she said. Boys could be physically aroused even in traumatic or painful situations. It didn't mean that they wanted the experience or understood fully what it meant at the time.

There was, she said, one more thing that set my case apart from other similar ones: the issue of Kohler's vocation. Kohler, like all priests, had a quasi-magical function, in bringing Christ's presence to the faithful. A priest was the closest thing to God on earth.

If you were close to the priest, therefore, you were close to God. Conversely, if you were betrayed by the priest, you were betrayed by God. What Kohler had done to me wasn't simply physical abuse. He'd also ripped from me the spiritual security that other children found with a consistent, unsullied belief in God.

It was soul murder.

On one hand, the Church preached enlightenment on issues such as poverty, immigration, and peace. In other areas it was still in the Dark Ages, and nowhere more so than in its attitudes to priests and their sexuality. Repressing natural impulses just encourages rather than discourages sexual abuse. If being gay was wrong, official thinking seemed to go, the best way to make up for it was to be a priest, and reclaim the lost moral ground.

Knowing all this was a help, but it wasn't enough. I knew Kohler had to be punished. I couldn't have been the only one he'd abused. Perhaps I could have saved a lot more kids if I'd only spoken up earlier; all that's needed for evil to flourish, after all, is for good men to do nothing.

I figured I could bring the case myself, and maybe others would join me once I'd set the ball rolling. There *would* be others, I was sure of that. Men like Kohler don't just offend once; they do it again and again. And when we found those photos in his desk, I knew. He wouldn't have touched all the kids in the pictures, sure, but some of them, definitely.

Remember that guy Guilaroff, Mara's agent, the one I went to see in LA? His picture was in there. Kohler did it to him too, sure as eggs are eggs. Everything Guilaroff said about Kohler, and about Sacred Heart. He hated the school, hated Kohler. He was one of the unlucky ones, like me. I'd bet a year's salary on that.

So, yes, I could bring the case myself. It wasn't the kind of thing I wanted my fellow cops knowing, but if that was the way it had to be, that was that. It would be my word against his, and Kohler would deny it, of course. His lawyers would send private detectives to sift through my trash and try to discredit me. I could deal with that.

I could deal with everything except my parents

knowing. I loved them too much for that. I had to sort it out without them. And that meant not sorting it out, everything else be damned.

I made two promises to myself. First, I'd do nothing about it while my parents were still alive. Second, I'd do *something* about it once they were no longer here. I wouldn't just sit on my ass and say, Oh, let bygones be bygones, let Kohler live out the rest of his life in peace, because it all happened a long time ago.

Not for me it didn't. The memories don't go away, and they never will. Nor does the legacy they've left. It's with me forever, shot through my core. I can't forget about it or get over it. The best I can do is keep it in a box, but it doesn't just stay there, docile. Every day, it wants out; and every day, I struggle to keep it down.

142

They sat in silence for long minutes after Patrese had finished.

There'd been enough hints, Beradino thought, if only he'd known how to look. There was Patrese's overarching dislike of religion, of course, even though Beradino still thought the reaction excessive. How could you hate an entire religion, all religion, because one man had done you harm? Beradino's own faith was stronger than that.

Beradino thought back to the night they'd found Kohler's body.

He remembered the thousand-yard stare on Patrese's face outside Saint Paul, when they'd been about to go in and examine the scene. Beradino had asked if Patrese wanted him to do this alone, and had said he understood. No, Patrese had replied. That *no* hadn't been to Beradino's offer to go in alone, Beradino now saw; it had been to Beradino's belief that he understood.

Beradino had also said Kohler was a special man, and Patrese had shot back a deadpan *you could say that.* At the time, Beradino had thought Patrese's mild sarcasm was in response to his understatement of Kohler's qualities. Now it turned out Patrese had meant something diametrically opposite.

Most obviously, Patrese had broken down that night while driving back to North Shore. *What kind of man could do those things?* he'd said through his tears. *What kind of monster?* He hadn't been talking about the killer. He'd been talking about Kohler.

"Why didn't you tell me earlier?" Beradino said at last.

"About Kohler, or about Mara?"

"Either. Both."

"Personal involvement with two of the victims, conflict of interest—you'd have thrown me off the case, wouldn't you?"

Beradino nodded. Here was his opportunity, served up as if on a silver platter. "And I still would. I am. Take a leave of absence, Franco."

Patrese shook his head. "I've got to see Shaniqua tomorrow."

"Don't worry about that."

"What do you mean, don't worry? She's got something for me. This could be it. This could be our breakthrough."

"I'll go see her."

"She won't talk to you, Mark, you know that. She trusts me, and me alone. She asked me to look out for Trent, you know."

"Franco, you're off the case. That's final. I'll cover for you, spin an explanation."

"At least let me go see Shaniqua, find out what she has to say—"

"No."

"—and after that, if you still want, *then* I'll take the leave of absence."

"I said no."

"Why? This could be the breakthrough, and you don't want to know? Why the hell not? Tell me why."

"It's not up for discussion, Franco."

"Why don't you want to hear what she's got to say? Are you worried about it? You think it's going to involve Jesslyn or something?" Beradino's face must have betrayed the truth of this, because he saw Patrese's eyes widen. "You *are.* My God, Mark. You know what Shaniqua's going to say, don't you? You never wanted me to go in the first place. You tried to steer me away from tapping Shaniqua, and—*steer me away*, that's it, it was you who ran me off the road that night outside Muncy, wasn't it? Of *course* it was. So stupid, not to see it till now. You knew where I was going; you had a reason to want me out of the picture. You stole that sedan rather than use your own car, so it couldn't be traced, and the next morning, when the sedan was in the police pound, you crawled all over it before forensics had gotten to it, so when your fingerprints were found inside, there was a perfectly rational explanation."

"You're talking nonsense, Franco."

"Tell me where I'm wrong, then."

"Nonsense. All of it."

"Yeah? Then let me go see Shaniqua, and we'll see once and for all."

"No."

"You can't stop me."

"Yes, I can."

"What are you going to do? Arrest me?"

"That's *exactly* what I'm going to do."

Beradino had his gun out almost before Patrese realized. Patrese's own Blackhawk was in its holster, hanging in the hallway. Beradino was standing, while Patrese was sitting in the depths of his sofa. It was no contest, in every way.

Patrese laughed, half in disbelief at the absurdity of the situation, half in nervousness that this was actually for real. "On what charge?"

"Well, we could start with five counts of murder, couldn't we?"

143

It was ludicrous, of course, but it was also strangely logical, once Beradino had outlined his reasoning.

Patrese had a cast-iron reason to want Kohler dead, that was beyond doubt. He'd also been Mara's lover, and who knew what had transpired between them? Men killed their lovers all the time. Perhaps Patrese had found out Mara was still sleeping with Howard and killed her in a jealous rage.

As for the other three victims; well, that was what questioning was for, wasn't it? You questioned someone when you didn't know all the answers.

Then there was the circumstantial evidence.

Serial killers typically need a trigger, something stressful or traumatic, to push them from fantasizing about murder to actually carrying it out. That trigger is usually one or more of the four *d*'s: death, divorce, dismissal, and debt. Patrese's parents had been killed a few weeks before Redwine's murder—and in a fireball too, the same way these five victims had met their end. Add to the mix Patrese's shooting of Samantha Slinger, and you didn't have to be Perry Mason to argue for a disturbance in the balance of his mind.

A vast proportion of serial killers—even by the most conservative estimate, more than nine in ten—have suffered abuse while growing up. Not all victims of abuse become killers, of course, but almost all killers have suffered abuse. Again, Patrese fit the bill.

And Patrese hated religion because of what Kohler had done to him. Kohler's killer had destroyed a crucifix and other religious imagery. The connection was clear.

"What about the old lady?" Patrese said. "How do you explain that the killer was me, when we've already decided it must be a woman using the old-lady disguise?"

"*We* didn't decide that at all. *You* told us it must be that way; and why wouldn't you, to throw us off the scent? And then you came into the incident room with the makeup on, after you'd been to the O'Reilly, and not a single person recognized you. If the makeup's that good, it doesn't matter if you're man or woman."

Beradino motioned Patrese to get up, very slowly, hands in the air. From a low, soft sofa, it was harder than it sounded. Patrese needed three attempts before he had enough momentum.

"Turn around," Beradino said. "I'm going to cuff you."

Real handcuffs, too, not the flexible plastic ties that were ten a penny. Beradino had come prepared. Patrese tensed his hands as the cuffs went on.

"Let's go," Beradino said.

144

Beradino put Patrese in the cells at North Shore. He needed Patrese out of the way for a day or two, somewhere secure, and he figured this was as good a place as any.

It was unfair, of course it was; Beradino knew that full well, and in any other circumstances he would have allowed himself the luxury of feeling sorry for Patrese. But he'd turned the problem over and over in his mind, and if there was a solution that involved hurting no one, he hadn't found it.

The simple fact was this: he had to sacrifice someone. If he hung Jesslyn out to dry, he wouldn't just be traducing his love for her, which he could never do. He'd also be pulling himself down: end of his career, public disgrace, possibly even time inside.

So Patrese had to be the lamb to the slaughter. There was no alternative. What that did to Patrese's career, or to their friendship, Beradino couldn't afford to consider. Ruthless? He preferred to call it pragmatic. Besides, hadn't he already saved Patrese's career after the Samantha Slinger shooting? A judicious word in the right ear after that, and Beradino could have had Patrese slung out on his ass. Perhaps he should have, the way things had played out since.

Yes, putting Patrese in the cells would set tongues wagging all over headquarters, but that didn't worry Beradino; quite the opposite. He didn't publicly mention the possibility of murder charges just yet, but he *did* drop into the incident room the twin pieces of news that Patrese was the unknown man who'd been at Kohler's house, and that he'd slept with Mara.

Cops tend not to be judgmental about their peers' personal failings—most of them have more than enough of those themselves—but they *do* take a dim view of anyone who withholds information vital to an investigation. These guys had been busting their chops for weeks, months, to find the killer. Patrese had held back at least two critical pieces of information. He wouldn't really be flavor of the month.

Beradino left strict instructions with the duty officers about how they were to treat Patrese. No one was to talk to him, bring him food or liquid, or even check through the door grille to see if he was okay. Whatever Patrese said, whatever wild accusations he might make, they were to ignore him. Patrese was in a world of trouble, Beradino said, and that went too for anyone who helped him, even in the smallest way.

What Beradino wanted was for Patrese to spend a night in complete isolation, and see how amenable that made him to walking away from the case. Beradino had even put Patrese in the last cell, right at the far end of the corridor, to keep him as out on a limb as possible. When Beradino came back in the morning, fed, watered, and rested—unlike Patrese—maybe they could come to some kind of arrangement.

The one concession Beradino had made was to take Patrese's cuffs off. There was no reason to keep a suspect cuffed when alone in a cell, providing laces, belts, and neckties had been removed beforehand. That was department policy. Besides, keeping the cuffs on would just give Patrese something to complain about, which might in turn tempt one of the duty officers to remove them, and get chatting, and then . . .

Patrese lay on the cot and stared up at the ceiling, his mind whirling. Once, he'd trusted Kohler, and Kohler had betrayed him. Now he'd trusted Beradino, and the same thing had happened. Idols had feet of clay. Wasn't that what the Bible taught?

It was cold down here, and the regulation-issue

blanket was too thin and scratchy to be much use. If he was to get any sleep, he'd need a coat, a woolly hat, maybe even some gloves.

Gloves made Patrese think of Trent, who'd been in a cell just like this, gardening gloves peeking from his hip pocket—

Not in a cell just like this, Patrese realized. In this very cell.

With the defective ceiling panel.

145

Maintenance should have repaired the ceiling panel by now—Patrese had put in a request the day after he'd caught Trent trying to escape—but clearly they'd still not gotten around to it. Patrese had lost count of the number of times he'd cursed bureaucratic inefficiency, but he'd never been so glad to find it as he was now.

Standing on the concrete bench, he could reach high enough to dislodge the panel. From there, it was simply a question of having enough strength to haul himself up through the gap. It had been almost a decade since Patrese had done pull-ups to the point of exhaustion at training camp, but he still had enough muscle memory and raw strength to make it. He was up and through on his second attempt.

He starfished himself, to spread his weight as widely as possible, and looked around. The panels were all part of a false ceiling, with the real ceiling a couple of feet higher. Electrical wires and three or four pipes snaked through the crawl space—the building's arteries and veins, hidden from casual view.

There was a small window at the far end of the crawl space. If Patrese flattened himself and leopard-crawled across the tops of the panels, he could make it to the window. He had no idea where it led to, but it had to be worth a shot, especially when he totted up his other options: a big, fat zero.

He went slowly, carefully. Time was not the issue. Beradino's interdiction against the duty officers checking on Patrese would work in his favor, since it should be many hours—with luck, not till Beradino himself arrived the following morning—before they discovered he'd gone.

No; the issue was stealth. The last thing Patrese wanted to do was alert someone by making too much noise or—worse—crashing through the panels into another cell below. So he took his time, testing his weight each time before moving forward.

Patrese didn't know how long it took him, since he didn't have a watch, but he was drenched in sweat by the time he reached the window.

The window was hinged at the top. He eased it open, looked through—and saw the underside of a car, parked a few feet away.

Of course. The cells were in the basement, so a window above their ceilings would be pretty much at ground level. This was the building's main parking lot.

Patrese waited a few minutes. No one walked past. It was night; the lot was pretty deserted.

He decided to risk it.

Moving fast now, he wriggled through the opening and onto the tarmac, staying low till he got his bearings.

Heinz Field was dead ahead. Beyond that, the river.

He thought about hot-wiring a car, but that risked drawing attention, and attention was the last thing he wanted. Better to go on foot. It was two or three miles back to his apartment. Not too long, if he ran it. Besides, running would keep him warm.

With no laces and no belt, he didn't so much canter as shuffle, but he didn't care. Every step took him farther from North Shore and nearer the Mountvue.

146

FRIDAY, DECEMBER 10

He didn't have his keys, of course, but that was no problem. The Mountvue wasn't anywhere near upmarket enough to have a doorman, but it *did* have a caretaker, Chad, who lived in a small basement apartment and had sets of every resident's keys.

Patrese buzzed Chad, feigned giggling drunkenness—a night out with the boys, he slurred, you know how it is—and got his spare key. Thanks, man. Appreciate it. Give it back in the morning. Sorry to wake you. Peace.

The clock in his apartment said it was past two in the morning, though Patrese felt wide awake. He changed into jeans and a sweatshirt, put his watch back on, grabbed a carryall, and began slinging stuff in it. He didn't know how long he might need to be on the road and he wanted to be as self-sufficient as possible, so he packed toiletries, warm clothes, and whatever nonperishable food he could find in the place. Then he strapped on his holster and put his wallet, keys, and cell phone into the pockets of his jeans. A quick check to make sure he'd left nothing vital, and then he was out of there; lights off, door locked, and who knew when he'd be back?

He checked both ways, up and down the street, before crossing the short distance to the Trans Am. It never hurt to be careful.

No one was around. The coast was clear.

The Trans Am started first time. Patrese smiled. Surely that was a good omen?

He nosed through deserted city streets, always wary of patrol cars—a couple came past, sirens wailing, but they were hurrying someplace far from him—and, almost before realizing it, he found himself on the interstate.

Next stop: Muncy.

147

Thornhill had said Patrese could come see Shaniqua any time from eight o'clock onward. Patrese was there right on the dot.

The security rigmarole seemed to take twice as long as he remembered, though Patrese knew that was just his impatience talking. As before, he surrendered every personal item: wallet, phone, coins, keys, and—of course—firearm.

After what felt like several eons, he was ushered through to the visiting room. A few minutes later, Shaniqua appeared.

"Okay," she said—no preamble or pleasantries; maybe she was as excited as he was, in her own way—"here's the skinny. I been talkin' a lot to that Madison bitch. She ain't all that bad, actually, once you get her to open up. I think she walk around puttin' on this big ol' don't-fuck-with-me act, but that ain't her at all, not really.

"Anyways. Accordin' to her, Mara had this ting with one of the guards. This *ting*, you know what I'm sayin'? Like a love ting. Love affair. Happens all the time in here. And not just any ol' guard, either. This guard, she be, gotta get the title right, she be deputy superintendent for facilities management, you know these people, ain't nothin' they love more than some big ol' job titles."

Patrese knew where this was going, but he kept quiet; not, he felt, that he could have gotten a word in edgewise. Once Shaniqua started off, you had to let her run her course.

"She's the boss player on the block. She's in charge of—let me get this right again—unit management, facility security, and all corrections officers. Like I said, she's the boss player, her word goes. She says jump, you say how fuckin' high, you know what I'm sayin'? Anyways, she gets a big ol' fuckin' bee in her bonnet about Mara. They get it on. And then, after a few months, Mara pulls the plug. This woman, this guard, she goes *bat-shit*. She wants revenge. No fury like a woman scorned, you know? Especially when it's another woman doin' the scornin'. Mara steps out of line, even this much"—Shaniqua held her thumb and forefinger a millimeter apart—"and her ass gets banged up in solitary.

"All this time, Mara's bein' cool and shit. She turns the other cheek, every time, like she's fuckin' Gandhi or somethin'. But everybody sees it, man; everybody sees what the fuck's goin' on, and peeps here don't like that shit, not when it's so fuckin' blatant, you know what I'm sayin'? Every motherfucker in here got a fuckin' sixth sense for injustice. So Madison says to Mara, either you complain, or I'm sure as fuck goin' to, 'cause this shit ain't right. So Mara complains—this is before she's released, you know—and it goes all the way up to the superintendent, and there's some other peeps called to give evidence, peeps like Madison, this takes, you know, some time, and by then Mara's released, so she ain't even here no more, and cut a long story short, couple of months back, this guard's given the sack, fuck you, bitch, *fuck you*, you Audi 500 O-U-T outta here, and you can kiss my black ass on the way through."

"Shaniqua?"

"Yo."

"What was this guard's name?"

"I ain't told you that? Sorry. Gedge. Jesslyn Gedge."

148

No wonder Beradino hadn't wanted him to come here, Patrese thought.

"That good enough for you?" Shaniqua said.

"Oh, yes. You can say that again. You're a marvel, Shaniqua."

"Shit, Detective. Sheeeit. Ain't no one told me that before. If I wasn't black, you could see me blush. Now, quid pro quo, like the doctor says to Clarice. My boy. Trent. You been lookin' out for him like I aksed?"

Patrese told Shaniqua about his encounter with Trent in the cop shop, what they'd talked about there, and how they'd gone to Heinz Field to watch the Steelers take down the Browns.

"Yeah, man," she said. "He a hell of a player. When Trent play in the NFL, we can go watch his ass. Hospitality suites, champagne and oysters, you know it."

"I'd like that."

"But you gotta keep on him, Franco. I know you a busy man, but once in a blue fuckin' moon ain't enough. You gotta build up a rapport with him, you know?"

"I know that."

"Else he gonna go to shit. He *will,* man; he will. He'll go to shit, 'cause I know what he capable of, man, I know he can get sucked in, I know he can be a dumbass, and then I'll be doin' all this shit for fuckin' nothin', you know? For *nothin'.*"

Patrese was about to reply, but something in Shaniqua's words jarred. He played them back in his head, trying to find what had caught his attention.

Two phrases, he realized: *I know what he capable of,* and *I'll be doin' all this shit for fuckin' nothin'.*

It seemed outrageous, what Patrese was thinking; and it also made perfect sense.

"Shaniqua," he said.

"Yo."

"Trent killed Weaver, didn't he?"

149

She said nothing.

Patrese was flattered, in a way. They'd obviously got to a stage where she wouldn't lie to him, not directly, even if she wouldn't answer him straight either.

He saw how it must have happened that day in Homewood. It had been Trent who'd been standing by the windowsill, next to the gun, and Shaniqua who'd been by the bed. Weaver had therefore gone for Shaniqua, not Trent. And it had been Trent who'd shot Weaver, not Shaniqua.

It made more sense that way, psychologically; that Weaver should have attacked his woman, his first target for abuse over the years; and also that Trent, unencumbered by blood ties to Weaver and ever-more cognizant of his own ascent to manhood, should have picked up the gun and said, that's it, enough is enough.

Then they'd swapped places, in every way. Shaniqua

had taken the rap for what her son had done. If she'd been the one to kill Weaver, she had a decent chance of pleading Battered Woman Syndrome and walking free, claiming that years of abuse had driven her to it. But if the killer had been Trent, he'd have no such defense.

Yes, he'd come to his mother's aid; but why only then, why not on all the occasions before? Patrese knew exactly how the jury would see him: just another Homewood punk, a fuckup-in-waiting. Likely as not, he'd have been found guilty, and that would have been it. His last, best, first, only hope gone.

Patrese was right; he knew he was. Nothing else could explain why Shaniqua had said *I know what he capable of*. Every other mother Patrese knew thought her son the Archangel Gabriel, even when confronted with direct evidence to the contrary. And it certainly explained why Shaniqua had been so happy to confess right off the bat. Any lawyer would have told her to shut the hell up, which in turn would have risked the truth coming out. This way, however, she could transfer all the heat from Trent onto her own shoulders right from the start, and bolster her chances with a sympathetic jury.

Patrese couldn't have begun to tell her how much he admired what she was doing.

"Trent killed Weaver, didn't he?" he said again.

"Franco, you got my confession. That's what happened, man. Just like I said."

He was about to ask her again, but stopped.

If she told him the truth now, what would he do? Would he go back to Amberin and say, look, here's what happened; let's lock Trent up too, keep Shaniqua in for obstruction of justice, and just fuck up as many lives as we can at one shot? Or would he think, this is what Shaniqua has chosen to do, because this is what being a parent is all about, protecting your own child, no matter the cost to you?

Put that way, it was hardly a question.

"Just like you said," he replied.

She smiled. "We understand each other, Franco, you know?"

He knew indeed.

150

Thornhill confirmed that Jesslyn Gedge had been dismissed for improper conduct. The Pennsylvania Department of Corrections maintained the highest standards of integrity and probity, and any officer who fell short of these . . . yadda yadda yadda.

"Mr. Thornhill," Patrese said, "I'm a police officer, not a press conference."

Thornhill gave a thin smile. "Of course."

"Do you have a copy of the proceedings I could see?"

"Of course."

Thornhill went across to his filing cabinet, opened the top drawer, flicked through the folders, brought one out, and handed it to Patrese. It was a full account of Jesslyn's dismissal: complaint forms, tribunal minutes, citation, judgment, legal counsel, the lot.

Jesslyn had written a longhand submission in her own defense. Patrese recognized the handwriting at once; it was the same as that on the two letters Mara had shown him in her apartment, one of them hateful, the other pleading for reconciliation, both of them liberally peppered with Bible quotes and admonitions about the Lord Jesus.

Patrese looked at the proceedings' relevant dates.

Mara had brought her complaint on June 23, and had been released on July 12.

Jesslyn had been fired on October 14. Redwine had been killed four days later.

Divorce, debt, death—or dismissal. From a job she'd regarded as a vocation.

You do the math, Patrese thought.

151

Patrese had been in the cell almost twelve hours, Beradino calculated. He'd be tired, cold, and hungry by now. Perfect timing to put the pressure on.

Beradino's first thought when he walked in was that he'd got the wrong cell. His second was that one of the duty officers must have moved Patrese, or even let him go, in direct contravention of Beradino's orders. Someone was going to catch hell for this.

Then he saw the hole where the ceiling panel had been.

152

"Thornhill."

"Mr. Thornhill, Mark Beradino here. Is Franco Patrese with you?"

"You've just missed him, I'm afraid."

"What do you mean, just missed him?"

"He was here with me a few minutes ago."

"What did he want?"

"He wanted to know about Jesslyn Gedge."

"What did you tell him?"

"I told him the truth."

"Mr. Thornhill, Franco Patrese is no longer part of the police force. In fact, he's a murder suspect. He escaped from custody last night. That makes him a fugitive from the law. Can you lock down your prison? Make sure he can't get out, if he's still on the premises?"

"Only if I activate the breakout alarm."

"Then do that, please."

"You have no jurisdiction—"

"I don't care. Do it, or I'll have you charged with obstruction of justice. *Now.*"

153

"Wallet. Cell phone. Keys, two sets. Coins, assorted. One sidearm, Ruger Blackhawk .357. Sign here, please."

Patrese held the inventory sheet flat with his left hand, scribbled his name with his right, and pushed it back to the prison officer. "Thanks."

"No problem. You have a good day now." She gestured toward the double set of security doors. "You remember how they work?"

"Sure. The outer set won't open till the inner set's shut."

"You got it."

The inner doors opened as Patrese approached. He stepped through them and into the small area between the two sets of doors. Patrese wondered what they called this area. An airlock? A pod? No-man's land?

The inner doors closed behind him.

The alarm was so sudden and loud that for a moment Patrese felt as though it was actually ringing inside his head. In the confined space, it seemed to come at him from every direction at once, wailing sirens and flashing lights hammering him, trepanning, like he was the unwitting subject of some giant experiment.

Through the bedlam, he realized something: the outer doors should have opened by now. That they hadn't meant the alarm must have overridden their mechanism, which in turn meant it couldn't be a fire alarm—a fire alarm wouldn't trap people inside.

It must be an escape alarm. Instant shutdown.

He looked at his watch. It was just before nine, easily time enough for Beradino to have discovered he was no longer at North Shore. Beradino would know instantly where Patrese had gone. He'd have called Thornhill, told him that Patrese had escaped custody, got him to shut the place down. . . .

Patrese looked back at the officer who'd signed him in and out. She shrugged, raising her hands in helplessness. *Nothing I can do, pal.*

Then he saw her pick up the phone, cupping one hand over her free ear and the other around the mouthpiece so she could hear and be heard over the sirens.

Her mouth moved in silent demands. *What? Can't hear. Speak up.*

She listened for a few seconds, then looked at Patrese; puzzled, suspicious.

They were onto him. Which meant he only had one option left.

He pulled out his Ruger Blackhawk and shot the hell out of the outer doors' lock.

154

Patrese crossed the lot to his Trans Am like an Olympic sprinter. No one else could get out of the building till the alarm was turned off, but he couldn't bank on his head start being more than a few seconds, a minute or two at most.

He flung open the car door and dived in.

Please start, he thought. *Of all the times, please start.*

It didn't, of course. Twice consecutively was too much to ask.

In the main building, the alarm suddenly stopped. They'd be out and on him in a flash.

Patrese jumped from the car, wedged his right

shoulder against the windshield pillar, and began to push.

Nothing. The car wouldn't move.

He pushed harder. *Come on. Come on.*

Still nothing.

The hand brake, he thought. *Didn't take the hand brake off. Doofus.*

He leaned inside, snapped the hand brake down, and pushed again. This time, the Trans Am began to roll forward.

A shout from the main gate. Patrese didn't even look. He was running now, the car gathering speed alongside him.

The crack of a bullet, the whistle of the air around his head as it passed by.

Lucky once. He might not be lucky twice.

He stopped pushing, jumped in, and twisted the key in the ignition, one seamless movement honed to perfection through years of practice with this damn machine. The engine fired and he was gone, fishtailing out of the parking lot with two snaking lines of black rubber behind him and the steering wheel bucking in his hands.

155

Patrese made straight for the interstate.

It was a risky strategy—freeways were much easier for the police to check than a myriad of minor roads—but Patrese wanted to get as far from Muncy as possible, as fast as possible. The local cops would throw up roadblocks at various distances from the prison, and he wanted to be outside them all by the time they did so. Besides, he didn't know the back roads around Muncy, and taking to them would just invite the police to run him to ground and corner him like a fox before hounds.

Patrese had already turned his cell phone off when he entered Muncy, but now he took the battery out too. Phones still send signals to the nearest towers every few minutes when they're off, but not when they have literally no power to work with.

If the phone links up with just one tower, that tower can judge the distance to the phone, but not the direction; that is, it could be anywhere along the edge of an imaginary circle. If a second tower gets the signal too, it can also plot an imaginary circle, thus narrowing the location to the sector where the circles intersect. A third tower will make the intersecting sector much smaller, pinpointing the location to within a few hundred yards. A few hundred yards wasn't much on the open road.

Then he turned on his police scanner. He didn't know the frequencies the cops around here used, so he set the scanner to search; lock onto a channel, listen for five seconds, hunt for the next one. A fire in Pennsdale. A water main burst at Seagers. RTA on Route 15 southbound out of Sylvan Dell, EMS en route.

And the Muncy police, together with the Lycoming County Sheriff's Department, rushing to the State Correctional Institution, all units to be on the lookout for a burgundy Trans Am, gold wheels, suspect armed and dangerous, use deadly force if required.

Well, Patrese thought, he'd shot his way out of prison and was listed as an escaped fugitive. What else did he expect?

The first thing he had to do was ditch the car. Silver Camrys might be a dime a dozen, but burgundy Trans Ams certainly weren't. Driving this thing around, he might as well put a neon sign on the roof announcing his identity.

There was a service stop up ahead at mile 194. Patrese pulled in, heading for the busiest part of the parking lot. The Trans Am would be less visible in the midst of a block of other cars than way out on its own at the edge.

He glided to a halt and turned off the engine.

The service-stop restaurant was filled with the breakfast-time crowd, all deep in their newspapers while chowing down their grits and waffles. If Patrese stayed low between the cars, the vehicles themselves would block him from the diners' sight.

He was looking for a car that was cheap and old. The newer the car and the more expensive it was, the better security it would have; Patrese needed to be in, out, and gone without screwing around with deadlocks or immobilizers.

Three spaces down from him was a two-tone Pontiac Sunbird hatchback that must have been a couple of decades old, and had definitely seen better days in that time.

Perfect.

Patrese got out of the Trans Am, clipping the police scanner to his belt as he did so. He popped the trunk, took out the carryall and another small canvas bag—the tool kit he always kept there—shut the trunk, and moved casually along to the Sunbird.

He opened the canvas bag and picked out a thin strip of spring steel a couple of feet long, an inch or so wide, and with two staggered notches at the bottom. A Slim Jim, the lockout tool beloved of locksmiths and cops worldwide.

Making sure the Sunbird was shielding him from anyone who happened to be looking out of the restaurant window, Patrese eased the Slim Jim between the passenger door's rubber seal and window glass, and slid it down into the door itself. There was a rod in there that connected to the lock, and if he could only find it . . .

There.

The Slim Jim's notch caught, Patrese pulled gently, and the lock popped.

He opened the passenger door, put the carryall in the footwell, and slid across to the driver's seat. From his tool kit, he took a screwdriver, a pair of wire strippers, and some insulated gloves. He'd had to hot-wire the Trans Am often enough when it was playing games with him. Now he'd do the same to the Sunbird.

Using the screwdriver, he pried off the plastic panels around the ignition tumbler, revealing six trailing wires: blue, red, purple, green, black, and orange. What those colors signified varied by manufacturer, and even between a single manufacturer's models, Patrese knew—but chances of the schematics matching were higher if you stuck with the same manufacturer, which was why Patrese had chosen a Pontiac. In his Trans Am, the "on" wires were purple and green, the starter wires black and blue.

Patrese put on the gloves and took up the wire strippers; pulling the four wires in question from the Sunbird's ignition, he stripped an inch or so off the end of each, and touched them all together.

The engine fired almost before the wires had sparked. If Patrese had believed in God, he'd have blessed every Pontiac engineer ever born.

156

Patrese headed toward Pittsburgh, into the eye of the storm.

There was method in his madness, of course. They'd be expecting him to run *from* them in his beloved Trans Am, at least to start with, so he'd blindside them by running *to* them in a Sunbird. Besides, he knew how to hide himself in Pittsburgh better than he did anywhere else, and he wanted—*needed*—to prove what Beradino had done. Quite how he was going to do that, he didn't yet know. He'd have to find some way of getting to Boone, or to Chance, and convincing them of the truth.

If he couldn't get it resolved today and had to hole up for the night—maybe several nights, given that tomorrow was the weekend—where would he go? The cops would already have been to see his family and friends, so there'd be no safe haven there. Hotels, motels, and hostels were too easy for the police to check. He could always hunker down in an abandoned building with the homeless and the winos, but half those guys would shop their own grandmas for a forty-ounce.

All of which meant he *had* to get it resolved today, one way or another.

The closer Patrese got to Pittsburgh, the better he could pick up city police chatter on the scanner, and what he heard alarmed him. Of the twelve channels used by the Pittsburgh police, Patrese was the prime topic of conversation on both Channel 8, frequency 453.950, which the detectives used, and Channel 12, 458.3625, reserved for tactical operations.

Again and again came his physical description. A voice from the Allegheny County Sheriff's Department, saying they'd disseminated the APB and were standing by for further instructions. Another voice said he'd spoken to the suspect's sister and told her to dial 911 the moment Patrese tried to get in touch with her family. There were men at Patrese's apartment, turning the place upside down. Someone said every local TV and radio station was carrying news of the manhunt.

Patrese flipped on the radio. They weren't lying. He was the lead item on that, too, top of the hour. *Law enforcement agencies have launched a statewide manhunt for Detective Franco Patrese, who escaped from custody last night and is suspected of carrying out the Human Torch killings that he himself was investigating.*

Beradino had gone nuclear, Patrese thought. He knew he had to get Patrese before Patrese got him, so he'd thrown the kitchen sink at him. Accusing Patrese of the murders was the only way Beradino could mobilize such a massive manhunt. If you were going to lie, Patrese thought, lie big.

Beradino must have known Patrese would be using the scanner if he was in Pittsburgh, but there was no way around that. You can't coordinate a manhunt on cell phones or secret frequencies; you have to keep everyone in the loop, otherwise one hand doesn't know what the other's doing. If a suspect is listening in, too bad. Even the most resourceful fugitive can't run forever.

157

"Clinton County Sheriff's Department, you've requested police assistance, how may I help you?"

"My car's been stolen."

"What's the make, color, and license-plate number, please?"

"Pontiac Sunbird. Light blue and dark blue—two-tone. Nevada plate, 740JEF."

"And your name, sir?"

"My name is Ryan Green."

"Thank you, Mr. Green. Where was the vehicle stolen from?"

"The rest stop on I-80. Mile one ninety-four."

"And that's where you are now?"

"Yes, of course. I can't exactly go anywhere, can I?"

"A patrol car will be with you within the hour."

"An *hour*? You can't get someone here quicker than that?"

"There's a statewide manhunt for an escaped fugitive. All our units are assisting with that. I'm sorry, sir."

158

In the suburbs now, stoplights making his progress jerky, Patrese felt more exposed. Drivers don't look at other drivers too much on the interstate; they do in urban traffic, picking their noses as they wait for the lights to go green. Sooner or later someone would recognize him, and they'd call in a description, send in the hounds.

Patrese flicked through the scanner's channels again, if only to know that the quotidian run of law and disorder went on without him, focusing on the three channels covering Pittsburgh's six police districts. First he turned to Channel 1, frequency 453.100, which covered Zones One and Two: downtown, North Shore, and the Strip, among others. The cops were waiting for him here, that was for sure, in case he chose to come back to headquarters or tried to take his case to someone in authority downtown—Negley, for instance, or Amberin.

Channel 2, 453.250, covered Zones Three and Six: Mount Washington, where he lived, and the South Side.

They were *definitely* waiting for him here. Half the force was probably at his apartment already, he thought; the other half would be at Fat Head's.

Which left Channel 3, 453.400, Zones Four and Five: Oakland, Squirrel Hill, Bloomfield, Homewood. Oakland was where Patrese had been to college; Bloomfield was where he'd grown up. Obvious places for him to head to, sooner or later.

Not Homewood, though.

Patrese smiled to himself. They'd *never* think of looking for him in Homewood.

159

Patrese's all over the news. A robot blonde stands outside police headquarters and breathlessly tells her microphone, the camera, and the nation in that order that this is the largest state manhunt in recent history, and that the Pennsylvania governor is considering calling in the National Guard if need be.

Robot Blonde says Patrese was arrested last night on suspicion of carrying out the Human Torch murders, but he escaped from custody sometime in the night. He was then involved in a shootout earlier this morning at the State Correctional Institution in Muncy, where Hollywood actress Mara Slinger, one of the Human Torch's victims, was imprisoned for killing her three babies, a sentence later overturned on appeal.

Robot Blonde clearly doesn't have a clue why Patrese

might have gone to Muncy, and she spends several minutes offering theories that get increasingly outlandish and ludicrous. But the cops—Beradino at least—must know that Patrese didn't do it. Which means Beradino must know why Patrese went to Muncy; because that's where the answer to the Human Torch is.

Which means Patrese has information Beradino would kill for. Hence the manhunt.

Patrese's alone, probably friendless.

Everyone's looking for him, including me.

Everyone's looking for me, too, including him.

The answer's obvious. We should collaborate.

Two fugitives, helping each other. But he doesn't know why I want him. He doesn't know what a lucky escape he had last night. He doesn't know I won't miss twice.

I'll help him, offer him a safe haven, and then I'll kill him.

Two fugitives, helping each other. One fugitive, killing the other.

160

The Clinton County Sheriff's Department had said a patrol car would be with Ryan Green within the hour. In the event, it was more than two.

A heavyset officer with a goatee too small for his face clambered out of the driver's seat. "Mr. Green? Sorry we took so long, sir. One heck of a busy day today. I'm Officer Schmidt."

Schmidt took a notebook from the breast pocket of his jacket. "Now, your vehicle—a Pontiac Sunbird, is that right?—was stolen at around what time?"

"I was eating breakfast in there from nine till around ten. Came out, car was gone."

"You didn't see anything suspicious?"

"Apart from a big gap where my car should have been?"

"Sir, you giving me static is not going to help matters, is that clear? I meant, you didn't see anything suspicious from the restaurant? No one acting weird?"

Green shook his head. "No."

Schmidt walked over to the restaurant window, wanting to see exactly what kind of view a diner would have of the parking lot. He looked back at the serried ranks of parked cars, and that's when he saw it.

A burgundy Trans Am. With gold wheels.

The one every law enforcement officer in Pennsylvania was looking for.

161

Knight was just about to begin a Bible study group when Patrese walked in.

"Hey, Franco," Knight said; as if nothing had happened, which meant Knight couldn't have known. If there was one place in Pittsburgh where folks wouldn't have heard the news, Patrese thought, it was Homewood. "You come to see Trent?"

There were a dozen or so teenagers in the room, Patrese saw, Trent among them.

"I was just, er, passing, and . . ."

"Then stay. Join the study group. Stay and pray with us."

"That's kind, but it's not really my thing."

"Come on, man," Trent said. "Just for a little while."

Patrese stayed.

Sitting in a spare chair, the only white guy there, he felt the tension and anxiety begin to seep out of him for the first time since the previous afternoon.

Knight began to talk about the way in which Jesus had always represented the poor and excluded, the easily despised, the demonized, those whose burdens were more than they could bear; and Knight did it all without once sounding superior or judgmental. He had a calm about him that was soothing. Patrese could tell from the faces of those in the study group that he wasn't the only one who thought so.

They weren't bored, fidgety, or disrespectful. They listened, they asked questions, they nodded when they got an answer that made sense. Patrese knew these kids weren't saints; few kids are. But nor could he sit here and reconcile what he was seeing with what he knew of how their record sheets down at Central Booking read.

Police work is marked by the underlying philosophy that might is right. Every year the cops declare war on the gangs, saying they're going to take Homewood back block by block, street by street, house by house. They call in help from an alphabet soup of agencies; SWAT, FBI, DEA, ATF. They lay confiscated weapons out like dead fish at press conferences and push slack-eyed gangbangers into the backs of cruisers in front of TV cameras.

And yet it seemed to Patrese, not to blow his own trumpet, that an afternoon at Heinz Field had probably done Trent more good than the endless cycle of arrest, trial, prison, release, and arrest had ever accomplished for any of his brothers.

Patrese thought of what he'd seen in Homewood and realized suddenly that the more pertinent issue was what he *hadn't* seen. He *hadn't* seen gyms or swimming pools, playgrounds or basketball courts, baseball diamonds or football fields, supermarkets or department stores. He'd seen vacant lots and boarded-up homes. That was pretty much it; and that was where the problem was, surely?

All the arrests the cops made—what did they accomplish? They took some bad boys off the streets and put them inside for a while, sure. Then out came those bad boys again, not changed in the slightest. Jail didn't make you better; Patrese had only had to talk with Mara to know that. Jail took people out of society's way, that was all.

If you've got a floorboard that needs fixing, there are three things you can do. You can leave it as it is, till one day it trips someone up and hurts them; you can put a rug over it and not think about it anymore; or you can get out your tools and mend it.

Those, Patrese figured, were society's options with kids like these: leave them as they were, which was more or less abandoning them; put a rug over them and lock them up, out of sight and mind; or do what Knight was doing, and try to fix things, turn them into productive members of society.

Patrese wasn't suddenly going to run off and sing songs with Joan Baez, but perhaps every cop needed, sometime in his life, to question what he was doing and why he was doing it. Patrese didn't know what the answers were—hell, he didn't even know what some of the *questions* were—but he realized now that the two cases that had informed his life these past few months, and the way in which they'd gradually become intertwined, were two halves of a whole.

Jesslyn was the Old Testament avenger, punishing people for who knew what, an eye for an eye until the whole world was blind. Shaniqua was the New Testament, a woman who loved her son so much she'd sacrifice herself for him.

And how could you understand the Bible when its two constituent parts were at such odds with each other?

Patrese dragged himself back from his thoughts to what Knight was saying. Knight had moved on from Jesus, it seemed, and was now talking about other ways in which the Bible sets out guidelines for how people should live their lives.

"How many commandments are there in the Old Testament?" he asked.

"Eleven." Trent, smirking.

Knight raised his eyebrows, playing along. "That so, Trent? I only remember ten, but maybe I'm mistaken. What's the eleventh?"

"Thou shalt not get caught," Trent said.

Everyone laughed, Knight included; then he was straight back to serious. "The commandments are there for many reasons," he said. "They're there to help us enjoy happiness, peace, long life, contentment, accomplishment, and all the other blessings for which our hearts long. They're there to show us the difference between right and wrong. They're there to protect us from danger and tragedy.

"The commandments cover the whole duty of man. They're the law of God, and the law of God is perfect, so the commandments cover every conceivable sin. The commandments are so serious, in fact, that in biblical times the punishment for breaking them was death."

That got everyone's attention, Patrese's included.

"And the other thing about the commandments people forget," Knight said, "is how restrictive they are. Of the ten, eight are prohibitions. Only two are positive exhortations to do things rather than injunctions against doing them."

Something tugged at Patrese here, something he couldn't quite place, but that he was sure was important.

"They're forbidding, the commandments," Knight continued, "and they're permanent, which was why they'd been carved in stone, on two tablets that Moses brought down from Mount Sinai."

There was a strange rushing in Patrese's ears, as though all the fizzing synapses in his brain had sparked their own electrical storm.

Wheelwright had said the Sinai Peninsula in Egypt was part of the Midyan terrane, where the pink granite had come from.

Two tablets, with the commandments on them, brought down. From Sinai.

Two stones at each murder site; two pebbles of pink granite. From Sinai.

Now Patrese saw what had tugged at him a moment earlier. In the commandments, there are only two dos, but eight don'ts.

Just as there had been in the e-mail that the killer—that Jesslyn—had sent them, about the dos and don'ts of the homicide investigation.

Jesslyn, with her Old Testament fire and brimstone. Jesslyn, railing against sinners.

That was why she was killing the victims. That was *why*. That was the pattern. They, her victims, had transgressed the commandments. That was what it said in the Bible, and so she took it as absolute truth.

As the word of God, in fact.

162

Thou shalt have no other gods before me.

> Thou shalt not make unto thee any graven image, or any likeness of any thing that is in heaven above, or that is in the earth beneath, or that is in the water under the earth. Thou shalt not bow down thyself to them, nor serve them: for I the Lord thy God am a jealous God, visiting the iniquity of the fathers upon the children unto the third and fourth generation of them that hate me. And

shewing mercy unto thousands of them that love me, and keep my commandments.

Thou shalt not take the name of the Lord thy God in vain, for the Lord will not hold him guiltless that taketh his name in vain.

Remember the Sabbath day, to keep it holy. Six days shalt thou labor, and do all thy work: but the seventh day is the Sabbath of the Lord thy God: in it thou shalt not do any work, thou, nor thy son, nor thy daughter, thy manservant, nor thy maidservant, nor thy cattle, nor thy stranger that is within thy gates. For in six days the Lord made heaven and earth, the sea, and all that in them is, and rested the seventh day: wherefore the Lord blessed the Sabbath day, and hallowed it.

Honor thy father and thy mother: that thy days may be long upon the land which the Lord thy God giveth thee.

Thou shalt not kill.

Thou shalt not commit adultery.

Thou shalt not steal.

Thou shalt not bear false witness against thy neighbor.

Thou shalt not covet thy neighbor's house, thou shalt not covet thy neighbor's wife, nor his manservant, nor his maidservant, nor his ox, nor his ass, nor any thing that is thy neighbor's.

163

Patrese began at the beginning, in every way.

If Jesslyn was murdering according to the commandments, she was surely doing so in strict numerical order; a pathology so precise in its insanity wouldn't brook random matchings of victims with transgressions.

So. First murder, and first commandment: Michael Redwine, and *Thou shalt have no other gods before me.*

Bianca had said Redwine was a typical Harvard Med School graduate, thinking God was his gift to the world rather than vice versa. Redwine was a surgeon, therefore he played God, whether he liked it or not; when you were under his knife, he had absolute power of life and death over you. At such moments, surgeons don't just think they're God; they *are* God.

Had Jesslyn killed Redwine simply because he was a surgeon, or was it something he personally had done? Something to do with Mara in particular? But they'd checked that already. Redwine had never operated on Mara, and wasn't involved in any of the awful business with her children.

Come back to that one.

Second murder, second commandment: Gregory Kohler, and *Thou shalt not make unto thee any graven image. . . . Thou shalt not bow down thyself to them, nor serve them: for I the Lord thy God am a jealous God.*

Crucifix, icon, stained-glass windows smashed, the Michelangelo reproduction defaced. All images of God, in one form or another; but the Bible holds that all men, even geniuses like Michelangelo, are mortal, and therefore by definition incapable of capturing the essence of a deity who has no shape or form.

It seemed a very literal interpretation of the commandment, Patrese thought; but then again, so was killing someone for transgressing it. Jesslyn's pathology might be extreme, but it was at least consistent.

Third murder, third commandment: Philip Yuricich, and *Thou shalt not take the name of the Lord thy God in vain, for the Lord will not hold him guiltless that taketh his name in vain.*

Yuricich's tongue had been cut out—for taking the Lord's name in vain.

Like all public officials in Pennsylvania, Patrese included, Yuricich had taken an oath: *I do solemnly swear that I will support, obey, and defend the Constitution of the United States and the Constitution of this Commonwealth and that I will discharge the duties of my office with fidelity.* At the end, the oath taker can, if he or she wishes, add *So help me God.*

Patrese hadn't done so on his turn, for obvious reasons. Yuricich would definitely have done so, for equally obvious reasons. But his handling of Mara's case, among others, had given the lie to that pledge.

Fourth murder, fourth commandment: Mara Slinger, and *Remember the Sabbath day, to keep it holy. Six days shalt thou labor, and do all thy work: but the seventh day is the Sabbath of the Lord thy God.*

Patrese didn't know what to make of this. Of all the many things Mara had been accused of, surely failure to observe the Sabbath wasn't one of them? Mara had been Jewish, so her Sabbath was Saturday—technically, Friday sunset through Saturday sunset—but did that make a difference?

While filming any of her movies, had she been on the set during those times? Almost certainly. She'd done theater too, so Patrese figured any Friday-night performance would technically have been a breach of her Sabbath. But was that really it? If you started killing people for breaching the Sabbath, you could pretty much pick any stranger at random, sure in the knowledge they'd transgressed at some stage. Even Jesslyn herself must have worked Sunday shifts at Muncy.

Was Patrese missing something? He wasn't sure. Another one to come back to.

Fifth murder, fifth commandment: Walter deVries, and *Honor thy father and thy mother: that thy days may be long upon the land which the Lord thy God giveth thee.*

This one was obvious. Even Patrese remembered enough from Bible school to know that the fifth commandment enjoins respect not merely on one's actual parents but on all elders, those in the twilight of their lives who've seen much of what the world has to offer and call it experience. Walter deVries had been charged with looking after these people. If the complaints of Old Man Hellmore and others were anything to go by, he'd failed them miserably.

Patrese slapped his face lightly to keep himself alert.

There'd been five murders already. If he was right about the pattern, there'd be five more to go, in strict sequence. Knowing what Jesslyn's criteria were might help him anticipate her choice of victim. He reviewed the list again.

Sixth commandment, the most basic and reductive one of all: *Thou shalt not kill.*

Patrese felt something warm and hateful clutch at his entrails.

He himself had killed, hadn't he? He'd killed Samantha Slinger.

164

She hadn't died instantly. He remembered that like it was yesterday: the hope, tight and burning within him, that she'd somehow make it, lying there with her life soaking the floor beneath her as the paramedics swarmed and injected and shouted, what kind of drugs has she taken, what kind, tell us *now.*

She'd been on life support. He'd wanted to go and see her. No way, Chance had said; absolutely no way. Him visiting wouldn't look good in legal terms, if this ever went to court. Patrese hadn't cared what it looked like, in legal terms or any other. He'd wanted to go see her, even though she was in a coma and wouldn't know he was there. He'd have been going for himself rather than for her. But he'd still wanted to.

Her family—Mara—had been there. She certainly wouldn't have wanted him anywhere near.

And eventually, after a few days, she'd turned Samantha's life support off.

Bianca had told him once that whether to end a life was a decision pretty much every doctor had to make at some stage during his or her career. In an ideal world, doctors would keep everyone alive for as long as they could. But this isn't an ideal world, and comatose patients take up time, resources, and bed space they never even know about.

So, sooner or later, a doctor will say to the relatives, listen, there's nothing more we can do. Your loved one might yet live for years in that bed, but they'll never regain consciousness. They're in a deep coma without detectable awareness. They are, to all intents and purposes, existing rather than living. They're brain-dead.

If the skill of the doctors is all that's keeping someone alive, Bianca had said, withdrawing that skill is what will kill them, or let them die, depending on your view of the semantics. As a doctor, you have to judge that margin, walk that line. You have to play God.

You have to play God.

Bianca would know. He needed to talk to her.

The police had already been onto her, in case he phoned. Maybe they even had someone sitting with her right now, especially if she was at home. He couldn't remember what shifts she was working this week. If she was at work, he could go through the hospital switchboard, but that would be lunacy; they'd put him on hold, trace him, and swoop.

Which meant he had to call her cell phone. But he couldn't remember the number.

It was programmed into his own cell phone, of course, but he'd never had cause to memorize it. So he'd have to use his own cell, and risk the cops triangulating his position. There are more phone towers in cities than in the countryside, and the accuracy of triangulation is therefore much greater—not a few hundred yards, but a few tens of yards, if that.

If he did this, he'd have to be on his way out of here straight afterward.

He needed to know. There was no way around it.

He put the battery back into his cell phone, turned it on, and hit Bianca's number on speed-dial.

"Jesus, Franco," she said the moment she answered. "What have you done?"

"Nothing, and you know that. It's a big frame-up."

"Are you okay? Where are you?"

"I'm fine. Where are you?"

"At the hospital."

"There any cops with you?"

"No. But they want me to call them when you make contact."

"Listen. In life-support cases, when the machine's turned off, do hospital records state which doctor authorized it?"

"What's *that* got to do with anything?"

"It might have everything to do with it. Please. Just trust me."

"Of course I trust you. And yes, they do state it."

"And that doctor—does it have to be the surgeon who originally operated?"

"No. Not at all. Any doctor senior enough can do it,

once they know the facts of the case and feel qualified to make a diagnosis."

The police had checked all the operations Redwine had performed, Patrese knew, but not every decision he'd made as a doctor.

"If I give you the patient's name, can you check for me?"

"Is this important?"

"Critical."

"Okay. Because there are computer checks, and they'll want to know why—"

"Samantha Slinger," he said.

Bianca caught her breath. "*Jesus,* Franco."

"It's related to the burning case. Trust me."

He heard the tapping of her fingers on the keyboard; then another intake of breath, much sharper and more urgent than before.

And he knew.

Bianca read it in a low monotone. "Cessation of Samantha Slinger's life-support mechanisms was authorized by Dr. Michael Redwine."

Patrese pressed hard on the bridge of his nose. Redwine had played God, even though there was little else he could have done, and he'd paid the ultimate price.

"Thanks. I'll see you. I love you."

Patrese ended the call, thinking furiously.

Was there no end to Jesslyn's obsession with Mara? Clearly not.

He was about to turn his cell off again when he saw he had a text message. He didn't recognize the sender's number. He clicked it open.

Looks like they're looking for us both. I didn't do it. I know you didn't too. I know who did. Let me help you. Meet? J.

165

Patrese worked out his options.

He didn't buy Jesslyn's claim of innocence for a moment, but that wasn't the point. What did she know? What did he know?

There was no reason for her to assume he'd worked out either her disguise or the pattern of the killings yet, which meant she didn't know he knew he was next in line. Therefore the promise of help was a trap; lure him, and then kill him.

He could turn this to his advantage. He'd meet her, apparently trustingly, but arrest her before she could do anything. That way, he'd have proof not only of his innocence but also of Beradino's complicity, which was why he'd come back to Pittsburgh in the first place.

Yes, it was a trap, but he'd be trapping her, not vice versa.

He didn't want to go anywhere private or enclosed, just in case she got a jump on him. She'd killed five people already; he had to afford her the respect of caution. What he wanted, therefore, was somewhere public, but not too busy. It was freezing outside, so he could wear a coat, scarf, and baseball cap without attracting attention, and that would shield his identity from any but the nosiest passerby.

He thought for a moment, wondering what would be a good location.

The idea came to him in a flash. He looked at his watch. It was just after one. He typed back:

Sure. Meet you at Warhol Museum at 3.

166

"Attention all units. Attention all units. Please be advised suspect's cell phone has been triangulated to Homewood district, corner Frankstown and Collier, error margin twenty-five yards. All Zone Five units to proceed to location immediately. Repeat, suspect believed to be driving two-tone blue Pontiac Sunbird, Nevada plate, number seven, four, zero, period, Juliet, Echo, Foxtrot. Suspect is believed armed and dangerous. Approach with caution. Use deadly force if necessary."

167

He hasn't given me long, a couple of hours at most. It'll only take me fifteen minutes to walk to the Warhol, but what about the makeup? That's a couple of hours in itself.

Which makes me wonder: Does he know about the disguise? Has he worked it out? If so, best not to risk it this time. Not if he's expecting an old lady.

I'll go as myself. That'll surprise him. And surprise, just a little bit, is all I need.

168

Beradino stood in the middle of the incident room and sucked his teeth.

Zone Five had just radioed in. They'd missed Patrese. They'd found out where he'd been—at the 50/50—but no one there knew where he'd gone, or if they did, they weren't saying. Zone Five was now asking whether Beradino wanted them to arrest everyone in the 50/50 and bring them in for questioning. They'd harbored a fugitive, after all.

Beradino thought for a moment.

"No," he said. "Even if one of those guys *does* know something, by the time we get it out of him, this whole thing will have moved on several stages. Besides, Knight does some good things for those kids. I don't want to start a riot in Homewood."

Where are you, Franco? Beradino thought. *Where are you heading?*

"Sir!"

Beradino looked around. One of the uniforms was brandishing a printout.

"What you got?"

"The old-age makeup kits."

Beradino had almost forgotten about them, what with everything else going on; and, in terms of keeping Jesslyn hidden, any news on this front was bad news.

"We've got slightly bigger fish to fry than that, haven't we?"

"Three kits sent to Magda Nagorska at the Pennsylvanian on Liberty Avenue," the uniform said excitedly. "That's where Redwine was killed, wasn't it?"

Magda Nagorska. The Pennsylvanian.

Beradino must have looked like a guppy, his mouth dropped so far open.

Magda Nagorska was the deaf old woman who lived beneath Redwine.

169

Arguably the three most striking of Pittsburgh's several hundred bridges are the coordinated trio of suspension spans painted in Aztec gold that cross the Allegheny at Sixth, Seventh, and Ninth Streets. They commemorate three famous Pittsburghers—Roberto Clemente, Andy Warhol, and Rachel Carson respectively—and Patrese had always been struck by the symbolism of that choice. It said much for the city, he thought, not just that a baseball player, an artist, and an environmental pioneer should be immortalized side by side, but also that such eclecticism was seen as normal.

He'd left the Sunbird in an out-of-the-way parking

lot in Polish Hill after hearing on the scanner that they knew he'd switched cars, and he'd walked the rest of the way into town, about an hour on foot. It was a cold day, and a man wrapped to the eyebrows attracted no attention, just as he'd predicted.

Standing on the riverbank, he waited a couple of minutes, just to check that there was no reception committee at either end of the bridge. If the police sealed it off when he was halfway across, his only option would be over the side and into the Allegheny, which was hardly going to be tropical at this time of year.

Satisfied that the coast was clear, Patrese crossed the bridge.

The Warhol Museum, a few hundred yards from the north end of the eponymous bridge, is a cream-toned, terra-cotta-clad warehouse, exactly the kind of industrial site the artist had used for his studios. Inside, it still feels like what it once was, with stone walls and airy, cavernous rooms.

Patrese paid the entrance fee, took a small map of the museum from the desk, and began to walk around, looking for all the world like just another art lover.

He checked his watch. Quarter to three.

170

A SWAT team went into the Pennsylvanian; they were taking no chances.

They split into four groups. One guarded the building's perimeter at street level, one took the rooftops, one went up the fire escape, and the fourth went with Beradino through the lobby and up the stairs. Once he'd realized there was no way he could call them off, he'd insisted on coming with them, in an ever-receding attempt to keep Jesslyn's identity to himself, or at least be there for her when her luck finally ran out.

No knock on the door, no polite request to have a word; a battering-ram to the lock and in they piled, eyes flicking left and right over the sights of their rifles, fast through the rooms, barking *clear, clear, clear.*

The place was empty.

Beradino stepped into the living room and looked around.

How the heck had Jesslyn afforded this place? How the heck had she stood in front of him the last time he was here, Redwine still too hot to touch, and presented a face, a body, a voice, an entire persona that wasn't her own? How the heck had he failed to recognize her, his own partner?

Then again, he'd also failed to recognize Patrese when *he'd* had the makeup on, and he spent more time with the two of them than with anyone else in the world. Just went to show, he thought, you never know anybody else, not really.

You never really know yourself half the time, come to think of it.

If Beradino knew where Jesslyn was, he could still lead them away from her.

There were books on the shelves, some unwashed dishes on the sideboard. She couldn't have left in a tearing hurry, since the place was pretty tidy; but it didn't look like she'd packed for a major journey.

Her cell phone was still here, for a start, sitting on the kitchen table. Beradino picked it up, his fingers brushing the keys.

The screensaver disappeared, and he found himself looking at the messages menu.

One message in the inbox. From Patrese.

Sure. Meet you at Warhol Museum at 3.

The SWAT leader was peering over Beradino's shoulder. Another second, and Beradino could have deleted it. Too late now.

"Let's go, sir," said the SWAT leader. "Let's go take them both down."

171

It wasn't the Campbell's soup cans or the Marilyn diptych that snagged Patrese's attention. Instead, it was Warhol's Death and Disaster series: *Orange Disaster #5*, orange-tinted photos of an electric chair isolated in a room with a sign blaring SILENCE; *Green Car Crash*, in a similar vein; a CAT scan of someone's skull.

These were Warhol's versions of old memento mori paintings, Patrese realized. Warhol understood death; he understood that we're little souls carrying around corpses, nothing more. And when you get to be that corpse, Patrese knew, it's not pretty. The body bloats, it purges, it bleeds. The only people to have it right in two thousand years, Patrese reckoned, were the Vikings. When it was his turn, he wanted to be like them; he wanted to be cast off in a burning boat and left to the flames.

He dragged his thoughts back to the present and checked his watch for what felt like the hundredth time. A couple of minutes shy of three o'clock.

Distant footsteps, echoing around the concrete spaces. The soft hum of machinery.

"Franco."

He spun around. No one there. Just soup cans and Brillo boxes.

"Over here. Through the pillows."

Off the main exhibit space was a smaller room, around which helium-filled foil pillows were being gently buffeted by a fan high on one wall. On the far side of the room, swimming in and out of view behind the pillows, was Jesslyn. She too was wrapped in a coat, hat, and scarf, clearly as paranoid as he was about being recognized.

Patrese closed his fingers around the Ruger Blackhawk in his coat pocket.

He remembered reading somewhere that these helium pillows represent a basic personality test. If you take the straightest route through them, bashing them out of the way, it shows you're no-nonsense but unimaginative. If you dodge and weave, working the angles and anticipating the gaps, determined that none of the balloons should so much as touch you, it means you see things from different angles and don't mind going off at a tangent.

All bullshit, of course; but he zigzagged anyway, jink, jink, breathe, and stop.

"We've got a lot to talk about," Patrese said as he reached her.

"We sure do," she said, unwinding the scarf from about her face, *and knowing that Patrese's shock when he sees me will buy me time* and the recognition was a physical blow, so much so that for a moment Patrese thought she must have actually reached out and punched him, right in the solar plexus.

It wasn't Jesslyn.

It was Mara.

172

Thoughts tumbled through Patrese's head like acrobats, logical deductions made lightning-fast, time slowing as his brain raced.

Two women had been in Mara's apartment that day. One of them had killed the other and then vanished. Beradino and, latterly, Patrese had both assumed Mara had been killed and Jesslyn had escaped.

Now Patrese saw the truth; it was the other way around. And because the body had been burned, and because there'd been three previous victims, no one had questioned whether it was Mara's or not.

For the switch to work, Mara and Jesslyn must have

been roughly the same size. Patrese remembered what Mara had told him about her arrival at Muncy, when she'd first met the woman who was to be her nemesis.

I expected her to be some big, butch dyke, all shaved head and tattoos, but she's nothing of the sort. She's pretty and petite, no bigger than me.

Pretty and petite, Patrese thought, *no bigger than me.*

Maxine Park had said people see what they want to see. If you've no reason to be suspicious, you can easily be fooled. The cops had seen what looked like Mara and what they'd had no reason to believe *wasn't* Mara. A lot of negatives in that sentence, but all adding up to one undeniable truth: they'd been fooled.

Patrese didn't even bother to consider motive. Mara had every reason to kill the victims; so much so that faking her own death was perhaps the only way she could have continued to evade suspicion.

When had the idea first come to her? Perhaps it had been less a blinding flash than a slow accumulation of realizations, starting with what she'd seen every day during her trial; the Ten Commandments, sacred text in all three Abrahamic religions and backbone of the justice system, printed on Yuricich's robes.

Then, when that system had failed her, she'd had countless hours in jail to brood, plot, refine, and watch as the pieces fell slowly into place; the final, crucial, achingly satisfying one being the fact that she could turn her tormentor Jesslyn into her patsy.

Jesslyn must have gone to Mara's apartment with malice on her mind; why else would Beradino have assumed Jesslyn was the killer and gone to such lengths to protect her? She'd probably never realized, until it was too late, that she'd been walking into a trap.

Mara had been unrecognizable as Eleanor Roosevelt in *First Lady*. On the set, she must have sat in the makeup chair day after day, hours each time, watching, listening, asking questions, seeing how she was gradually transformed into someone else.

It was a hell of a plan, and a hell of an execution, in both senses of the word; Patrese had to give her that.

All this flashed through his head, sensed and understood if not properly articulated, in a couple of seconds; during that time he was too stunned to do anything other than stand and stare.

Which was exactly what Mara had counted on.

Patrese wasn't even beginning to draw his gun when Mara pulled from behind her back the makeshift weapon that had served her so well: battery in a sock, the staple prison weapon. Up fast and around she whirled it, hard against Patrese's temple before he could block it, and down he went as though someone had cut his strings.

173

For a moment, when Patrese came around, he had no idea where he was, and he felt no pain. Then the recognition of the gallery—Mara had closed the door of the side room, sealing them in with the silver helium pillows still bouncing happily around—together with the agonies pulsing in his head and the realization there was a gag in his mouth, all hit him at pretty much the same time.

The room swayed, and he put his hand down to stop himself falling; except his hands were fastened behind his back and he was already sitting down, his butt on the floor and his back against a wall, so he toppled sideways with a lack of elegance that would in other circumstances have been embarrassing.

Very clever. He'd have thought about applauding if his hands were free.

She'd secured them with plastic cuffs; he could feel the texture against his skin. A few years before, plastic cuffs had been pretty much the preserve of the police, but now you could get them anywhere; uniform and equipment retailers sold them in stores and online. Hell, you could make half-decent ones yourself just by going into a hardware store and buying some electrical cable ties. It wasn't exactly arduous to get a gun in America; why would it be hard to get some plastic cuffs?

But they had their limitations too. They could be broken by people who were very strong or very strung out on drugs, and they could be cut or melted.

Patrese wasn't either of the first two, and if the other murders were anything to go on, by the time the cuffs had melted, he wouldn't be around to take advantage of it. So if he was going to get free, he'd have to somehow cut them himself.

But how?

She'd leaned him near a small niche where the wall jagged away at a right angle to accommodate a window alcove. If Patrese leaned slightly to his right, he could place his wrists against this right angle; and if he rubbed hard enough and fast enough, he might be able to wear away the plastic on the cuffs enough to split them.

It would hurt like hell, because whatever damage he was doing to the cuffs he'd be doing to his skin too; but it was that or die like a human barbecue. Put that way, it wasn't much of a choice.

Keeping his body between his wrists and her so that she couldn't see, Patrese began to rub in small, quick motions. Even if she saw it, he hoped she'd think he was simply shaking with fear; not an unreasonable assumption, given the circumstances.

She came across the room with the gasoline can. The top was off; he could hear the gasoline sloshing inside, and smell the rich fumes as they wafted into the room.

Splashing it on him now; it ran into his eyes and nose as he gasped through the gag for air, panicking for a brief moment that he might asphyxiate here and now even before she ignited the flames.

Patrese kept rubbing his wrists against the concrete. His skin was wet with what he presumed was blood, and each abrasion sent jagged shards of pain darting through his body, but he didn't care. Pain was good. Pain meant his plan might be working, he might be rubbing the plastic away.

Pain meant he was alive.

She had the torch in her hand, and was flicking the lighter open.

Patrese had a sudden, hysterical urge to know whether she'd ever really cared for him at all; but he guessed here was his answer, right here.

He looked away. Pleading would do no good. Nothing would stop him from dying apart from his own ability to free himself.

He wasn't going out like the others, he told himself. He was younger, and stronger, and he was a cop, and she wasn't going to beat him, not as long as there was breath in his body.

He's shaking, his body giving little jerks against the wall. He's scared. Good.

He knows what happens next, he's seen it five times already. He knows how the bodies look, how they smell. He knows what a horrible, horrible way it is to die.

He deserves it, and he knows that too, deep down.

I remember what we shared, what we did together. It means nothing. It never did.

I turn to him and speak.

"Isaiah, chapter fifty-nine, verse seventeen. For I put on righteousness as a breastplate, and a helmet of salvation upon my head; and I put on the garments of vengeance for clothing, and am clad with zeal as a cloak."

There was more give in the cuffs now, Patrese was sure of it. His wrists were agony, from being scraped against the wall and from the cuffs themselves, but he gritted his teeth against the inside of the gag and kept going, *Drive on, drive on against the pain.*

Then a snap, so sudden it made him jump, and his hands were free.

174

He comes up fast from the floor, his arms swinging around to the front, all wet and slick with blood and the cuffs falling away from them, and somehow he's managed to break free.

I spark the flame on the lighter and thrust it in his direction. He sways away fast and scared, a fencer dodging an attack. He's not wild-eyed; he's calculating, and that makes him more dangerous. I could rush him and touch the flame to him, but he's bigger and stronger than me, and he could grab me and hold me to him so we both burn.

He pushes his matted hair back from his forehead, rips the gag from his mouth, and snarls. I pick up the gasoline can again, to use it as a shield if need be.

And then the world explodes.

They come flying through the door: men in body armor and hockey helmets, sighting down the barrels of rifles that are as much a part of them as their own limbs, hollering and whooping to disorient me and keep their own adrenaline high.

Then they stop dead, because I've got the lighter in one hand and the gasoline can in the other, and Patrese's drenched in gasoline from head to foot.

"Drop 'em," they shout. "Drop 'em, and step away."

"You won't fire," I say. "None of you will fire."

"Hands EMPTY!" they shout.

"None of you will fire," I say as though I haven't heard, "because bullets create sparks, and sparks start fires. So even if you hit me, he'll go up in flames."

And while they process this, I flick the lighter shut, lift the gasoline can, and empty the rest of it. Over my own head.

175

"No!" Patrese shouted.

It's something they train you for at police academy, because any officer might face it one day: the moment in a situation when the perpetrator realizes it's not going to end the way they'd intended. That's when things really get dangerous.

That was the point Mara was at now.

She'd missed killing Patrese, let alone whoever she had in mind for the last four. So this was going to end only one of two ways—their way, or her way.

And she was right; they couldn't shoot, not without risking that fatal spark.

She took four quick steps backward, right to the other side of the room, just in case they tried to rush her; and she flicked the lighter open again.

"I have walked the same path as God," she said. "By taking lives and making others afraid, I have done God's work."

"Not this way, Mara," Patrese said.

"Yes," she said. "This way."

It would be dark outside soon, Patrese thought; and with sunset came Shabbat.

Mara sat down, sparked the flame on the lighter, and touched it to her face. Flames billowed beneath rolling clouds of black oily smoke, transforming and destroying her: the high, salty odor of burning flesh, her skin blackening and charring, skin and clothes melting into one; and all the time she burned, she never moved a muscle nor uttered a sound.

176

Even the highly trained SWAT team took a few moments before they fell on Mara, beating and smothering the flames with their own bodies.

Patrese looked around for Beradino, whom he'd glimpsed behind the SWAT team. He was nowhere to be seen.

Patrese went out into the main gallery. The few visitors there were hurrying down the stairs in barely concealed panic, away from the alpha-male yells of the SWAT team.

No Beradino; not with the soup tins, or the Marilyns, or the memento mori.

Patrese followed the fleeing gallerygoers down the stairs; faster than them now, breaststroking his way through the scrum, outraged mutterings bouncing off him. "Police," he yelled. "The fuck out of my way. *Move.*"

Down in the foyer, he caught a glimpse through the main doors of a trailing leg, moving fast. By the time Patrese was on the sidewalk, Beradino was thirty yards up the street, heading toward the river.

"Mark!"

Beradino turned, saw Patrese, and began to run.

There was no way Beradino would stay ahead of Patrese all the way across the bridge, and Patrese understood instantly.

Beradino had no intention of getting to the other side of the Allegheny.

He was aiming for the river itself.

Jesslyn was dead, his career was in tatters, and he'd be facing charges: unlawful imprisonment, aiding and abetting, hindering an investigation, and obstruction of justice, at least. Whichever way you cut it, he was looking at a stretch inside, and cops tended to be not much higher than child molesters in prison pecking orders. Even for a Christian who believed suicide was a sin, Beradino had very little to live for.

This time of year, the Allegheny would be damn near freezing, cold enough to kill a man in minutes, if he hadn't drowned first.

Patrese gave chase.

Beradino reached the bridge. He grabbed hold of the nearest vertical suspension cable and hauled himself up onto the top of the railing.

"No!" Patrese shouted. "Mark! No!"

A passerby, approaching, hesitated. Patrese held up his badge. "Police! Back off!"

Beradino looked down at the water, then at Patrese.

Patrese was five yards away. Near enough to be heard; too far to make a grab for Beradino.

"Stop right there, Franco," Beradino said.

"You don't have to do this, Mark. We can sort something out."

"Like what?"

"We'll think of something."

"There's no 'we' anymore, Franco. Not after what I did to you."

"I understand why you did it. We can still save something."

And all the time, Patrese was shuffling forward, tiny baby steps like the ones soccer players take when defending free kicks; each step so small as to be imperceptible, but an inch became six inches, six inches became a foot, a foot became two, and gradually the gap was narrowing.

"You did it for love," Patrese said. "Love makes people do the strangest things."

"What the heck do *you* know about love, Franco? I wanted you out of the picture. You could have been killed. If I were you, I sure as heck wouldn't be forgiving."

"You're a good cop," Patrese said.

Four yards between them now.

"*Was. Was* a good cop. No way back, not now. But you're right, I was a good cop. I've always fought for what I thought was right. And now I ask: why? There are still bad people out there; always have been, always will be. I've tried to keep it in perspective, to remember that just because death and violence are the norms of my life, they're not those of most people's."

Three yards. Beradino was on a roll, and Patrese didn't dare interrupt; the more he kept Beradino talking, the closer he could get undetected.

"Most people want nothing more than to be happy, you know? Happy. They might disagree about what makes them happy, but they want to get there. That's all I was looking for. Happiness. That's all. Is that too much to ask? Me, you, all of us, Franco, we're that little Dutch boy with his finger in the dike. You can never conquer evil, but maybe you can keep it at bay, keep the darkness at one remove. If that's all you can do, that has to be enough."

Two yards.

Yes, Patrese thought. Not only did it have to be enough, but it *was* enough. The darkness only won if you let it.

Patrese thought of Kohler, and the vile things Kohler had done to him, and he realized that already he was seeing that at one remove. He'd never have killed Kohler himself, but he wasn't in the least bit sorry that Kohler was dead.

Kohler had known what kind of man he was. He hadn't needed a trial or a jail sentence to show him. His own torments, let alone anything his God might choose to inflict on him, were punishment enough.

One yard now, close enough for Patrese to make a sudden leap; but even as he did so, he saw Beradino's hand uncurling from the suspension cable as his body began to tip forward, Patrese clutching at the material of Beradino's coat, feeling the roughness against his fingertips as Beradino fell away from him, feet sliding off the railing, body marking a parabola against gray sky and grayer water, down, down, and the only sound Patrese could hear was his own scream of disbelieving frustration.

Beradino in water, Mara in fire; both of them facing their fates in silence.

177

Beradino's body was fished from the Allegheny a quarter mile downstream.

Mara and the SWAT team were taken to Mercy. The SWAT guys got away lightly, all things considered. Several had suffered epidermal burns and a couple of dermal ones, but none had gone full thickness, down to muscle or bone.

Not so Mara.

She was horrifically burned, third-degree over more than half her body. She'd survive, but would need multiple grafts; how many, the doctors couldn't say. What they *did* know was that the fire had damaged her larynx so badly she'd never talk again, and smoke inhalation meant she'd have respiratory difficulties for the rest of her life.

Patrese went through Mara's apartment in the Pennsylvanian and pieced together what she'd done.

After killing Jesslyn, Mara had taken Jesslyn's car, keys, and phone, driven to the Punxsutawney apartment Jesslyn shared with Beradino—Beradino, of course, being at the murder scene—and taken enough items to make it look like she'd gone on the run. And after *that,* she'd disappeared to the Pennsylvanian—she was officially dead, and very recognizable to boot—and only ventured out in full old-lady makeup.

But swapping places with Jesslyn was only the half of it. In fact, Mara had created an entire new identity for herself. A new identity meant a Social Security number, a bank account, credit cards, passport—everything she'd need to start a new life. An identity started with a single piece of paper, without which nothing else was possible: a birth certificate.

But Mara couldn't have got just any old birth certificate, especially one of someone else who was still alive. The risks of the duplication being discovered were too great. Nor could she have got one of someone too old still to be alive, as the Social Security computers would have picked it up.

What she'd needed was the certificate of someone who was no longer alive. Identity fraudsters frequently trawled graveyards or cemeteries, looking at headstones to find someone who fitted the bill.

The Allegheny County clerk of courts, located in the main courthouse on Grant Street, had issued a passport at the end of July to one Magda Nagorska, confirmed by her birth certificate to have been born in Cleveland, Ohio, on May 14, 1932. What the ersatz Magda Nagorska had understandably failed to add was that the real version had died little more than a fortnight later, on May 31 of the same year, and was buried in Saint Stanislaus' Church in Cleveland's Warszawa district.

Patrese remembered from Mara's story that her Polish grandmother had lived in Cleveland between the wars. Magda Nagorska, in fact, had been Mara's aunt; one of her grandmother's children who'd died in infancy of what Hellmore had later identified as long QT syndrome, a connection that had been the starting point for getting Mara's conviction overturned.

Mara's choice of the Pennsylvanian might have seemed counterintuitive—surely the more people around, the more chance of her being rumbled—but Patrese knew the number of people is far less important than their attitude. Large apartment buildings are full of transients, people staying a few months here, a few months there. They often work or party long hours, and have neither the time nor the inclination to get to know their neighbors. In smaller communities, on the other hand, everyone notices a stranger, and everyone knows everyone's business.

Mara had kept detailed files on all her victims, past and future.

Howard was to have been next in line, for violating the seventh commandment, *Thou shalt not commit adultery.*

Number eight, *Thou shalt not steal,* was Mara's agent Guilaroff, who had indeed been stealing from her. She'd made meticulous lists of the amounts. It wasn't that she hadn't known; she'd simply chosen to bide her time and exact her own revenge.

Number nine, *Thou shalt not bear false witness,* was Lockwood, the man whose testimony had done so much to help convict her in the first place. He'd sworn on the Bible to tell the truth, the whole truth, and nothing but the truth. He hadn't done so.

The last one, *Thou shalt not covet,* was Ruby, and covet she certainly had. She'd been Howard's neighbor before becoming his lover, Patrese remembered. Ruby, like everyone else, had coveted what she'd seen, especially what she'd seen every day.

Beradino hadn't been on Mara's list, but she'd destroyed his life just the same.

178

SATURDAY, DECEMBER 11

Amberin stopped by Patrese's apartment after breakfast.

"I can't stay," she said. "My mom's in the car outside. I just wanted to check that you're okay."

"Probably not yet, but I'll get there."

She kissed him once, very softly, on the mouth, and then drew away.

"I'm sorry," she said.

"Don't be." He tried to smile. "Don't be sorry at all."

"Well, I am."

"Why?"

She touched his cheek and buried her head in his shoulder; then she looked him straight in the eye. "My mother's taking me to an Islamic dating convention."

"An Islamic dating convention? That as bad as it sounds?"

She laughed. "Worse. The tenth circle of hell. Dante

would add one specially for it if he was still around. Five thousand people at the convention center down by the Allegheny, you know? Po-faced miked-up facilitators marching around saying"—she put on a mock-solemn voice—"*It is important to the family system of Islam for our sons and daughters to match well.* Matrimonial registration forms, everything your future mother-in-law could want to know, and they want to know *everything*: hobbies, sports, visa status, height, weight, religious participation, family information. Fathers wanting to get daughters married off before they go to college so they won't be single during spring break. My mom will scope out every man there, and she'll tell me about each one: 'Yes, his looks matter. His personality matters. But if he's not aware and fearful and loving of Allah, he's not going to be right. If he doesn't follow Allah's laws, he won't be able to treat you right.'"

It was Patrese's turn to laugh. "Okay. But why does this make you sorry?"

"Why do you think?"

Patrese flushed. "Well, I wasn't sure whether you . . ."

"Of course I do. That night you took me home, I wanted you to stay more than anything. But my parents are traditional. They wouldn't understand what I see in you, and that's nothing to do with who you are or aren't; it's simply the color of your skin and the God you worship, or in your case don't worship. They want me to find a nice Muslim boy, settle down, have kids. They don't want me dating white men, people who aren't from our race or culture."

"But you're—you're you, Amberin. You have a mind

of your own. Hell, more than anyone else I know, pretty much. You really care what they think?"

"Yes. Of course I do."

"No, I didn't mean it like that. I meant—"

"I know what you meant. And I see why you think it. But I could never do it to them. No matter how much I like you—and I do, believe me, I do—I couldn't even introduce you to them. They could never know you even exist. I had to tell my mom I was picking something up from a girlfriend." Amberin wiped at the corner of her eye with the end of her little finger. "And that's why I'm sorry."

179

Three minutes after Amberin had left, the phone rang. Patrese picked up, hoping it was Amberin calling to say she'd changed her mind, and knowing it wouldn't be.

"Franco? Allen Chance here."

"Hello, sir."

"Just calling to check how you're doing."

"I'm okay, thanks."

"Good, good. You need any help, you know where to come, right? The channels are well established, and there for you."

Which was, Patrese knew, Chance-speak for "Go see the shrink if you want, but for God's sake don't mouth off about this whole thing outside of the department."

"Yes, sir. Thank you, sir."

"You're welcome. Oh—and we won't be having an official funeral, of course."

Official funerals were quite something. Police car lights flashed far into the distance; officers wore white gloves and black bands on their badges; guns were fired, bagpipes were played, the flag was folded across the coffin. Then, right at the end, the dispatcher called for the fallen officer over the radio. Three times the dispatcher called; three times he received only silence and static. Finally, softly, the dispatcher said "10-7": officer number out of service.

Official funerals were given to officers who had perished in the line of duty. They were not given to officers who had jumped off a bridge to avoid disgrace.

And yet, and yet . . . if anyone deserved one, Patrese thought, it was Beradino, even after what he'd done. Beradino had been a good cop, a hell of a good cop, for round about a quarter century. All the cases he'd cracked, all the bad guys he'd locked up, all the rookies he'd mentored—they must count for something, right? If you'd drawn up a ledger for Beradino's career, good in one column and bad in another, he'd still have been way in credit, even now. What Beradino had done to Patrese wasn't what Beradino had been.

How did the saying go? *Hate the sin, but not the sinner.* That was it. The Church had taught him something after all, Patrese realized.

"Sir," Patrese said, "I really think . . ."

"See you on Monday, Franco," Chance said, and was gone.

Patrese looked out of the window, across the cityscape. The glittering office blocks downtown seemed a little indistinct, and Patrese was reaching out to rub the window clean when he realized it had nothing to do with the glass.

It was him.

This place he loved so, he was seeing it through a gauze. Beradino was dead. His parents were dead. Mara was dead. Bianca was still here, of course, but she had her own family, her own unit of laughter and love and light.

It was time to go.

The thought had never before occurred to Patrese—he'd always been convinced he'd live all his life in Pittsburgh—but in the moment it came, he was absolutely convinced it was right. He could always come back one day, but for now, it was time to go.

He wanted to stay in law enforcement. It was all he knew how to do; besides, he was good at it. He could start in another police department; learn a new set of routines, patterns, lingo. Cops moved around the country all the time.

Or, or . . .

He picked up the phone and dialed.

"Caleb Boone."

"Caleb, it's Franco."

"Hey, buddy. You okay?"

"Not really."

"Anything I can do?"

"Matter of fact, there is. Two things, in fact."

"Shoot."

"One, come and drink a shitload of beer with me tonight."

"You got it."

"And two, tell me how a Pittsburgh homicide cop would go about getting a transfer to the FBI."

180

SUNDAY, DECEMBER 12

It was two days before they let Patrese see Mara. She was so heavily bandaged that only the doctor's notes at the end of the bed and the permanent presence of a policeman by her bedside could confirm her identity.

Bianca sat with him before he went in. He had to ask Mara some questions, all of them strictly official, about the murders. There were other questions to which he knew he'd never get answers, at least not ones he could be sure were honest. Bianca had met a few like Mara, she said, women who had become so used to manipulating others that they no longer knew how not to.

Mara had exploited Patrese not just to get inside information on the police's progress in her killings, and not just to drive a wedge between him and Beradino, but primarily for her own pleasure. Whether she'd even been attracted to Patrese at all was now as moot as it was irrelevant.

Since Mara couldn't speak and her hands were too badly damaged to write, the hospital had rigged up a laptop for her to communicate. The pinky finger on her right hand had escaped the worst of the fire, more by luck than judgment. It was the only digit she could put any pressure on whatsoever, so she'd peck away at the keyboard with that. It was painfully slow, but better than nothing.

"I'll ask, you type," he said. "Is that okay?"

Yes, *I tap.*

I wonder if he'll understand; really understand, that is.

I was tried, convicted, and sentenced under a legal system based not on God but on the blindness, stiff-neckedness, foolishness, and self-righteousness of the idiots who think they have the power, righteousness, and wisdom to make laws. Only God can govern us through His most perfect and holy laws—the Ten Commandments.

My God is not a God of benevolence, but one of justice. He moves in mysterious ways; what seems incomprehensible today may, with His guidance, be crystal clear tomorrow. So I asked Him: Why?

You were not meant to be a mother, He replied. You are a warrior princess, hardened by the ordeals you have suffered. I have tested many, and discarded them all; they were weak and unwilling, so I cast them by the wayside. What I've put you through has shown the true nature of those who stood before you and deprived you of everything you held dear. They clothe themselves in the garments of the righteous, but when the scales fall from your eyes, you will see them in their true colors, and you will know what you must do.

The Book of Hebrews says there is no forgiveness without the shedding of blood.

They'll punish me here on earth for what I've done, because they're pygmies and understand nothing. But God won't punish me. Everything I've done has been for Him. Every life I've taken, the ones too good for this world and the ones who deserved punishment alike, has been for Him, because He told me to do so.

I've done His work, and He knows that.

I turn my attention back to Patrese.

"We'll take this slowly," he says.

I nod.

"Okay. Let's start at the beginning. Let's start with the first murder, when you killed Michael Redwine."

I type with excruciating, exquisite slowness, a letter at a time.

Michael Redwine was not my first murder.

Read on for a sneak peek at

DANIEL BLAKE'S

riveting new novel,

CITY OF THE DEAD

Coming July 2012 from Gallery Books

PROLOGUE

DECEMBER 26

KHAO LAK, THAILAND

The sea ran back down the beach.

Franco Patrese felt the warm sand between his toes and smiled. There might be better places to be in the world right now, but none sprang to mind. It was sunny and hot, he'd spent the last six nights with an English girl who had the dirtiest laugh and nicest smell of anyone he'd ever met, and the most strenuous task he faced today was sorting out the precise sequence of swimming, sunbathing, lunch, beer, and sex.

Exactly two weeks ago, Patrese had sat in a Pittsburgh hospital room and listened to a murderer's confession. It had been the culmination of a case that had consumed him for months and taken with it much of his faith in human nature. Exhausted and traumatized, he'd searched online for last-minute holidays and ended up among the palm trees here in Khao Lak.

The first week had been an open-water diving course—a refresher course, in Patrese's case, as he'd done a lot of diving in his youth but hadn't been for a few years now. It was there that he'd met Katie, the English girl currently asleep in his beachfront hotel room. They'd dived to reefs and wrecks, swum with

Technicolor rainbows of marine life: cube boxfish dotted in yellow and black, nudibranches of solar orange, shrimp banded in Old Glory red and white.

Now Patrese had another week in which to do the square root of nothing. For the first time in months, perhaps longer, he felt—well, not exactly happy, given everything that had happened back in Pittsburgh, but certainly carefree. Tension was leaching like toxins from his body with every day that passed.

He kept walking toward the sea, waiting for the next wave to roll up the sand and lap round his ankles like the licking of an eager puppy.

The water continued to retreat, almost as though it were playing a game with him. Through one wave cycle, then another, and still it receded.

Patrese's brain was so firmly in neutral that it took him a few moments to realize how unusual this was.

In the shallows, swimmers laughed in amazement as the water drained around them. Tourist canoes were left stranded on ropes suddenly slack; beach vendors picked up fish writhing on the sand. Patrese heard questioning voices, saw shoulders shrugged. No one had ever seen such a thing, it seemed.

He had.

A Discovery Channel program, he thought, or maybe National Geographic. They'd reconstructed a historic earthquake—Lisbon, that was it, sometime in the eighteenth century—with CGI effects, talking heads, and a narrator whose voice was set firmly to "doom." The program had shown many of Lisbon's residents fleeing to the waterfront to escape fires and falling debris in the city center. From the docks, they'd seen the sea recede so far and fast that it had exposed all the cargo lost and wrecks forgotten over the centuries.

And after that . . .

"Tsunami!" Patrese shouted. "Tsunami!"

A couple of people looked curiously at him. Perhaps they thought he was calling for a lost dog. A lobster-colored Englishman in a black-and-white soccer shirt clapped and began to sing. "Toon Army! Toon Army!"

A posse of Germans were twenty yards away. Patrese ran over to them.

"Move! You've got to move!"

"Hey!" One of the Germans clapped him on the shoulder. "Chill out, man."

"There's a tsunami coming!"

"Tsunami?"

"Tidal wave."

The Germans looked out at the ocean. The water was a carpet of azure as far as they could see.

"I don't see no tidal wave," said the shoulder clapper.

They all looked at Patrese with a sort of benevolent wariness, clearly bracketing him as slightly demented but probably harmless.

"It's coming, I tell you," Patrese insisted.

"Whatever you're on, man, can you give me some?"

"Please leave us alone now," said one of the German women.

Patrese opened his mouth to say something else, but the Germans were already turning away from him.

He kept moving, telling everyone he could find: leave the beach, go inland, get somewhere high. Some people packed up their stuff without a word and did what he said. Some ignored him or feigned incomprehension. Some, the smart ones, took off to other parts of the beach and began to spread the word.

A white crescent on the horizon now, awesome in its grace and beauty. For a moment even Patrese stood spellbound, watching as the crescent began to grow.

Then he ran.

Behind him, the tsunami reared up, an angry cobra of seawater. It flipped a fishing boat over and swallowed it whole. Urgent voices around Patrese, a dozen different languages and all saying the same thing: *Move, run, keep going.*

Katie was standing at the entrance to the hotel, wearing one of Patrese's T-shirts over her bikini. Her hair was tousled, and her eyes were still bleary with sleep.

"What the hell's going on?" she said.

Patrese grabbed her without breaking stride. "Move. Come with me."

"Franco, what the fuck . . . ?"

"Just do it!" He had to shout to be heard above the roaring.

The tsunami smashed through the swimmers who hadn't managed to get ashore in time and raced up the beach with murderous intent. It was every monster from every nightmare bundled together and made real; surging into the hotel, devouring whole rooms in seconds, tearing husbands from wives and children from parents.

Water all around Patrese and in him, holding him up and dragging him down. Water does not strive. It flows in the places men reject. Chest and spine pressed vise tight and harder still, a balloon expanding from within. Bubbles around his head and ringing beyond heart thumps in his ears; air, life itself, scurrying away into mocking oblivion. The camera's aperture of consciousness closing in, light shrinking from the edges, dim through flashes of jagged crystals. Thoughts slowing, panic receding, resignation, acceptance, dulled contentment, blue gray flowing around, sounds gone, and this is how it ends, this is it, just let go and slide away, like falling about in a green field in early summer.

Then suddenly the water went out and the air came in; coughing, spluttering, frenzied inhaling, man's reflex to survive. Patrese opened his eyes and saw that the tsunami was gone, pulling itself back out of the hotel and down the beach. Bodies spun like sticks in the surge. Patrese felt a wall at each shoulder and realized he'd been pinned in a corner, facing away from the beach. Blind chance. Anywhere else in the room, he'd have been swept straight back out to sea.

From the dining room upstairs came voices, giddy and shrill with relief. Patrese climbed slime-slippery steps and looked around the room. Two dozen people, he reckoned: the quick ones, the lucky ones.

Katie wasn't among them.

NEW ORLEANS, LA

It could have been very romantic. Private room in one of the city's most expensive restaurants, hard on the shore of Lake Pontchartrain. Just the two of them: him handsome in a swarthy, weathered way, not quite yet ruined by the years; she with skin the color of barely milked coffee under an orange-and-black madras headdress. They wouldn't have been young lovers, that was for sure, but it was anyone's guess as to exactly how old they were: they weren't the kind of people to keep their original birth certificates. The best estimates put her somewhere in her late fifties and him half a decade older. Whatever the truth, they weren't saying.

It could have been very romantic, were it not for the four men who stood outside the private room—two of them hers, two his, all of them armed—and were it not also for the FBI surveillance van that sat at the far end of the parking lot, listening in through the microphone attached to the underside of the wine bucket. The Bureau had guessed the room would be swept for listening devices before the diners arrived, but not after that. They'd guessed right. Now all the listeners needed was something incriminating: something they could hear and, even better, something they could record. These were two big fish, and the Bureau desperately wanted to net them.

The male fish was Balthazar Ortiz, a senior member of Mexico's Los Zetas drug syndicate. Los Zetas were somewhere between a faction of the Gulf Cartel and a private army of their own. The organization was full of former Mexican special forces soldiers like Ortiz, and they were ruthlessly good at what they did. Los Zetas had sprung two dozen of their comrades from jail somewhere in Mexico a couple of months back; they'd killed the new police chief of Nuevo Laredo six hours after he'd taken office.

And *she* was Marie Laveau, one of the kingpins—queenpins?—of the New Orleans underworld. In particular, she was Queen of the Lower Ninth, a hard-scrabble district perched at the corner where the Mississippi met the Industrial Canal. The Lower Ninth, uneasy by day and terrifying by night, reeked of poverty and drugs. It was overwhelmingly black, of course; that went without saying, that was just the way it was in this city.

The original Marie Laveau had lived in New Orleans in the nineteenth century and had styled herself the Voodoo Queen. A hairdresser by trade, she'd also claimed to be an oracle, an exorcist, a priestess, and much more. For every known fact about her life, there were a hundred myths. So, too, with this one, the current Marie Laveau. She claimed to be not just a descendant of the original but the very reincarnation of her. She also styled herself the Voodoo Queen, but with the proviso that the spirit of the Voodoo Queen was immortal; she was only the temporary guardian of it.

Marie gestured across the shimmering darkness of the water. In the distance, headlights slid along the Lake Pontchartrain Causeway, the twin-span interstate bridge that connected the city to the north side of the lake.

"The second Marie Laveau—daughter of the original—she was conducting a ceremony on the lake when a storm came up. Swept her out into the middle of the lake. She stayed in the water five days. When they found her, she didn't even have exposure."

Ortiz nodded. "Shall we get to business?"

Marie sighed, as if his lack of interest in small talk was somehow discourteous. "If you like."

"Now, I don't know how you did it before, with my, er, predecessor . . ."

"Just like we're doing it now."

"Good. That's good."

"Round about this time, every year. See how the arrangement's gone the past twelve months, see how we want it to go for the next twelve."

"Okay. And the arrangement; how is it for you?"

"The arrangement's not the problem."

"Then what is the problem?"

"You."

"Me?"

"You. You're the problem."

The folds of Marie's green caftan seemed to shift and rearrange themselves, and suddenly she was holding a Magnum Baby Eagle pistol with an extended barrel to accommodate the suppressor on its end.

Ortiz just about had time to look astonished before Marie shot him straight through the heart.

INTERLUDE

Patrese stayed in Khao Lak for three weeks after the tsunami. Every day of those three weeks, from before dawn to after dark, he worked with a frenzy born of knowing one sure thing: that once he stopped, he'd never start again.

He helped carry corpses—one of them Katie's—to warehouses stacked to the ceiling with coffins, body bags, and cadavers. He helped dig through rubble with his bare hands, dragging bodies out into the open and off for whatever dignified burial their families could give them. He helped pin photographs of the lost and missing on walls; he listened to the impotent bewilderments of each newly arrived wave of relatives. He helped pile debris into trucks, and helped drive those trucks to landfill sites. He helped aid workers hand out food, helped doctors distribute medicines, helped hammer up walls and roofs for makeshift shelters.

He helped everyone but himself, knowing that he could wait.

And at the end of those three weeks, he suddenly knew it was time to go. There were more people helping with the reconstruction than were strictly needed, and they were beginning to get in one another's way. Hardened professional aid workers were scorning fresh-faced Western volunteers as "disaster tourists"; locals were chafing at soldiers who ordered them around.

The night before Patrese left, he was taken to see Panupong Wattana. Wattana was five foot two on a good day, always immaculately turned out in what seemed an endless rota of lightweight suits, and he'd been around Khao Lak pretty much every day since the tsunami: giving interviews to the world's media, glad-handing those unfortunate souls who'd lost everything, and generally strutting around like some latter-day Napoleon. As far as Patrese could make out, Wattana was a hybrid of politician and businessman. Clearly, the two roles were seen as complementary, even indivisible. Equally clearly, the concept of a conflict of interest was a very remote one round these parts.

"The great Stakhanovite!" Wattana exclaimed, clasping Patrese's hand in both of his own. "I have heard much about you; the American who works like a Soviet!"

Patrese mumbled something noncommittal about just doing his bit.

"Come, come, Mr. Patrese. You are too modest, and we all know it. I just want to thank you on behalf of the people of Khao Lak, of Takua Pa district, of Phang Nga province, of Thailand itself . . ."

Patrese half-wondered whether Wattana was going to keep on, rather as he had addressed envelopes when a child: name, street, city, country, earth, galaxy, universe.

". . . and to tell you that if you ever need anything in America, three of my sons are there, and I've instructed them specifically to do anything you ask."

"Where are they based?" Patrese asked, more out of politeness than a genuine desire to know.

"Johnny's in Baltimore. Tony, New Orleans. Mikey, San Diego."

Johnny, Tony, Mikey—damn, Patrese thought, they sound more Italian than I do.

"Well, I'm in Pittsburgh, but if I ever go visit any of those places, I'll be sure to look them up."

The Bureau might not have caught Marie discussing anything concrete about her drug business—the "arrangement" she'd spoken about could have meant anything—but they'd gotten something better: audio evidence of a murder. The cough of the suppressed pistol hadn't been loud enough to carry outside the room, so neither Marie's bodyguards nor Ortiz's had heard; but it was clearly audible on the surveillance tape.

Backup had been there inside three minutes: barreling through astonished diners into the back of the restaurant, shouting at the bodyguards to not even fucking think about it, and into the private room, where Marie was sitting calmly across the table from a very dead Ortiz.

The surveillance might have been a Bureau operation, but the murder squarely and clearly belonged to the New Orleans Police Department. Homicide detective Selma Fawcett took charge of the investigation. Selma—named after the Alabama city of civil rights movement fame—was black, which didn't make her a minority in the NOPD, and female, which did.

Short of actually catching Marie with a smoking gun, this seemed to Selma pretty much as clear-cut as cases went. Marie was so guilty, she made O.J. look innocent.

Under Louisiana law, murder in the first was reserved for killings with aggravated circumstances. Since none of those circumstances applied here—there'd been no kidnap, rape, burglary, robbery, and the victim hadn't been a member of law enforcement—Marie could only be charged with second-degree murder, which in turn meant the maximum sentence she could receive was life rather than death.

That suited Selma fine. She'd seen firsthand what Marie's kind of drugs did to people, and if the last, best option was putting Marie inside to the end of her days, then that would have to do. Selma was less keen on the fact that the second-degree charge allowed Marie to be released on bail—$500,000 bail, to be precise—but since there was little Selma could do about that, she tried not to let it bother her too much.

The world and his wife grandstanded on this one. The Bureau trumpeted the success of their surveillance operation. The police department pointed to the speed of their officers' response and the efficiency of their investigators. The assistant district attorney took personal charge of the prosecution. Even the state governor himself went on television to restate Louisiana's commitment to drug-free streets. Impressively, he even managed to get all that out with a straight face.

Marie said she wanted a quick trial, as was her right. She also said she wanted to defend herself. This, too, was her right. She started to keep a tally of everyone who quoted to her the maxim about a man who is his own lawyer having a fool for a client.

Trial date was set for late June; and pretty much everyone who came across Marie said that, for a woman facing the prospect of life imprisonment, she seemed about as concerned as someone putting the cat out for the night.

It was ten below freezing when Patrese arrived back in Pittsburgh, and the welcome he got at police headquarters wasn't a whole lot warmer. He'd worked there almost a decade, he'd always thought of himself as fairly popular, yet pretty much not a single person asked how he was, said it was good to have him back, or suggested they go for a beer. They must have known about the tsunami: even the most inward-looking of America's TV networks couldn't have ignored it. They just didn't seem to care.

Patrese knew why, of course. The case that had so consumed him had done in his partner, Mark Beradino. Beradino had lost his career and more because of it, and since Beradino had been a legend in the department and the department didn't like to see a legend brought low, they'd looked around for someone to blame. Patrese was clearly that someone. That this was unfair—Beradino had brought all the bad luck and trouble on himself—was irrelevant. A scapegoat, a sacrificial lamb, had been sought, and Patrese was its name.

There'd been a time, perhaps as recently as a month ago, when Patrese would have said, "Screw the lot of you," and put up with it until people came to their senses. But as he walked through the endless institutional corridors, catching snatches of discussion about the Steelers' upcoming championship game in Foxborough, he realized that he simply couldn't be bothered. He'd just spent three weeks among people who really had lost everything. The static he was getting now seemed so petty in comparison.

He found an empty meeting room and dialed his old college buddy Caleb Boone, now in charge of the FBI's Pittsburgh office.

"Franco! Man, am I glad to hear from you! Been trying you for weeks."

"Caleb, you want to grab a beer?"

"No."

"No?"

"No. I want to grab many beers."

Patrese laughed, relieved. "I believe that's the recognized international signal for a serious FatHeads session."

"I believe it is. Seven?"

"Sounds good. And listen, we can talk about this more when we're there, and I mentioned it before but I was wondering . . . I was wondering if the Bureau has any vacancies. For a cop."

"Vacancies? In the Pittsburgh field office?"

"No. In any field office *apart* from Pittsburgh."

The FatHeads session indeed turned out to be serious; seriously liquid and seriously long. Patrese stumbled to bed sometime nearer dawn than midnight and trod gingerly through the next day as a result. He was just about feeling human again by the time he went to his sister Bianca's for dinner, and for a few hours he lost himself in the uncomplicated and riotous warmth of her own family's love for him: her briskly efficient doctoral clucking, her husband Sandro's watchful concern, and the endless energy and noise of their three kids.

"Here," Bianca said suddenly, as they were clearing away. "Meant to give you this."

She reached up to the highest shelf and pulled down a small jar. There was some kind of fabric inside, Patrese saw. It looked old and frayed.

"What's this?" he said.

"It's your caul. I found it while packing up Mum and Dad's stuff." Their parents had been killed in a car crash a few months before.

"Funny thing to keep around the place."

"Mom, what's a caul?" said Gennaro, Bianca's youngest.

"Some babies are born with a membrane covering their face and head."

"Yeeuch!"

"Not 'yeeuch,' honey. It's perfectly natural; it's just part of the, er, the bag that holds babies inside their moms' tummies. Uncle Franco was one of those babies. And having a caul is special."

"Why's it special?"

"Lots of reasons. If you have a caul, it can mean you're psychic . . ."

"I wish," Patrese muttered.

". . . or you can heal people, or you'll travel all your life and never tire, or—"

Bianca stopped suddenly and clapped her hand to her mouth.

"What?" Patrese said.

She spoke through her hand. "It doesn't matter."

"Tell me."

She took her hand away, put it on his shoulder, and looked him squarely in the eye.

"It means you'll never drown."

Boone called as Patrese was driving back home.

"This a good time to talk, buddy?"

"Er . . . sure."

"You okay? You sound a little, er, distracted."

Patrese glanced at the caul jar on the passenger seat. "No. Just driving."

"Okay. You asked about the Bureau? Got a name for you: Wyndham Phelps."

Patrese laughed. “Sounds like someone from *Gone With the Wind.*”

“Good Southern name. I told him all about you, and he wants to meet with you.”

“Where’s he at?”

“He heads the field office in New Orleans.”

A stunning novel of faith and reason from
#1 New York Times bestselling author
JEROME R. CORSI
THE SHROUD CODEX
A NOVEL
"EXCELLENT . . . A MUST-READ FOR FANS OF SCANDINAVIAN CRIME LITERATURE." —BOOKLIST, STARRED REVIEW
THE ICE PRINCESS
A NOVEL
CAMILLA LÄCKBERG
Blockbuster thrillers
from Pocket Books!
NEW YORK TIMES BESTSELLING AUTHOR OF
THE JURY MASTER
ROBERT DUGONI
A NOVEL
BODILY HARM
AUTHOR OF ROGUE WAVE
BOYD MORRISON
A NOVEL
THE ARK
AN INDIE NEXT NOTABLE PICK!
Available wherever books are sold
or at www.simonandschuster.com
POCKET BOOKS
A Division of Simon & Schuster
A CBS COMPANY
26628